"This supremely talented writer has stit[...] the ancient world with those of Gatsby or Faulkner or O'Connor, delivering to his reader a deeply satisfying and wholly original read for the twenty-first century. Is reparation possible in the modern world? An ambitious debut novel asks no less of its flawed and affecting hero."
                                                    —Antonya Nelson

"A strong narrative line . . . and his graceful, wry writing about the Southern legacy of the Caldwells lend the book an elegant charm. The narrative is richly atmospheric as Elliott examines the complex Southern heritage of gentlemen landowners and their slaves, good old boys and rednecks, whose values continue to influence their descendants . . . Elliott shows promise as a solid, assured stylist."
                                                    —*Publishers Weekly*

"Here at last is a deliberately old-fashioned Southern novel—rich in family history and sense of place—that neither condescends to nor takes advantage of its subject. In the pages of *Coiled in the Heart* we find tattered Tennessee gentry; we find the haunting residue of tragedy; we find the new south inexorably squeezing out the old. Not only does Scott Elliott write gorgeous sentences one after the next, he understands these people and this place. Reminiscent of writers like William Styron, like Robert Penn Warren, while re-maining wholly original, *Coiled in the Heart* marks the emergence of a very real and durable talent."
                                                    —Michael Knight

"History-ridden and proud of it, *Coiled in the Heart* teems with all grades of trouble: venomous serpents, fallen aristocrats, brash young millionaires, whiskey, and guns. Scott Elliott's shrewd debut is at its best when delineating a far subtler danger—the past in the present, and the crazy way it alters the heart."
                                                    —Michael Parker

COILED *in the* HEART

SCOTT ELLIOTT

BLUEHEN BOOKS   NEW YORK

BLUEHEN BOOKS
Published by The Berkley Publishing Group
A division of Penguin Group (USA) Inc.
375 Hudson Street
New York, New York 10014

Copyright © 2003 by Scott Elliott
Book design by Chris Welch
Cover design by Jess Morphew
Cover photo of farmhouse © David Robin/Graphistock
Cover photo of tree © Davis O'Connor/Graphistock

G. P. Putnam's Sons hardcover edition: July 2003
BlueHen trade paperback edition: July 2004
BlueHen trade paperback ISBN: 0-425-19701-8

The Library of Congress has catalogued
the G. P. Putnam's Sons hardcover edition as follows:

Elliott, Sott, date.
Coiled in the heart / Scott Elliott.
p.   cm.
ISBN 0-399-15038-2 (acid-free paper)
1. Young men—Fiction.   2. Murderers—Fiction   3. Tennessee—Fiction.
4. Twins—Fiction.   I. Title
PS3605.L45C65   2003   2002037116
813'.6—dc21

Printed in the United States of America

10 9 8 7 6 5 4 3 2 1

FOR MY FAMILY

I'd like to thank Elizabeth, Robert, Greg, and Andrew Elliott; Henry Gordinier; Jenna Terry; Clift Jones; Heather Hart; Laura Hansen; all my helpful teachers and colleagues at UC-Boulder, Columbia SOA, and UH; Aimee Taub; Greg Michalson for his good faith and keen eye; Alice Tasman for her steadfast belief and intrepid enthusiasm; and everyone else who expressed interest and offered support during the writing of this book.

COILED *in the* HEART

ONE

Tʜɪs ᴀꜰᴛᴇʀɴᴏᴏɴ we're celebrating the erasure of another house. To this end, one at a time, I carry five fold-out tables from the cellar to the backfield, unfold their legs, and set them up on the newly sown grass where the house used to be. I arrange the tables in a horseshoe facing the Grand Old Caldwell Place and spread over them portions of material my mother bought in Aix-en-Provence not long before she came back to Tennessee, suffered a stroke, and collapsed into her tomato plants. As I wave the cloth, sunlight runs through Mediterranean blue, golden fleur-de-lis, and alternating rose dragon- and peach butterflies stitched in mid-buzz and flit just above the open mouths of lime serpents.

Beyond the tables, at the end of a vacant driveway in an abandoned cul-de-sac, stands the window- and doorless facade of the next house in our plans, blue sky and trees at the margin of the field visible through its Georgian shell. Beside the house, the driving crane, jib, and five-thousand-pound cast-iron ball we have named Old Havoc awaits its next call to service.

I gather the food Tonorah has spent all morning preparing, with my negligible help, and carry it from the kitchen to the horseshoe where the ends of the cloth are fluttering in a soft breeze. The old Jackson china is heaped with fried chicken, corn on the cob, cheesegrits, pasta and fruit salads. There are wicker baskets filled with cornbread and beaten biscuits. There are silver buckets filled with champagne on ice, two pitchers each of sweet tea and lemonade. I stand back to admire the spread.

After a time my father strolls across the lawn. At six-three, he is a thin, vigorous-looking man with intense blue eyes and prominent neck and temple veins that stand out when he yells. He is a steadfastly polite man whose sad, fake smile plays often, his wise, authentic one, rarely. Stories from unexpected sources trickle back to me on occasion of the hellion exploits of his younger years. Now, that time is far behind him and, except for rare, instantaneous flashes of angel-demon mischief in his eyes, those wild days may as well be credited to another man. He's wearing a canary cotton polo shirt with a few grey hairs curling over the collar, soft worn khakis, scuffed loafers, no socks.

When he sees the spread Tonorah and I have arranged, he nods his approval. We stand beside each other, on this new patch of grass, in this field we're expanding, on this land that's been in our family these two hundred years. We push into the bluegrass with the soles of our shoes, rock onto our toes, and wait for our guests.

Who arrive soon enough. Bank Shankhorn and his crew of deconstruction artistes, as we call them, and whom I convinced my father we ought to include in our celebrations, drive up in pickups, El Caminos, and pinging Pintos as do a select number of our benefactors, sympathizers, various friends of Rollback Inc., old friends of the family in Lexuses, Rovers, old Mercedeses, and Cadillacs. They climb out of their cars and walk across the lawn—our benefactors: doctors, lawyers, professors, inheritors, money managers, all of them dressed like my father and me or more formally in jackets, ties, dresses, glinting jewelry. Bank and his crew are mostly in beaten-up baseball caps and jeans.

Two weeks ago my father and I took turns manipulating Old Havoc's hand and foot levers so that the jib moved to the right and, at the precise moment, slightly to the left. The great cast-iron ball swung on its cable and gathered momentum as it came back around to impact, with a thud of satisfying finality, into the side of the house. In little time at all, through a tumult of dust and noise, chalky in-then-down-crumbling brick, another house was reduced to rubble, beaten out of existence, out of time. Destroyed. Then completely erased.

The next day Bank Shankhorn and his crew came in with their excavators, front-end loaders, and trucks to cart the house's shards off to the appropriate places. They recycled what they could and threw away what they had to before refilling the cavity with soil, in which, over the course of the following weeks, my father and I sowed and watered new grass.

After the initial greetings and when everyone has found a seat—all of the construction-come-deconstruction workers, I notice, sitting at one end of the horseshoe, our benefactors at the other—my father says a brief blessing. Then, with a raised glass of sweet tea, he toasts Rollback Inc. and wishes me a happy birthday. All around the horseshoe our guests raise flutes of gingerly blinking champagne. I am toasted, and I thank the toasters and we dig in.

Except for my father, who continues to sip his sweet tea and look across the yard in the direction of the Grand Old Caldwell Place in a way that makes me imagine he must be waiting to see Aunt Marcy wheel my mother across the lawn to join us. There's a hard longing in the way he's staring into an unaccountable distance that makes me think he's willing his contrition at her. My mother has been invited, through me and at my father's request, to all seven of these picnics, one for each of the Golfhurst subdivision houses we've erased so far, but in her steadfast rage against my father, she has yet to show up for any of them.

In my father's mind, these picnics are gestures of reconciliation and have been put on, one and all, for the benefit of the one guest who has never shown up. *If only she would show,* I imagine him thinking, *she would see how well we're doing.* He would prove his contrition and how much he loves her despite the wheelchair and the brief, he would say, meaningless affair he had with a younger woman shortly after her stroke. Perhaps he would admit he needs to feel a forgiveness only she can grant him.

I watch him spend a polite half-smile and nod for the benefit of Ms. Byrd, our staunchest supporter and benefactress and a good friend to my late Grandmother Pearl, who has caught him looking at nothing in particular. He focuses on his plate and forks up some cheesegrits.

MY FATHER AND I work in the new spaces of yard where the houses had been. We've planted a large garden back here. There's sweet corn, okra, cabbage, tomatoes, cauliflower, carrots, onions, lettuce, sweet peas. And we've set in a number of trees—oaks, pines, magnolias, larches, ashes, redbuds, dogwoods, a few weeping willows, and some thin, hopeful-looking pecans. Some of the trees are vulnerable when they're first in, so we wrap wire rings around the fragile trunks to remind the world they're there and keep them from harm. I'm not sure—we've never discussed it—but I suspect that for both of us these trees are also gifts for my mother—if she ever comes back to see them, if she ever shows.

EIGHTY-EIGHT-YEAR-OLD Fenton Monroe arrives typically late. He moves toward us across the lawn, shadows in the wrinkles of his white seersucker suit shifting with his steps and a stained leash, red as newly loosened blood, extending from his wrist to what appears, on first glance, to be a malignant black colossus, some vile monster waddling beside him. It's Fenton's alligator snapping turtle. I jog my mind to recall the Latin which sifts gradually into focus, a relic from a time in my life when I was a sort of hybrid herpa-toxicologist, to ripple in a whisper off my tongue: *Macroclemys temminckii.*

Fenton calls the turtle Eddie, and over the lawn, as if he's just been called from the ooze of a bygone era, Eddie waddles our way, craggy carapace rising and falling with the slow rhythm of his scaly black legs.

Many of our guests have never seen Eddie, and, speaking for the group, Dr. Bass, a thoughtful history professor who, with his wife, is a new benefactor, asks for an explanation. So I tell them all Eddie's story and my connection to it. Tell them how, on the morning of the day I was born, Fenton found nine-month-old Eddie—who had hatched, like all snapping turtles do, the previous June, down near the creek—and brought the poor bewildered creature to my mother's hospital room to mark my birthday. Both my grandmothers, in whom the turtle engendered visions of a noseless or otherwise tragically disendowed child (there I was, Tobia-the-Bald, newly minted, swaddled, and cooed-over) not to mention the unsanitary considerations, lectured Fenton for some time for bringing in the unwanted guest. They commanded him to cleanse the room at once of the vile beast and later wondered, laughing, after Fenton had left the room, how he'd managed to sneak it into the hospital in the first place.

Fenton remains the kind of man who doesn't understand why anyone might think it odd to bring a snapping turtle around to celebrate the advent of a child or why an older man in a seersucker suit shouldn't jump fully clothed into a swimming pool. I love Fenton for ignoring decorum in these ways. Since that first reception in the hospital, Fenton has kept Eddie, these twenty-eight years, in bigger and bigger stainless steel drums. Every year he brings the turtle, which now must be close to two hundred pounds and whose head is the size of a seven-year-old boy's, to visit me on my birthday. In this way, I mark time with a turtle. I may be aging better than Eddie, but he will probably outlive me.

Behind approaching man and beast the back of the Old Caldwell Place rises above the green lawn, looking comfortable in the shadows of its surrounding trees. Looking, I think, pleased, inasmuch as a house can project a pleased aspect, with the increased greenery in its view since the subdivision houses have fallen.

Apparently, Fenton has taken the liberty of checking our mail at the bottom of the driveway. He is clutching a bundle of letters and magazines in his left hand and cradling a package against his right hip in the same hand in which he holds Eddie's leash.

"'Lo there, Mr. Monroe. And hello . . . Eddie," my father says, glancing down with a tolerant scowl at the equally disdainful turtle.

I stand and offer Fenton my hand. "Hey, old man."

"Happy birthday, QBTC," Fenton sings in reference to my college quarterbacking days. He sets some of the mail down on the table, ignores my hand, and hits me on the head with a rolled magazine. The rest of the guests look from man to beast. The ones who know Fenton call out their own hellos, and he smiles and waves back.

"Went ahead and picked up y'all's mail," he says, meaning him and Eddie. "This," he addresses my father, giving the package a small lift against his hip, "is for you. From Costa Rica this time."

Fenton hands me Eddie's leash and holds the package out for my father. I reach down to pet the turtle's head. Eddie opens his beak, revealing the pinkish white inner mouth, the lure on his tongue for wiggling to bring fish within snapping range. When my hand is close, Eddie hisses and leaves his beak open to show me he means business. I look into his cold survivor eyes.

"Nice to see you, too," I tell Eddie and slowly withdraw my hand.

My father accepts the package from Fenton and checks the return address, his light blue eyes sparkling in a repression. Fenton and I share a glance. We both want but refuse to ask my father what's in these packages he's been getting from exotic locales. We wonder when he'll break down and tell us. We have our theories. We connect them to the peace offerings he has me deliver to my mother every week. Our guess is that these packages contain butterflies from around the world for my mother's collection.

When it's clear my father's not going to talk today, Fenton says some more hellos, serves himself a healthy plate of food, and pours a fluteful of champagne. When he's settled in his chair and has downed most of the bubbly so you can see it shimmering in his periwinkle eyes, adding an extra ruddiness to his already red cheeks, he launches into his favorite subject.

In his life's gloaming, Fenton has distinguished himself with the prediction that very soon the New Madrid Earthquake is going to awaken from its slumber to rattle this part of Tennessee. Fenton claims that day by day he's closing in on the exact date and time when the New Madrid will shake things up around here.

He says he can feel the plate tectonic tension reverberating up from deep rifts in the earth to hum like a distant radio signal in the heart of his marrow. When he walks barefoot through the grass with his trousers rolled he says he can feel the rustling hint of a great disturbance on its way, a faint but no less colossal rumbling in the earth's belly. With unconquered flames roiling his fine old eyes, Fenton'll tell anyone who'll listen, he's almost pinpointed the moment when the tremors will commence.

Fenton sits back in his chair and, with no preamble whatsoever, lights into a tale of the 1811–12 New Madrid quakes, the big ones. He gains the immediate attention of our guests. It occurs to me not everyone could pull this off. The tale he tells is one of rivers reversing direction, the earth oceanlike and rolling in great swells, foundations cracking, roosters crowing well past midnight, hounds howling, flocks of birds motivated to premature migration, the scent of sulfur released from the darkest bowels of the earth.

While Fenton tells his tale, I begin absentmindedly to sort through the mail he has set in front of me. I flip through the bills and mailings—

wasted words tripping over themselves with false urgency—*act now act now don't delay act now*—until my eyes fix on a name on one of the return addresses that stops my sorting and, for a moment, my heart: *Merritt Wilson.*

It is a name that represents someone I once thought it best I never see again. A boomerang name. I imagine it spinning through the air and back to me, end over end, after all these years and over a great distance, with the sound of sliced air: *MerrittWilsonMerrittWilsonMerrittWilson.*

I tether Eddie to my chair, excuse myself, and stand from the table. Fenton's voice, the mild chuckling and inquisitive tones of his audience, fade as I move away across the lawn under the towering trees that placed me, happily, under their spell when I was growing up here on the Grand Old Caldwell Place and felt the trees' power but didn't yet know their names. I walk in the green light under their branches, which are recently leafed-out and lush from last night's rain, toward the house my ancestor Joshua Jackson homesteaded in 1798—the house to which I have returned and, it could be said, the house I've saved.

Down the hill, the creek twists through its minor valley. Insects run through with sunlight spiral up and up above it. I walk up the cracked, moss-covered front steps of the old house, sit in a wicker rocker on the porch, and tear open the envelope to read:

Dear T,

Six years since Starlight. Six years!

I've mailed this to "The Old Caldwell Place." I got your cryptic letter which said almost nothing about what you're up to. Lost the envelope with the return address, probably used it to start a fire for boiling water. It occurs to me you're probably milking a moccasin or drawing blood from a sheep, even as I scribble this.

Was surprised and pleased to hear from you here, in Angola. As you must already have found out I'm working for the Red Cross.

We're near a refugee camp in Saurimo. 100,000 land mines remain in the ground. 70,000 amputees, at the very least, so far. I work with children who've stepped on forgotten mines and had their flesh torn from their limbs, their bones turned to shrapnel. This, in addition to being hungry and covered with mange. There is precious little fresh water. Last week we were driving by a herd of cattle. One of the cows stepped on a mine. Gory little cow pieces rained down on the wind-shield. Our job is to try to get kids, who've known nothing but war, to smile.

Some days I walk through the fields, on unsapped land. I step. And I wait. And I step. And I wait. I don't know why I do it. Maybe for the thrill. I think I once tried to explain to you the stillpoint rush I get when I put myself in real danger. My way of feeling alive. Letting God make the decision to let me live. Or not. If there is a God. Sometimes, seeing what I'm seeing here, I wonder.

I have to admit I've been thinking about you more than I want to. Still. I have no idea how it will make you feel to read that. Not just because of your peculiar letter. Even before it arrived, I was thinking about us in that shack. Naked in the mud . . . meeting your dreadfully beloved moccasins. Are you still down there? Torturing those poor sheep? What were their names?

What made you write me after all this time, T?

Better go. Feel I've said too much. Your letter was so cryptic. . . . There's a good chance I'm coming back to Haven to visit Ben's grave. And to see you. We have much to discuss, you and I, peace of our own to make, after all this time, don't you think?

M.

If I didn't know better, I'd think old Fenton's quake had found its moment. Such is the effect of the letter, in large part, because I have written Merritt Wilson not a single letter of any kind in over ten years. How could she think she's received a letter from me?

Coming back to Haven. The phrase spins to settle from a great height, like a flaming leaf falling from the limb of a tall tree, to light on a field of dry wheat. This will burn through me for some time.

Coming back to Haven. Much to discuss . . . peace to make . . . kids, who've known nothing but war.

I look up from the letter, over the front porch, and down into the creek's shadowed valley. Bursts of golden light wink up from its surface, as if in recognition.

T W O

IT WAS MY STREAM. I'd lift the rocks, feeling, on their undersides, the fossilized forms from ages past, and crayfish would push themselves backward with their segmented tails through the murky water for new havens.

I was the stream's keeper. I meted out a justice that ran in a rhythm with my seven-year-old whims. The crayfish fought one another for my sport or were left to build their clay towers in peace. I amputated their claws if they failed to cooperate with my imagined decrees, or I left them alone.

Minnows skittered and darted away when my shadow fell on their pool. Or, fearful of the second shadow on the creekbed, they leaped and sprinkled the surface with their falling.

Every morning that summer at least three silver chubs with black stripes flopped against the osier weaving, worked their tiny round mouths for air in the old trap I'd baited with bits of stale bread. They were at my mercy. I'd slit open their slippery white bellies with my

rusted Old Timer pocketknife and let their entrails glisten in the sun. I'd
cut off their heads and throw them in the bushes; or, I'd let them squirm
out of my hands to their freedom.

Whispers and whims guided me through illimitable-seeming summer afternoons. I'd lie on my back and watch the drifting of clouds on
the bridge I'd built across my creek by stretching three faded old boards
from the bank at the bottom of the hill to an island in the stream and
then to the opposite bank. The boards had once formed a dilapidated
shed that Father and Grandfather Thomas said had been there since before they were born. The boards of the shed were still relatively strong.
Mother had it torn down because it wasn't safe for me to play around it.
For a long time after the shed was torn down a few of its old boards the
workmen had forgotten to truck away were strewn along the bank of
the stream. When I peeled the planks from the dirt that was beginning
to claim them, red ants, termites, black ants, and grubs scattered to find
new hiding places; a garter snake poured itself off through the grass. I
used these boards to make my bridge.

Grandfather Thomas said that slaves had built the shed. And slaves
had made and set the brick for the house and laid the stone fence. These
slaves had been black people who my ancestors *owned*. When he told me
that, I asked Father to repeat it so I would know I hadn't misheard him.
He repeated that, yes, these slaves had been owned in a time that had
passed, a time when our house was the only house for miles around and
Father's great-times-two grandfather Tobit had lived there and ridden
with John Hunt Morgan's Raiders in the War for Southern Independence, and before that.

The great Stonewall Jackson, they said, had met with other Confederate leaders in the parlor when they were trying to decide how best to
stop the Yankees from taking Tennessee. And adjoining our family grave
plot the field of graves I often played in was the final resting place for
fifteen hundred Confederate soldiers who Tobit had lost under his command at Chickamauga and arranged to have buried on his land to try to

alleviate his guilt, a last gesture of devotion for the poor volunteers who had followed him and lost their lives.

In those summers Grandfather Thomas would sit drinking on the front porch and tell stories of the old days. When the adults finished their juleps I'd volunteer to take them to the kitchen and on the way I'd tilt them back and let the inch-thick sugar at the bottom of the glass— the mint, water, and just a trace of bourbon—slide onto my tongue. Glasses deposited in the sink, I'd rush back to sit at his feet and hear more. I was only five or six, but listening to him made me think he had grown up in a better time. The men of his generation had won their big war, and before his time, the war our family most liked to remember had been lost honorably. There seemed to be a bittersweetness to hav-ing lost that made for better storytelling. The lines in his world seemed clearly drawn. Father would listen to him tell his stories and half smile, a little uncomfortably at times. Mother would laugh and laugh; she loved her father-in-law, seemed to, more than my father. I knew that Grandfather Thomas had been a senator, and, though I had no real un-derstanding of what that meant, the way my parents pronounced the word when they told me about it made me associate it with a lost grandeur.

I anchored the old boards with some rocks I lifted from a stone fence that Father and Grandfather Thomas said had been laid by slaves. One of the rocks had a name carved into it that was hard to read but felt like "Abel." I would trace the indented letters with my finger and think back to when a gnarled black hand or a smooth, strong black hand had carved that name in the time of these slaves. My favorite thing to do on a hot afternoon was to dangle my feet in the cool water under my bridge and idly trace the name in the rock over and over. And when there was a breeze, even a hot summer one, I found myself whispering whatever words the wind brought me.

A red-tailed hawk would alight on the limb of a particular elm in my kingdom, and I would hail it from below. I was especially interested in the hawk after I'd seen it swoop down, grip a squirrel in its talons, and lift off and away with it. I imagined seeing my kingdom with hawk's eyes. If I saw the hawk flying above me, I would run under it until it had crossed the borders of my kingdom where the construction sites and busy roads began.

Before we'd had to sell so much of the land, I'd defy Mother's rule that I stay within sight of the old house. I'd carry the butterfly net she had given me to the farthest reaches of my kingdom, where I'd set it down and dig for buried treasure with a rusty trowel. In the woods the bulldozers were knocking down, near the mounds of earth where my father said the Indians had left their things for safekeeping, I found flint-chipped arrowheads, whiskey bottles whose labels advertised the Monroes' long-defunct distillery, Coca-Cola bottles, beer cans, mason jars, Indianhead pennies, spent shotgun shells.

In the family graveyard where my ancestors lay and in among the fifteen hundred Confederate graves, the whispers increased their intensity so that they took on a steady susurration that sometimes sounded benevolent and often did not. The gravestones always felt cool under the ash trees' great looming limbs despite the most intense heat.

In my small kingdom, at three-foot-four and scarcely fifty pounds, I was a giant, a ruthless, whimsical king.

In the old house with the paint beginning to peel away I was still small and inconsequential. My dimensions seemed to change the moment I crossed the threshold. Up the hill, I was still my mother's little Tobia. Her errand runner and plaything, her precious little boy who caught and carried to her—their dusty wings pinched between his fat, dirty fingers—the live butterflies she would identify in a leather-bound book and kill in the killing jar and pin to the felt backing of her collection case. Sometimes, she would flip to a page in the book—the soft cotton of her sundress floating across her smooth freckled skin—and say, "Oh, look, Tobia! Run and find your mother one of these Gulf fritillaries!"

Up the hill from the creek I was my father's sissy son who had quit the swim team earlier in the summer and was not yet old enough for football, yardwork, or political discussions. I was the boy my father would just as soon ignore for a few more years. Up the hill, transfixed by his weighty presence, I was a spy, a fly on the wall, a specter—a tiny shade of the giant I became down at the creek.

I watched my father to see how he did things. Watched the way he moved, observed his manner of engaging the world. When he went to work in the morning, I'd watch the old silver Mercedes wind down the driveway. I'd practice his aristocratic swagger in the bathroom mirror. I aspired to his stoic grace and imagined the day when I would wear the power I read into his aloofness, his manly coolness.

At night, when a ponderous hush breathed through the house, I'd hide behind the statues of the Rhodesian Ridgebacks, those lion hunters in the hallway. I'd spy on him, reading his documents, managing our dwindling resources, haggling on the phone with developers and real estate agents.

Other times Mother would have me take him cool whiskey drinks that he would accept from me, wordlessly, ice clinking, his breathing the only sound between us, rapt as he was, on his work, on finding loopholes so that we could hold onto the land. Or, I would take him drinks in the den when he was watching the news or football. For years I thought the only things anyone could watch on television were football or the news. At those times when it was just me and my father in the room, I wanted to say something to him that would cause him to listen to me, but I had no idea what that might be.

The whispering voices reached a crescendo in my seventh summer. They would find me when I was sitting on the boards of my bridge. Sometimes my lips would form strange words I'd never known but that I came to think of as my secret, a power I had, the only friends of an only child.

On some nights that summer I couldn't sleep for all the images flickering through my head. The old house, too, was sometimes aswarm with whispers. I'd climb out of bed and take walks under the conjoined canopies. The trees on those nights seemed to be whispering about me, protecting, or, perhaps, threatening me. The leaves were having conversations about what would become of me.

On a few of those nights when I'd sneaked out to wander the yard and look up into the boughs, a cat I had never encountered during the day would appear from the darkness. The cat was entirely grey and would come into focus and look up at me as if to say, "Isn't that something. Here we both are in this place on such a night as this." The cat would rub against my legs, and I would lift it up and cradle it in my arms. Its fur was softer than most cats I'd held, and when I buried my face in its coat, I could feel its heartbeat. It smelled clean and kinetic, like the places it had been—crabgrass, honeysuckle, jonquils, wild onion, like the rocks under the creekwater, and faintly, I imagined, like the blood of young rabbits, moles, and squirrels.

The cat purred when I held it under the whispering trees. I saw it on perhaps three or four of my night wanderings that summer, never during the day. The last time I saw it was the night before I first saw the snake.

WHICH APPEARED in the place where I'd been staring, materialized out of the hot thick air. It was the color of a tire dusted in places with ash; it had a wide head and small bituminous eyes. Seeing it produced the same effect as a loaded gun pointed and cocked with its cold eye on me. This snake seemed ready to burst with deadly potential. It was magnificent, longer than I was, thick as my arm. I knew as soon as I'd seen it that it was poisonous.

The snake had composed itself in the shallows with its head resting just above the surface in the leaf-broken sunlight. Below the water I could see its body intertwined with the roots. I stood up quickly on the old boards of my bridge. It was unsettling that the afternoon's silence—only the distant whine of a chainsaw—remained steady with the snake there, this new thing that had slithered into my life. Two urges flared: one to run up the hill into the house; the other to find a stick and destroy the intruder in the heart of my kingdom. I scampered up the bank and into the cool air of the house.

I knew my father was the one to ask about snakes. After dinner that night when he was standing up from the table to go upstairs to his study and Mother had taken some plates back into the kitchen, I told him about the snake, leaving out the part about how I'd run away from it. I felt uneasy telling him, as if the snake had been a secret between me and the snake.

"What color? Flat head? Long? Thick?" he asked, and I told him. "Sounds like you found yourself a cottonmouth. A water moccasin," he said. "You leave him alone, Tobia, and he won't bother you," he said, turned, and walked up the creaking stairs to the study, where he often went after dinner to squint down over his documents.

I thought about the cotton soaked with alcohol old nurse Dickson rubbed on the smooth skin of my arm before she inserted the needle and pushed down the syringe—the smell of rubbing alcohol, the cold feeling before the little sting. I thought about a buckskin moccasin falling without sound on a rock submerged in a flowing stream.

The next day I approached the stream with great caution. I stood on my bridge and was surprised to see the water passing as it always had. Even though I couldn't see the snake, the air was thick with the intensity of its possible appearance. I searched the banks for its shape among the leaf shadows and tried to peer underwater among the twisted roots. I waited for it to show itself, to slither out and be accounted for. I threw rocks at the twisted roots, but the snake didn't show itself. I shouted for it, threatened it, taunted it, called it names. It never revealed itself.

There was a splash in front of me. When I looked up, I saw a boy facing me from the opposite bank. The start he gave me was the same as when I'd first seen the snake. I started to run up the hill, but after a few steps the boy was saying something. This stopped me. I turned to face him.

"I said, what's yer name?" the boy said in a raspy voice. He was wearing an untucked red-striped shirt and dark jeans, despite the heat, and his voice was unpleasant to my ears. I'd spied on this boy when he'd been moving into the first finished house in the new development going up on some land we'd had to sell. I'd told my mother I didn't want the houses to be built there because I liked to explore the fields and the patches of wood over there. I had a tree fort on that land. But she'd said not to worry because there would be lots of new friends moving in for me to play with. Once all these new friends moved in I wouldn't be so lonely, she said.

I'd seen this boy playing while his family unloaded the moving van, and I'd seen him throwing rocks into the part of my stream in front of his house. His father was tall and hawk-nosed. I'd seen the man yell at the boy for getting muddy and for not helping them unload the van. The boy had shuffled his feet, looked down at the ground, and sulked back toward the house. I wondered how, exactly, the boy would become my friend and imagined several scenarios in which our friendship came to pass. I wondered if he liked to fish, if he'd ever caught a snapping turtle like Eddie with chicken gizzards or been out for ducks or found an arrowhead. He had a sister I heard them call Merritt, who was his twin. I had seen her scold her brother for dropping one of the boxes. Their chubby mother had shiny golden hair, wore a wide sunhat, and was continuously fanning herself in the heat and saying, "Be careful with that one. Be *careful*." The boy's name was Ben. Ben Wilson.

"What . . . is . . . yer . . . name," Ben Wilson said, again, enunciating as if he thought I might speak another language, or might be a little slow.

"My name's Toby. That's my house up there," I said, pointing at our old house up on the hill. Ben looked up at the house, then back at me.

"Well. You can't play in this creek. You better stay away from it. It's mine now," he said. I tried to get a better look at him through the shadows of the oak tree, but I couldn't really see his face.

I felt myself give in to my fear, and I turned and ran up the hill where I could be small and safe in the cool air of our house, up the stairs down the creaking hall, into my bedroom and leaped on my bed. I punched my pillows, and imagined what it would feel like to punch Ben Wilson's face. It was cool in the room and the cool sheets felt good on my skin, but my face and my body were still hot, and the tears poured as I pummeled the soft pillows.

"I'll show him. I'll show him," I said. A chorus of other whispering voices echoed mine through the room. I was suddenly afraid that my father would find out I'd run away from the boy, and thought how there would be many things in my life I couldn't tell him.

I didn't stay away from the stream. That would have been impossible for me. I went down every day to look for the snake. I poked and stirred a long stick between the roots, but the snake was never there. I also watched out for this Ben Wilson.

A week later he caught me sitting on my bridge dropping twigs and leaves into the desultory current.

"You better get off that bridge," he said. He came out onto my bridge. I watched him coming and stood to face him in stunned surprise. We scuffled briefly before he managed to overpower and push me into the creek. All at once, I was looking at the bottom of the stream. I flailed, and I was frightened when I remembered the snake. After the splashing, I went running in my soaked clothes up the hill and home, his laughter diminishing behind me.

At the top of the hill I turned and looked down at him.

A FEW DAYS later my mother said, "I want you to deliver this pie for me, Tobia. They're our neighbors. Their name is Wilson. It's polite to make a newly arrived family feel welcome. They have a little boy who is going to be your friend. And a little girl who is his twin who will also be your friend."

All day, as I'd been coming in and out of the house on my rounds, I'd been smelling the pecan pie. When I saw it cooling on the counter, I started looking forward to eating a piece or two of it, preferably with some vanilla ice cream, that night after dinner.

I looked at my mother and considered telling her about my encounters with Ben Wilson and how they had not augured well for our ever becoming friends, but I didn't say anything because I knew she would probably tell Father.

By the time I was crossing through the stand of trees separating our yard from the Wilsons', I'd pulled two or three of the sweet pecans from the pie and eaten them myself.

The Wilson house was a two-story brick Neo-Georgian. Only a few weeks before I'd seen workmen rolling out green sections of sod on top of the construction dirt.

I stood on the front porch holding the pie in its tin and pressed the doorbell button, heard it chime inside, heard footsteps. The door swung open to reveal Mrs. Wilson. "Oh-oh. Hello, young man. Can I help you?"

I held up the pie.

"Oooh—look at this. For us? What a treat." Her voice was raspy and funny-sounding like her son's. Her r's were hard. She was pretty but not as pretty as my mother, and she was plump and her skin was pasty and white as milk and so smooth it didn't even seem like real skin.

I stepped cautiously into the house, which smelled aggressively new, like fresh paint and enamel. Boxes with labels that said ATTIC,

LIVING ROOM LAMPS cluttered the hallway and rested on the landing of the stairs.

"Benny! Mer! Come down here, please," the woman sang into the house. "We have a visitor." She landed hard on her *r*'s. She smiled down at me.

"My mom said," I began. "My mom said this is for you and welcome to Haven." I thought after that I would be able to turn around and go home.

"What a little gentleman. And what's your name?" she asked.

"Tobia Caldwell."

Ben and Merritt Wilson peeked over the banister. When they saw me looking up at them, they giggled and ducked down behind it, as if they thought I couldn't see them through the slats.

Mrs. Wilson said, "Come down and say hello."

They came down the steps, Merritt first, then Ben, who stopped on the landing next to a box that said CHRISTMAS DECORATIONS. He looked at me for a moment. Then, as if he had decided I was not in his house to get him in trouble, he allowed himself a faint, mischievous smile.

"Benny, Merritt, this is . . . what's your name again, dear?"

"Toby Caldwell," I said, looking at Ben.

"Oh . . . yes. Your family lives in the house up the hill, over through all those big trees. Oh, my," she said. "I've heard about . . . It's nice to meet Tobia Caldwell. *Isn't* it, guys? "

Ben came down the last of the steps. "Nice to meet you, nice to meet you," he said in a cartoon parody of an adult's greeting. He shook my hand wildly—way up way down—as if he'd never seen me before. I felt like laughing but wasn't sure if that was the appropriate response. Merritt joined him. Each of them shook one of my hands—Ben my left, Merritt my right—way up, way down.

"Nice to meet you, nice to meet you," they both said and laughed together as they shook my hands.

"Nice to meet you, too," I said, looking at Ben.

Their mother shook her head. "You sillies," she said.

Merritt was slightly more slender and taller than her brother, and her hair was curly like her mother's, but she had her father's thinness, his hungry cheekbones and big eyes. She looked very much like Ben; it was clear they were twins, but equally as clear they were not identical. In his squint-eyed chubbiness, Ben leaned a shade toward his mother; Merritt, in the burgeoning semi-angularity of her features, a tinge toward her father.

Merritt looked at me with what I took to be keen interest. She said, "He lives in a mansion with big white columns? Like in your books, Mother."

"That's right," she said. "Let me take this to the kitchen. I'll be right back. You two stay here and keep Toby company," Mrs. Wilson said.

I looked at Ben. "My mom says," I began, emboldened by his parodic greeting, feeling its clownishness had given me an opening. "My mom says maybe we'll be friends, someday," I said.

Ben looked at me and made his eyes into slits between smooth cheek and brow. He shrugged. "Yeah, maybe," he said. "And maybe NOT!" he said and shook with a burst of fake laughter.

Merritt looked at me. "He'll be your friend. He was complaining this morning he has no one to play with around here," she said.

Ben ran up the stairs and once he'd reached the top of the landing looked down at me. "I'll never be your friend," he said in a singsong voice.

Merritt shook her head. "Don't worry about him. We'll whip him into shape," she said. The way she said it made me think she was repeating something she'd heard her mother or father say, a chorus about troublesome Ben.

"Anyway, I'll be your friend. I mean, if you're desperate for friends," she said.

"All right," I said, wondering whether or not a girl could be your friend.

A short time later, Mrs. Wilson came back into the foyer. She thanked me for the pie and told me to thank my parents for her and sent me back out into the heat everyone was swimming in that summer. I walked slowly toward our house where, when I returned, Mother asked me for a full report. The thing I remembered most about the visit was Merritt standing on the Wilsons' new porch and waving goodbye and how she said she would be my friend, but I didn't tell my mother about that.

A DAY OR TWO after I'd made my delivery, the doorbell chimed through our old house. Mrs. Wilson and the twins had brought over a casserole. I watched from between the railings of the mahogany banister as my mother let them in. I listened to them moving into the kitchen and heard Mother talk to them in a superanimated tone. Then her voice rang through the house on my name.

"Tobia, come down here. Oh-oh, Tobia?"

I ran to my room and pretended not to hear her. I didn't want to have to be polite to this Ben Wilson in my own home. Mother came upstairs to my room. I could tell she was angry by the way she pushed open the door.

She said, "Tobia, come downstairs with me this instant. Honestly. Come and talk to our new neighbors." I followed her grudgingly down the steps.

"Of course, you've met Tobia," my mother said as we walked into the kitchen. My father was excusing himself, telling Mrs. Wilson that it was nice to have met them, that he appreciated the casserole, but he had some work to do if they would please excuse him. Mrs. Wilson said her husband was at home getting some things squared away himself in their new house or he would have come over. My father nodded and smiled and walked away, passing us as we came into the kitchen.

The woman looked at me. "Hello, Tobia," she said and smiled at my mother with her red lips. She was wearing an off-white sundress dotted with dark blue violets. "Moving's hard on a child. Ben's very glad to have Tobia so close," she said. "And Merritt is, too, for that matter."

Merritt stood beside Ben and looked at me. I noticed again how Ben was chubby like his mother, that he had her full cheeks and deepset eyes, which he squinted slightly as he stood in my kitchen smiling at me. I looked at both of them standing there. Merritt was slenderer and bigger-eyed. I thought of them coming into the world at the same time and wondered how it would change my life if I had a brother or a sister, a twin.

"Tobia's glad Ben's here and Merritt, too. There aren't many boys Tobia's age around here, at least not within biking distance. I'm sure you two will be fast friends," my mother said, looking from one to the other of us and smiling, the smile a trifle icier than it would have been had someone she considered on a par with her, socially, come to call. Ben stared at me from behind the island counter, grinning, his eyes full of mischief. Merritt put a hand on Ben's shoulder, and he shrugged it off.

"Why don't you boys go outside and play?" my mother said. I shook my head, but she persisted. "Oh, Tobia. Silly. Go on now. Show Ben your new bicycle."

I felt like reminding her that my bicycle wasn't new. I'd had it for two years. It was a rusted one-speed with a banana seat and backward ten-speed handlebars like a ram's horns. My mother shook her head and smiled about me to the boy's mother.

I walked out first into the heat and to the side yard at the top of the hill above my stream. It was so hot that if you moved, even slightly, you'd start to sweat. Ben came out afterward and when I glanced back I could see our mothers smiling at us from the doorway as if they might have been musing on their sons' long future together. The door shut and just when I was about to make a suggestion about what we could do, Ben put his leg across my feet and pushed me over so that I fell and went tumbling down the hill. I let myself roll down the slope to the edge of my stream. When I stopped rolling, I stood up, turned around, and looked up the hill where Ben was standing and laughing down at me.

I wondered what Father would do in this situation. I searched my mind for references. I'd seen him yelling into the phone at someone: "Well, you change that, or I swear to God, I'll have your head mounted on my wall!" And I'd seen him blow a raccoon's head clean off with the shotgun for tipping over our trashcans.

"I am the king of the hill!" Ben shouted. "Now you have to come up here and try to push me off."

"Hey, you," I called up to him. "Hey, you, Ben Wilson. Come down here. I want to show you something," I said.

"What?" he said.

"Come down here. I'll show you something."

He came down the hill slowly. But then at the last rise, he ran.

"See these roots, here?" I said, walking to the edge of the stream. "The ones down there reaching in the water?"

"Yeah?" he said.

"I lost a silver dollar down in those roots," I said.

"So?" he said.

"So, I bet you can't find that silver dollar. I bet you don't have the guts to reach down in those roots and get that silver dollar."

He looked at me.

"Why don't you reach down there your own self?"

I shrugged. "Maybe I got plenty of silver dollars."

"I'm not afraid of those roots."

"Then do it. If you get the silver dollar, you can keep it."

"No, I'm not afraid, and if I get that silver dollar, I am keeping it. It's all mine if I get it out."

"I don't care. I got plenty," which was true. Aunt Marcy gave me one every birthday I ever had, every visit from Turtle Eddie. Seven.

"I'm gonna get that silver dollar," he said, and he hurriedly yanked off his shoes and socks and waded into the stream to the place where the roots were all tangled up. "Where is it?" he asked when he was standing in the middle of my stream, turning skeptical when he saw the over-expectancy in my face. "Wait," he said. "You better not be trickin' me. Is it really down in there? Where is it?" he said.

"Way down in there. Pretty deep," I said. "You'll have to reach your whole arm in, probably," I said.

He looked at me. "Why'd you drop it down in there anyway?"

"I told you. I got those other ones."

"Is it down in here?"

He reached his whole right arm down in the deepest part of the tangles of roots and groped around at the bottom of my stream. In my mind flashed the alcohol-soaked cotton, the nurse pushing down the syringe, the short sting, the puffy sort of feeling when the medicine was in you. Just after or just before the impulse to tell him to stop, he shrieked and pulled up his arm. He shook it and the water splashed around him. Something dark and long was obscured in the furious water. Ben's face contorted. The long dark snake rippled down the stream, angry and fast. It was frightening to watch it ripple on down— creekwater dancing under its belly, ripples curving out behind. Ben ran through the stream toward the Wilsons' house. His feet broke the water in sharp staccato splashes. He was holding the bitten arm against his side and grasping it with his other hand so that he wobbled and almost lost his balance several times. He was screaming and running up the stream toward his new house sounding like he was laughing when I knew he wasn't. I stood on the bank and watched him running away.

I looked up at the fan window of the old house and saw some movement in the frame.

A short time later, Merritt Wilson ran down the hill toward me.

"Where's Benny?" she said.

I lifted my arm and pointed up the creek.

"Come and help me find him?" she said. "We'll make him play with you."

I had no intention of moving.

"Come on," she said.

I shook my head, but when she went I followed. We walked up the creek on the trail I'd made, ducked under limbs, leaves and sticks cracking under our feet.

"Did he go home? That turkey," she said.

I nodded.

We rounded a bend in the creek. Ben's body was a splash of color in the center of the stream. He was lying facedown in a little rapids that trickled through some mossy green rocks. His soaked shirt was undulating in the slow current, and his brown hair was rising and falling like strange eelgrass.

Merritt screamed, "Benny!" and splashed in, kneeled beside him, and turned him onto his back. "I don't think he's breathing!" she said.

I took up his swollen, discolored right forearm and helped her drag him to the bank. Merritt examined the place where it was turning blue and knotting up. She pinched his nose and tried to breath into his mouth and hit him in the chest.

"I'm going for my dad. You stay here," she said and ran up the hill toward the Wilsons' house.

I watched her running away and thought this has not happened. I looked down at Ben. His wide-open, hazelgrey eyes were staring up at the clouds. I put my hand in front of his mouth and waited for a time. I thought I felt something stir against my palm, but I wasn't sure, so I waited a little longer, straining to feel his breath on my hand. My own breath caught in my chest. After a time, Ben sucked in a great gasp of air and clutched at my arm and stared wildly up at the sky before going completely limp and still.

There was a hubbub up at the Wilsons' house. I heard them coming.

I heard the opening of the door, tense, clipped voices—Ben's father asking questions, Merritt's answers. I stood up beside the creek and thought about what I should do. I was thinking this has not happened. And then, when the voices were closer but before I'd seen them, I left Ben and ran and hid myself behind the stone fence. I crouched and slunk along behind it. I could hear them finding him, hear them trying to help him, hear them gathering him up. I kneeled behind the fence and watched the car race away.

Later, I ignored my mother when she called for me.

"Tobia! Tobia Banes Caldwell!?"

I let my name fade behind me and under cover of the trees, I ran through the side yard and behind the house where our land still spread back. I ran until the tangled weeds that were taller than me and growing in careless profusion at the edge of the cultivated part of the yard, slowed me down. I kept running till our land gave out.

THE NEXT MORNING I hid behind the old walnut tree at the top of the first small rise of the hill and watched three men search the stream and kill the snake. One of the men was Ben Wilson's tall, hawk-nosed father. The other two were men in long black jumpsuits from some kind of animal control organization. One of them was carrying a shovel, the other a pair of tongs. I saw them corner the cottonmouth in the shallows between the oak's roots. The man with the tongs poked them down in the roots and flicked the snake up onto the bank. It struck and struck at the men, almost sank its fangs into one of them in the leg above his boots. The man jumped back, cursing. But then the man with the shovel hacked off the snake's head with a quick guillotine motion, and its severed head still struck and chomped as if it thought it could bite itself back to life. It sure wanted to live. You could see the fangs in its white mouth, its cottonmouth, venom squirting—the same kind of venom it put in Ben Wilson. The long black body squirmed and flipped around. The man with the shovel handed it to Ben's father so he could give the snake's still-striking head one last vengeful cathartic *whack* with the flat of the shovel. Three more times: *whack whack whack.*

When they had all walked away, I went down to where the snake's head had been smashed into the mud. It surprised me they had just left it there. I looked for its body but I couldn't find it. I assumed it must have already sunk to the bottom of the stream. With a sharp slate rock I dug the head out of the mud and scooped it up. It had been smashed in such a way that you could see its fangs sticking out on either side of its head, which was heavier than I had expected, like a large rock. I thought for a minute what I should do with it, and then I knew. I walked to where the oak roots made the shelter in the stream, tangling down into the deepest place and tying themselves up in knots. I dropped the head down in there and watched it spiraling and seeming to watch me the whole way down.

THAT NIGHT at supper the phone rang and Father answered. He talked for a while and then he came in and sat down.

"That was Mr. Wilson," he said. "Their boy died." He looked at me.

My mother, who was standing behind me, gasped and hugged me and kissed the top of my head. "Thank God," she said. "That could've been Tobia. Tobia's always playing in that creek. I send him down there to hunt butterflies. Thank God that dreadful creature didn't get its fangs into our precious little Tobia," she said and again she kissed the top of my head.

I looked at my father.

LATER THAT NIGHT I sat in one of the white flaking wicker chairs on the front porch looking down into the small dark valley my stream had carved and tried to think what it would be like to be dead. How long, exactly, was forever? Dead forever. I said the boy's name. Ben Wilson.

I didn't turn when I heard the screened door creak open and clap shut and my father's footsteps moving across the porch. I knew he was coming to talk to me. He sat in the creaking swing above the other end of the floor and stared into the increasing darkness far beyond the porch until he had worked up to tell me. He said he thought he had a pretty good idea what had happened. He said the boy's father told him how they'd killed the snake. But the boy's father said that didn't feel like justice; he wanted to know what had happened.

"I didn't know what to tell the man," he said, and it was a question.

THREE

A SERPENT'S HEAD breaks the riffles of the creek. Its ancient eyes return glints of moonlight. Without a ripple, it vanishes beneath the water to reappear a moment later in the creekside grass. It slides up the bank, the fluidity of its movement mirroring the stream in which its tail is, now, no longer immersed.

Moments later, Ben Wilson emerges from the same place in the creek. His head breaks the surface, and he stands in the shallows. Drops of moon-suffused water fall from his body. He fixes the old house up the hill with a look of otherworldly determination and sad, ineffable loss. He steps onto the bank—a grown man, one year older than me, as he would have been—and follows the serpent up the bank.

I sense the serpent's history. It has flown the papyrus of the Egyptian Book of the Dead, left Genesis in the dust. This is the serpent that sent Eurydice to the underworld, one half of the Aztec rain god Tlalac. This is the Chinese demon Nu-kua. It is the serpent on the staff of Asclepius,

Greek god of medicine. It s-curves through the creekside grass and slides up the rise, slowly, on its belly, as the Bible decreed.

The March air is cool and does not give much warmth to the serpent's blood. The moon lends its skin a silvery-blue tint. Its tongue flick-flicks for news. With each flick it pulls in and, with Jacobson's organ, tastes the air.

This serpent has molted recently, slithered out of the translucent shell of its old skin, reborn into a fresh portion of the eternal life it snuffed from Gilgamesh. When it coils, the serpent is immortal. Its tail *was;* its head *is.* And then its head *was* its tail *is.*

The serpent glides easily up the four cracked and moss-covered steps and slides across the flaking paint floorboards on the front porch of this old house. It slithers between the legs of the wicker furniture and pauses there at the base of one of the Doric columns. It flick-flicks its tongue to taste the air. Its head rises slowly, lifts around . . . gains purchase and, so, it spirals neatly up the column and sloughs down onto the floor of the second-story porch just outside the window of my childhood bedroom. It peers in the open window and whispers, *Ben Wilson is coming is Wilson Ben.*

I open my eyes to darkness, reeling with the realness of the dream. I sit up on the edge of my childhood bed and put my bare feet flat on the fringe of a threadbare kilim. I stand into a wavering slice of moonlight, pull some clothes from the dresser, and throw them on.

I walk down the old stairs. Especially late at night, the boards in this house creak and groan under my weight, seeming to engage one another in a conversation, the loudness and harshness of which my mother softened with her presence when she lived here.

I walk across the back porch, let the screened door clap clap clap shut behind me, and move out across the grass toward one of the houses Bank and his crew are in the process of dismantling. It stands before me, an enemy soldier, its wounds strangely enhanced by the moonlight and the cool air.

Inside this demi-house I take up a sledgehammer one of the work-men has left behind. I feel its weight in my hand and carry it upstairs and let it throw me into a blind spin. I spin counterclockwise. Sledge-hammer extended, I let the weight spin me through the house until the sledgehammer finds a wall or a window or until I'm too tired to continue.

Glass shatters. Sledgehammer on brick makes a dull thud. Bricks chip, dent, crack. Tiny white sparks appear to enjoy their split seconds of life in the cool air. Drywall explodes chalky white. Boards splinter, break, or hold fast to stop my spinning.

Thus halted, I rest for only a moment before I pick up the hammer and let it let me regather momentum. I spin into fresh assaults and the spinning reminds me of the time I spun Merritt Wilson over the grass one day when she asked me to do that for her for fun, and I obliged, re-luctantly, afraid I might hurt her. We clasped each other's wrists, and I leaned back, and when I spun she rose into the air over the grass.

On nights like this, in these houses we're erasing, I spin counter-clockwise and close my eyes to better remember how it felt to spin Mer-ritt in our first summer together, ten years after Ben was bitten and died. Tonight, as on the other nights, I spin with the hammer, feeling the memory. I am still spinning in the room when I hear a voice.

I let the end of the hammer thud to the floor.

"Please, stop. Please. Please . . ." A child's voice, and on the verge of tears.

I open my eyes and see Kippy Goodhope standing in the doorway, a laser gun holstered at his hip. This is the Goodhopes' seven-year-old son. It occurs to me he must have been playing in one of the upstairs bedrooms of this partially demolished house and suddenly realized his exit was blocked by a crazed man with a sledgehammer. I shake my head with the realization of what he must have just seen and what he must think.

"Hello there," I say. "It's all right. I'm not going to hurt you."

He looks at me, his eyes wide with fear, and begins to slide around behind me to the stairs and his exit. I stand out of his way. Before he reaches the stairs, just when he's poised to go down, I make another attempt to talk to him.

"When I was young, I used to sneak out and walk around this yard, on this same land. Just like you," I say. "So . . ." But I can't quite think how to establish the connection.

He pauses for a moment, fixes on a point somewhere to my right and behind me. He begins to say something, but then he thinks better of it and disappears down the steps. I hear his footfalls going across the downstairs floor. I imagine him leaping out the gap where the front door had been.

I walk over to what had been a window and watch him sprint across the yard. He runs through my ancestors' graves on his parents' property and into the last intact and inhabited house in this part of the Golfhurst subdivision.

I let the handle of the sledgehammer fall to the floor and try to account for the emptiness Kippy's leaving has set loose in me.

After a time, I put the sledgehammer where I found it and walk back across the moonlit lawn to the old house. Lights have come on at the Goodhopes' and their golden lab, Ballooloo, releases a volley of barks that fall flat on the night air.

I open the back door, walk across the screened-in porch, creak up the stairs, settle back into bed and sleep. Sleep and nothing. Just sleep.

FOUR

I STARED AT THE CEILING and tried to grasp the concept of complete, unappealable absence from the world. I was five when Grandmother Pearl died, and the two intervening years had hushed her service beyond recall. Grandfather Thomas had been given a hero's funeral at St. Andrew's before his empty casket was buried in the backfield beside Pearl and our other ancestors, not far from the graves of the men Tobit had lost at Chickamauga. Later, the gravesite was covered by a stone mausoleum. Everyone talked about what a great man my grandfather Thomas had been, how full his life, meaningful his impact, and numerous his achievements. In his and Pearl's heyday people of import, substance, and real worth, people who'd done big things with their lives, had come to visit our house and filled it with their stories. I thought how Ben Wilson hadn't even had the chance to come to such an end.

When the wind touched the leaves outside the window, the grey shadows lifted on the wall, and in the upper corners of the room the greyness darkened to the color I decided was the color of death.

As I watched the leaf-shadows moving on the wall, I revisited Ben Wilson's run through my creek and its aftermath. I saw it again and again. He ran away holding the bitten arm. His feet churned the creek-water. I stood on the bank and couldn't move. Ben Wilson disappeared around the bend. I watched the creekwater flowing and saw how it was holding the secret, already uncreased in the places where Ben Wilson's feet had broken it, already reassuming its ceaseless forgetting.

I looked up from the water and stared in the direction in which Ben Wilson had run. I turned and looked downstream where the cotton-mouth had danced atop the water. A numbness coursed my veins. *What have I done and what should I do? What have I done and what should I do?*

Merritt came out of the front door of our house up the hill. She stood between the columns looking down at just me. She ran down the hill and skipped toward me down the last rise. We went to find Ben, where he'd fallen and his hair was waving like eelgrass in the current. She went to get help, and I waited with him, the unmoving boy, who was supposed to be my future friend.

I replayed it again and again that night as I still do and always will. His wide skyward-looking eyes, his final gasp.

MY FATHER interrupted my replaying of the events that night. His shadow joined the shadows of the leaves. He sat down in the chair beside my bed. I looked up at him. It was not unusual for my mother to tuck me in at night, but if my father came in, there was usually a reason for the visit—some business to discuss, a lesson to learn. I knew we were going to have a talk.

"How you making it?" he asked.

"Making it," I said.

"I need something from you. I need you to tell me exactly what happened down at the creek the other day. I want you to tell me just what you remember."

I looked up at him.

"Did you say something to Ben Wilson before it happened?" he asked.

"Yes."

"What did you say to him?"

"I told him he better watch out for that snake," I said.

My father narrowed his eyes as if he'd had a whiff of my mendacity.

"So you knew the snake was there?" he said.

"Yes, sir. In general."

"In general you did. And that boy pushed you down the hill?"

"Yes, sir."

"Were you angry with him for pushing you down the hill?"

"Yes, sir. I fell and . . . I let myself tumble to the bottom of the hill. I was angry with him."

"Of course you were. Anyone would've been. But, then, why so suddenly did *he* run down the hill and take off his shoes and socks and wade into the creek? I was watching. I saw it happen."

"It was hot."

"I see, that's right. It was hot outside so the boy—Ben Wilson—impulsively ran down that rise and pulled off his shoes and socks and rolled up his pantlegs and jumped into the creek? That's what happened?"

"Yes, sir."

"And you had nothing to do with the decision he made to take off his shoes and socks and roll up his pantlegs and wade into the creek."

"Well . . . I told him. I told him it was . . . that it would feel good if he did it."

"So you suggested to him that it might cool his feet if he jumped into the creek. You offered him the water of your portion of creek. That was neighborly of you. But, then, why did he reach down into those roots? Did you suggest to him that it might feel especially good if he reached down into the roots? I could see him groping around in there while he was talking to you."

"No."

"You didn't?"

"No."

"What did you tell him?"

"I told him there was nothing down in those roots that he needed to be reaching down in them . . ."

"So you didn't warn him about the cottonmouth?"

I searched the shadows on the wall behind him as if my answer would appear somewhere in their midst.

"Don't lie to me," he said.

I sat up. Tears streamed down my cheeks. I leaned toward my father. "Don't tell Mother," I whispered. "Please don't tell her what I said."

"Stop crying," he said. "Straighten up and fly right."

I tried to reverse the outward motion of my sobs.

"You need to tell *me* what you said to him before I can make a decision about whether or not we need to tell your mother."

I told him what had happened. I told how the strange boy had appeared on the opposite bank one day. I told him how the boy had pushed me off my bridge. I told him again how the boy had pushed me down our hill and how I went tumbling, at the end letting myself tumble. And then I told him about the silver dollar.

And after he'd heard, he nodded and breathed and leaned in close so I could feel his breath when he whispered, "Listen to me. There are certain things people need not tell anyone else. And everyone in the world keeps at least one of these things close to them." He clinched his fist and brought it in close to his chest and looked away for a time, out the window at the leaves lifting and falling on the breeze. "Do you know what justice is, Tobia?" he said.

"Just us," I said quickly.

He shook his head.

"Fair? That people should be fair," I said.

He nodded. "We'll have to find the way to be fair in this matter. Between us we'll decide what's fair. You need to do something to set yourself right in God's eyes and in your own eyes," he said, pointing up at the ceiling and then at my eyes.

"In God's eyes?" I said.

He nodded.

LATER THAT NIGHT my mother came into the room and sat down on my bed. I feigned sleep. I felt her fingertips spread a remaining tear to dryness across my cheek, the touch of her lips to my forehead.

"Sweet dreams, Tobia," she said.

I opened my eyes and watched her moving away.

THERE WAS GOING to be an interrogation of sorts. The Wilsons wanted to get a better sense of what had happened down at the creek. The snakebite was troubling them deeply. They wanted to ask me some questions because I had been the last one to see their son alive. They thought I might know something that could help them with their pain.

When the time came, my father drove us over to the first of the subdivision houses that would follow. From the shotgun seat my mother said, "Just tell it how it happened and everything will be all right. Ben Wilson was hot, right, sweetie? It doesn't get quite so hot, so humid, up in Ohio, so he decided to go for a wade in the creek to cool himself. And . . . what happened then, Tobia? He saw a crawdaddy on the bottom and he reached for it and . . . what, Tobia? Maybe you ought to practice your story, honey. Tell it in your head so you don't even sound like you're not telling the truth which you will be." She looked at my father whose eyes I had met in the rearview mirror as we turned through the gates of the subdivision.

We stood on the porch until the door swung inward to reveal the Wilsons.

Mr. and Mrs. Wilson, all four of Ben's grandparents, and several aunts and uncles were standing in the foyer to give us a solemn welcome. A grandmother, or maybe an aunt, was going around asking if people wanted tea or cookies. Merritt stood at the bottom of the stairs where she and Ben had shaken my hand the day I'd delivered the pie, way up way down. Three days before she'd stood behind Ben in our house and leaped into the creek when she saw his hair waving like eelgrass, his eyes staring at nothing.

In the Wilsons' foyer, my parents offered grave, soft-spoken condolences, which the Wilsons accepted with downturned heads and small nods, except when Mr. Wilson raised his gaze, suddenly, from his shoes and up at me, and I saw that his brown eyes were alive with a thinly concealed mixture of what looked to be fury and guilt. I heard Mr. Wilson speak, then, for the first time in a half-buried Tennessee twang that contrasted as much with my parents' soft r'd lilt as it did with Mrs. Wilson's Midwestern brogue.

Mr. Wilson asked my parents if it was all right if they questioned me in private. My father didn't answer immediately. He narrowed his eyes. "Well," he said. He clearly thought it an odd request, one he wanted to refuse.

My mother stirred at the suggestion. She shot a nervous glance around at the strange, solemn faces in the room, probably worrying almost as much about the effort it was going to take to maintain a conversation in that living room as she was about protecting me.

"I don't see why not," my father finally said, looking into Mr. Wilson's eyes. My father looked down at me. I looked up at him. He nodded.

"Tell them exactly what happened, Tobia, so they'll know and have that peace of mind," my mother said into the otherwise silent room. "In the past, Tobia has always been an honest child," she announced and smiled into the room a smile reminiscent of the smiles she and Mrs. Wilson had had for Ben and me just before we'd walked outside and he'd pushed me down the hill.

I followed Mr. and Mrs. Wilson past Merritt at the bottom of the steps. She looked at me in a still, dazzled way that suggested she thought I was being led to my execution.

We went into a sort of den that had been partially moved-into on the second floor. On the wall was a framed antique menu with outdated food for low prices that said FRED WILSON'S RESTAURANT on top, and on the other wall hung a framed, mostly orange Tennessee Vols football poster. On the desk facing me stood a photograph of the Wilsons, Ben included, out of which the whole family smiled in a strained sort of way, all of them wearing white turtleneck sweaters, and sitting on grass in front of a tree among big, crunchy-looking leaves. The room afforded a view down onto that part of the creek flowing in front of the Wilson house. I was strangely comforted by the sight of the water of my creek and the knowledge that it would flow beneath my bridge in a matter of minutes.

They had me sit down in a maroon, leather easy chair, and they sat behind the desk. Mr. Wilson looked as if he hadn't slept or eaten in a week. There were tiny grey cirques under his eyes broken by even more minuscule black cracks. He said, in his slow, even, half-buried drawl, "We just wanted to hear from you exactly what happened, son."

Both Wilsons were looking at me in a way in which I was not accustomed to being looked at, having never been in a position to address neediness in an adult.

I didn't see suspicion in their faces when I searched for it, unless Mr. Wilson's fury and guilt-grappling eyes betrayed a wish for ascription of blame that was running so strongly in him, concealed though it was beneath his slow Tennessee manners, that it approached a certainty of guilt. Hadn't I fled the scene? Couldn't I have done something to help his son? Might I have done something to harm him?

In Mrs. Wilson's face, which was to prove the more concealing, I perceived no trace of anything but a raw, lachrymose yearning toward the truth. There was no mistaking, in both of them, a leaning forward to me—seven-year-old, and not-at-all-innocent, me—as a bearer of their placation. Mrs. Wilson fumbled a cigarette out of its pack and shakily lit it.

After the lengthy silence, during which I found myself to be frozen, stealing glances down at the creek, Mr. Wilson started speaking, and I realized then that they had been waiting for me to say something. "Let me tell what I know. Let me tell you my half of the story. Then, you give me your half. Does that sound fair?" he said.

"Yessir."

"All right," he said. "Two days ago, Saturday, I was arranging some things up here in this room. I was unloading that box right there of its knickknacks, and I was putting them away in this desk. I happened to look out the window down at the creek, and I saw Merritt tearing up the yard toward the house here. I could tell something was wrong. I met her down in the kitchen. She told me how she'd left him down there. She said you were with him. She led me down there where he was. But when we got to the creek, you weren't there anymore. You were gone."

They both looked at me. I couldn't speak.

"You may have seen the mark on his inner forearm." He pointed there on his own forearm. "Here. In the autopsy it was confirmed that it was the bite of a pit viper . . . a water moccasin. It's not common that anyone dies of these kinds of bites. But because he ran so fast, it accelerated the effect of the venom and, as you saw, he tripped in the stream. But . . . the snake. We'd like to ask if you saw it when Ben saw it, if you saw it bite his arm. We wondered if you could tell us exactly what happened down there. Tell us how this happened to our boy."

I shook my head slowly, deliberately, no, because of all the things I didn't want them to know. No, I told them, I didn't remember having said anything to him before it happened. I didn't say that their son had reached for his own death on my suggestion or that it was his greediness that killed him or his miraculous bad luck or his pugnacious demeanor or his curiosity, or that he was supposed to have been my friend or that I didn't understand what I had done, or what it meant to be dead, or to be alive, yet, in the numbness of my youth and my numbness in the face of death or that I was sorry it had happened.

I recounted the details, told his actions, without my words. I told it to them the way I wanted to believe it had happened. I wanted to believe it had all taken place the way I'd told it to my father the very first time, before he'd gotten the truth out of me, and the way I imagined he had told it to my mother, who had never herself directly asked me any questions but had only accepted my innocence. I said I remembered their son taking off his shoes and socks. I said, I remembered him climbing down into the creek. It was hot. He was hot. He wanted to cool off. He sought the coolness of the creek on that thick-aired day. Maybe he said something about the heat because it wasn't quite so hot, so humid, in Ohio. Maybe his arms were hot, too, and he wanted to cool them off, too, in the slow-flowing creekwater. So he reached down into the water and . . .

That was not enough. They had more questions. *You told us that you didn't tell him anything, but we never said you told him anything, so why would you deny what we did not accuse you of? Do you understand why that is suspicious to us? Did you know about the snake? Had you seen it before then? If so, did you warn Benny? If so, why didn't you tell him before it struck? Why did you run away before we came down to the creek to get him? Why did he reach down in those roots? Did you tell him to do it? Tobia? Did you lead him to the snake, somehow? Of course, surely not, but tell us. What happened? Tobia?*

I answered them carefully without really answering them. I stuck to my story and, when their questions fell one after the other faster than I could answer, I looked down at the beige-carpeted floor and let it swim in my gaze. I felt as if I were hovering over myself and watching me not answering their questions.

Suddenly, Mrs. Wilson gave in to her rage and exploded my numb, seven-year-old equanimity.

"Do you even care?" she said very distantly. "Do you even care? My baby's dead!?" She stood and screamed at a volume and with a fury that sent me flying from the chair and halfway to the door before she'd said "baby." My parents came running into the room and when the door opened, I saw the Wilsons' relatives lined up out in the hallway, their faces studies in curiosity and gravity. My mother rushed over to me and took me under her arm. My father looked at the Wilsons and stood straight and tall, his chest out-thrust, scowling, surprised at the situation that had developed, poised and waiting to see what, in the possible insanity of their grief, the Wilsons might do beyond this and trying to discern just how much I might have told them.

"I'm sorry," Mrs. Wilson said almost immediately, returning to herself. "I don't know what came over me. I'm so sorry," she said. She stepped out from behind the desk and seized me, hugged me, violently, close to her. She smelled like purple perfume and cigarette smoke. I suffocated in her girth, my head crushed between her soft arm and ample belly. From this suffocation, I looked up at my mother, who had taken a step back from us, shocked and reaching for an empathy with this woman's fickleness of emotion at the same time that she was wondering if I was in any danger against which she would need to defend me.

"I'm so so sorry," Mrs. Wilson said. "So so sorry. So sorry," and she started sobbing so that I thought I must be feeling the very rhythm of her sorrow.

Mrs. Wilson's sobs and the voices of her comforters backgrounded the grave, deeper-than-usual voices of my father and Mr. Wilson, which registered in my head as murmurs and buzzes lost as I was to my numbness. We ran the gauntlet of the grave curious faces out in the hallway.

Merritt's was the last, the only young face, in the row. She turned her head to watch me pass, her face composed in silence and stillness and hyper-receptivity.

THE NEXT MORNING, just before Ben Wilson's funeral service, a thunderstorm rolled over Haven. By the end of the service the sun had brightly asserted itself and burned away the clouds.

My ears were ringing with my numbness. I remember the priest's reference to the serpent in the garden, its time-honored grudge against God and God's children. I remember Mr. Wilson's speech about Ben's unique promise and ready energy.

Unevaporated droplets on the window of the Mercedes blurred the world outside. The dark clothing, the mourners' skin, their faces under black umbrellas floated by as we glided out of the parking lot. The scene reminded me, vaguely, of Grandfather Thomas's funeral, except that his service had been at St. Andrew's Episcopal before the burial at the old house and my mother had said that it was a grand farewell, a lovely way to go.

My father said he didn't think it was necessary that we go to the burial, that, in fact, it would be a breach in decorum. But my mother insisted that we attend it because the Wilsons were our neighbors. They didn't know anyone in Haven. It would send the right message. It was the proper thing to do. Father acquiesced, silently and grudgingly. He drove us to the cemetery well behind the lights-on motorcade.

Water droplets were beaded out on the flower petals. I thought the gravestones looked like bad grey teeth stuck at random in a colossal monster's green gum. I clutched my mother's warm hand as we walked under the white canvas tent under which the short white casket in which you could see your own reflection, had been set down. My mother kneeled down on the muddy green carpet, still holding my hand, and whispered, "Watch after this child in his journey beyond."

My father stood by. In my head I told God I was sorry and to watch after this child in his journey beyond and wondered what landscape that journey spanned, what pit stops and challenges. I looked up at my father, who was wearing a fifty-yard stare, and I imagined he must have been thinking about my justice and our just us. The sun was bright and birds were singing. Merritt Wilson wasn't crying as were many of the Wilsons, across from us, on the other side of the tent. It seemed to me that she was staring at me, but I couldn't tell. I looked across at her and tried to tell if she was staring at me; it looked like she was, but I wasn't sure. Mr. Wilson put his arm around his wife's plump shoulder. Her mascara had blackened her tears. She turned into him and sobbed into his chest.

Merritt trained her eyes down into the grave.

FIVE

THE FAN WINDOW in this study looks out onto the trees in the yard.

Our estate is blessed with wonderful trees: trees with lanky, distended shadows in the morning and at dusk; oaks with magisterial boughs and Herculean branches; maples hosting grackles; a blasted ash where a single turkey vulture sifts Machiavellian secrets on the sole hangman's branch; trees with new leaves, as now, three weeks from Easter, alive in the breeze in a symphony of motion: the slow sway of a hundred-fifty-foot bough, the mad synchronous flurry of each individual leaf, the *shhhshhshhh* of the wind; the sycamore ribbed with climbing planks, my tree fort in its upper branches, the chainsaw growling then ceasing, white wood cracking, the long, slow-seeming fall; the larch with its fallen needles, bough straight as a pirate's dream-mast; redbuds and dogwoods laughing with their blossoms; locusts barren and naked in the brown November lawn, thinnest branches cracks in the slate sky.

Full canopies overarching the driveway, racing overhead in a phantasm of shadow, streaming sunlight, and a verdant translucency, or in the kaleidoscopic colors of fall, in my adolescence, in the morphine glow of that nostalgia, when I let my head fall back, looked up, felt myself laugh, deep in Indian summer with Mother's blue Fiat top converted and Merritt Wilson at my side; post-rain drips in glissando down waxy magnolia leaves; trees an interactive auditorium for crickets, cicadas, and frogs; trees a hundred years old; trees two hundred years old; the holly where we strung the Christmas lights; the red-tail's elm; grandmother oak's tangled roots in the stream where the cottonmouth hid.

I'VE BEEN WORKING up here all morning. Grandfather Thomas pored over cases up here, wrote speeches, planned political and business strategies, and my father has spent hours at this desk trying to keep the Caldwell Estate from complete dissolution these twenty years. And now, I've taken my place up here. I sit at the same desk, surrounded by almost identical decor, look out at the same view—the leafed-out trees I can see out the great fan window, the eye of this house—and oversee the partial re-extension of our holdings.

I think it's amusing that I'm up here. Though, I'm not sure of the nature of my amusement. I'm not sure I find humor in it because of my past professions, if I see myself as an underdog stacked against the other men who've sat at this desk, or if I think it's funny because I'm still young enough that any job I undertake feels diminished, its gravity lessened, simply because I'm the one who's undertaken it.

At any rate, all this morning, between spells of wanton procrastination and involuntary daydreaming, I've been paying bills, preparing invitations, balancing books, looking over new tax laws, making phone calls to ask for donations, and, in every other way, carrying out the civilized pencil pushing that is a quiet parallel to last night's sledgehammer session. A session that has left me as sore as I've been since my football days. With the slightest motion in this chair the soreness rises to rake the muscles of my lower back.

The man who developed Golfhurst, Martin Felter, was good enough to let us have an original blueprint of the subdivision. My father and I set it up on an easel in the corner of this study. The blue lines erase like a night's dreams. Each time the crew has finished with one of the houses and we've done our part with Old Havoc and the crew has come in with their excavators and trucks to haul everything away to be recycled or thrown away and have covered the cavity with dirt, my father and I convene in the study to erase that house from the blueprint.

We make a small ceremony of it. I run an industrial eraser over the lines. When I blow on the page, the eraser particles engorged with traces of blue pencil scatter and fall to the floor. My father climbs briefly off the wagon for these occasions. We clink glasses of bourbon and toss them back under the intense, watchful eyes of Gabriel, the Tennessee Turtle, whose portrait watches us from the wall. We talk about the future of Rollback Inc., and sometimes my father talks about old times.

My father has seen ghosts in this house. He says Gabriel himself appeared before him one night. The old Turtle began civilly enough, my father says, but by the end of his visit, thick ropy veins were bulging from his neck and his face was contorted in a rage so fierce that it seemed possible a pure strain of rage itself ran in those veins. My father decided his grandfather was yelling at him for having sold off the land and driving my mother away with his indiscreet affair and for otherwise being unworthy of the Caldwell name.

On another night, my father says, old Colonel Tobit strolled into his bedroom and stood before him, as if reincarnated as a young man, wearing his finest greys. By the end of the visit, Tobit, too, had worked himself into a rage befitting his reputation as a firebrand and hawk. He brandished his saber and shouted, also voicelessly—accusations, censure, blame, admonitions. My father sat up high on the bed shivering and breathing out a string of apologies one after the other. Before he left the room, Tobit leaned in and said one audible word: *ruinous,* before he strolled out, presumably to return to the unrest (thanks to my father) of his grave.

My father insists these ghosts were of the traditional, supernatural variety, and I believe him. Several times on this property I've felt a distinct tap on my shoulder and whirled around to find nothing there. And yet, though I don't discount the possibility of their having been genuine ghosts, I imagine the hauntings are mostly in his mind. Or that these were the sort of ghosts who fly out of whiskey bottles; both of these visits occurred when he was mired in the murkiest portion of his year-long binge.

Anyway, it doesn't matter. To wonder about whether these ghosts really exist or not is beside the point. What matters is that they are real to my father. I have no doubt that, for him, these ghosts, whatever their origin, are as real as the hands at the end of his arms and that he carries them with him in a way from which I've been spared.

They crowd his dreams and whisper admonishment when he's awake for having let the Grand Old Caldwell Place fall into such peril. In my father's imagination, these are men who are worthier than he can even hope to be. They are men who carved out our place on this land and led the Caldwells to prosperity in this country. In his mind, these are men who would never have let our land be overtaken by the development, as he has.

OUR HOUSE now rests on forty acres, the biggest wooded patch in a five-mile radius. Before Rollback Inc., the estate had diminished to five acres surrounded by ten new cluster mansions. We gained back five acres with each of the seven houses we erased. Now, only the Goodhopes' house, the hollow house I spun around in last night, and another one Bank's crew has yet to touch, remain of the ones in our immediate plans.

On the other side of the stream, down the hill in front of the house, the slave-laid fence of lichen-covered stones runs its ramshackle course along Caldwell Trace. Across the road another new development is going up on land over which I used to ramble.

The house in which I'm daydreaming, this Grand Old Caldwell Place, is a gleaming white three-story Greek Revival plantation house with a porch on the first two floors, each level fronted by six Doric columns, green shutters on the windows.

Behind the house the fields used to spread back. Even in my grandfather Thomas's day, when my father grew up here, there were a thousand acres. Still longer ago, our ancestors planted cotton and hemp. They had an overseer to look after hundreds of slaves. This still amazes me. There were slaves here. Sometimes, walking the property I feel their presence and hear their whispers and remember that it was not long ago in the course of time, that they lived and worked and suffered here. I mull on this sometimes when I'm sitting in this study. It's difficult to believe; there were humans working this land for my ancestors who my ancestors thought they owned. Here. On this land. Not all that long ago. My thinking goes only so far before awe hits rewind. Sitting up in this study, looking out the large fan window at the trees in this lawn when I'm supposed to be working, I let my mind work over my blood connection to that peculiar time.

Now, where the fields and woodland had been, there are one hundred or so houses of the Golfhurst subdivision, the ones we will likely never be able to afford to touch. Lexuses and Rovers crawl over the speed bumps on the blacktop avenues between the sod lawns, gazebos, and swimming pools and feed yawningly into the steady flow of traffic to course between the messy sprawl of suburban commerce—mirror-windowed office parks, lube shops, tire stores, supermarkets, flower shops, beauty salons, fast-food joints—over the twenty miles to the desolate and ever more dangerous downtown.

In the opposite direction, away from the city, the sprawl ends in the mess of several construction sites, which will soon be new links in a chain of chains. Beyond the construction sites—much-interrupted stretches of field, farm, forest.

THE TELEPHONE on the desk in front of me starts ringing. I sit and look at it for a few moments in a way that suggests I may never have seen a telephone display this sort of behavior. Gradually, I let the rings—one, two, three, four—bring me back into the room. I lift the receiver.

"Hello."

"It's me," says Robin Sackett.

"Hi."

"Am I interrupting something? Hold on a sec."

"Sure."

"No. That needs to go out today," she says. "I made that clear. Well, you better get on it then. Yes, now. Now. All right. All right. Sorry," she says. "It's been crazy here all day."

"Sounds like it."

"How are you?"

"Fine. I've been trying to gain some ground on the . . . project out here."

"And?"

"Coming along . . . coming along." I would never admit to hard-working Robin that I've spent most of the morning daydreaming.

"Meet me for lunch at Dan 'n Dave's, okay?"

"I suppose I could tear myself away."

"One-thirty."

"All right."

DAN 'N DAVE'S is the brainchild of a prominent gay restaurateur couple. The couple themselves are named Dan and Dave, and the restaurant's sign and logo (a silhouette of two buckskin-clad pioneers holding hands) suggest a fictional homosexual union between Daniel Boone and Davy Crockett. In a cartoon bubble above their heads, Davy delivers the famous quote attributed to him: "Make sure you are right. Then, go ahead."

The subtle, completely fictional suggestion of a homosexual relationship between the two has created a rift in the usual place; there are some who think it's funny and others who think it's the worst kind of blasphemy. You don't see the latter crowd at Dan 'n Dave's, which adds a further irony to the restaurant in that the decor suggests it's exactly the kind of place in which the people who will never set foot in it would feel most at home. The walls are filled with animal carcasses, black-and-white photographs of stiff-bodied, long-necked, unsmiling, turn-of-the-century families, advertisements touting, with anachronistic straightforwardness, the newness, freshness, and effectiveness of long-obsolete products. It's over-the-top and tongue in cheek, and a little unsettling for its out-of-control mock-authenticity despite its being all in good fun, and—considering its proprietors and some subtle, refined touches here and there if you're looking for them—layered thickly in irony. The decor is the couple's way of saying, When in Rome . . .

I step under the sign with its controversial depiction—it's been stolen twice—and into the restaurant. I'm glad not to see Dan or Dave. They're fond of Robin, and if they see me they'll come over and fuss over us. I have nothing against Dan or Dave. I think both of them are charming, but their fussing over our table exhausts and embarrasses me, so I'm glad when I don't see them.

I locate Robin and walk toward her table. She's sitting under an ad for Kentucky Plug Tobacco. Painted on a long rectangular plank, the ad depicts a buckskinned, coonskin-capped Daniel Boone readying himself to stab, with a mean-looking bowie knife, an Indian, who's threatening to brain him with a tomahawk. Oddly, for some reason, both Boone and the Indian are smiling so that it seems as if the Indian himself has realized and accepted the inevitability of his death at Boone's hands—destiny manifesting itself, I suppose. Boone will win this one.

Robin smiles when she sees me. She stands to greet me, and we hug and meet in what I expect will be a peck on the cheek or a kissing of air next to ears, but what Robin turns into a real kiss with slightly parted lips. Here. In public. In the middle of the afternoon.

Her long blond, face-framing hair shines in the light from the low-hanging bulb in its funky fixture. Her lips are red with lipstick. If she's stressed out by work, she doesn't show it at all. There are no dark circles or drawn features for Robin Sackett. Seeing her engenders a rush of excitement, and the kiss leaves me a little dizzy. I sit down, heavily, smiling at her like an imbecile.

"I ordered you an iced tea," she says.

"Thanks. Sorry I'm late."

"I just got here."

"So, what's new?"

"Talked to Pam today."

"What's new with Pam?"

She shakes her head, crosses her eyes, one of the weapons in Robin's social arsenal, something she does when she's fired up about something, or declaring the ridiculousness of something or someone. "Same old. Complaints. No boyfriend, no life, future's bleak. Where are all the men of quality? Alas, all the true gentlemen have vanished from the world, gone the way of the dodo, leaving nothing but dodos. I gloated a little. She agreed that you're a gentleman. I told you, she told me she thinks you look like a young Paul Newman. The black-and-white one. Like Hud."

I shake my head.

"I said I could see it—the eyes. But you're better-looking." She smiles.

"You're full of shit and so is Pam."

She holds her smile, shrugs. "How's Rollback Inc.?"

"Been preparing invitations just about all day for our big reclamation party. Made a few calls."

"I'm psyched about that party, T. Did I tell you my mother told me she always wanted to go to your mother's November Ball?" She shakes her head. "Never got the nod."

"How's the wonderful world of Pinkmellon Computers on this fine afternoon?" I ask her.

"We're still completely jammed, as is to be expected, considering . . . I had to work miracles to be here with you, actually, TBC." She smiles and nods and holds me in a gaze that demands my acknowledgment of how special I am to have been granted her company on this busy afternoon.

"I guess I'm a lucky man. I *am,* in fact, a very lucky man," I tell her and watch her bask, or, at least, pretend to bask, briefly.

The waiter comes over and waits. "Have you made a decision?" he asks, and, for a moment, because of the grave, deep-voiced way he's said it, it seems possible he might be talking about something of greater import than lunch. Have you made a decision? A question like that could get under a person's skin, could crawl into someone's mind and make him decide to change his life. Have you made a decision?

Robin and I laugh about that for a time. "He's jealous," I say. "That's why he's so serious. Wishes he was in my shoes and it's got him down. Wildly covetous of your company," I tell her. She registers the compliment in the shallower depths of her wide and deepsome blues. And I smile briefly, until I remember Merritt Wilson's letter—*coming back to Haven*—which erases the smile and sends my gaze down at the table.

"Eon tells me he called you a while ago and you never got back to him," Robin says. "He's not used to people failing to return his calls."

"I've been busy."

"Yes," she says. "You've seemed preoccupied the past few days. Ever since your birthday, you haven't been yourself," she says. "I told you how sorry I was I couldn't make it, didn't I? I'm glad it went well. As it turned out I got a lot of work done. I can't believe the big day is this Friday."

"Yes . . . that's right . . . the big day," I say, trying to recall what big day she's talking about. "The big day," I say again to stall.

Robin widens her eyes and cocks her head.

I remember what it is and smile at her. She's been preparing for the grand opening of the technological super-place, the Pinkmellon Computer–sponsored Dipsy-Do Club. The party in celebration of its opening is this Friday, and I am expected to attend it on Robin Sackett's arm. The "To Do" column in this morning's paper said, *The Dipsy-Do Club plans to be something of a phenomenon. How would one categorize this place? It is nightclub meets country club meets cafe meets cyberbar meets video arcade meets cinema meets honky-tonk . . . and this weekend it is THE place to be.*

Everyone who worked at Pinkmellon when Eon first pitched his idea for the club has their own version of his speech. The battle lines had been drawn within the company. The bean counters knew that the club, as Eon had conceived it, was too extravagant to make money, but Eon was blinded by a gleaming idea of the place. It came to a head one day in the top-floor boardroom. I'd been gazing out the window, down at the wide, muddy river and its rusty barge traffic when Eon made his case.

During a brief silence in the discussion, Eon suddenly unfolded his long frame, paced in front of the windows and circled the table talking the entire time, one idea bumping into the one in front of it, like toppling dominoes, a trickle on its way to becoming a torrent. A scribe typed every word anyone said at these meetings, and a projector hooked up to the computer put it up on the wall for all of us to see.

At the height of his speech he said, "This place must exist! There is no question. This is tablets handed down from God to Moses. This is a burning bush talking. No matter what it costs. We must build this. Do you understand? I will pay out of my own pocket any cost deemed exorbitant by a watchdog committee made up of my most zealous critics. What we are building is a contemporary temple. This is an upholstery stud to hold up and define the fabric of our culture and times. Nothing less. The place where the newest and latest, the most exciting technology available, will meet with its first assimilation!"

Knowing glances were exchanged around the table—crazy Eon acting crazy again.

But the glances softened after a time to assent. It was Eon's baby, what did we have to lose? He could be held to his pronouncement. Arrangements for the watchdog group were drawn up immediately. Eon resumed his pacing and when he was behind me in his back-and-forth route behind the table, I could hear him whispering further plans for his club.

"That's right. Dipsy-Do," I say. "Of course. Dipsy-Do. I don't know what I was thinking," I say, attempting to gauge Robin's reaction, so that I might elevate my level of excitement to suit her.

"I don't know what you were thinking, either," she says and dimples. "I think even you'll have fun, Tobia. I'm really *really* excited about it. I think once it's finished this place is going to be one of the coolest places on earth."

I nod. "So, do you have any responsibilities at this affair?"

"You know how it is. I'll have to make sure the investors have a good time. I'll be expected to make the usual rounds, squeeze and hold the usual hands, blow smoke, flash a few mirrors, trot out a few dogs and ponies. All you'll be expected to do, you'll be happy to know, is relax and enjoy it. You'll be expected to play a starring role as your natural, charming self—well . . . And— Oh! There's something about it I can't tell you right now, even." Her eyes sparkle just thinking about this fabulous thing she can't tell me as she narrows them. "It's a wonderful surprise!" she says and widens her eyes at me, which, for some reason, as with her talking to me as if I'm a little boy, makes me feel as if my chest is expanding and my head has lost blood.

"Robin, I'm a little concerned about this party," I say when the excitement has worn off.

She shakes her head. "Don't worry. No one cares. People still like you at the Big Pink, Tobia. Don't be silly."

"I can't keep up with you at these affairs. I'm losing my ability to play along—having more and more trouble acting congenial. Maybe I'm getting too old. I feel like it's doing me psychic damage. I feel like I'm being false to what I believe and . . . where I come from. I'm tired of pretending to have fun at these things when I'm not. Do you agree that we pay in unpredictable ways, for the false things we do?"

She regards me for a moment without speaking, then looks down at her salad. I can see her mood shift. It has been clear from the beginning that Robin will go only so far in indulging my hang-ups with the grand opening of the Dipsy-Do Club and my ideas about the direction in which the human race is heading.

I brace myself and momentarily consider backtracking and patching up before it comes, but decide, instead, to weather it.

"Tobia," she says and lets a tone of imminent reproach support the word in the air between us for a moment. "I didn't want to have to dive into our favorite argument. I wanted this to be a nice, relaxing lunch. But I have to say what I'm thinking."

I look at her and wait for it.

"You're twenty-eight years old, first of all. That's not old. It would be so much easier on you and me both if you would allow yourself to act your age. If you weren't all the time looking for noble causes, hanging your decisions on lost codes," she says. Another pause to let that sink in. "We've been over this. It's not healthy, if you want to talk about psychic damage, always groping around to find some principle to fight for. Wondering what one of your ancestors would do in this situation, what they would want you to do in that one. These Confederates who lost the war. Can I say, once again, that I think you need to learn to accept the way things are. The way things are *now*. Late twentieth century. Information, digital age. You would be so much happier if you let yourself ride along in the direction you seem so bent on resisting. Do you really want to become a farmer? Do you know what it means to become a farmer? Are you going to ride around on a horse? After your money runs out, are you going to be some kind of hermit, haunting that property of yours out there until the debt collectors come to cart you away? If you quit fighting these battles you invent, you would be so much happier. Quit worrying so much about the best way to live so you can start to live. I think it's as easy as that."

Listening to her, it occurs to me, while she's talking, that rather than being chagrined, shocked, angered, enlightened, or put on the defensive by Robin's lecture (thought there is the chance it will burrow in and make me deeply consider it later on) I am mostly touched that she cares enough about me to deliver it. I want her to keep going. I'm enjoying the show, feeling buoyed by the care it demonstrates. I decide to hear her out completely and, also, when it's over, to accept whatever she suggests, even if it involves my going to the Dipsy-Do Club with a smile on my face and incurring the psychic debt.

"And, if you have to pretend for a while to get there, then maybe that's what you should do. Go ahead and pretend to be aligned with the way things are, let yourself take part in the inescapable direction of things, until it becomes real and you're not pretending anymore. Eventually, you'll just . . . be happy and you won't remember why you were ever upset in the first place. You should try it. There's nothing to be afraid of," she says in a certain tone and with a strange smile and the smallest hint of what could be irony (trace evidence of her own decision to pretend) playing in slightly deeper depth of her eyes, which, if it weren't there I might stand from the table and leave the room. She lets what she's said hang in the air and waits to see how it's hit me.

In response, I give her a wide pretender's smile. "Please don't get me wrong," I say. "I'm afraid you're misunderstanding me," I say. "I'm looking forward to this party as much as you are. I can't wait to see this surprise you're talking about. If you say this party will be fun, sign me up. I'll be there. Front and center. Consider me your beau, my beautiful, beautiful belle. I'm sure we'll have a wonderfully fabulous time." I hold the smile.

And she returns it, suspiciously. "You're damn straight we will, Tobia Banes Caldwell," she says and narrows her eyes at me, which intensifies their lustrous sparkle. And then she pouts so beautifully I'm almost tempted to gnaw on my palm like a cartoon character gone loopy and bug-eyed with midafternoon lust.

SIX

IN THE AFTERMATH of Ben's funeral, I began to hear whispers. Sometimes I thought I was imagining them; other times I knew I'd heard them. There was a rumor in circulation around Haven about me and the Wilson boy. No one knew what, exactly, my part had been in his death, but they had heard I was the last one to see him alive and that I'd acted mysteriously. There was a story in circulation about me and a moccasin, the premature death of a boy. There was something about that Caldwell boy; I was separated from the other children now, not just because I was a Caldwell, but because of the new rumor. I could feel myself holding people's interest a little longer. I heard, or thought I did, a chorus of whispers wherever I went. *Watch him. Keep an eye on that one.* Everywhere in Haven, I felt it, or thought I did, until the cumulative susurration, real or imagined, formed an unshakable shadow under which I moved.

I heard whispers in my class when school started in the fall. *Moccasin . . . My mom says . . . Tobia Caldwell . . . Wilson boy . . . died.* Mother said, "They're jealous of you, that's clear as day, pay them no mind." People turned their faces to talk to each other, keeping their eyes on me, when I made a second trip to the buffet line at Sweet Hollow.

People wondered about me, and the more I heard them wondering, or thought I did, the more I wondered about myself. I waited for Father to talk about how my justice would be served and how we would put this right in my eyes and God's eyes. I wanted to serve my sentence, whatever it might be, so that I could move on. Whenever he was about to speak to me, and I didn't have a clear idea of what he was going to say, I thought, *Here it comes here it is,* but it was always something else.

One Saturday, not long after Ben Wilson's funeral when I was still looking for him to discuss my penance, he drove me to the YMCA for the little league football draft. I'm not sure whether or not he intended this to serve as a method by which I might earn extenuation, but I saw it that way. In the beginning it seemed like a punishment, but I was willing to accept it if it would speed my rightness in God's eyes. Otherwise, I might have refused to do it.

Fathers and sons pulled into the parking lot and walked out to the fields together. Some of the fathers talked to one another about how quickly the season had rolled around. Some of the sons ran around in spastic abandon and chattered about how good they were going to be, how they would win the championship. Others, like me, the rookies, kept silently close to our fathers, listening to and watching, with wide, scanning eyes, the louder veterans of the league.

We were lined up from biggest to smallest in the middle of one of the fields. Once the fathers had us situated and quieted down, the coaches huddled up for an intense discussion about how to conduct the draft. A few of them raised their voices at one another till they'd worked out how they would do it.

The draft began. Except for a number of instances when it was clear that the coaches knew of an especially talented smaller player or wanted to pick their own son, or were making good on some other prearranged deal, they went down the line grabbing the biggest kids first. Because I was smaller than most of the kids and young for the age group, I stood in the shortest three-fourths of the line. The coaches were still sorting through the more desirable picks when the chubby kid to my left started talking and didn't stop.

"I hope I get to be a Ram this year. A Ram or a Dolphin. Last year I was a Cowboy, which was okay. I hope I get a cool uniform this year. I only get to play if we're clobbering the other team or if a lot of people are on vacation. But my dad's a coach this year so . . ." He kept talking. I looked at him; he made me feel better about my own chances in the league. He had round flushed cheeks, big blue eyes, and his bright, clean jersey, with its outsized number, 00, looked like it was a size too big for him. Altogether, he gave the same impression as a cub from a species of big cat. There was a hint of underlying grace in his conformation, but for the time being, he was all feet and eyes.

"My name's Bradley Sackett," he said. "See that big kid with the number thirty-four? He was our quarterback last year. His name is Jason Bornshine. He's fast and he's got a major arm. I was—"

"Zip it, Nut Sackett," said a bigger kid down the line.

Bradley looked down at the kid, back at me, and shrugged. "What's your name?" he asked.

"Toby."

"You want to be on mine and my dad's team?" he asked.

I shrugged.

When it came time for us to be chosen, Bradley's father skipped me and picked Bradley. In the next round, when I was still available, I saw Bradley whisper in his father's ear, and Mr. Sackett picked me. When they had the drawing to see what names the teams would have, Bradley's dad drew the Saints.

After the draft we assembled for a makeshift practice in which we learned the stances and blocking, ran laps, and did wind sprints. Bradley wanted to be my partner for blocking drills, but I intentionally paired up with the biggest kid on the team, a nine-year-old who looked like he was only a year or so away from shaving. When he knocked me down, I got back up so he could knock me down again.

At the end of practice, while Mr. Sackett and his assistant were working out the schedule, a few of the kids rallied us into a game of "smear the queer."

"The secret to this game is to never get the ball," Bradley told me.

One of the kids tossed the ball high in the air. No one caught it. It hit the ground and bounced straight to me. I stood still for a moment before running.

Bradley ran alongside me, leaping and shouting, "Run, run!"

One of the kids caught me and dragged me down, and some of the others piled on. I went after the ball every chance I had and ran until the other kids hit me and dragged me down. They threw the ball up into the air for anyone to catch. I saw Father pull up in the old Mercedes and ran under the ball and caught it. He climbed out of the car and stood watching. Our eyes met. I stood frozen while one of the boys ran full speed into me, and I felt the impact of the boy then the ground. On the way home, he asked how the first day had been, and I told him I liked it and we drove the rest of the distance in silence.

"TOBIA. You have got to keep yourself cleaner when you play that vile sport. Leave some grass on the field, sweetheart," Mother called out while I soaked in the bath she'd drawn for me.

I developed an affinity for the taste of grass and dirt, the metallic tang of my own blood. I learned how all three tasted mixed together. I learned about a good kind of pain—the sting of a strawberry, the throb of a bruise—that let you know, with a stabbing insistence, that you were alive. When school started, I worked at the scabs during my classes.

One day after practice when Father came to pick me up, I heard the assistant coach tell him I was a tough little sucker. "He can take some serious punishment." I felt my chest inflate with pride.

Bradley and I rarely saw any action as Saints. We stood on the sidelines eating the halftime oranges and playing with the water bottles. One time he made me laugh by putting an orange half in his mouth, taping water thermoses to his feet and trying to walk on them. He let his arms hang down at his sides, rotated his eyes back in his head, and made orangutan noises. Mr. Sackett turned around just as Bradley toppled over, and for a few seconds fixed his son with a look of deep disappointment before shaking his head and turning back to the game. Bradley spit out the orange half, looked at me, and shrugged so that it seemed to me that this was his powerful, all-purpose gesture for surviving the world's unfairness and derision.

After the games my father was always angry about my lack of playing time. Mother would say I looked cute in my uniform, her little Saint, and that of course I had no talent for such a barbarous sport. "Tobia is better than that. He's more suited for cultured pursuits. One day he'll be a famous pianist, a great composer—maybe a poet."

THAT WINTER WHEN ice was just beginning to form on the creek in front of the old house, Bradley and I stood on the bank pelting the flaky crystals with rocks. When Bradley got too close to the roots of grandmother oak in his reaching for rocks, I stood over him and told him to look somewhere else. When he didn't move, I grabbed him by his jacket collar, pulled him up, and said, "I mean it—don't look there."

"What? Jeez. What?" he said, looking up at me with his wide blue eyes.

I could feel the Old Timer pocketknife against my thigh. Just a few days earlier, Fenton had showed me how to sharpen it with a whetstone.

"Can you keep a secret if I tell it to you?" I asked him.

He looked at me. For all his silliness, Bradley has always been able to turn serious on a dime when it is required of him. He nodded.

"I mean never tell anyone about it ever."

He nodded.

"You ever heard of a blood pact?"

He shook his head, no.

"We cut our thumbs. With a knife. And press the blood together. Like this. And, after we've done it, it means you can't tell what I tell you to anybody."

He breathed whitely into the cold air, threw the rock he'd picked up into the creek.

We ran the recently sharpened blade across our thumbs. Me first, then Bradley. It took us a while to summon the resolve to do it, and after we'd done it, we grimaced and tried not to make a fuss about it and looked down at the warm dark crimson that had been loosed from us into the cold air. We pressed our thumbs together and mingled the blood.

We sat across from each other, Indian style, and I told him what had happened with Ben Wilson and the silver dollar and the snake. I told how Merritt had appeared between the columns and come down the hill. How we'd found him and his hair had waved like eelgrass. How I'd dropped the snake's head down into the roots and watched as it spiraled down, the eyes watching me as it disappeared.

Bradley looked at me as I told him the story, in a very serious way. After he'd heard everything, he looked at the ground and gulped. I felt drained of anything else to say and didn't know what I expected of him. After a few moments of silence, we ran downstream to see if the bigger pools were frozen.

ONE DAY that spring Bradley and I rode our bikes through one of the fields in back of the old house toward one of the new houses going up on some of the land we'd sold, tires rattling over loose soil and rocks, someone hammering at random intervals at the construction site.

Bradley stopped to look at something coming up the drive they'd put in to connect the new houses to Old Cherokee. I stopped and dismounted, aware of the sound of a motor competing with, then drowning out, the sounds of the hammer in the house.

A boy wearing a helmet was driving a go-cart along the new road. We got back on our bikes and pedaled quickly, stopping in front of the point he would soon reach, to watch him go by. The boy saw us. Bradley waved, and the boy stopped the go-cart and turned off the motor, talking before the motor had silenced: "My name's Elvis Orville Newcomb. And I bought the kit for this go-cart from my egg-selling money, and I built it myself." His hair was brown and long in the back, his eyes were dark and long-lashed, and his voice was high-pitched and twangy. I thought he must have been our age or younger. "My father works in that house over there, he's a builder, and I'm bringing him his lunch—a pimento cheese sandwich, 'cause he's sick of chicken and pork, an apple, and some tater chips." He held up a rusty lunch pail. "He forgot it when he left this morning because he has a lot on his mind."

"You made this thing," Bradley said, admiring the go-cart.

A deep voice from the house interrupted us. I was aware of having heard the hammering stop. A man in jeans with a ring of dark curly hair encircling a sunburned head stood on a mound of rock-flecked dirt under what would be the threshold of the house, motioning with an index finger for the boy to come to him.

Elvis Newcomb left the go-cart where Bradley was still admiring it, and walked with the pail to give it to the man, who stood on the dirt mound fixing us with an expression that suggested he was considering telling us to leave. The man took the pail from the boy and said something to him in a low tone I couldn't make out. Then, the boy walked in front of us, to his go-cart, climbed in, and started it up.

"Can we ride in it sometime?" Bradley asked over the motor.

"Sure, later," the boy shouted above the noise. "I gotta go help my momma with our chickens and pigs—twenty-five chickens and ten pigs, five of the pigs, piglets."

Bradley and I watched him turn around and zoom down the new drive, leaving us in a thin pall of smoke. His father also watched, as if to make sure he was going to leave instead of hanging around to give us rides, only opening the lunch pail when the sound of the go-cart had completely diminished.

Early that summer, after Bradley had had his turn, which I thought would never end, I rode in the go-cart with Elvis Newcomb. He drove us along a busy stretch of Old Cherokee and through the shotgun shacks of Nerrytown, where curious kids jealously looked on from their jump rope and milk-crate basketball, and occasional hounds roused from under porches to give brief chase, teeth flashing in mouths that moved as if barklessly, due to the roar of the go-cart's engine.

We passed through a stretch of fields spreading back from the road and came to a long gravel drive with grass growing up between the tire ruts, fronting a trailer settled under a small grove of catalpa trees. Some juicy green-and-black catalpa worms were crushed against the dusty white gravel. At the head of the drive a sign with handwritten lettering said FOR SALE BY OWNER and gave a number. We scattered chickens as the go-cart labored through the gravel, spitting rocks behind us. To our right, in a half-dry pond, a few gigantic pigs rolled side to side on their backs in black mud.

When we neared the trailer, a woman in a dress that looked to have been fashioned out of drapery, came out onto the porch and began moving her mouth, wider, faster, her expression turning angry. I glanced at Elvis. He looked frightened for a moment, then gave a small, apologetic smile, before turning us around. As we turned, two boys who looked older than Elvis appeared at the side of the trailer; two girls who looked younger than Elvis came from around the other side of the trailer. All of them moved their mouths, but we couldn't hear them for the go-cart's din. The boys gave chase and gained on us, until we reached the pavement and shot off to lose them. Wind in our hair, we started back toward the new subdivision. I looked back to see the boys stop running. One of them shook a fist. I turned around and smiled. Elvis grinned briefly, before his expression turned more somber.

We left the traffic on Old Cherokee for the smooth blacktop of the subdivision's principal artery, and when we neared the new house where Elvis's father had been working that day, I saw my mother standing beside Bradley, hands on her hips.

"Turn that thing off," she said when the go-cart was idling in front of her, and as it was quieting, she said, "Tobia Caldwell. I have been worried sick about you."

Bradley, who was looking sheepish in front of her, attempted a shrug.

"And who is this?" she asked me. "Who are you?" she asked Elvis.

"Elvis Newcomb," I said for him.

"Elvis Newcomb," she said, "take that dreadful, dangerous machine away from here."

Elvis immediately started his go-cart, and Bradley and I waved as he zoomed away.

"Honestly, Tobia," she said. "Making me come all the way out here to find you."

I GOT BETTER at football, came to know its controlled madness and rage. Grew accustomed to its equipment. Started to earn respect in it. My muscles developed to meet its demands. I grew.

I played little league for eight years before high school. I began to seek on the field a very personal sort of glory and extenuation that no overarching concept of team could dissolve. I saw myself as a lone predator. I had my own very personal mission. I sought out victims on the field. I punished receivers. Ran on the battery of my bloodthirsty desire

for interceptions, for the good kind of pain that came when I hit someone with a teeth-vibrating solidity.

When I was filled up with my mother's, my father's, my teammates'
approbation, it gave me the energy and drive I needed to leverage my
way into further glory. My mother, when I was in the thick of my silent
rage to glory, became a bigger football fan, nearly better knew its terms
and armchair philosophies than my father. She was there to greet me,
arms open wide to hug me, after every game.

"The way you stopped that receiver—that was wonderful. But, oh, it
looked so so painful. Are you all right, sweetheart? And when they
threw the ball and you knocked it down. Fantastic. Wonderful," she'd
say. "Did you hear your mother cheering for you?" I told her I did.

I WAS FOURTEEN, in eighth grade, when Mother called me into the
living room to read to the ladies of the Garden Club a poem I'd written
for which I'd won a creative writing award at school. The poem she
wanted me to read was called "Time." What she did not know was that,
on my own, I'd been working on another poem. Late at night I'd been
waking up with strange words coming to me, which I scribbled onto a
page in my notebook.

Instead of reading "Time" to the ladies of the Garden Club, I read
the poem I'd been working on late at night. I was calling it "The Serpent." The women in the living room smiled, arranged themselves in
anticipation, readied themselves to give an appropriate show of appreciation. I scanned them with adolescent unease and sensed, unpleasantly,
the way they wanted to pigeonhole me into tight expectations for who
and what a fourteen-year-old boy should be and the way, in spite of
themselves, they wanted to see me fail and think I had failed even
as they smiled and clapped so they could think better of their own
children.

For what it did, it was torn apart.
Rejoined in time by mysterious art.
Its start is its end and its end is its start.
When it comes up from the creek,
And coils in my heart.

After I'd read it, the words hung in the air for several long moments. The women exchanged glances. Some of them clapped hesitantly. Of course all of them knew I'd been the last one to see Ben Wilson alive. My mother smiled. "That's not the one, that is certainly not the one I had in mind, Tobia," she said, smiling angrily. She stood up and shook her head to the ladies about me and ushered me out of the room, shaking her head and explaining, so very silly, boys at this age.

THE HIGH-SCHOOL football coaches—Rapport Glass and Grain Tiller-back—would speechify before games in an effort to fire us up. Red-faced, husky-voiced, veins bulging, they spouted platitudes. *There's no I in team. Are you eagles or prairie chickens? Lions or gazelles? Monster bass or night crawlers? Swordfish or ballyhoo? I need y'all to have tunnel vision down the Great Hall of Victory! You'll pass out before you die, girls!*

My teammates, in their dunderheaded pregame roughhousing, didn't understand my silent preparation for the games, and I didn't understand their need for so much hoo-rah!-ing. I was openly disdainful when they called my silence into question. Who were they anyway? I sometimes thought to myself when I needed to make them small. I was better than they were, wasn't I? Of course I was. When all was said and done, under it all, no matter what, I was a Caldwell. Who the hell were they?

You better get fired up, Caldwell! What the hell's the matter with you anyway, Caldwell. TC stands for too cool or maybe it's too chicken.

They beat their heads against the lockers, head-butted one another, growled, and screamed to prove how ready *they* were. If I hadn't become, as I did, fast and cruel and powerful and graceful on the field my attitude would have been inexcusable, and they would have punished me for it, duct-taped me to a heating pipe running through the locker room like they did the equipment managers. As it was, I remained an enigma to them. I wasn't quite right. I moved in a dark aura; there was that shadow with me, but because I was good and they needed me, they respected and eventually defended my silence.

Bradley Sackett talked his way onto the team. He never played, never dirtied his uniform. He'd sit next to me on the bus and remind the others of the sanctity of my silence, in his precocious and evenhanded manner, a manner that was so quick and well developed, even then the PR man he was to become at Pinkmellon, that it disarmed even the worst of them. They left us alone.

Before my senior year in high school, the coaches switched me from end to quarterback. *Hillcrest High Pins Its Hopes on Caldwell,* said the football preview in the paper. My parents put the article up on the refrigerator. Old Fenton Monroe took to calling me QBTC. Little freshmen whose names I didn't know and did not bother to learn would diffidently wish me good luck in the hallways on game day, and I'd grant them a nod before they scurried away.

One time a skinny kid with wide, adoring, rabbit-scared eyes and curly hair came up to me and asked if it was true what they said, if it was true that I'd killed someone and gotten away with it. I looked down at him in his puniness and stared at him, not saying anything because I didn't know what to say, until his resolve crumbled and he ran away between the lockers, his feet echoing, the blurred reflection of him following him on the newly waxed floor.

I was nicknamed Tobuddha. Over time my teammates came to celebrate my pregame silence. There were banners in the crowd that said, simply, "Tobuddha." It was never enough. Never enough glory.

As quarterback and captain, I insisted that everyone on the team observe a two-minute silence prior to the time when the music and banter could begin. We'd sit in the locker room, our uniforms clean, the smell of Ben-Gay and the sound of fans arriving outside. Old Doc, the trainer, who was rumored to have killed people in Nicaragua and who fixed the faded yellow bus whenever it broke down, taped people up. We'd sit in front of our lockers, not saying a word, imagining our imminent paths to glory on the field with "We Will Rock You" blaring from the speakers, the deafening drums of war making the entire room vibrate—a roaring in the head.

At dinner one night, my father said it didn't surprise him I'd achieved so much on the field. Football was a form of war, a conduit for the warring impulse in man, and the Caldwells had never shied away from a fight. He told me again how my great-times-three grandfather Tobit, my namesake, had been a colonel for the Confederacy. After most of his command was wiped out at Chickamauga, he'd ridden back to our house to check on his three daughters and make sure things were running smoothly on the plantation. Things were not running smoothly by any means. Some of the slaves had seen their chance and run for it. There were whispers in the quarters about freedom. Federals were thick on the primary roads.

Suspecting pursuit, Tobit is supposed to have come in through the front door, kissed his oldest daughter, Lucy, my great-great-grandmother, on the forehead, urged strength in her, and escaped through the back door, where a Kentucky Thoroughbred held by Jones the liveryman was ready and waiting. He shot off across the fields for the forest, just as a Federal officer rapped at the front door. Eventually, he would find John Hunt Morgan's Raiders, the band he rode with for the remainder of the war, bringing to the war the guerrilla tactics they hoped would have the same effect as they'd had against the British. Later, Colonel Caldwell escaped with Morgan from an Ohio jail. Earlier in his life he'd injured a man in a duel. I listened and nodded, fascinated with the story, as I was every time I heard it, but not knowing what to make of this ancestor or how, exactly, to connect it with my glory on the field.

My mother said, "Who cares who cares who *cares*. From the Phinster side, you've inherited your sweet, peaceful nature and your prodigious intelligence. Your Charleston relatives were merchants before, during, and after the war. Not one of them ever fought in that bloody travesty. Though, they suffered from it, like everyone else. They survived it better than most, however, because they thought ahead and saved provisions when they heard the hawks raging. Football is just a silly game. I want you to remember that, sweetheart, no matter how good you are at it and how proud we are of you for being good at it. It's nothing more than a silly game," she said and shot my father a glance. He didn't make any more comparisons that night.

But other times when I heard him make these vaunted comparisons based on my newfound football prowess, I wondered if his making them meant I had been forgiven for what had happened with Ben Wilson and came to decide that it did.

SEVEN

Back from lunch with Robin and up in the study, I start back to work. I type up some invitations, make a few calls, but it's not long before I'm leaning back in the chair and daydreaming again. There's not an object in this house that isn't held in place by the weight of a story.

The bookshelves up here are still filled almost exclusively with my forebears' books of law, but I'm carving out a place for my own books of older laws and inscrutable phenomena. You can see my pocket forming. My books about reptiles and snakes are up there now alongside several books of toxicology, chemistry, zoology, agriculture, animal husbandry, literature (all the works of Wendell Berry, *I'll Take My Stand* among others) and also books and documents about the history of this particular part of Tennessee and documents pertaining to this particular house. My father's self-published account, *The Caldwells of Tennessee,* is up there on the shelf as is the Tennessee Turtle's memoir, *In the Deep Green Hills of Old Tennessee,* in which I read just last night his hypothesis that the Cherokee might have been a lost Hebrew tribe. Part of his evidence for this was that they share several words with the Hebrew. For example, "Abel" in both Hebrew and Cherokee means manslaughter.

On the west wall I have hung a five-by-seven-foot tapestry of an uroboros: a multicolored serpent stitched in serpentine interlace on an off-white background biting its own tail. I talked my father into letting me hang it up there. I convinced him it was a perfect symbol for our project here. It is Egyptian and was a gift from Merritt Wilson. She gave it to me when we were living together in a shack at Reelfoot Lake, and I hung it on the door to keep away what needed keeping away.

The emblem now hangs in the same place in this study where once had hung an amateurish painting (the neck was all wrong) of a horse named Texas Kisses on which my great-grandfather Gabriel and my great-grandmother Lida once won some money. After one of Texas Kisses's races Gabriel was approached by the painter, one Timothy Dewdrop, who claimed he just happened to have a painting of Texas Kisses with him. His new winnings fresh and loose in his pocket, Gabriel bought the painting.

I used to imagine who this T. Dewdrop might have been. As I saw him, he was desperate for patronage and haunted racetracks in the Southeast with a load of mediocre horse paintings just outside the track walls. Some chestnuts, blacks, bays, a few greys, all of the horses rendered just generically enough to pass as everyhorse. Perhaps old T. Dewdrop even had some white paint out there so he could get a white star on a nose just right or could conveniently erase a caricatured black stable boy if a Yankee owner had won the race, before he presented it to the newly flush potential buyer. The painter, I imagine, would tactfully approach whomever celebrated the loudest after a race. My great-grandfather hung the painting over the mantel on the west wall of the study, or so my father claims my grandfather Thomas always insisted, as a representation of how fate has always smiled on the Caldwells. The black stable boy and a black jockey are in evidence. Gabriel had recently been part of a syndicate of Tennessee men who wanted to breed a strain of Thoroughbreds they hoped would one day rival or surpass those being bred to the north in Kentucky. Gabriel kept several of the horses on this land, and the success of Texas Kisses, he thought, proved that the venture would succeed in time. I took Texas Kisses down in favor of the uroboros.

On the wall to the left of the uroboros, glaring out into the room, as if in stern reproach and indignation at the replacement of Texas Kisses by the uroboros, Gabriel himself fixes the study with his withering gaze. His longish grey hair, surrounding his otherwise bald head, stands in riot all around and his eyes are afire and yet they still smile despite his otherwise imposing sternness.

Elsewhere in the house other portraits of my ancestors stare out from the walls. Especially when I was just old enough to be left alone in the house, I used to imagine I heard them whispering to me. Or, I would suddenly become aware of them, their knowing eyes following me around a room. I'd stop whatever I was doing, stop reading my book or playing pick-up pairs or solitaire (I rarely watched television) and wait for something to happen.

My favorite painting in the house is a large one that hangs in the foyer. In it Colonel Tobit poses with his triplet girls and a trusted hound. The Colonel looks pleased with his situation, but, as with Gabriel, there's a bright sharpness in his eyes that foreshadows his imminent role as a warrior and someone who once badly injured (possibly killed) a man in a duel over a matter of honor. The portrait was commissioned three years before the beginning of the War, and, for some reason, I imagine it having been painted not long before one of the balls Tobit was famous for throwing. I can imagine him in the parlor with the other men, discussing the quality of horses, bourbon, and slaves, forging the noble facade of their despotism. The painter has captured the beauty of the three belles who were Tobit's triplet daughters with their curls and bright hoop skirts. The advent of these three had killed their mother.

All of them look as if they've guessed at how this painting will immortalize and freeze them in time. It seems as if they are mulling over the knowledge that their slight, enigmatic smiles will be their passports to survive the years with the appearance of eternal freshness and youth. The one on the far right, Lucille, is my great-great-grandmother. She was married, just after the war, to a young Kentuckian and a friend of her father's named Justin who had also ridden with John Hunt Morgan's Raiders.

My second favorite portrait is one my mother inherited from her family in Charleston of another one of my namesakes—Banes Phinster—her great-grandfather, who was, as she is, and, so, am I, a descendent of the "three ships." One of our ancestors was aboard the *Carolina* when it landed in Charleston in 1669 after saving as many passengers as possible from the other two, doomed ships. Banes, a benign-looking man, with long dark hair and grey-ish eyes, was a wealthy merchant during the War, who miraculously and mysteriously, according to my mother, survived it without declaring sides and without financial ruin.

On the mantel over the fireplace—one of four in this house—and under the uroboros rests a gift my father has wrapped, perfectly, in solid crimson with a navy bow. The gift is meant for my mother. I was supposed to have delivered it to her last Sunday, but her sister, Aunt Marcy, told me my mother wasn't feeling at all well—that she was "gone"—by which she meant that my mother had retreated more deeply into aphasia's maze.

I'm willing to bet that before the day is over my father will have another gift for me to take when I go over to Marcy's tomorrow. He sends my mother a gift a week as part of a second courtship.

Next to the gift is a framed photograph of Grandfather Thomas and Grandmother Pearl standing outside their cabin at Reelfoot Lake. They're both laughing, full-on, at something. Both Grandfather Thomas and Grandmother Pearl disappeared in Reelfoot lake, she just one year before him. She was on a bird-watching, he, on a bird-shooting outing. Last Sunday I was conscious, as I was when I lived there, of gliding over their bones, and every time I had a snag I couldn't help but wonder if my hook had slipped into an eye socket or twisted around a collarbone.

My father says Grandfather Thomas used to say, with typical jocularity, that because the New Madrid had created Reelfoot Lake in 1811–12, the next time it shook the land Grandmother Pearl was going to come back to life. A year later, he joined her. He never rendezvoused with his buddies, Fenton Monroe among them, at the cabin after hunting geese all day at a secret blind. Now, it's a running joke with my father, Fenton, and I that, after the next rumblings of the New Madrid, we'll have to set *two* extra places at the table.

I barely remember it, but I'm told we went to the lake when the authorities were sounding for Grandfather Thomas. I was only six. They got me out of school, and my father and Fenton explained to me how they were dragging the shallow bottom near the place where they thought his blind must have been, just as they had dragged for Grandmother Pearl the year before. They never found any trace of either one of them. Fenton went to the lake every day to help out the authorities. His obsession with the New Madrid began shortly after the unsuccessful search for the remains of his lifelong friend.

One night, not long ago, at a black tie affair down at the Halcyon club, Fenton approached me. He was well into his bourbon. He came in close, and with sad blue eyes and whispery breath, told me he thought Grandfather Thomas might have killed himself at Reelfoot that day, taken the initiative and gone on to join Pearl. Or, maybe, he wondered aloud, he'd erased his previous identity, gone on to assume a completely different persona. Maybe the two of them were living another life together somewhere. That would explain the surprising (especially for my father) paucity of his estate after he died.

After Fenton had said this to me, the idea of it left me breathless. I had no response for him. He'd become a grandfather to me. It wasn't true, I assured him, when I'd gathered myself to say anything at all.

"Why would he do that, Fenton?" I asked him and managed a smile that acknowledged the seriousness of what he was suggesting.

Fenton didn't answer. He only stared at me as if to say, *Yes, Tobia, son, you believe that. It's best for a grandson to believe his granddaddy was a hero.*

"Love you, T. Good old QBTC," he said and gave me a hug that nearly knocked the breath from me and gave me also a red-faced, almost tearful smile. "And, I'm sure you're right, son," he said in an old southern way that means, *You're not right at all of course but let's pretend you are because it'll be easier on both of us and life is short so why not layer it with charm and grace and well-meaning lies to salvage this moment.* "Now where's that date of yours," he said, snapping himself out of his missing my grandfather and laying the suspicions on me. "You oughta be dancing with some lithe young belle. Sharp-looking rake like you. Hell, I plan to get out there myself, here directly."

THERE'S A NEW COMPUTER in front of me on this desk that could provide me access, in seconds, to the records of Pinkmellon Computers which records rest in a database in the Pinkmellon Concourse downtown. Bradley and Robin Sackett and Eon now run the show at Pinkmellon. Not long ago I had a hand in its affairs. My investment of some of the money my father and I made from an antivenin patent Henley Dempster and I developed, effectively began Pinkmellon, and for three years I served on its board and drew a salary for my services in the marketing department.

I drove to work every weekday morning at the Pinkmellon Concourse, a distance of about twenty miles that used to be farm and woodland and is now covered, without a break, by the concrete, chromium, glass and neon chain of chains. Driving down Old Cherokee from the old house to work, it used to occur to me on certain mornings and nights that if it were possible to transport someone seamlessly, in a millisecond, and without warning to another chain of chains in another American city a thousand miles or more away and this person were asked to identify, quickly, where he was, gauging only from the collection of shopsigns he could see out the car window, he would have not the slightest idea where he was though his mind would reel and reel like the sound of the film rolling through the projector when the film's over. On some of these same mornings and nights, driving to or from work, I would think about how tenuous it all was, the whole commercial facade, how directly under Old Cherokee Road, Fenton's New Madrid fault was biding its time.

When I started working at Pinkmellon, I felt central to the effort. Every day I'd sit at my desk and brainstorm ideas for new products, niches in the market we hadn't explored. People came in to get my opinion on projects they were developing. At the end of the day I'd pass my ideas to a team of MBAs, marketing gurus, and number crunchers who would cull through them and later advise movement on the ones that seemed workable and nix the ones that didn't. It was customary for me to be in the office till long after midnight, high on the competition and the possibilities of the products we were producing. For a time at Pinkmellon I became Tobia-the-Marketing-Juggernaut. Every morning I devoured the trades, the *Wall Street Journal, Forbes.*

Robin popped into my office three or four times a day to chat and bounce ideas. As time went on, we started to flirt, although we wouldn't start dating, officially, till about six months after I'd left Pinkmellon. She was conducting a long-distance relationship, at the time, with a Miami Dolphin.

It's difficult to say when the staring sessions began. In the middle of an ordinary working day, sitting at my desk high in the new Pinkmellon building, the dark-windowed symbol of our new success, I would come to myself and realize I'd lost a space of time—five, fifteen, thirty minutes, lost. After starting off the day like any other, performing my brain-storming, thinking of ways to capture new markets and make more money, putting all these ideas into memos and reports for Bradley and his team, I would zone out, lose a space of time.

So, this is your life, Tobia Caldwell, I thought to myself when I returned, looking at the computer screen and the desk, the phone, the computer, the fax and copy machines. *This* is your life. After a time it changed from statement to question. Late at night after many brain-storming sessions at Pinkmellon I looked at my reflection in the plate-glass window. *This is your life?*

I began to long for the simplicity I'd found during the time I'd lived at Reelfoot. I wanted to learn to properly love the land I felt I should have known so much better than I did. I vowed to rediscover, for my-self, the broken connection between the production and consumption of food. I would plant a garden; I would get some chickens and a cow, some pigs. I was tired of having to feign excitement (in the interest of selling) over enhanced resolution, faster processing time, larger memory, efficiency, convenience. I was losing blocks of time to daydreams and feeling the gnaw of a colossal emptiness. I wanted to take up my own lost cause, to make an eddy for myself against the inescapable stream of time and tasks, the overhyped myth of progress, to figure out how to live and feel like I was living properly. It seemed to me something had been lost that I wanted to recover. Working at Pinkmellon didn't feel like living properly.

My father is retired from his brief service with Pinkmellon, and I liquidated my investment just after the company was bought for a large sum by Kelly Industries, and I used the money to start Rollback Inc. and afford myself time to sit up here in this study considering the objects in this room and the stories they suggest.

Despite the fact that, once started, the nature of Rollback Inc. allevi-ated some of the guilt I felt about being another cog in the wheel of endless economic expansion, especially just after I had liquidated, I was subject to pangs of regret over what I was doing with the money. The destruction of the Golfhurst houses seemed such a costly affair of infinitesimal gain, given the rampant, ubiquitous "development" taking place. Sometimes I would, and still do, sit up in this study and think of escape, of all the places I could go, all the real estate I could buy in other, more desirable locales—waterfront, slopeside property. I also wondered, and still do, what good we could have done with the money had we given it to a good charity. Gradually, I fully invested myself in Rollback Inc. to the point where I could see nothing beyond the day-to-day tasks of the project. Now, so close to the end, more and more, I'm finding myself sitting up in this study, the brain of this house, and wondering what's next for Tobia Banes Caldwell if it doesn't have to do with computers, which I hope to God it does not.

MY FATHER steps into the study with a second gift. The ribbon is gold, the paper azure. He likes solid colors. I don't think it has occurred to him that Mother might prefer a floral pattern or a lepidopteran design. He stands in the doorway, patient, childlike, with his gift, as if he is afraid he will untrack important thoughts I've been having about Rollback Inc. He doesn't know I've just been daydreaming.

My father is showing the effects of his aging by the day and the fact of it sometimes surprises me. His hair is more grey than sandy now, his stoic manner has become more ponderous, his natural silence more fertile to a listener's imagination. He steps into the room to deliver the gift. He receives and delivers packages now. That seems to occupy an inordinate amount of his time.

He wants me to deliver this gift along with the other one when I visit her tomorrow afternoon.

My mother doesn't know what's in these packages. All three of us know she will place these newest two in her closet, unopened, with the rest of the cast-off gifts. Nevertheless, he is persistent in his second court-ship despite her resolve to keep him out of her life.

The nasty truth that he can't and God knows she can't forget is that six years ago my mother had a stroke and shortly afterward, he had an affair. He was poor, drunk, and deluded at the time, and his only son was wasting his life—rotting away—down in the same swamp that had claimed his parents, researching poisonous snakes, of all things for a Caldwell to do with his life. Piecemeal, my father was selling his birthright. Apparently, he was indiscreet. One night, my mother heard young, throaty feminine giggling coming from somewhere in the house. He had told her he was going to be out of town and expected her to be at Aunt Marcy's. There had been a mix-up. She saw them to-gether and left him for good the next day.

Aunt Marcy, her younger sister, was happy to take her in. The devel-opment was marching down old Cherokee Road. Her leaving him didn't help him hold onto the land. In fact, it hurt him worse than any-thing that could've happened. At any rate, I don't think I would be sit-ting here, helping him with this project, if he hadn't repented his part in it, as he has.

"How you making it?" my father asks.

"Making it."

He stands in the doorway of the study and nods.

"Tom Goodhope called a while ago. Said he and his wife could talk to us tomorrow morning at nine. We can make an offer then. Or just feel them out."

He nods, raises his stern, thin eyebrows.

"Count me out," he says. "You handle it, T." He walks into the room and sets his gift on the mantel next to the guncase, beside the other gift. He lifts it up again and asks me if I'll deliver it with the glance and by releasing a strangling sound through his nostrils.

I nod. "I'll take it over tomorrow afternoon. After the Goodhope meeting." He looks pleased for a moment till he glances, accidentally, at the uroboros. He shudders, mutters something under his breath that sounds like *hideous,* or *hideous thing.*

"You know," he says, "I can't get used to that thing, that 'robrous or whatever you call it. I don't care what you say it stands for. I miss Texas Kisses." He smiles, shrugs, and holds his shrug, raises his eyebrows. "But you're the one who spends the time up here now, I suppose. Tonorah's cooking supper," he says, turning to go.

I had guessed Tonorah was cooking by the scent of garlic wafting up into the study. Tonorah is a fantastic cook. She cried when my father let her go not long after Mother had left him. He was in a whiskey funk. We rehired her as soon as we could afford it. Tonorah releases a wise laugh no matter what you might say to her. You could say, "Tonorah, the house is on fire!" and she'd chuckle at that. *White people are all crazy—the more money they have, the crazier,* is what her chuckle seems to say—*may as well just laugh, take the check, and go your way.* Tonorah still works for my mother. My father has tried to enlist her, as he has enlisted me, in his campaign to win my mother back. It's difficult to tell if Tonorah is helping or hurting his cause. My father and I both know that Tonorah is a spy in this house. She fills my mother in on every detail of our bachelor existence here. It is my mother's way of exerting a measure of power over us even in her absence and from behind aphasia's wall.

"Should be ready soon," he says. "If you're hungry."

"I am if Tonorah's cooking," I say. My father is no chef and knows it.

He nods but doesn't spend a smile.

I nod back.

His expression turns suddenly grave. "You have trouble sleeping last night?"

I realize what's coming.

"I thought I heard the steps creaking," he says. "And then I heard you playing the destructive somnambulist. Again. Even after our discussion. I came down and opened the door and heard the racket out there. Sounded like all hell. And then, strangest thing, I saw the Goodhope boy run out of the house and across the lawn. He wasn't making all that racket."

"I don't know what came over me."

"We're paying people to do that for us, T. And do it neatly. We have Old Havoc for the rest. Plus, it's dangerous. You might hurt yourself. Or, worse, that little boy. Think of the liability."

"All right. I see your point."

"I hope your head's still in the game," he says, pointing to his own head. "This close to the end of this project. Or—this phase of it."

"I don't know if it is or isn't anymore," I say. "I couldn't sleep again last night and I felt like doing some work on the house so I went out and did it. That's all."

"Oh, you did some work all right. No question about that. Looks like a rogue rhinoceros ran through there with a grudge. What happened to the systematic dismantling we've talked about? How're Bank and the boys supposed to salvage all that ruined material? It's something of a waste."

"Well, Dad, I don't know what to say. Actually, there's a lot I could say, but I don't think you want to hear it. It might reveal the degree to which my head's not in the game." I think about telling him about the letter I've had from Merritt.

He looks at me, a flash of what? in his eyes. Fear? Then it's gone; he has chosen to ignore my last comment. He doesn't want to know. "What's going on with those invitations?" he asks.

"They came back from the printer's today." I fish one of them from the desk and hand it to him. It reads:

You are invited to a Gala event on April 10th at eight o'clock P.M.
Come, dance to the music of Around the Bend, make merry, learn the details of the

Rollback Incorporated Caldwell Reclamation Project.
Donations Welcome. Black Tie.
RSVP

I see, with regret, that the envelope I've handed him is addressed to Brandon Campbell, care of the Tennessee chapter of the NAACP. I spoke with Brandon on the phone about the event some time ago, and he expressed his interest. Then, with a trace of challenge, he mentioned the probability that his ancestors had been slaves on this property. I said I thought that was fascinating and that we'd have to talk about that at the party, and tried to steer the conversation to more comfortable ground.

My father reads the invitation slowly, looks again at the envelope. I wait for him to see those particular letters together on an invitation to our big party and wonder if I will always crave my father's acceptance, even in the smallest things.

"NAACP?" he asks, eyebrows raised, chin thrust into neck. "This a joke?"

"I spoke to a gentleman named Brandon—"

"What in the world is this?"

"It's good for PR for one thing. For another, I've talked to Brandon about groups of some of these kids who've never seen a field or a real tree in their whole lives coming out from the inner city to use the open space, once it's established."

No, he doesn't like it. He puts down the first envelope and reaches for another one, which does nothing to alleviate his concerns; it is addressed to John Redbear, care of the American Indian Movement.

"What in the name of all that is graceful and pure . . . ," he says, showing me the address and furrowing his brow. "I didn't even know there was such an organization. I thought we were clear on this." A pause. "New money. Old friends of the family. Invite all your Pinkmellon buddies, the Blinker International crowd. Remember what we discussed?" A vein thumps at his forehead; he gives me a look.

Which raises my hackles. A healthy injection of Caldwell bile comes up into my mouth, and I think, *Who's been up here taking care of all this crap? Who dragged you into rehab when you were deep in the bottle, who saved you, who saved this house?*

"Would you like to take over?" I ask him. "Or don't you have time now, given these packages you're dealing with."

We look at each other. There is a brief silence between us. Who do we have in this old house except each other? I take a deep breath, look away first, reach down and pick up the package that arrived this morning.

"This came for you," I say. "From Indonesia. Irian, Jaya." His eyebrows elevate slightly, he exhales, steps over to take the package from my hand.

I wait to see if he'll explain it, knowing he won't. There is a code between us that will not permit me to ask him what's in it. He must volunteer the information, and I know he won't.

"Ah," is all he says and thanks me under his breath and creaks back out the open door of what used to be his study.

After signing checks for some of the bills on this desk and readying them for mailing and preparing twenty-five or so of the invitations, I stand up and walk down to the kitchen where, by the smell, I can tell Tonorah has once again outdone herself. She's left a plate of lasagna in the oven, a salad in the fridge. I pour myself a tall glass of sweet tea, thank Tonorah, and dig in.

Tonorah has just finished the dishes my father dirtied. In a few minutes she will climb into the Honda Civic for the five-mile drive to Nerrytown, the predominantly black neighborhood originally founded by slaves who had fled from this and other plantations during and after the War. There are a lot of Caldwells and Monroes in Nerrytown. When my class photograph was taken in high school, there were black Caldwells in front of and behind me in line. I remember looking at them and thinking how strange it was that, quite probably, my ancestors had owned theirs. I wondered if they considered this possibility and hoped not. When Tonorah gets home, her husband, Charlie, will have returned from his construction site on the fringes of the chain of chains, expecting a supper of his own.

"This is fantastic, Tonorah," I say, to which she smiles and releases a safe dollop of her all-purpose, long-practiced shell of laughter. But before she leaves and as I'm just starting to really get into the lasagna, she approaches the table.

"Tobia, I want to ask you something," she says.

"Sure," I say. It's rare that Tonorah says anything to me despite the fact that I've known her all my life. Yet every so often she surprises me. Once, when I was no more than ten or eleven, Tonorah was vacuuming the hallway, vacuuming and humming along with the radio the way she always does. I was in my bedroom. I had thrown myself into a tearful rage over some trifle. She turned off the vacuum and came and sat on the bed. I'd buried my head in my pillows after giving them a beating. Both my parents had told me to get it together and abandoned me.

She put a hand on my back. "You're a child with big feelings. That's all. It's gonna be all right," she said. Her words and the way she said them and the strangeness of her speaking to me at all had a profoundly settling effect. In all the time since, she's been content to chuckle at me and leave it at that. I sometimes wonder if she remembers that day. I've never asked her and have been content to let our acquaintance rest on the safest platitudes ever since. But I remember it.

"I talked to your daddy about letting Jacob and some of his friends be valets at this party coming up," she says. "When I asked him, he looked real serious. And then he said he didn't think it was such a good idea because of Jacob's past troubles." My father has helped get Jacob out of some speeding tickets and, a year ago, helped get a shoplifting charge lessened. Tonorah's daughter, Janice, is studying violin on scholarship at the Manhattan School of Music, so, especially by comparison, Jacob's delinquency worries Tonorah and her husband considerably. "I wondered if you wouldn't mind talking to your daddy about giving him the job. He could sure use the money."

"I'll talk to him," I say.

"I'd appreciate it," she says, chuckles.

"He's a stubborn man, isn't he, Tonorah?"

She chuckles again. "Not nearly's stubborn as yo' mother. Shooo!" Her eyes shut; her whole body shakes.

"That's true," I say and find I'm chuckling with her. "That's really true," I say. "How do you find her, Tonorah? How's she doing, in your opinion?"

"I find her better than most think she is," she says and looks at me out of the corners of her eyes, eyebrows raised, chuckles some more.

I wait for her to elaborate, but that's all she's going to say.

EIGHT

Bradley Sackett and his sister, Robin, achieved a minor celebrity among a certain set of high-school kids for throwing large parties in their parents' house, which dwarfed its lawn in the Kingshaven subdivision less than a mile from our house. Some of these parties were sanctioned and overseen by their parents, but most were not.

At one of these parties toward the end of the summer, Bradley and I leaned against a wall of the spacious living room armored with a calculated indifference that had its roots in insecurity. We surveyed the mix from a cool remove, our bodies sore and tan, strained muscles relaxing after two-a-days, feeling clean and slick from our after-practice showers.

I stared at her for a few moments before I recognized her. She was across the room and slightly withdrawn from some of Robin's friends from Faith High. She looked over at us and twisted a strand of hair around one of her long thin fingers. I had heard she was going to boarding school in Maryland, some school named after a forest, but I hadn't seen her for several years. The girls talked and laughed. We made eye contact, and I thought I saw the shadow of her having recognized me cross her face. I nudged Bradley, but he didn't know what I wanted him to see, and I didn't have a chance to explain.

She walked over to us. Her clothes were looser and darker than the other girls' at the party, and she let her hair hang straight down her upper back, wore little or no makeup. Her eyes were a large, galvanic hazelgrey, and her face had gained some ground on them in the intervening years. My heart beat faster as I watched her approach. Two urges flared: one to leave the room and run miles away; the other to stay and do I knew not what.

A few tacit beats passed before she spoke. "Remember me?" she asked and fixed me with an unblinking gaze that was at the same time sad, stimulating, and semi-mischievous.

I shook my head, no.

"I remember you," she said.

"You do. Who am I?" I asked.

"You don't remember me?"

"No," I said; it felt as if something was unraveling in my chest.

"I don't believe you," she said and cocked her head and looked to be holding back a smile. She narrowed her eyes. "I think you know who I am."

"You can think that if you want to."

"I'm your neighbor. There's your hint."

"I have a lot of neighbors now."

She further narrowed her eyes at me. "I'm . . ."

"Merritt Wilson," I allowed.

She smiled, slowly, at having been properly named. "Why'd you say you didn't . . ."

"He didn't want you to know he was keeping track," Bradley said, smiled, and wiggled his eyebrows.

Merritt looked at him with her sharp, galvanic, hazelgrey eyes. Then, she took hold of one of my hands and led me onto the Sacketts' living room floor. I let Bradley see my surprise at her boldness. We moved around on the makeshift dance floor, a space cleared by the removal of furniture. The couches and chairs that had been moved to the periphery were bright, new, and florally upholstered; their fabric smelled so new you'd get a disorienting headrush if you inhaled the scent too deeply. A glass coffee table resting atop a plaster nude had also been pulled aside to accommodate the young dancers. As we swayed to the music, Merritt watched me closely with her quick, intelligent eyes as if she thought I might make a sudden move against which she would need to defend herself.

It seemed as if it should've been forbidden for us to move as we did, though I scarcely moved at all, on the shiny parquet floor. There were new books—how-to, finance, and best-sellers—on all the shelves. The Sacketts' state-of-the-art stereo was playing "Video Killed the Radio Star." A dozen kids moved and laughed on the floor with us, doing dances their parents and older brothers and sisters had taught them, and ones they'd made up.

Mr. and Mrs. Sackett were chaperoning this party, and every now and then one or the other of them would cruise by on the outskirts of the room, attempt to engage one of us in conversation, or just look on and smile at how time had flown and hadn't it been yesterday when they were the ones out on the floor and dancing to Elvis or the Beatles or Buddy Holly, or Chuck Berry or the Rolling Stones. I think both parents were a little drunk. Earlier that night Mr. Sackett had cornered me for a conversation about football tryouts. He wondered what I thought of Bradley's chances. Mrs. Sackett had asked me several questions about my mother's November Ball, the answers to which I did not know, which seemed to upset her.

Merritt swayed in her dancing. She did a weeping willow in the wind, feet planted, new curves and arms waving. I moved stiffly, carefully, as if I thought I might break if I gave in and really moved. I watched her. I could see Bradley in the background not watching me from the doorway. Several of Robin's friends had him surrounded and were poking him in his marshmallowboy stomach. *You're going out for football?* I imagined them asking him and everybody laughed.

I thought about how I was going to get free from Merritt. Swinging in the willow dance, her body seemed to move more than it was actually moving. It was as if my nervousness were enhancing her motion. I felt dizzy. She fixed me with her eyes, which seemed to want to ask a burning question, and I wondered what she wanted. The lyrics of the song were about a point beyond which it was impossible to rewind. Her eyes fixed on me like rivets. She was beginning to remind me of exactly the thing I wanted to forget.

I couldn't hold up under her gaze. Before the song ended, I mumbled an excuse, broke free, ran out onto the Sacketts' backyard, and took in gulps of the crisp night air. I stood on the edge of a patio where the yard began, wondering what I was going to do.

Little orange glows shone from the darkness under the trees and hedges on the fringes of the lawn. I stood listening to the conspiratorial giggling and nervous banter. Someone had the inevitable beer or liquor, acquired at great risk, hidden back there in the underbrush. Behind them, the gigantic Kingshaven houses dominated their lawns, seeming to say, *Look how well we're doing!* Someone said, "I'm starting to feel something."

I lit out on the Kingshaven avenues. Walking home seemed a good idea. The sounds of the party diminished behind me till they were gone, and I only heard the clip of my shoes and my breathing. When I was a quarter of the way home, I changed my mind and decided to go back to the party. I walked back and stood looking at the lights of the house, wondering how I would avoid Merritt.

She was suddenly beside me. When I realized she was there, twenty neon underskin millipedes ran down my spine and balled themselves up and did forward rolls into my fingertips. "What are you doing out here?" she asked.

"Would you like some punch? I was thinking of heading back inside. I can go in and get you some punch," I offered.

"You're a friend of Bradley's?" she asked.

I nodded.

Someone yelled into the night: "Davis just puked!"

Merritt looked in the direction of the voice, shook her head, and smiled at me. "Do you know Davis?" She took a cigarette out of its pack and lit it.

"No," I said.

"I've been wanting to ask you. Do you remember what happened that day, down at the creek?" she asked, and looked at me, exhaling smoke.

"When?"

She looked at me. "That day. Down at the creek."

"Not very well," I said.

"My parents think you knew something you didn't tell them. They say they could tell you were lying to them when they asked you questions." She looked from one to the other of my eyes.

"You sure you don't want any punch?" I asked.

She smiled and shook her head, no.

"That was a long time ago," I said. "I was just a kid."

"My father says something," she said and drew in the smoke, the cigarette tip glowing orange, and exhaled. "He says, 'People change. But not all that much,'" she said. She gave me an appraising look out of the corners of her eyes.

I was about to leave, but before I excused myself, she asked me a simple question about football. I answered it and asked her if she liked boarding school. We talked in front of the house, the music inside just making it out to our ears, the kids talking, laughing, sitting Indian-style, drinking and smoking under the privet hedges. I began to relax. Then, very suddenly, she kissed me on the cheek and withdrew to see how her kiss had left me. I was breathless in the aftermath of it. Why would she do that? I looked at her as coolly as I could, terrified as I was and spoiling to run.

"Sorry," she said. "I know that was weird of me to do. I don't know why I did that," she said and threw the cigarette to the ground and stepped on it, looking at me the whole time. "Was that okay? How did you like that?" she said.

"Yes, I guess so," I said.

"What is it about you?" she asked.

"I don't know. I don't think there's anything about me," I said and told her goodnight and turned around and walked home.

A YEAR LATER Bradley and Robin had a get-together that was smaller and more select than a party. This one was not overseen by their parents. Due to a territorial dispute in the planning phases of the get-together, the Sackett siblings had agreed to entertain in separate areas of the house. Robin and her friends would stay on the upper floors; Bradley's friends were to remain in the basement. This was an arrangement that suited us. The lowest floor of the Sackett house was equipped with an entertainment system, a pool table, a Star Wars pinball machine, Atari, two bedrooms, a bathroom, and kitchen. Also, that night someone had stolen from their parents' liquor cabinet, or had otherwise arranged for a fifth of Wild Turkey, which we sipped and chased with Cokes.

By this time, my football prowess, that glory engine, was up and purring. Moving through my life, down the halls of school, stark against the cool white sheets of my bed at night, I could feel the warm certainty of my power coursing through me. I felt I was having an impact on the world, that it had better take note of me. I convinced myself that I had forgotten the old Tobia. There were football trophies resting on the bookshelves in my room. My father had found time to keep a scrapbook chronicling my exploits that he kept up in the study next to some other relics of Caldwell success in the world. Mother was there after the games, smiling, overdressed as if a football game was a sacrament. There she was, waiting to give me a post-game hug. A circle of fans would gather around and wait for me to come out of the locker room to hug my mother.

The Sacketts' house was much newer and more polished than ours. At the time, I thought it was how a house should be. At the time, I was happy to leave our old house as often as I could for a house like the Sacketts'. It was clean and reflective of a prosperity that Bradley with his immaculate haircuts, cherubic face, and fabric-softener smell, himself exuded. It was as if Bradley had struck up a deal and had himself exempted from the awkwardness of adolescence. I aspired to Bradley and Robin's effortless-seeming charisma and grace, and I thought that such a charisma and grace could only thrive in the environs of a household like the Sacketts'. I envied the smell of the new paint, the fresh carpet, and the soap-opera-commercial shine on the waxed wood floors and brass fixtures.

Our house was old and creaky. Our floors were slanted. Our house needed a painting and a thorough cleaning beyond the reach of any vacuuming or dusting Tonorah could ever give it. We walked on hardwood or faded Orientals. The Sacketts' feet sank into plush carpet that threw out an intoxicating, fresh-from-the-factory smell. I began to envy that antiseptic newness.

Mr. Sackett was an executive at Blinkers International, a corporation that owned a handful of restaurant chains and chemical factories. His Saturday golf game at Sweet Hollow, where my father had voted on him, maybe blackballed him, in his green alligator pants, was observed with strict devotion. Mrs. Sackett wore enough makeup for two women despite being an attractive woman underneath it. She liked to bake Mississippi Mud cakes for Bradley and Robin's friends. Her blue eyes gleamed and her cheeks dimpled so much you expected to hear a little bell go *ding* when she smiled. You would have been hard-pressed to dirty a dust mop in the entire house. Still, their maid showed up every day. Five years later Mr. and Mrs. Sackett would be divorced and fighting like alley cats over the house, their beloved possessions, their children.

I remember how excited I felt the night of that get-together in particular. Excited and scared. Merritt was upstairs. I remember repeatedly thinking, *Merritt Wilson is upstairs. She's just upstairs.* Nervous jolts of excitement swam through me like schools of guppies. I tried to keep them under control in front of the other boys as we did Wild Turkey shots. I was trying hard not to slip and turn the conversation around to the girls upstairs. I didn't want to let the boys know I cared. It was cool not to care about anything, and we all wanted to be cool. Bradley demonstrated his uncanny talent for Atari games in the basement that night, which was frustrating for us because we were accustomed to blowing by him on the field. We passed around the fifth of Wild Turkey and made our faces and released our rebel yells after we'd taken our shots.

The bourbon gradually eroded or exacerbated our cool. I talked a lot, then, about whatever came to mind, which was, then, and is, now, very rare for me. We could hear the girls' footsteps on the hardwood floor upstairs. Distant, wonderful peals of laughter floated down to us like promises.

Later that night when the Wild Turkey and some of our eyes were flying at half-mast, the girls progressed downstairs for a lark. They wanted to pay a visit to the juniors. When I saw her on the stairs—she walked down third of seven—I was frozen in want. I was held in thrall by a murky, subterranean yearning that I associated with the newness and promise of the Sacketts' house; and the unbalanced, full-on excitement of adolescence; and the singing in my blood when I blew by the linemen and crushed the quarterback (I had yet to be switched to quarterback myself) and heard the cheering of the crowd; and the Wild Turkey strutting around in my head. I fell into a dazed silence while my friends took up a steady babble as if someone had promised them a dollar a word. Drunk, they tried to put on a show for the older girls. I'd suddenly lost my words. My cogs spun in silence.

The other boys whipped their banter into greater silliness. Many of them were irrevocably drunk. I watched and laughed and couldn't think of a thing to say in the presence of Merritt. She had supercharged the room with her presence. In my eyes, the basement was Merritt's alone.

When she laughed at something, her quick, intelligent eyes disappeared from view in the blink so that it seemed as if she was trying to relish that bit of laughter. When I watched her the rate of my heartbeat increased, my breath came heavy in my chest. I felt like running away, felt like my blood had thickened, felt dirty. I couldn't stay and I couldn't go. A few times she caught me looking at her, but I looked quickly away.

After a time the Wild Turkey was gone. The girls went back upstairs.

Merritt stood out of the depths of the leather couch. As she walked by, she looked down at me and said, "Goodnight, Tobia Caldwell," with just a touch more Tennessee in her accent than she'd had a year earlier and blew me a second kiss. I felt enfiladed with joy and dread. I mumbled something unintelligible.

As Robin and her friends walked up the steps, a hush fell over the room. As soon as all the girls had disappeared, and we could hear them laughing about us and moving to the upstairs bedrooms, my friends fell to whooping and hollering. Several of them clapped me on the back.

"You're crazy if you don't go up there right now, Tobuddha," they said with their loosened tongues. "If I were you I'd go up there right now," they said. "I guarantee she's waiting for you."

I smiled as coolly as I could. The guppy schools raced and multiplied and scattered to hide before returning in my dream. There was no way I was going up there.

NINE

I SIT UP IN BED, place my feet on the threadbare kilim, take a deep breath. A whippoorwill in the maple outside my window is up and trilling this-will-pass, this-won't-last. Through the sun-splashed leaves haloed in green light, I can see the Goodhopes' house. They're due here in thirty minutes to discuss its sale.

In the beginning my father and I tried to keep our reclamation project a secret. We had associates at Pinkmellon buy the houses for us, engaged in all manner of banking gymnastics, set up accounts and shell companies for our accomplices, let the Golfhurst houses sit unoccupied for months after we purchased them.

After a time, as expected, the neighbors started talking. Many of them asked us directly what we knew. In a few cases we set up renters in the houses who took care of the lawns and paid us healthy rents while we waited to buy the rest of the houses.

We didn't tell any outright lies; we danced around the truth a little. While I was up in this study, working out some detail or another about the project with the window open to catch the breeze, I'd hear my father saying to one of the neighbors from the subdivision, "Yes. I find it surprising that no one has moved in yet. They're renting. You don't say? I agree. Yes, the yard is getting ragged." Like that, he would chitchat them on the front porch.

We bought as many houses as we could over a two-year period, before, finally, a year ago, with five houses bought, we were unveiled as the culprits, the atavistic lunatics. The neighbors dug their trenches, kept their distance from us, discussed how they would hold out for as much money as they could get. That's when Father pulled some strings with some old friends and got us permission from the zoning commission to start tearing the first houses down. To our neighbors' well-voiced surprise, we erased five houses.

Then we paid outrageous prices for the other four. I suppose we could have done worse. But we paid much more than they were worth, and it took its toll on the diminishing Pinkmellon money. After we had bought them, we erased them.

Now, on the land we've set out to reclaim, the Goodhopes' is the only house we don't yet own.

The doorbell rings just as the grandfather clock in the foyer tolls the last stroke of nine. Tom and Trish Goodhope are standing on the front porch and, to my involuntary disgust, looking bright and cheerful this morning. Why should that bother me? I decide that it shouldn't and compose myself for optimal politeness and cordiality.

I open the door. Tom's blond hair is aggressively parted to the side so that a well-defined line of pink scalp is revealed on the upper left side of his head. He is wearing a multicolored, short-sleeved polo shirt tucked neatly into his khakis. His wife, Trish, wears a yellow cardigan sweater, khakis, and a pink blouse. Both of them went to school in North Carolina—Trish to UNC, Tom to Duke. Both are rabid basketball fans. Tom was an SAE, Trish a Tri-Delt. Anyone who knows them at all knows these two facts about them. Tom is a doctor, Trish is in hospital public relations.

Tom has a hearty handshake for me and a booming, "Mr. Caldwell." Trish says, "How *are* yew!"

I let them in.

They follow me into the dining room. We take our seats. I have a pitcher of lemonade and glasses filled with ice on the table. I offer them lemonade. They both accept. I pour the lime-green liquid into three tinkling glasses of ice. After we've all had our first sips, I begin.

"You know what we want," I say. "Surely, there's no secret about that. No need for me to tap-dance here. Your house is the last one in our plans." I don't say, "the most important house because of the graves." I glance down at the notebook in front of me, the $650,000 figure written there. Dr. Tom Goodhope smiles and glances over at his wife.

"You're right about that. No secret about that. But what if," he says. "What if I told you we didn't want to sell at any price." He punctuates this statement with a little hug for Trish. "What if I told you we like the new open land around us. Kippy and little Laura enjoy it. We're happy right where we are. We're not planning on going anywhere anytime soon. What if I was to say that?" All smiles and hugs for Trish.

I nod. "Okay," I say. "You won't sell? Not at any price? Well, then I guess . . ." I shrug, there's nothing more to be said. Tom doesn't realize how tired I've grown of the project, how much I want it to be over with, one house short or not, graveyard or no graveyard. My father made a mistake by not attending this meeting, I think. Is he testing my loyalty? Is he off somewhere with his packages?

"Well. I suppose there could be a price, but I'm afraid it's going to have to be a great deal of money. A great deal more than anyone else got." He nods and narrows his eyes and lets his ample forehead furrow; it is a very doctoral, bedside-manner look, this.

Trish nods. With very odd timing, through a tight terrier's smile, she asks, "How's your mother doing?"

I look at her and look away without answering. "You may have heard about our reclamation party," I say. "Our goal in throwing this party is to raise enough money to be able to make you pleased with our offer. Today, I wanted to see if you could name a fair price you would entertain. You're going to be invited to the party, by the way. I hope you'll come."

"Wait a second. Time-out," Tom says, like coach K. He's one of those guys who's always calling time-outs, a Cameron Crazy to the core, his life a sporting event. "Let's see if I got this straight. You're inviting me to a party the central purpose of which is to try to raise money so that you can buy the house that I don't really want to sell you?" All smiles and half-certain of my insanity.

"That's right," I say, smiling back, crazily.

"Sometimes I think you have lost it, Mr. Caldwell. You and your father." He laughs. "Attempting the impossible. This 'going back in time' stuff. 'Rollback.'" He's referring to an article about our project printed under that headline—Going Back in Time. "Are you really against all technological advances? You should come visit us at the hospital."

"Can you name me a figure, Tom?" I say. "Something that would make it easy for you to part with your house, but that's within reason."

"Is it true your father saw a ghost telling him to carry out all of this? Trish and I were curious. That's what the rumor is. One of the ghosts from the graves in our yard flew to him and told him to start this demolition." Tom's mention of the graveyard reminds me of our earlier negotiations with the Goodhopes regarding the purchase of only the land with the headstones and the fruitless wrangle that turned out to be— completely frustrating. They didn't want to make their lot any less than its five acres, for resale purposes.

Trish gives her husband a disapproving glance.

"You can believe what you like, Dr. Goodhope. More lemonade?"

"No thanks," he says. But Trish pushes her glass forward and I pour her another glassful. She looks at me with an expression that makes me think I'm keeping her guessing, which pleases me. I want to keep the Trish Goodhopes of the world guessing.

"And, on the subject of ghosts, you realize that your house was built right smack on top of fifteen hundred Confederate graves. The developer ripped them right out, plucked them out of the ground like bad teeth. And then, in went your house."

Their jaws drop. Trish looks at Tom. "I thought you said that wasn't true."

"It isn't," he says, shaking his head dismissively. "It's just a vicious rumor. No truth to it whatsoever." He turns to me with an expression of repressed hostility.

I consider showing them a photograph of the hastily removed graves with our family graveplot in the background, but think better of it. It won't do me any good to antagonize these people. I smile at them and shrug—believe it or don't, fine with me.

"Three million," says Tom Goodhope, ready to change the subject back to the matter at hand. "I don't think we're ready to entertain anything less. We had to work very hard to get into Golfhurst, Mr. Caldwell. That house you want to destroy is the culmination of a lot of hard work for us. Medical school, residency, internships, a lot of patients, a lot of blood, lives saved. We like it here in Haven. There's plenty of greenery, now, especially given your . . . eradication of our neighbors. We're putting down roots. It'd sure be a pain to have to move now. We'd enjoy being next to a park. So, you'll certainly have to make it worth our while."

"We really like the school district," says Trish, nodding and smiling as if conspiratorially.

"Yes. Three million," says Tom, nodding. He puts his arm around his wife's shoulder. They both smile at me.

I nod. I have an urge to remind the Goodhopes that their house is worth six hundred thousand dollars at the very most. Looking at them, though, a part of me admires them for going for all they can get. Why not? I'm reminded of how strange I must look to them—a twenty-eight-year-old—I'm guessing, seven or eight years younger than Tom, in charge of a project whose object is the erasure of the symbol of progress in their lives. Their home. Why shouldn't they get rich off of our obsession?

"All right. Yes, you *must* like the school district," I say. "You've given us something to work toward. A ballpark figure. I hope you will come to the party." I stand up and so do the Goodhopes. I follow them to the door.

"I just love this neat old house," Trish says as we walk across the creaking floorboards of the foyer. "So many neat old things. So much charm."

"Thank-you," I say.

"Yes, it is quite a place," says Tom. "Not many places like this anywhere anymore. It's a real gem. How old is it?"

"The foundation was laid in the early eighteen hundreds," I say. "Since then it's been through several manifestations and refurbishments."

"Isn't that fantastic?" says Tom as if he is genuinely impressed. Who knows? Maybe he is. In another life, if things were different, perhaps he could've been my friend.

I wave goodbye from the front porch and watch the Goodhopes move across the lawn toward their three-million-dollar, five-hundred-thousand-dollar house.

I PASS MY FATHER at the bottom of the front steps. Sometimes it seems as if we wander through this house with our own agendas, passing each other at random like travelers on a rural road, archaeologists at a dig site. It occurs to me at times that my mother is still the principal connection between us despite the bond of Rollback Inc.

"How'd it go?" he says.

"Not so good."

"Break it to me gently."

"Cool three million," I say.

He clenches his jaw. "Greedy, yuppie bastards," he says. "We can do that, can't we?"

"If we think it's really worth it. There's a chance. It depends on the party. If we match that, it'll mean we're dependent on Rollback Inc. from now on."

He looks worried. There is no question in his mind that it certainly is worth it.

ON THE THIRD FLOOR I gather up my father's gifts. I walk down the stairs, out the door, climb into the car, and drive the ten miles to Aunt Marcy's. It is roughly a fifteen-minute drive depending on traffic, which is heavier than usual today. Sun glints on metal and glass to the right and left in the streams of cars rushing in opposite directions between the chain of chains.

I'm told my mother left the house with tears of undiluted rage condensing her grey eyes into beads of devouring ice. Aunt Marcy, who is something of a saint and who has never married, took my mother in. After the divorce, whenever my father tried to visit her, she shut herself off in a room of Aunt Marcy's house and refused to come out till he'd driven a safe distance back out of her life.

When I pull into Aunt Marcy's, three of her nine dogs and five or six of her twelve cats gather in the driveway to greet me. I can never keep their names straight. "Hello, Buster, Maggie, George, Heffe . . . Now, who are you? You're new." I pat some of their heads, and they part to let me pass.

Some movement in my peripheral vision catches my eye, and I'm surprised to see Bank Shankhorn and some of his crew working on a foundation out in the yard. I see his truck and see him from the back, the ever-present faded orange UT hat. He and his workers are squatting next to a circular foundation of sorts.

"What do you say, Bank?" I call out.

He turns and squints over and, recognizing me, nods with, what seems to me, undue seriousness. It's unclear whether or not he's recognized me. I try hard with Bank, but he seems bent on regarding me as a college puke. I suspect he might have lost money because of me when we beat his beloved UT during my brief tenure as quarterback in college.

"'Lo," he says, squinting over.

"What are you doing over here, Bank?"

"Some work for your daddy."

"What's it going to be?"

"Sort of a greenhouse-type deal," says Bank and turns back to his work.

I shake my head. Typically, my father has told me not a word about this. "So, now we've got you tearing down houses over there, and putting them up over here, huh, Bank?"

"I reckon," Bank allows without turning back around.

Full of tricks, I mutter to myself as I walk into the house past all the animals, *full of tricks. A greenhouse-type deal.* Marcy is waiting for me just inside the front door. Some of the cats and dogs manage to squeeze into the house with me, others are stopped by the closing door.

"Well, hello, Tobia. Give me a kiss," Aunt Marcy says in her warm way. Her speech reminds me of how it used to be to hear my mother.

I kiss her on the cheek. "Hi, Aunt Marcy. How are you?"

"Fine fine. I'm glad you're here. Perhaps you can tell me what that father of yours is up to out there?" She's looking out the window at Bank and his crew.

"I didn't know about it before today," I say, shaking my head.

She shakes her head, too, and clucks. "All I can say is we never asked for this. Never asked for any of it." She looks down at the gifts in my hands. "How does he know we didn't have other plans for that part of our little yard."

I shake my head.

"Well. Go on back, she's waiting for you."

"Thank-you."

My mother is never cold to her only son. I push her wheelchair around the block of Aunt Marcy's house to a little pond—called Gibble's Pond, for Old Gibble, who my father says used to run him and his friends away from there with his shotgun and underfed hounds. Mother remembers that story and I think that's exactly why she likes the pond now. I push her around and around. The pond is encircled by a concrete path. The land around it has been made into a tiny park in the middle of an upscale apartment development. Who knows, maybe even Old Gibble searched his heart before he died and donated this small portion of his land for use as a park.

Today, as I wheel my mother around, I enjoy her continued delight in the passing scenery which she expresses in chirps as if she is a bird gone flightless and remembering the way a gust in the wings used to lift her unexpectedly up. I remember what Tonorah said about her: *She's doing better than most think she is.* It seems to me that what she expresses in the small way is the momentary brimming of feelings that have achieved a great depth inside her.

My mother does not even try to speak, though, if she wanted to she could. She's too proud. She knows her malady. Knows her words would come out all mixed up. She refuses to be a laughingstock. Her speech, tainted, would be too painful to hear given its mellifluousness before the stroke.

My mother and Marcy grew up in Charleston, with little money, but with the connections and social privileges of one of the old established families there. I used to love going to Charleston or to their family's house in the North Carolina highlands. Marcy moved to Tennessee years ago to be close to her younger and much admired sister, not long after my birth and after she was jilted by a Citadel boy. Now, both women are unified in a strong distrust of all things masculine. It's a wonder they let their guard down for me.

Some days, in fulfillment of my father's request, I talk to my mother about coming back to the old house. I tell her he feels terrible about everything that's happened, feels rotten about what he did. I sometimes try to convince her of how much he's changed. She listens, but I suspect the only reason she's so patient is that I'm her son, and she feels compelled to indulge me.

She hasn't stopped being a mother. Trying. Even after the stroke and me a grown man, I'll sometimes see her face move into a sour expression as she looks me up and down and know that she disapproves of the way I'm dressed or of the shagginess of my hair, or is noting the fact that I've neglected to shave that day. When I worked for Pinkmellon she used to enjoy seeing me in my business suit and close-cropped hair and the ties she'd given me. I knew that if she could she would have told me I looked super-sharp.

Now, she'll inquire, with a certain solicitous glance from the corner of her eyes, if I'm seeing anyone "special" as she used to say. She makes no secret about being ready for grandchildren. Most of the time I shake my head, no. Given Robin, I could answer this question in the affirmative, but that's not in our time-honored script. I wouldn't dare upset her by talking about the projected return of Merritt. Not yet. What is in our script is that after my "no" she'll shake her head, haltingly, so that I know if she could, she would remind me what a worthy candidate I am for some "little girl's" affection. In these ways, she has remained an excellent communicator even without speech.

There are times when I go to wheel my mother around Old Gibble's pond and deliver Father's gifts that frighten me as much as anything else I've experienced. Marcy calls these her "gone" times. Sometimes, a distance moves in and covers her like a shroud. She'll look up at me, on these days, as if she doesn't know me and make no effort at even tacit communication. This is so unlike the mother I know her to be that it unhinges something in me, makes me unable to fill the silence that needs filling more than ever at those times.

When she could still speak I had grown used to being distant with her. That had developed into my role in the game we played. She would flush the words from me while I acted like I didn't want to tell her anything. I would remain aloof but I'd still be hanging around in the knowledge that everything would be revealed through our game in its own good time. Most things would be revealed, anyway. Many things. She would pursue and I would slowly reveal. She would ask and I would grudgingly tell.

It was a serious feat gaining distance from her. On these days, it's difficult to find her.

Now on these gone days my greatest fear is that she's decided to turn forever in on herself. Decided to leave those who have disappointed her with the husk of her absence, her chrysalis. I wouldn't be able to stand it if she ever completely gives up on me. And my betrayal, here, as I imagine it, is composed of a thousand micro-negligences that have built and built up to equal one macro treason. On these "gone" days I wheel her around Old Gibble's pond in silence. She stares straight ahead and far away. I try to take on the role she's always played in our game—communication facilitator, question asker—and hear myself fail miserably, fall far short of her mastery. I try to tell her stories, but they sink like stones in the pond. I sometimes think on those days when she is distant that I have lost my mother and gained my father when it had once been so much the other way around.

Today, though, she's not gone. She's in as good a mood as I've seen her for some time. Her eyes are mirthful. She sits up straight, pivoting slightly to take it all in. I wheel her around Gibble's wind-rippled pond, and we toss bread crumbs to a pair of mallards. As predicted, back at Marcy's, she tucked away both of my father's gifts, unopened. The pond is so wind-rippled today that the bluegills' nests in the shallows are obscured beneath tiny waves. As I wheel her, I think about Merritt's letter. Because it's so much on my mind, it's difficult for me to keep from talking about it, but I don't bring it up. This is her time, and pretending nothing's wrong is something I learned from her. I push, she chirps.

We stop and throw some bread to the ducks. My mother throws the pieces of bread, with her good arm, as hard as she can, straight at the drake's viridian head. She looks up at me and smiles her rage.

TEN

I STOOD IN THE FOYER for last rites, my hair wet and combteeth-furrowed, feeling caged in my tuxedo, already regretting the pinch of the narrow shoes. Mother buzzed around after this and that. Father leaned against the doorjamb, his bourbon and branch cocked. Beads of sweat broke out on my forehead and threatened to drip. Mother went to get me a handkerchief. Father had me hold his drink and took out his wallet, pulled from it two twenties. I took them and handed back his drink. She gave me the handkerchief and went to get the camera.

"Have fun tonight, Romeo," he said.

"Thanks. I'll try."

"And why not let's let this be your only contact—first and last—with this Wilson girl."

I nodded.

He winked and shook his head. "A strange business," he said. "Be careful out there." He smiled sadly.

"Come and give your wonderful, beautiful, charming, adorable mother a farewell kiss," my mother said. "You look so handsome. Dashing," she said. "A real killer diller. It's a shame you're wasting it on that old Wilson girl."

"Interesting choice of words," Father said, under his breath.

Mother stood on the front porch watching me walk to the car. She waved goodbye as I turned her Fiat around and sped down our driveway under the trees.

It had rained a few hours earlier and already the trees and grass looked greener. Frogs glowing in the headlights leaped ahead of me on the road just avoiding the wheels at the last moment. Or, maybe I squashed some of them under the tires. Driving, I was struck by the awareness that the old Tobia, a previous version, would have stopped to marvel at these frogs, but the new one didn't stop because he had other things to think about—dealings in the complicated realm of human interaction.

As I drove the short distance, the sweat kept flowing as if it was a continuation of my preparatory shower, a continuation of the flow of sweat on the football field. The sweat poured out as if my nerves were making a case for their greater future expression. I mopped my brow and neck with Father's monogrammed handkerchief; halfway to the Wilsons' I could have wrung it out.

I parked in the Wilsons' driveway and sat there sweating and thinking how good it would feel to take off my tie and unbutton the top buttons of my shirt and open up the Fiat on one of the outlying country roads, how it would feel to let the wind dry the sweat and to never turn around for a girl or anybody.

The world was not like that. There were things you had to do. Bradley had come to me one day after school and told me that one of Robin's friends had a crush on me. Robin had a lot of friends, but from the beginning, I knew that it must be Merritt. Though there were a lot of football groupies who would have been interested in going to the dance with me, there were no standout prospects; so, I agreed to be set up.

I marched up to the door. Mr. Wilson swung it open before I'd knocked so I was caught on the doorstep with an elevated fist. The last time I'd seen him, besides out in his car or working in their yard on a few occasions, had been when he'd questioned me that day when I had been a much younger version of myself.

"Listen, Tobia . . . ," he said, stopped short. The way he said it made me think he'd been meaning to tell me the date was off. But then he said, "Come in," and offered a small, tight smile and took my hand in a quick shake, his ring digging in. I followed him into the living room.

"She might be a while," he said.

"All right."

"What are the prospects for next year?"

"Sir?"

"Football."

"Very good. A lot of guys coming back." I kept myself from looking at the portrait of Ben above the fireplace on the mantel, frozen at eight years.

"Congratulations on all-region. I saw that in the paper."

"Thank-you, sir."

Despite his effort and goodwill, and my nervous determination to keep up appearances, our conversation sank into a silence that grew heavy and pushed at the seams of the room. I felt a drop of sweat loosen and slide down my back.

Mrs. Wilson came into the room. "She'll be a minute," she said. "Would you care for a soda? Can I offer you anything at all? What a nice night for you for this," she said. "Now that the rain's gone. How're your parents? I haven't seen you in a good while considering you live so close. Isn't that interesting? Neighbors and yet . . . It's those big trees on the edge of your yard. You've sure grown up into a . . . young man. And, as you know, Merritt is . . . starting to really assert herself in things. Off to college next fall. I'm glad we got that rain. A lot of people complain about it, but I'm glad. There's something so cleansing and refreshing about rains like that. Don't you . . . How's your mother?"

I was about to try to say something when the sight of Merritt descending the stairs stopped me.

She was wearing an old dress fashioned from the kind of delicate fabric—a lacy pink-and-white chiffon—that's unsettling to a high-school boy with no sisters to have prepared him for it, no sisters to have diffused, through familiarity, the heady, exotic power of its super-femininity.

"Well, what do you think?" Merritt asked.

"You look fantastic. Unbelievably great," I said, shaking my head, meaning it. I stood and stepped forward to meet her at the bottom of the steps. I demonstrated and then tried to pin the corsage my mother had bought for me for Merritt to the delicate chiffon, but I couldn't do it due to a malfunction of hand-eye coordination that worsened the closer my hands came to Merritt's breathing body beneath the taut material. Another droplet of sweat slid down my back, another loosened from my forehead and fell to the floor. I started several times and held back. I was seized with the irrational fear that I might break her skin with the pinpoint, or that I might lose control and stab her. My football-playing hands started shaking once they felt the body heat coming through the fabric, once I heard and saw her breathing.

Mrs. Wilson stepped in, grabbed the corsage, said let me help you with that and how truly lovely it was, and affixed it to Merritt's dress.

Relieved and bewildered, I stepped back. Merritt stepped toward her mother and, pushing Mrs. Wilson's head to the side and leaning into her ear, whispered something with an emphatic expression. I met Mr. Wilson's eyes for a moment. His face was expressionless. I looked down at the tiny glistening drop of my own sweat on the hardwood floor.

Mrs. Wilson came away from her mini-huddle with Merritt wearing a tight, pained expression, almost a wince. She forced it into a smile. Merritt stepped toward me, smiling, as if in apology, and effortlessly pinned a boutonniere to my jacket and looked up at me: *Just stay cool and we'll be out of here soon.*

"BE CAREFUL with our girl," Mrs. Wilson said. "Twelve-thirty." They stood in the doorway watching us leave.

On the way out Merritt grabbed a backpack resting under a coatrack and slung it into the backseat. I thought I heard her mother sobbing over the sound of the car engine as we pulled away, but I wasn't sure for the frogs and their singing about the rain.

"You have no idea what I had to go through to be here with you tonight, Tobia Caldwell," Merritt said, and we sped away.

WE ARRIVED at school, and I parked outside the gym, but when we stepped out of the car and saw how it was going to be, Merritt looked at me and looked at the open gym doors where the couples were filing in.

Someone in the parking lot started yelling, "Tobuddha! Tobuddha! Woo woo woo woo!"

"Do you really want to go in there?" Merritt asked.

I shook my head, no, and smiled. It was as if she had read my mind. My skinny tuxedo shoes were prying at my feet. There was an unsettling racing in my chest.

"Give me your keys," she said.

"I'm sorry?"

"Give me your keys."

"Why?"

"Please trust me. Give me your keys," she said, holding out her hand palm up. She kept her eyes on me, kept her palm out, till I tossed her the keys. She walked around the front of the car and hopped in the driver's seat and adjusted it to suit her. I walked around the back of the car and hopped in the passenger's seat. She started the engine. I looked at her.

"What're you doing?" I asked and smiled and shook my head.

We raced away.

Neither of us spoke during the fifteen-minute drive, although, now and then, at stoplights, she glanced over with a small, mischievous smile.

SHE DROVE US straight to the cemetery. In the parking lot, she switched off the ignition. The only sound around us was the engine pinging and the frogs. The last time I'd been there was for Ben's burial almost ten years before.

"Here we are," she said and looked at me.

"Yes we are, but why are we here?" I asked. I looked at the black wrought-iron gates.

"Let me tell how we came to be here. Okay?"

"Okay."

"First I told my parents I was going with another boy," Merritt said. "Do you know Rusty Green? He goes to Maxwell. Tennis player. Cute. A little immature, emotionally. I was planning to tell you to pick me up somewhere else so they wouldn't know. Robin gave everything away. She must not know much about . . . our past. Robin let it slip on the phone. She asked if I was excited about my date and so my mom goes, 'Oh? Big date?' They had *the big talk* with me that night." She looked at me for a time without speaking. "They asked me why I would want to go on a date with you, considering. Then, they said, 'We absolutely forbid it. How could you consort with that boy who was there. . . . Do you even know him, Merritt? Do you want to torture your mother?' Like that. On and on they went."

"What did you say?"

"I told them they have no proof that you did anything wrong and that I know how to judge people. I can tell about people. Then, I just told them. I'm going to go with him, I said. It was my idea. They couldn't believe that. They want to think it's your scheme. I'm seventeen and soon enough you'll be rid of me, I told them. I told them I could make my own decisions." Merritt was looking out the front window. She seemed to be enjoying the recounting, and so was I.

"Later, they had a talk in their bedroom. I don't know what it's like in your old house, but in ours you can hear vibrations. I can tell what kind of conversation they're having by the vibrations their voices make in the airducts. You catch a word here and there. Even when I can't tell what they're saying, I can listen and tell a lot by the tone. They decided to let me go. Not that I would've let them stop me anyway. I can't help it. I'm curious about you. Yes, there, I said it, and I feel better for having said it. I have been since that day." She looked across the seat at me, looked away, at the cemetery gates. "They're still hoping you'll turn out to be a creep so I'll never want to see you again."

"I noticed the performance back at the house," I said.

"You notice things like that, huh? Are you sensitive?"

"No," I said. "I . . ."

"I think you are." She pulled the keys from the ignition and reached in the backseat for the backpack, took from it a pair of tennis shoes, took off her dress shoes, put on the tennis shoes, gave me still another small, crafty smile, opened the door, and went running for the cemetery gate.

I sat and watched her run up to the gate, which, I was surprised, swung open to let her pass through. After a time I shook my head and stepped out of the car and followed her.

I walked into the cemetery and called for her and, judging from her answers, jogged till I could see her grey-pink form moving among the stones.

"What in the world are we doing?" I asked her. "Maybe we should've stayed at the dance."

She looked back at me, increased her pace. "You'll see. We didn't want to go to any silly dance."

I fell back a second, considering, then caught up. We wandered between the headstones, the mausoleums, our feet crunching on the gravel of the groundskeeper's road, and we went through some grass and through three or four rows of stones and stopped in front of Ben's grave.

"See what it says?"

I looked down and read the stone.

BEN WILSON. 1969–1977
WONDERFUL BROTHER AND SON

"Simple. And true. Not overdone," she said. "Do you like it?"

I looked at her and looked back at the stone. "Yes, it's fine," I said. "You're right. It's simple and not overdone."

"And true."

She sat down Indian-style, which took some folding-in of her dress. I sat down, knees up, next to her.

We were silent for a time. Then, Merritt told me how they'd left Cincinnati and followed the moving van down to Haven. How her father had earned a promotion in Blinkers International, and her mother was planning to teach at the university annex. Her father was returning to Tennessee where he'd grown up poor, the son of a big-hearted cook. Her mother was moving farther away from her native Chicago. Merritt told me about the telephone poles and the black fences flying by against the rolling hills through certain parts of Kentucky. Thoroughbreds bent with stunning equine grace to pull at the grass her father said was blue when the wind caught it in a certain way. *No it isn't,* Ben had said. *Not really. Where's the blue?*

"He could be difficult," Merritt said. "He wasn't a saint or anything. He was just a kid."

They'd stopped at Claiborne farm to see the great Secretariat on the way down, that god of a horse whose heart in the autopsy proved twice as big as a normal horse's.

Mr. Wilson had been prone to smile and whistle as he'd driven because he was going back home to Tennessee. Mrs. Wilson was worried about the upheaval. She wondered if she'd be able to write the romance novels she published under the pseudonym Gracie Harmony in Tennessee as successfully as she had in Ohio. She suspected she would. All of her novels were set in the garden district of New Orleans, and in Tennessee, she would be that much closer to the garden district. As the car rolled along, Merritt and Ben had been thinking about the friends they'd left back on the other side of the river for which their former state was named.

After a few hours they'd grown restless and Ben was sometimes difficult. He got hyper in the car. He and Merritt had wrestled and had pinching wars in the backseat and they'd been scolded mildly, later threatened with more severe punishment. They hadn't had a chance to have any good times yet in Tennessee before everything had happened.

Merritt unpinned her corsage and placed it on the grass in front of Ben's headstone. She looked at me, and I realized what she wanted and unpinned my boutonniere and set it down next to hers. The two conglomerations of lace and flowers rested about seven inches from each other in front of the stone. I could hear my heart beating in my ears. I'd started to sweat again. What was I doing here?

"I think it's terrible, what happened," I said.

It occurred to me, then, that it might be better to tell Merritt everything—the twisted roots of grandmother oak where the cottonmouth stayed, Ben's bullying, the silver dollar—wipe the slate clean regardless of the consequences. I loosened my tie. I looked at her. She was scanning the dark shapes of the trees spread out here and there through the cemetery. She looked down the hill where there was a pond with ducks, swans, and, I imagined, in the depths, lugubrious snapping turtles like Turtle Eddie that the old Tobia would've wanted to catch and observe.

"So," Merritt said. "Not that you asked, but this is how Ben was. He was pure boy. If he'd lived, he'd be bigger than you, and, no offense, but he'd probably be better at football than you are and maybe in school, too. I don't care how good you are. He'd also be stronger than you. He wouldn't be as quiet and sort of like mysterious as you. He'd be more up front. He couldn't keep still. He was vivacious. We have this picture of him—my favorite picture of him. He's sitting on the little front porch of our house in Cincinnati with his arm around our neighbor's beagle, Rumply. I have that in my room. There's another one where he's sitting in this field of buttercups with just his fat little face poking out and cows in the background looking at him. And, of course, because we were twins, there are tons of photographs of us together." She looked left and right with her eyes. "Do you sense something?" she asked.

I shook my head.

"Don't know?" she said. "I thought *you* might be able to sense something," she whispered, leaning toward me, looking from one to the other of my eyes. "You must have experience with ghosts. Living in that big old place."

I shook my head.

"Really? None? No ghosts?"

"I'm starting to think you're a strange girl," I said.

"Good strange or bad strange?"

"I don't know, yet," I said.

"When will you know?"

"I don't know. Do you come here often?"

"No. We come as a family like every other Sunday or something. . . . I've talked a lot. What do you do besides play football? What goes on in that big old house?"

"Remembering."

"What do you remember?"

"The past. The great lost glory of the Caldwell name," I said.

"Oh?"

"Yes."

She moved closer and kissed me, quickly on the lips.

I pulled a short distance away from her. "We should go somewhere else," I said. "If we're . . ."

She shook her head and kissed me again. "I knew it," she said, during a pause.

"What?"

"If you're as bad as my parents think, there's no way you could kiss me. Here. Like this. You know? Unless . . . you're really really bad." She looked at me.

"What if I am really really bad?" I said.

"Then, I don't know," she said and kissed me and we fell into it again.

While it happened I thought how I should be honest with Merritt in light of our kissing and my liking it more than I wanted to, and the pulsing in my groin and a sudden urge, a promise burgeoning, that I would protect her and treat her better than I'd ever treated any girl I'd ever known. I felt afforded a prescience. I thought I saw a clear path down which Merritt and I could travel cleanly despite or maybe because of everything.

"What?" she said, pulling away.

"Nothing."

"What?"

"I'm surprised you'd want to kiss *me* here. Anyone *here*. In a graveyard. In front of . . . ," I said, looking at the grave.

"If any part of Ben is still around, I think he'd like to see me living," she said. Again, she moved in close.

"You're a strange girl. I'm not sure . . ."

"You don't like kissing me." She spoke into my lips.

"No— Yes I do, but . . ."

"Can I ask you a question?"

I gulped and nodded.

She whispered into my lips, "What happened down at the creek that day, Tobia Caldwell?"

Her question was horripilant; for a few seconds I sat there, so close to her, feeling stunned. "That was a long time ago," I finally managed, pulling away.

Her eyes afforded themselves with some distance. She regarded me. "Now, *that's* strange," she said. "Because, *I* remember it all very clearly. Standing in your all's kitchen. How you and Ben got excused and I had to stay inside to listen to our mothers' girl talk. How I excused myself and came down the hill and saw you standing there like you'd seen a ghost. How you and me . . . found him. How we tried to make him breathe, then I went and got my dad and thought you were going to stay with him. How we came back down the hill and how you were gone."

I took a deep breath. I was troubled, more than anything else, by the fact that I wanted to tell Merritt everything. "I got scared," I said. "I was seven years old. I'd never been alone with a dead body. We should get out of here," I said.

"I see," she said, nodding and looking at me, narrowing her eyes. "Yes, okay," she said and gave me a look of sideways appraisal.

I braced myself.

But then, all at once, she turned irenic; I watched the judgment melt from her eyes. Neither of us spoke or moved as we settled into a long, sanctuaried glance that pulled me toward her. Then she turned away, stooped to kiss Ben's headstone—"Night, Benny"—and ran off, her pink-and-white chiffon sounding like a percussion instrument, the sounds of her footfalls, her tennis shoes on the gravel, diminishing as she moved away till she had disappeared in the darkness.

My next breath was spiked with an angry energy; in its wake, I was afraid to move. When I could no longer hear Merritt's footfalls on the gravel, I shook myself loose, turned, and started jogging after her. When I heard the car start, I ran as if something dangerous were chasing me.

ELEVEN

I WAKE UP and roll over in bed. My view: leaf-shadowed wall, ceiling, the window, and this morning's portentous sky, which looks like a Church sublime: grey stratus clouds suffused with a peach light burning to carmine at cloud-edge and blood-colored low in a thin line on the horizon. I wonder what old Fenton Monroe, with his eye for omens, will make of such a sky.

I wind down the driveway under the canopies of the trees. Drive across the limestone bridge spanning the creek at the bottom of the hill. Take a right onto the dappled ribbon of Caldwell Trace. Then a left to zoom down Old Cherokee with the workgoers—traffic light to traffic light—between the expanding chain of chains. A right onto Stonewall Lane to race up and down hillocks—subdivision to subdivision: Brookmill, Oldhearth, Raven's Gate, Mallard's Roost, Stag's Stand, Millbrook. I can remember when all of this was farmland or rolling hills and trees. I stop at a four-way stop, then take a right into the parking lot of the Olde Guarde condominium complex.

When he was sixty-four and I was four, Grandfather Thomas and Grandmother Pearl moved out of the Grand Old Caldwell Place, so we could move in. They took a condominium near Fenton, here in the Olde Guarde, and, in the year before Pearl vanished at Reelfoot, left often to travel the world, always returning with gifts for the old house. An oil painting from Italy of red poppies in a meadow they thought would look just about right over the mantel in the foyer. A stone sphinx and a multi-tiered lunch box for me from Egypt. Ornate kilim rugs from Istanbul. A butterfly book from Paris for my mother. An antique split willow fishing creel from Inverness. They sometimes stayed for a weekend, and we'd gather around to listen to their stories. My father's customary, worried aloofness, which he had slipped into with the new responsibility of the house, after the—by all accounts—wildness of his youth, cracked open just a little to reveal his former spirit on those occasions, and my mother glowed with obvious affection, seeming to love her father-in-law even more than my father.

I park, step out of the car, climb a brick staircase, walk down a corridor to 222 and stand outside Fenton's door. The brass knocker is supposed to be a rendition of the bust of the graceful Evangeline from the Longfellow poem. I knock three times—and wait. When Fenton takes a long time to answer his door, I begin to fear the worst.

I don't think most people my age see Fenton's appeal. Robin and Bradley Sackett and some other of my former colleagues at Pinkmellon have asked why I visit Fenton so often; they wonder why I bother at all. Most of my contemporaries think Fenton is an atavistic old fumbler, a joke and a flake and that his company, his dusty stories, are a waste of a young person's time. They know that in America, history is erased as it's created. *What's wrong with you?* I can see them wondering. I've tried to explain to them that I visit Fenton because I enjoy his company, love those dusty stories, his charm, but, also, I come to the Olde Guarde on these days out of respect for a long-standing bond between our families.

The Monroes and Caldwells have always been close, my father says Grandfather Thomas used to say. Our ancestors came together from North Carolina to take land grants after the War for American Independence. And then our families helped each other climb back to prosperity in the lean years following the Lost Cause, the War for Southern Independence, the War of Northern Aggression—whichever you prefer. We endured the carpetbaggers and scalawags together during reconstruction and were Redeemers together.

I hear the deep, reluctant barking of Fenton's aging Rhodesian Ridgeback, Treffen, then, to my relief, Fenton's footsteps.

The door opens a crack, exposing a portion of his momentarily quizzical face to the waxing morning light. A blue eye gleams in the center of a tortoiseshell frame. The sun glints white on a lens. The door swings open. Fenton's white hair is swept, cavalierly, straight back over his forehead. A well-established network of laugh lines furrows, which makes me smile. You never know when someone in their eighties will greet you with an empty stare.

"Young T.C. Come on in, son," Fenton says, grasping my shoulders in still-strong hands, ready fire and an appreciation of mischief sporting just under the surface of his eyes. We walk into the condo.

"Notice the sky?" he asks.

"I was wondering what you'd make of it."

"Very interesting. I did a watercolor this morning. It's trying to tell us something. I've noted it, believe me. Prior to certain earthquakes, as far back as the Greeks, people have noticed pneuma in the air, electrostatic phenomena. That may be what animals pick up on. I think that's what we're seeing out there this morning. Did you know, also, that most animals, including humans, have a small measure of magnetite in their systems, which keeps track of earth vibrations," he says. "Very interesting."

Treffen used to growl and keep his distance when I came to visit. But gradually the dog has come to know me. He sniffs my hand and halfheartedly aims a lick in my general direction. Then, he shuffles over to his faded plaid dognest in the corner of the loggia, circles, curls, sighs, blinks, shuts his eyes. An excess of skin on his face makes Treffen look as if he's deeply concerned about something. Fenton says the dog's worried about the quake. I think he's probably more concerned about his master's obsession. Treffen was named for the castle in which a dog's whining and hurling of itself at a barred window saved the Lord Grotta von Grotteneck from the Corinthia earthquake of 1690. The lord and his sons, Siegfried and Franz, rushed to window niches inside the castle to see why the dog was making so much noise and, there, were safe as the castle crumbled around them, killing eleven people and eleven horses.

When I catch up with him, Fenton is standing in one of his own window niches and looking out at the sky. The colors are fading—the violets bleeding into the light blues, the carmines cooling to a faint pink.

"Yes. This has been duly noted," Fenton says as if to himself.

At the Superstore that buried Goodall's Grocery I've seen small crowds take time out of their shopping to gather around and listen to Fenton hold forth on the turmoil under our feet, our structures, our lives, the great shaking he says will give the lie to our smugness about ourselves. Make eye contact with Fenton in the frozen foods aisle and the passive and kindhearted are going to hear what'll happen when the New Madrid stops biding its geological time. Pause to listen in the deli, the video station, the bread aisle and the indulgent and truly interested will hear how Fenton's *this close* to narrowing down the exact date when the big one's going to strike. *This close,* he says with an infectious delight, right index finger approaching right thumb and shaking there.

Linger long enough in the glut-of-choices cartoon brightness of the Superstore's cereal aisle and the considerate and curious will hear how it's going to happen soon. And when it next rages, according to Fenton, it's going to shake the earth for the oldest reason in the book: God is angry. He's fed up with the haughtiness of human "progress."

On other visits Fenton has told me, as he told our guests at the picnic the other day, how almost two hundred years ago, in 1811–12, the last big New Madrid measured over eight on the Richter scale, forced the hopeful settlers of the planned metropolis of New Madrid, Missouri, to abandon the settlement the Spanish and the French had abandoned before them. It reversed the flow of the Mississippi, shot sulfurous clouds of smoke and dust into the sky to choke the sun, toppled trees, wrecked Yankee chimneys as far away as Maine, rang a church bell in Boston. Tuned-in livestock frenzied in their stalls. Flocks of fluttering-hearted birds flapped into mass exodus through the enshrouded sky. Hounds fell to howling. The land rippled and rolled in swells of earth like the surface of some apocalyptic never-ocean. Reelfoot Lake was born, former lakes erased.

The quake destroyed the Monroes' fledgling whiskey storage barns. The barns fell apart, the barrels broke, and the whiskey swept down a hill and into Three Bullet Creek, catching fire en route and running burning and backward on the surface for three miles.

My paternal grandfather Thomas used to tell the story of the barn's collapse as if he had been there himself even though it had occurred one hundred years before he was born. He said you could have picked up channel catfish off the surface of the creek already cooked for you in a bourbon sauce. Ready to eat.

There is evidence of the power of the 1811–12 New Madrid Earthquake in the Old Caldwell Place. A year before he died, just a few days before he and Pearl moved out and we moved into the house, my paternal grandfather Thomas showed me a thin fissure, no longer than six inches, in the limestone foundation of this house. He bent down, and I leaned in close to see the thin line running up the dimpled rock behind his shaking finger. Then he stood up and made his fist a silhouette against the sun in a demonstration of what I have come to think was defiance at any force—natural or human—that would attempt our house's destruction, that would dare threaten what we Caldwells, and before that, the Jacksons, had built up in this part of Tennessee since just after the War for American Independence. The old house would survive whatever dared oppose it.

Grandfather Thomas tousled my hair and laughed that day, and I felt a weight and a power in his hand—a current flowing from the bones of our ancestors whose bones were resting then as now under the weathered grey stone on what used to be our property, and is now in the Goodhopes' backyard. A connection of blood in some metaphysically rigged vein flowed through the years and through my grandfather's hand and into me. I was five.

Fenton points out unusual activity on his very own seismograph. He shows me graphs he's compiled that take into account moon phases, weather patterns, people's moods, water table levels, animal behavior, his dreams and intuitions, cloud patterns, sky coloration.

He introduces me to three new finches in an oriental wicker cage darting around in what looks to be a complicated game of musical perches.

"The one with the yellow swathe on its wing is Bohai," says Fenton. "The one with the splash of blue, Yuxi. That one, there, missing an eye, that's Tangshan," Fenton says. "All named for Chinese quakes."

"They've been trained to sense seismic activity?" I ask.

"By God . . . old Tango sure likes you," Fenton says. His grey cat strides by, purring and going up on its hind legs to better rub against my leg. Tango is named for a Japanese quake, I suspect. "These little guys already know. It's hardwired into them from the get-go."

"Well, if they're already skittering around like that, how'll you know when they really mean it?"

"You know how you can tell when it's a fish on the end of your line and not a snag?"

I nod.

"Like that. I'll just know. I think they're bouncing around a little now due to the pneuma. Their magnetite sensors may have been engaged."

"The birds read the earth and you read the birds."

"Among other things," Fenton says. He points to three semicircular entrances recently cut into the wall at the floor—the kind of holes in which cartoon mice make their homes. "I got a deal on some rats," he says.

"Rats?"

"The other day I told the young fella I had a snake, and he sold me these little white suckers with pink tails at a special discount. They're really abominable creatures. Gives me the creeps seeing them scurrying around."

"I'm sure Tango appreciates them. All for science?"

"Sure. They'll stay in their little holes. Until something's up."

"What about these fish? I don't believe they were here last time."

"Yes. They're new. Little catfish. In Japan earthquake prediction with fish is a centuries-old art. Plus, I've started feeding them to Eddie. I like to give him something alive from time to time. Keeps him sharp." His mention of feeding Eddie makes me recall a story about one of Fenton's affairs. It was Easter and the distinguished older woman with him was delighting in Fenton's little Easter chicks while Fenton was in the other room preparing to leave for some sort of function. Fenton came into the room, casually lifted one of the chicks from the cage he had them in and dropped it into Eddie's tank. The woman, horrified when she saw Eddie awaken to notice the chick, reached her hand into the tank to rescue it, and almost lost a finger as Eddie snapped the chick down whole. I think that was the beginning of the end of that particular affair. Eddie's stainless steel tank is in a corner of the room.

Fenton is cultivating the ability of earthquake prediction in himself as well. He once told me he went for a walk directly above the faultline in a park in Memphis—a park adjoining a wealthy white neighborhood and a poor black one—and felt a great pressure swelling up to meet him, a leaden weight of earth-shifting potentiality that turned his legs to "quivering Jell-O."

"In the Tan-tung area of China, not long before a quake there, snakes roused from their underground burrows and froze in great numbers. Curious farmers lifted snakes from the ground like sticks. Do I have your solemn promise that you'll report to me on any unusual behavior of snakes in the area, young TC?" Fenton says with mock gravity and a deep, nearly undetectable irony, a nod to my former profession.

"Of course. Rest assured, I'll let you know if I see anything unusual."

When Fenton's in the grips of his quake talk, I usually listen with one ear. It's not that I don't believe him or find his stories interesting, it's just that I've already heard most of them. I nod and smile with the quiet, gentlemanly agreeableness, the cool remove that is my MO—or so I would like to believe.

Fenton's place is stuffed to bursting with the dusty remnants of his family's lost grandeur. Almost four hundred years of Monroes distinguishing themselves on American soil has come to this—come to rest in a condo. I pace the floors, half-listening, half-exploring. I take in the claw-footed chairs and tables. All around us are portraits of Fenton's ancestors in gilded frames, all manner of trinkets and curiosities, the musty scent of mildew, the sinewy scent of survival, of smoky earth, a thickness in the air suggesting the presence of shaken-up and clinging ghosts. And, also, a foreknowledge in the room of impending auction and dispersal. I have an urge to tell Fenton about Merritt's return and how things are good but not great with Robin, about my guilt at wildly lusting after her without being sure if I will ever love her, and ask for his advice, but decide to keep it all to myself.

Fenton's bright experiments in impressionism from his early thirties hang alongside the portrait of his hero, the Shawnee chief Tecumseh, who was supposed to have predicted the last big occurrence of the New

Madrid. In the portrait the chief is holding the red stick that, with the rumbling of the earth, was intended to have been a rallying symbol for the confederation Tecumseh had organized to throw out the upstart white settlers—mine and Fenton's ancestors. I take in the heavy antiques—mahogany, oak, and cedar—upon which rest black-and-white photographs of Fenton and my grandfather in plaid shirts, wool pants and caps, with their retrievers, guns, strings of ducks and geese. There are several photographs of Fenton and Grandfather Thomas, in Italy in their World War II regalia, on the streets of Paris afterward. Some of the same guns from the hunting photographs are locked up in a guncase under a portrait in oil that Fenton did of his father aiming a shotgun at a chevron of geese flying over the dark cypress of Reelfoot Lake.

Mounted game with glass eyes rest in the margins of the apartment's central room—lions, tigers, cape buffalo, and grinning hyena wrapped in dusty, moth-eaten coats, many of them posed in perpetual menace, all of them relics of Fenton's father's safari phase. I was surprised Fenton kept them, and now they crouch in the corners, as if, like the earthquake Fenton's talking about, they're waiting to regain their lives, waiting to pounce, to charge someone, to stalk and tear flesh, and taste blood again.

A garbage truck roars into the parking lot of the Olde Guarde, rattling Fenton's windows. He crouches into the stance of a surfer on a Turkish kilim, knees bent, hands spread out for balance as if he's expecting the carpet to launch into flight around the room.

"What's that?" he stage-whispers, rigid, his eyes madly scanning the room. A lock of his white hair comes loose and falls over one eye. The truck passes. "Hoooo," Fenton says. He lets his body relax. "I thought that might have been the beginning."

"Of the end," I say, wondering what it would feel like to live in constant anticipation of apocalypse. That's exactly what's keeping Fenton alive, I think.

"Unthinkable," he says with a shudder. He stands up, shakes it off, offers me a drink.

Because of his ancestors' interest in business, money has never been a problem for Fenton. His has been a life of leisure. He's skied the Alps, barged the Danube, rafted the Amazon, camelled the Sahara, made love overlooking the Seine, motored the autobahn, climbed Kilimanjaro, ridden elephants in for a glimpse of a man-eater in Thailand, feasted his way through Italy, visited an artists' commune in Marrakech, driven through all the national parks in the western U.S., country-clubbed in Tennessee. There was a phase when he was a beloved fixture at Sweet Hollow Country Club (up to date on all the spreads with the bartender/bookie Old Red, privy to the inside information kicked around by the good-old-boy network there). The men who had paid their dues like Fenton just fine. He is an excellent golfer, after all, and his family name still carries a certain, dying cachet.

WE DRINK SPRINGWATER fortified with a splash or three of Maker's Mark for color, Fenton says, sitting in a large bay window facing a common garden in the Olde Guarde's courtyard. It's a little early for me, for bourbon, but because I'm with Fenton it feels all right for some reason. Below, a few grey residents are sitting on a cast-iron bench and tossing pink pistachios to fat squirrels with bushy, frosted tails. The squirrels here at the Olde Guarde have it good. I wonder if Fenton ever opens the guncase, pulls out the .38, and keeps them honest.

I think Fenton appreciates my visits. For my part, I borrow a necessary weight from his stories, his endurance, his pseudo-madness, his charismatic failure, his stacks of well-intentioned canvases, which he describes as his ballast, a description which has always suggested to me that if he didn't have them, Fenton might just float away.

Including my father and his older sister, I am the last of our line of

Caldwells in Tennessee, and Fenton, who is a confirmed bachelor, is the last of the Monroes if you exclude his sister Berenice, who moved to New York to be a Broadway star and has not been heard from since. Fenton doesn't discuss Berenice anymore. Fenton once went up and found her, but she pretended not to know him—walked down Bank Street in the opposite direction and kept on walking. Fenton says he doesn't blame her, considering that he represented so much that she had wanted to escape.

"I wanted to tell you about the party we're having in a few weeks," I say, turning from the courtyard. "It's going to be a sort of fund-raiser for our reclamation project. You'll get an invitation in the mail, but I wanted to let you know about it now."

"Be delighted," he says. "How is the dismantlement coming along?"

"We need more money to complete it properly."

"Isn't that always the way?" Fenton says and smiles and shakes his head. I nod.

"If you don't mind my asking . . . what happened to all that computer money?"

"We spent most of it erasing the houses we've done so far. It's almost gone." In the past when Fenton has asked me to remind him of the timeline of our new wealth, I've explained how the antivenin patent money stopped coming in after someone else developed and patented an excipient that caused even fewer instances of serum sickness than ours. Fortuitously, the Pinkmellon investment returns started flowing in not long after the patent checks dried up.

"I see," says Fenton. "You know when I first found out about your coups—your all's success in that newfangled what-have-you—I thought, 'For the first time in our families' storied association, the Caldwells are going in an opposite direction of the Monroes.'" Fenton raises both his arms, looks around him to indicate all the things crammed into the condo—all that is left. There is both a heavy sadness and a relieved resignation in his blue eyes and on his face. "We lasted longer than most," he says. "People like me and . . . you, too, TC, were rumored dead long ago. And, you know what, it could be said we never existed. Do you know what I mean? That we were inventions from the beginning? But who is not an invention? And we were—are?—better than most, eh, QBTC?"

I nod.

"Will there be dancing at this party?" he asks, brightening.

"Actually, there might be, yes."

"Excellent," he says. "Marvelous." He smiles, takes a healthy gulp of his bourbon drink. "Count me in."

"You still like to dance?" I ask him, smiling.

"I enjoy watching you young people dance."

A short time later I notice Fenton gazing bemusedly at the framed photograph of him and my grandfather Thomas in their World War II uniforms, both of them smiling despite the war. I see a story well up in Fenton's eyes before it spills.

"Did your granddaddy ever tell you the story about the time we . . . met those Germans in a cave?" Fenton asks.

"I'm not sure if he did or not," I say, which is a lie. Grandfather Thomas told me the story a handful of times. In fact, I've heard it several times from him and my father and, when she could still speak, from my mother, too.

"I should hope he would've told you that one," Fenton says. "We were in Italy, on temporary leave, out rambling the countryside like Don Quixote and Sancho Panza. I don't have to tell you which of us was which. When we came across several crates of wine back in a cave. This was the good stuff, too—some of it at any rate. Someone had cached it back there for safekeeping. Or perhaps that was their regular cellar. Who knows? Of course your grandfather and I and someone else who was there with us got into that wine. We went ahead and got man-jack-skunk drunk on the stuff.

"We were sitting there, drunker than a bunch of nine-eyed you-know-whats, swapping stories—when we heard voices coming from the mouth of the cave. We could see shadows moving on the walls. The voices were guttural—unmistakably German. We put two and two to-gether—we were a sharp couple of boys, your grandfather and me. So, we put two and two together and decided these were German soldiers. We thought we were in trouble because we didn't have our guns with us, for some reason. We thought that was it for us when they rounded the corner with their guns preceding them.

"Well, to break the horrible tension that was mounting—brilliantly, bravely—your grandfather saluted those soldiers with the bottle in his right hand. He raised it, held it up high, and tilted it in salute. Like that.

"It worked. Nobody in that cave wanted to fight. There were two of them. One guy was this big blond fellow who smiled and chuckled with his shoulders, the other one was a shorter dark-haired guy who was a lot more somber and uneasy. Nervous. Anyway, we sat there and got pretty well schnockered with those two Krauts. Just had a ball.

"After a while, we were ready to return. Dusk was falling. The two Germans huddled up and had a discussion. That husky blond one bent down and drew a map in the dust showing us how to get back to our lines. The Germans had moved since we'd set out on our little hike, or, somehow, we'd messed up and got ourselves behind their lines. We were a reckless couple of young fellows—your grandfather and me—back then.

"If we'd gone back the way we'd come, it's likely we would've been captured, maybe killed."

"That's a little different from the version Granddaddy used to tell," I say.

"Oh?"

"I think in his story you were the one who toasted the Germans."

"Toasted, yes. He was being humble."

Fenton's expression shifts, suddenly, to something darker. When he speaks it is as if he is looking out of a dark cave to someone at its mouth.

"In his version, did your granddaddy ever tell you that after we left the cave with the wine, he pulled a pin from a grenade and tossed it back behind him into the cave. And there was an explosion. Did he ever tell you that part of it?" He lets that story hang in the air between us.

"No. That is certainly not the version he used to tell. And . . . that's not true, Mr. Monroe. I mean I don't believe that for one second."

"All right," he says. "You believe what you like," he says and smiles serenely, the hint of darkness gone.

"I will believe what I like. . . . I'll believe the truth. You just made that up. You're pulling my leg."

"Believe what you like, young TC."

"I will. I don't believe *that*."

We sit for a time in silence. I decide to let the story go, to forget it, to dismiss it as an idle fabrication, a brief surfacing of false meanness in an otherwise pleasant man. I bury it right then.

A short time later, our drinks are finished. Fenton returns to the quake, smiling, saying, "I mean it about those snakes. They may just be the key. See some of 'em walking upright, doing the fox-trot, tying themselves up in knots, slithering like hell out of town, let me know and I'll come over to y'all's place," he says, milky blues ablaze.

"Remember, Fenton, there's a fissure in the foundation of our house. It may not be it's such a safe place," I say, returning his smile.

"Oh yes, a fissure in the Caldwell house. Let me assure you, young QBTC, that I know this quake, and I know which places will be safe and which will not." He winks.

Despite my protests, Fenton walks me, very slowly, to the car. I thank him for an interesting morning and leave the Olde Guarde in my rearview. Fenton stands, drink cocked in his right hand, and waving from the parking lot.

TWELVE

W E WOULD SPEED along a straight stretch of an outlying country road far from the new developments and the lengthening
chain of chains. The greenery, the occasional house, blurring by. We
flew past cornfields, fencerows intersecting green fields, ponds, grazing
horses and cows. When we reached the crests of the hills, we decided it
felt as if our hearts were tracing zigzags in the air like sparklers. We
stopped the car as dusk was falling, got out, and raced each other between rows of corn.

The stalks whispered as we rustled through them. *There won't be any
poisonous snakes in here, will there, Tobia?* In August they were taller than
we were and hid most of the sky. *Why would I know that?* We ran along
together. In time, we lost each other. The one behind ducked into another row and kept running. After that, the game was to yell out and try
to find each other again. We called out to each other, called out nonsense, made-up names, inane insults, sang verses from songs we hadn't

known till the moment we felt them in our throats. Eventually, we met again, lost together deep in the stalks.

We called each other when our parents weren't home and talked for hours about what I don't recall, and when they were home we lied about where we were spending our time. We met often at the Sacketts', told our parents we were spending time with Bradley or Robin. I'd walk across our yard and through the trees to find Merritt up in her room leafing through old *National Geographics*. She loved to find out about the places, people, animals, and things in the strange world. She was enthralled by its marvelousness, its beauty and ugliness, its wealth and poverty-strickenness, its bountiful complexities. Shrinking fisheries in Labrador, the haunting eyes of an Afghan refugee, wolves on the tundra, disappearing tigers in disappearing jungles. She told me often she would see these places one day, and I told her I was sure she would, if that's what she wanted.

I tried to keep myself from looking at the photograph of Ben and the beagle on her nightstand or any of the numerous photographs of both of them together. Looking at the photos, it was impossible not to notice how much Ben resembled the younger Merritt and impossible to avoid thinking of what had happened. Nevertheless, sometimes my eyes would wander to these photographs as if of their own accord. And when I found myself looking at them too much, a weight accumulated so that it seemed as if Ben had entered the room with us, and I felt a pressure to tell Merritt everything, which drove me from her house. I would tell her I had to go. I couldn't leave fast enough when I was gripped by the sudden claustrophobia, and it wasn't until I'd walked outside that I felt I could breathe again.

I was more comfortable with her in our house when my parents were gone. Merritt seemed to enjoy perusing the accumulated material of two hundred years of Caldwells in Haven, and I enjoyed showing her the dusty relics and telling her what I knew of the stories behind them.

We walked the halls, our knees and legs reflected in the mirrors under the petticoat tables, and I showed her portraits of my ancestors and she told me she didn't know who any of her ancestors were before her grandparents.

We spun the old globe in Father's study and closed our eyes. Wherever our finger stopped the spinning was where we'd live when we grew up. Our fingers stopped the globe on Gibraltar, Rouen, Petra, Chwaka, Omaha. We'd say what we'd do to make a living in that place, what our house would look like, what we'd eat, what kinds of animals we'd see. I don't think we ever once stopped it on the spot that would have marked Haven, Tennessee, or Angola, Africa, for that matter.

After a time we would turn to each other. Find a bed and pursue each other—eager, tentative hands on sharp shoulder blades, tracing the small mountain range of spine, running along smooth, downy thighs, tentatively expanding the territory of our exploration, sometimes in rapt silence, other times laughing together at the strange wonderfulness of it.

We came to have our places. The train trestle a mile down the creek from our houses where it widened and deepened and you could jump off like Peyton Farquhar or let the "helicopters" from the oaks spiral down to the slow current below; the Dairy Delight where we got soft ice cream that melted so quickly late that summer we had to lick the drips from each other's fingers; Sweet Hollow with its sunbleached clay courts, well-watered green links, and the pool with black lane lines on a robin's-egg bottom; strawberry slush puppies that stained our lips an eminently kissable red, juicy burgers, and grease-sizzled fries from the snack bar.

One day that summer, in the yard of the old house, Merritt said, "Spin me."

We gripped each other's wrists. I leaned back, and started to spin.

"You sure you want to do this, Mer?"

"Uh-huh."

I leaned back against her weight and started to spin. Her body elevated above the grass. In midspin I thought I heard her screaming for me to stop, but, as it turned out, she was laughing. I was afraid I would lose my grasp and send her flying off across the lawn to bruise herself on a tree trunk or a rock or worse.

Some workmen on one of the new houses going up were eating their lunches and watching us. In getting Merritt spinning, it was inevitable she would scuff the ground a few times. When this happened I cringed and redoubled my efforts to get her airborne. The workmen must have wondered if it was something they should have been interfering in, if some sort of violence was being perpetrated while they watched. But once she was up in the air and spinning, they laughed at us—coupla bored kids with nothing better to do on a weekday summer afternoon, so hot, late July.

The world, the lawn, the leafed-out trees and lucifications of winged insects, the blue and white sky—all of it spun around us. All of it disjointed, ablur, renewed in strangeness. The blood must have been rushing into Merritt's head. She was still laughing when I slowed our spinning. My forearms started to burn, I grew too dizzy to keep my feet firmly planted, and I tried to bring Merritt's spinning to a graceful denouement. I wanted to be very careful with Merritt. But that was impossible given the nature of the game. She hit the ground once, twice, three times, each time less forcefully.

"Are you all right?" I said.

"Do it again," she said, breathless, her hair spread out on the grass, eyes mostly closed. "Do it again, Tobia."

"I don't want to hurt you," I said.

"Please please please please," she said.

"Don't please me. You know I can't say no when you please me like that."

Later that day we were lying in the grass. Merritt placed her head to my stomach to listen. She said she could hear a grumbling in my gut. Boys' stomachs were always so grumbly. She remembered that Ben's had been. I put my ear to Merritt's stomach and concentrated on my listening until I heard a sound like the sound of surf in a whorled seashell.

IT WAS the very end of summer. Merritt and I were sitting and talking on the bridge across the creek. Dawn was not far off. The fireflies were drifting up into the trees and sinking into the underbrush. I'd relaxed a little after a few furtive glances up at the old house, which was dark and perched on the hill, my guilt and conscience. I knew that inside, my mother was sleeping with one eye open. They let me keep my own hours, but I could sense her waiting, even in sleep, for the sounds that would tell her I was home.

After we'd met in the woods, we'd gone to see a movie and after that had driven by a party where we'd split up for most of the time and talked to different people. Bradley and Robin Sackett were there as were many of my teammates. Two-a-days had started, and we talked about our prospects for the coming year, made fun of our coaches, did their voices, talked about our summers, and drank beer. Merritt found some of her friends, and they sat under an umbrella by the pool and had their own conversations. Somewhere in the course of the party one of the guys—someone I didn't even know, a boarding-school guy—got really drunk, took off his clothes, and ran naked around the lawn. We all watched and cheered him on. A few of the girls were scandalized and went inside to sit it out, others were critical of his equipment. When the party was over, Merritt and I reunited, climbed into the old blue Fiat, and headed home.

When we neared our houses, Merritt asked me not to take her home.

"Where do you want to go?" I asked.

"Down to the creek," she said.

We dangled our feet in the current the way I had on countless days when I'd been a different version of myself. I was thinking about going back to school in a few weeks, about the switch I was making to quarterback, and about Merritt's leaving for college and how much I would miss her. This was to be our last night together. It was some time, sitting there over the creek, before Merritt broke the silence.

"Tobia?"

"Uh-huh?"

"I had a dream about Ben last night."

I looked at her.

"I didn't see him. I just woke up with a feeling of him, you know? I still carry him with me every moment of every day."

"Yes."

"Do you ever dream about him?"

"I don't think so," I said. "I rarely remember my dreams."

"Do you ever think about him?"

"I can't not, sometimes. Every day I do."

"Really?"

"Yes."

"Tobia?"

"Yes."

"Do you think there're any poisonous snakes in here, still?"

"I haven't seen any since I saw your father kill the one in those roots there," I said. "They hacked off its head and its head kept striking so they smashed it into the mud. Later, I picked it up and dropped it back down in the creek. It's late, isn't it?"

"Yes . . . Tobia?" she said.

"Yes?"

"Nothing," she said and pressed herself against me. "Here," she said and kissed me. We fell into our kissing ritual. Our clicking mingled with the trickling creekwater. Our clothes, after a time, were slid along our skin and off and scattered on the bank like shed leaves. Our breathing came faster and promised more. We moved tentatively toward what we had been approaching all summer.

There was little pleasure in it. It was overwhelming and breathtaking in its newness and rawness and strangeness. It didn't feel anything like I'd expected. Afterward, there was some blood possessed of a singular sheen in the moonlight.

"Merritt?" I whispered. Her head was obscured in darkness. She'd moaned some, but I hadn't been able to tell what sort of moaning it had been. "I'm sorry. This was wrong. I'm sorry."

She propped herself on an elbow. "It's okay," she said. She rolled off the bridge and fell into the creek and sat up in the water. "Is it safe now? Are there snakes? Would you warn me if there were?" The water-droplets fell from her body like liquid moon, and it occurred to me that she was beautiful. She shook her hair and combed it back and settled into the creekwater three yards from the tangled roots of grandmother oak.

"Yes, of course I'd warn you," I said.

"It's pretty cold," she said.

"There's a spring not too far upstream. That's why the water's so clean here. And cold." I cupped water up onto myself. My head felt hollow. It was almost morning. The gurgles of the creek seemed to be trying to hypnotize me. "Are you sure you're okay, Merritt?"

"I'm fine, I'm fine, TC TC," she said in a faraway voice. "Tonight, this. And tomorrow I'm gone."

"I can't believe it. I wish you weren't going."

"Me too."

"You're sure you're all right?"

"I'm okay okay, TC TC."

"Oh . . . we shouldn't have done this here, I'm thinking."

"Why not?" she said with the same faraway tone.

"We got carried away. It's late," I said.

"We got carried away and it's late, but it's fine. I'm happy," she said and smiled up at me on the bridge. "It was good to do here, I think. I was ready for it. It's going to be healing or something. So late it's early," she said and laughed. "I wanted this, here, so don't worry, TC," she said. "It's all right. I'm thinking now, what it means. It'll take some time to figure that out."

I pulled on my clothes. The creek in that place would only have come up to her knees, but she was using her hands to swish her body back and forth over the rocks and crawdads, the arrowheads, and the fossils from the time when everything had been under an ocean. She pulled herself up onto the bridge and sat there, naked and beautiful in a hydro-luna-crepuscular glaze.

"I'll walk you home," I said.

"How much do you love me, Tobia Banes Caldwell?" she asked.

"Very much . . . very much," I said.

I did not tell her how an unsettling had found me. That I was nervous again. I glanced up at the house, imagining that I was seeing lights come on. The familiar sight of the grassy hill seemed abuzz with a new energy. The world seemed to have been recast. I was worried about us. I felt a threatening force in our midst. The grass blades seemed liable to whisper, to be filled with spies. It was as if the crickets were roaring information to a higher power about Merritt and me. I thought I heard my father or Mr. Wilson yelling down at us, but it was just a riff my ears had found in the crickets' roar.

We walked along the path by the creek toward her house, and she leaned into me and I put my arm around her and felt her warm wet hair against my neck and chin.

WHEN I ENTERED our old house through the front door I was surprised to find it so quiet, my parents apparently asleep. I creaked up the stairs and lay down on my bed and stared at the ceiling as sunlight began to play into my room through the leaves of the maple. Images of Merritt and the creekwater broke in waves in my head. The way it had felt to do what we had done. The sinking into it. A tangled riot of erinnic whispers intensified when I brought my hands to my ears to try to stop them.

I stayed on the bed, staring up at the ceiling, through the beginning of the afternoon. I listened to my parents moving around the house, heard them reading the paper in the kitchen, heard my mother watering her in-house plants.

Occasionally, I glanced over at the bedside table clock. The time rolled beyond the time Merritt and I had set for our goodbye meeting in the woods between our yards. Two or three times I drifted into sleep to awaken a few minutes later with fleeting images from strange dreams arollick in my head, the persistent thought that what had happened the night before had also been a dream. The whispers tangled together.

A little after noon, the doorbell rang, and I heard the sound of unintelligible voices, high- and low-pitched, at the door. My father's voice called my name.

He was standing at the bottom of the stairs. Merritt Wilson was in the doorway, features indistinct in the sunlight. My mother stood in the doorway opening onto the foyer from the kitchen, a few steps back, so that I could see her but Merritt could not. Both of my parents watched me walk outside into the heat on the front porch and shut the door between them and Merritt and me.

"Where were you?" she asked. "I'm leaving now. My parents are wondering where I am. I wanted to see you before I left."

My eyes were not accustomed to the sunlight; her features looked bleached and indistinct. I looked down at the grass, then down the hill to the creek. The golden glints on the creekwater seemed to want to erase what we'd done the night before, and I willed them to do it.

"What's wrong?" she asked.

"Nothing," I said and shook my head to see if I could clear the whispers.

She found my eyes. "You sure?"

I wanted to tell her about the whispers, that I hoped they'd resulted from a lack of sleep. I told her I was going to miss her and meant it, though I was unable to look into her eyes when I said it.

She threw her arms around me and squeezed, her chin at rest atop my right shoulder. I held her as tightly as she held me and lost myself in the creekwater, fulgid as it was, in the sunlight.

THIRTEEN

Tonight, Robin and I are off to the Grand Opening of the Dipsy-Do Club.

In preparation, I've showered, shaved, steamed the tux with the Jiffy Steamer, shined my shoes, arranged myself in the bathroom mirror, and assured myself, repeatedly, I will have fun and utter not a word of derision tonight. I will do my best to appreciate the Dipsy-Do Club for the future-gazing, cultural everyplace its creators would like it to be. I will make the beautiful Robin Sackett proud in my attempt to be the perfect, Apollonian date-deal, with a splash or two of Dionysian vim when appropriate.

Thomas Jefferson said, "In matters of principle, stand like a rock; in matters of taste, swim with the current." Tonight, I plan to grow fins and gills and become a fish in the current despite the distant thought that now might be a good time to stand like a rock.

"Who's that young man on Robin Sackett's arm?" people will say, and the answer will be, "Tobia Caldwell of the Haven Caldwells. Isn't he charming?" And on her arm will be . . . a better-seeming version of me. So successful will my pretending be that in time, as per Robin's prescription, the new version will permanently eclipse the old. I will be happy, unburdened, available, tonight, and the hope is that this will launch me into a new life unencumbered by the weight of dusty old stories. Underneath the wish: a clutch of doubts about whether or not I'll be able to pull it off.

Earlier, my father warned me about the club's dangers. "Don't let yourself be fooled by what you see there tonight, T. It's all glitter and flash. Keep in mind why you quit working with those folks."

"I won't desert you, Captain," I assured him, thinking, I'm going to desert you, but only temporarily, to see how it feels.

When I'm as ready as I'm going to be, I walk outside to wait on the front porch, hearing my father call through the screen door just after it's shut behind me, "Give my best to that stunning Robin Sackett. If you think of it, remind her I think she's the one to one day have my grandchildren."

"Will do," I say, shaking my head, rolling my eyes, feeling a pleasant early-night breeze, hearing a faint rhyme in it: *Young night: cleansed of lore; open door, more, more.*

I sit on the front porch, imagine the unveiling of the new Tobia Caldwell, and will some distance from thoughts of Merritt Wilson amid a horde of gaunt, hollow-cheeked children who've known nothing but war. I sit and rock and wait, concentrating on settling into the role I'm about to play as I wait for the limo.

Which pulls up—long and black with tinted windows—precisely at eight, and in which the driver and I zoom down Caldwell Trace en route to pick up Robin Sackett at the Arbor Pointe condominium complex, which is located about halfway down the chain of chains toward the city from our old house and the building of which spelled an ironic death for a thousand trees.

Robin clicks across the sidewalk in a black backless wraparound evening gown, a gleaming-eyed serpent clasp around her throat. My mental image rarely lives up to the real Robin; her beauty is an opened gift her absence wraps. Seeing her walking out to the car reminds me how lucky I should count myself to be in her company at all.

She slides in with a bright hello, filling the carspace with the rich, edgy scent of her designer perfume and letting a licked-cherry-lollipop smile reveal perfect white teeth, pink upper gums. We meet midseat for a minty-toothpaste, friendly passionate kiss hello.

"See?" she says and turns and thrusts forward her chest so that I might have a better view of the dirty silver snakehead clasp pulled taut at her throat, the snake's iceblue, lanceolate eyes glimmering in the light from the parking lamps.

"It's great!" I say. "I like it a lot," I say.

"Good," Robin says. "I thought you'd like it." And we're off.

AT PARTIES such as the one toward which we're flying, Robin hones in on the heart, the epicenter. She establishes herself in the most advantageous place for her to work the rooms—gracefully, genuinely, with little or no hint of artifice. She learned how to do this in high school and honed her ability as social chairman for the Tri-Delts at Vanderbilt. Once she's found the center, she relaxes into social brilliance. But the heart of a party is never a fixed location. There is always a better place to be. Consequently, there is never a moment's rest for Robin at a party. When I happen to be with her, she pulls me along on the party's currents; I begin to feel as if I'm white-water rafting. I find her fascinating in this element. I miss conversational cues for watching her eyes brim with intent, a predator's eyes—registering levels, coming to understandings, plotting new advances. She remembers to have fun, but she also establishes new connections, strikes deals, solidifies existing alliances, exchanges winks and nods, runs down trails, begins and puts a rest to rumors. When I was caught up in the three-year whirlwind of the computer industry at Pinkmellon, Robin, like her brother, Bradley, was invaluable at winning and solidifying business contacts.

We cruise down the expressway, above the chain of chains, smoothly as you please, in the river of headlights. The streetlamp reflections float backward atop shiny hoods. The car shadow makes a dual-appearance in the emergency lane. Robin suggests I make us some cocktails, and I oblige: a vodka martini for her, Maker's and water for me.

"You are not going to believe all the news I heard today," she says.

"What is it?" I mix and shake up the martini and take a sip to see how I've done.

"Remember how I told you about John and Ann going to Charleston for the weekend?"

"Did he propose?" I pour the drink into a glass and hand it to her.

She nods, accepts the drink, takes a sip. "They were overlooking Charleston harbor. Strolled into a gazebo. He took a knee. Popped the question."

I sip my Maker's and water and smile. We race on an overpass above the chain of chains, billboards and storefront signs screaming for our attention.

"She said yes, of course. We all kinda thought it was coming. Did I tell you that? Guess who else?"

I try to think of other likely candidates but finally have to admit I don't know.

"Adam Gold proposed to Betsy Granger in a chairlift over a skislope in Vail. And that's not all!" she says.

I glance over at her. We whoosh through the river of headlights. "Wow," I say. "They're dropping like . . . Busy weekend," I say.

"Patsy Tullman proposed to John Erickson. Can you believe it?"

"Brave girl," I say, feeling the first blurry insinuation of the bourbon.

"All on the same day. I'm going to be a bridesmaid for all of them," she says.

I look away from the lights on the expressway, and our eyes lock for a moment through the dappled cardarkness. Robin has refused marriage proposals from three perfectly legitimate candidates, one of them her Miami Dolphin. A steadfast glimmer in the depths of her burner-flame eyes that almost looks like a rippling for the light and shadow flowing over us, suggests a split-second flash of what feels like prescience: Robin and I promised to each other for eternity, our children in the backseat. I feel a sudden dizziness.

"So there," she says, "you've had your warning. There are lots of weddings in our future, Tobia Banes Caldwell," she says and looks at me in a certain way. I hold fast to our mutual gaze a second longer, then look away at the whizzing lights, still feeling her looking at me, though I'm imagining Merritt Wilson walking over desolate ground, holding hands with a stricken-eyed child.

A SHORT TIME later we come to a stop. The driver opens the door, and Robin and I step out in front of the Dipsy-Do Club's screaming mirror-and-neon facade, in front of which has assembled a long, eclectic line of hopefuls. Robin does not ever wait in lines, and tonight is no exception. I follow her across a red carpet, past the people in line to the attentive bouncer who has been expecting us. He greets Robin with a slight bow and opens the door.

Inside the club, a large dance floor dominates the room reflected by a mirror on the ceiling, which doubles the images of fifty or so dancers. Many of the people on the floor are attempting a line dance to a Buck Kelly tune. A few couples in cowboy hats and boots appear to know what they're doing—some of them embellishing the known steps with extra twirls and flourishes. The other people on the floor—in a staggeringly ecumenical array of fashion sensibilities—mimic the cowboys and girls in varying degrees of earnestness and undisguised and—in some cases—acerbic parody. One of these mimickers—a black man in baggy pants, a bandana riding low on his head so as to almost cover his eyes, a Tennessee Titans jersey, and a gold dollar sign necklace—gives the impression in his movements that he's confident the next song will be more to his liking.

Robin smiles back at me to see how I'm enjoying things so far, and I return her smile, amping it up to please her. As we continue walking, I peripherally notice men's eyes taking *all* of Robin in—the snakehead clasp at her neck, the skin left exposed by her gown.

An article in yesterday's paper said that several caiman and a fifteen-foot reticulated python (*Python reticulatus*) were to have been released in an atrium on the lowest level of the club. Some people standing on the floor and seated in plush bronze couches beside it are staring straight down as if into the dance floor itself, and when I step closer I'm amazed to be able to see *through* a remarkably clear plastic to the swamp below where several orange-and-white koi glow between white lilies on green pads.

For some reason the article hadn't mentioned the see-through floor. Kneeling beside it, as much as I search the recesses of the thick foliage on a small patch of land, I can't see any evidence of the reptiles. It was a reticulated python, I recall, that was proven to have swallowed a Malaysian boy.

A man with a shaved head, wearing thick, black-framed glasses and red clogs with giant buckles, notices that, like him, I'm peering down into the swamp. In the distance I see Robin moving through the bar to some doors in the back fronted by more bouncers.

"At midnight," the man shouts above the twanging music, "they're going to put a pig in there for the python to munch on."

I look to see if he's joking.

"No shit," he says. "A friend of mine is a friend of one of what's his name—that Eon guy's—brothers, and he told me it's going down. At midnight. They're going to put them both in the same little glass aquarium."

We return our gazes down through the jungle.

"I *do not* want to see that," the woman next to him yells over the music.

"Well. *I* am not going to miss it," he shouts.

I look up and see Robin talking to one of the bouncers, glance down once more into the foliage of the man-arranged swamp, assure myself the man has fed me a rumor I will not dignify by spreading, and move quickly across the rest of the room—through raucous laughter, sudden cheers, bleeps, robotic voices, three kinds of music, multiple news broadcasts, the play-by-play of basketball and baseball games—to the doorway where Robin is waiting. I stop and look back at the scene we've passed through, then turn to face her, eyebrows elevated, eyes wide. The bouncer smiles, thinly.

The silver door, which, contrary to appearances, turns out to be an elevator door, slides open, and we step inside. Robin inserts a silver key-card into a slot beside the control panel.

"What's up?" I ask. "We're leaving so soon."

"No," she says. "Just rising above all the . . . randoms. Wait till you see what's up here. You will *just love* it."

"I saw what's below us," I say.

"I thought you'd like that, Tobia. We talked about that at the investors' meeting. Maintenance will be expensive, but it got voted in, so . . ." She shrugs. "Eon wanted it for some reason. Especially the snake," she says again and looks up at the mirrored ceiling of the small compartment in which we're floating upward.

I consider telling her what I've heard about the pig. But, as if to change my mind, Robin steps over to give me a quick kiss on the neck, and, I suppose, in her excitement about the floor toward which we're escalating, she does a little step-step dance.

We progress one floor before the doors slide open to reveal a room the same size as the one we've left below except that the ceiling is twice as high. When I look down, I see that the mirror on the ceiling below had been one way! and that the dancers have given up the line dance to gyrate beyond any fixed order in the erratic light. Some of the diners on this level are leaning over in their chairs to point out their favorites. Under the dancers, when they move to make room, the dense foliage on the island and the finning orange-and-white koi in the water come into view. Now, I also make out the silhouette of a caiman's jagged head.

Tables have been arranged at intervals on the clear floor in the center of this level. Candles flicker in glasses of oil, gently illuminating faces above grey tablecloths. Fluted Corinthian columns at each corner of the room are festooned with fake ivy. Digital reproductions of masterpieces on thin screens on the walls slowly morph, section by section, into other masterpieces. On one wall Mona Lisa morphs into Water Lilies. On another, a protean Warhol soup can has halfway altered, as if exploding, into a Jackson Pollock. The conversations sound distant, muted, with someone's laughter occasionally rising above the even hum. At the edges of the room people are playing virtual-reality games, entering hidden rooms. Servers in what look to be silver pajamas scurry to and from the kitchen.

An unbidden thought finds me: *It's not too late to leave. Make an excuse. Go home, fix up a nice, tall bourbon and branch, sit on the front porch, rock, think, use the time to mull and mull on distant stars, pliant earth, gurgling streams, returning lovers. Find your father and talk with him about the recoverable past.*

I clear my head of the notion and reassert the vow Robin suggested—to pretend, pretend until it's real—as I follow her across the floor.

Our party is seated against a far wall of the room, at a large, rectangular table situated, with several other tables, on a platform elevated about two feet above the dance floor. When he sees us, Bradley Sackett's cherubic face lights up in recognition, as does his wife Clarice's.

Bradley still looks like he did when he was eight years old and we played for the Saints. His ever-more-adroit social dexterity and charisma surprises me as much as Robin's beauty. It, too, tends to dull in my memory and is re-brightened when it's at work in front of me. "Mr. Caldwell," he says. "Look who's come out of his shell? Welcome, welcome," he says, giving me a you-old-devil grin. He stands up and we shake hands. He hugs Robin, kisses her cheeks, gives her a "hello, big sis," and tells me with a wink I'm a lucky man to be with his big sister. Clarice also stands, and we exchange greetings until someone suggests we sit down, at which point Robin excuses herself and disappears to work the room.

"Bradley, Clarice. How've y'all been," I ask.

"Toby, do you know Buck Kelly?" Bradley asks.

"We've met," I say.

The chisel-cheeked man in the ten-gallon hat, Buck Kelly of Kelly Industries, reaches across the table to shake my hand. He's an old-school country-music has-been who refashioned himself, in a Lonesome Rhodes kind of way, into the billionaire owner of a holding company. Bradley thought it would be a good idea to have Buck resuscitate his music career by using one of his songs for a Pinkmellon ad, and Buck agreed. Later, he bought the company. Bradley and Buck get along like old friends, despite the twenty-year age gap; they golf, hunt, and fish together.

"And this is Grace Lamar," Bradley says. The pale, gaunt-faced girl sitting next to Buck—his twenty-four-year-old girlfriend (Robin has informed me)—offers up her wilted hand, and I take it in mine for a moment, surprised at its coldness.

The other guests around the table are primarily young CEOs Bradley is schmoozing for Pinkmellon. In fact, the room is filled with some of the most powerful businesspeople in the Southeast. I watch some of them walking around in their suits and cocktail dresses, drinks in hand, observing the expansiveness, the information-age splendor, of the Silver Room. Some of them pause and interact with a computer kiosk, play one of hundreds of virtual-reality games, sit in on clips from movies in one of the film booths.

"Have you and Robin entered yourselves?" Bradley asks.

"Don't you think that's a little personal?"

"You've been away too long, T," he says, smiles, and slides a laptop across the table to me on little rollers.

"What's this?"

"Just follow along. It'll ask you questions about your preferences in music, films, food, drink, lighting, decor—things like that—and the central processing computer will generate a chip for you to wear. If all goes well and we get this up and running, the next time you enter the Silver Room, your preferences will register as votes for music, artwork, decor, lighting, food, etcetera. When we've perfected it, it will take votes from everyone's chips and produce a consensus. Instant, true democracy. It's all something Eon dreamed up."

"Maybe later," I say, "I'll enter myself."

Bradley looks disappointed. "Well, at least take one of these," he says, producing a silver card from his inside jacket pocket. "Good for two hundred dollars' worth of entertainment points."

I smile and thank him.

The servers in the silver pajamas pour champagne into flutes out of a gigantic, silver-labeled bottle. Bradley tells me he has a good feeling about the place, especially since Eon used so much of his own money to soak up the debt. He explains that the Silver Room is to be an exclusive club. Several of the city's big shots and celebrities, including Buck and a good number of the new order of wealthy families, have already signed on and will soon be paying monthly dues. An even more exclusive set will belong to other levels upstairs, which have yet to be completed. Someone better warn the old boys down at the Halcyon Club, I think. "You, of course, will be given an honorary membership to all the levels, Tobia," he says. "To show our appreciation for your initial faith."

"All right. Thank-you," I say, wondering if tonight is the debut of a version of myself who will take advantage of such a membership. "Where's Eon?" I ask.

"No one knows," Bradley says, flatly, then calls out to an older man down the table, "How's the golf swing, Grant!" After Grant has answered and they've had a laugh, Bradley says, "You should've invested in this one, T."

Across the table, Buck nods—I should have.

For some reason, just then, I have the urge to tell Bradley, away from the buzz of the table, about Merritt Wilson's return.

"Hey—you're the snake man?" Buck says.

I have just felt the first kick of the champagne, bubbles climbing over the bourbon I had in the limo, percolating up to my head. I don't quite know how to answer.

"Yeah, Gracie, this's the snake fella Brad was telling us about. Used to be on the board at Pinkmellon. Before that, he was a college quarterback—the . . . whatever-it-was Gentleman. We made this son of a bitch a rich man, then he up and quit on us," Buck says and smiles. "Took the money, like a gentleman, and whoosh, he was go-one," Buck informs Grace, broadening his grin.

Bradley smiles, too, beaming at everything tonight, his perfect teeth almost glimmering, even in the room's dull light, his eyes, like his sister's, the blue of burner flames. He's clearly told Buck and Grace about my career as a herpa-toxicologist, the antivenin I developed with Henley Dempster.

Farther back in the room, I see Robin skate across the clear floor to alight at a party of young politicians and other well-connected people our age—all of them sharp, silver-tongued movers and shakers of the sort with whom Robin would be well matched, and their dates. This would be my set, I suppose, if I had a set. They give her a rousing welcome. A young lawyer and aspiring politician, whose name I don't recall—a master at delivering undetected insults that carry a lingering sting, phrased in the moment just delicately and humorously enough not to invoke any rejoinder from a polite listener—stands and embraces Robin. I entertain a thought about how different my life would be if I was sitting among them. If, like my grandfather, I had chosen law and politics. If, like my mother, I had a taste for society.

"Bradley, is there something planned tonight involving a pig?" I ask.

"No," he says, furrowing his brow, shaking his head, smiling. "Unless you're talking about the pork loin on the menu. What an odd question. Why do you ask?"

"Nothing. No reason," I say.

Bradley, perhaps newly reminded of my eccentricity, turns to Buck and Grace. "Not only is Tobia here an expert on the slippery subject of snakes and venom, but he's also interesting in that he and his father are tearing down part of a subdivision over there off Old Cherokee."

Grace cocks her head to one side. Buck's head moves backward on his neck, and his face screws into a scowl. Clarice looks down at the table and suppresses a giggle.

"Come again?" Buck says. A grey-haired man two seats down dislodges himself from the conversation in which he was involved and stares over at us. Others down the table also look at me, some of them whispering to one another.

"Yeah," says Bradley. "Him and his father live in an old plantation house. Their family's sold the land to developers over the years, but now they're buying subdivision houses back and tearing them down."

"I'll be. Folks' homes," Buck says and shakes his head. "What on earth possessed y'all to do that? Too much money on your hands after you hightailed it out of your old job? Couldn't wait to throw the money away?"

I see Robin leaving the table of young politicians and heading to another table (perhaps to see a group of German and Japanese investors I've overheard people mention) still farther back in the room. Buck and Bradley, Clarice and Grace, and some of the other faces farther down the table are awaiting my answer. The sounds of the room echo in my head—the murmuring voices, the clink of silverware, the tinkle of glass, the faint peals of laughter, the beep-bleep, buzz, click, and blip of the computers. I think I can distinguish Robin's voice rising above the rest for just a moment. A voice in my head whispers, *Escape at all costs and immediately.* I don't have at the tip of my tongue a quick answer, a good pretender's answer, a funny-guy answer, to Buck's question. I don't have an uncomplicated, self-assured soundbite loaded up to feed them.

At first I say the word "trees," as if that's a good beginning, then manage to say, "I'm planning to take up farming," and put on a wide, pretender's smile to try to buoy it with some conviction: "I'm going to learn to live closer to the land."

Buck breaks into a volley of laughter.

Someone else down the table says, in a head-shaking way, "No money in that, son."

Yet another asks, "Wasn't he the Five Game Gentleman awhile back?"

Bradley sighs, still smiling. Clarice looks down at the candle on the table. Many of them are still looking at me, some of them shrugging to one another.

"It's a heritage thing," says Bradley. "Right, T? Reclaiming the homeplace and such."

"I got it," Buck says. "Your people are mansion-on-the-hill types. Just like Mr. Sackett here." He aims his rugged smile at Bradley.

Just then, Robin returns to the table and stands behind me, massaging my shoulders.

Grace mouths a word that looks like "trees," and stares into a great distance. Then again, "Trees," as if it's a concept she's trying to recall.

"No, now wait a second. Our father came up through the ranks at Blinker International," Bradley says, looking to Robin for backup. " Just like you, Buck, and just like Eon—a self-made man. With Tobia here, I suppose the term would be more accurate. His family is as old as they come in this country. But you're a 'mansion-on-the-hill type' now, Bucko," Bradley says. "Wouldn't you say? That's the beauty of the American-dream machine." Bradley widens his smile, as if he has explained everything in the world.

"Mansion on the hill's ass," says Buck. "I am and always will be pure redneck. Now I'm just a high-tech redneck! Like the Possum sings about."

I want to ask why Buck feels he has a right to appropriate this redneck pride, despite his honky-tonk singing career, if he has never worked on the land, which I suspect he hasn't. I feel like reminding Buck and everyone else at the table that the original rednecks were yeoman farmers, beloved of Jefferson, gracefully, artfully living close to the land, and that, however unlikely it will ever happen, I'd like to see the term used, even now, in a tone of reverence. I want to let him know I plan to join their number and encourage others to do the same. I want to let them know this is my lost cause—to die as Tobia-Yeoman-Farmer.

I open my mouth to speak, wondering for a second how my fist might feel flattening the cartilage of Buck's nose, but to save me the humiliation Robin looks down at Buck with undisguised superciliousness and says, "Come on, T." Grace looks up at Robin, wide-eyed, an expression of undefined yearning on her vacant face. Something in Robin's tone reminds me that Buck once propositioned her. "Eon's on the kiosk screen," she says.

I stand up and walk with Robin toward the center of the Silver Room.

"I ain't done with you, snakeman," Buck says from the table, chortling, enjoying the sport, perhaps reminded how much he likes having someone to rib, someone against whom to flex and test his hard-won power.

There's also something cold in his eyes that reminds me of what I sometimes see in the eyes of Bank and his crew and which I've seen in Eon's
eyes—something ancient and restless, grave and driven, and more than
a little unsettling.

THE KIOSK where Eon's face has appeared is located at the center
of the clear floor. It is a computer terminal on rollers atop a marble
pedestal. In the future, at Eon's request, this kiosk will be, alternatively,
a center of riddles and acrostics, and a place where club visitors can interact with the artificial intelligence robots he's developing.

Some Pinkmellon employees, some of my former colleagues, who
are gathered around the kiosk, greet us as we approach. Internet soft-
ware guru Ferdinand De La Garza says hello.

Eon's gaunt face fills the monitor. His large, dark, generously lashed
eyes shift left and right behind circular glasses with no frames, as he con-
siders his answers. His hair is cut short and slightly spiked, more out of
genuine than practiced insouciance, and there are two small dark circles
under his eyes that make him look perpetually sad and diverted, even
when he smiles. I watched these circles form slowly as the company rose
from the ground, while Eon was giving up sleep for days at a time to ensure its success. Now, even though he can afford to rest, to delegate, the
dark circles have remained, making me think he's too young to have the
concerns the circles suggest.

There is a brief on-screen delay between the movements of his face
and the arrival of his words. Some of the braver employees around us
are teasing Eon for having stayed home on the night of the big opening.
Eon's lips move in speech, then he smiles slyly as we hear, "How do you
know I'm not in the building?" in reaction to which his workers guess
where he might be.

One by one, the employees and fans drift away after having had a few words with their boss and host, so that Robin and I are the only ones in front of the monitor with no line behind us.

"Looks like a big success," says Robin.

"So I'm seeing and hearing," says the face on the screen.

"Congratulations," I say.

His eyes shift to take me in. A moment after his lips have begun moving, we hear, "Tobia. Tobywahn Kenobe. I'm surprised to see you here. I'd have thought you'd be off somewhere destroying perfectly good real estate." His lips on the screen stop moving. He shuts his eyes and gives me an extended nod, as the speakers say, "Burrowing back into the past like a blind mole."

"I'll get back to that tomorrow," I say. "I'm enjoying myself tonight."

"You'll get back to burrowing into the past in the near future," he says. "He's crazy, Robin. You know that, don't you? He's a crayfish. A pair of lonely claws."

"I know he is," she says, putting an arm around my shoulders and squeezing. "That's why he needs us."

"You would have been the man of honor tonight. Why didn't you show up, in person?" I ask.

"I've been telling people all night that I'm here, in the building. Do you think I would have missed this? In fact, I want to show both of you something."

"You're on the third floor," Robin says.

"We have a winner," says Eon. "Ding, ding, ding, ding."

"The gold floor," Robin says. "Can we see it?"

"You know, Tobia?" Eon says, ignoring Robin for the moment. "If not for your initial investment, there's a good chance none of this would be here today." His lips form a slow smile as he watches me through the screen's eye. "I'll bet you lose sleep over that."

"You would have found someone else," I say.

"Perhaps," he says. "And perhaps not. I like your clasp, Robin.

Appropriate, considering your date," he says. "Which reminds me . . . don't move. Stay where you're standing."

A few minutes later a tuxedoed bouncer approaches and extends to Robin, in a white-gloved hand, a golden key.

"Thank-you," she whispers in a little-girl voice and winks at the man, who turns on his heel and walks away.

In little time we're through the door in the back of the Silver Room and in the elevator and ascending. One level up, the doors open onto a room as big as the Silver Room, but more dimly lit from track lighting below the mirror at the top of the twenty-five-foot ceiling. The room is empty and silent as a church. Robin looks around expectantly, takes my hand, and we move out onto the clear dance floor. It's a heady experience, from this height, looking down through three clear floors to the bottom of the atrium.

"Bradley wanted to open this up tonight. But I guess Eon and his boys say it still has some bugs. Some copyright problems, I believe," Robin says, executing a twirl. "I wonder where Eon is. I thought he'd be up here. Hmm? Where could he be?" There is only the welcome silence around us. It occurs to me that this alone—a silent, empty room—is accomplishment and surprise enough for me.

Robin singsongs, "Eon, oh, Eon," as she approaches a wall of the room in the middle of which some hidden double doors slide open. She turns, smiles, shrugs, and motions me after her.

Inside the thin, peripheral room, Eon is sitting in front of twenty large color surveillance screens that have been set into the wall. He gives no sign of having noticed us come in. As I approach, Robin puts a finger to her lips, and I join her in watching what Eon is watching.

His hands, the right one on which there is a tattooed *E* on the flesh between his thumb and index finger, rest on a black board filled with meters, knobs, dials, buttons, and levers. I once overheard a Pinkmellon employee ask Eon if the tattoo stood for his name and Eon answer that it stood for anything, everything but.

All of the screens, with the exception of one showing the vacant room through which Robin and I have just passed, are alive with crisp representations—captured from various angles and in varying degrees of closeness that shift as Eon makes adjustments on the control board—of a single, crowded table in the Silver Room, at which are seated a man and a woman who look to be in their sixties; three younger men and four women, several of whom are heavyset and all of whom look to be in their early to mid thirties; and eight or more young children of various ages.

On one of the screens, in slow motion, a wild-haired girl in a maroon velvet dress flings a handful of peas across the table. Almost before the last pea lands, one of the thirty-something women rises from her chair with a ferocious expression, yanks the girl to a standing position, and spanks her. The girl's face howls. The tape stops, rewinds, and plays again.

The older and middle-aged people look vaguely familiar to me.

On the live-sequence screens some of the children, including the now-recovered and laughing wild-haired girl, are climbing on chairs and crawling on the floor under the pulled-together tables. Other children are scattered around the table—retrieving flung forks, plastic action figures, and dolls, chasing one another, running to play or back from playing virtual-reality games, going to watch sections of films.

Eon continues making adjustments—zooming in, now, on the face of the oldest man, at the head of the table—crow's feet around the lost-looking eyes shifting to fall on different places in the Silver Room, lips and mouth, around teeth with multiple crowns, moving to say, "Well, when you think he'll finally show up and see his folks?"

On another screen, the oldest woman's mouth moves in answer, over the continuous babble and occasional louder cries of the children: "Don't know. We oughta just try and enjoy ourselves till then."

On still another screen, isolated in his own medium close-up, the biggest of the thirty-something men at the other end of the table, who has a beard, dark-tinted glasses, stringy black hair, a tan, iced drink cocked in his right hand, looks up from his plate of food to say, "He ain't gonna show up and see us. He'll pay the bill. And he'll send an e-mail sayin' he hoped we had an old-fashioned blast. But the only way we're gonna see Eon or Eore or whatever the hell he wants us calling him these days—is on a screen. If that."

Eon makes adjustments on the board. Just after the bearded man has said "that" the isolated close-ups on the three screens stop, rewind, and reappear to repeat the conversation. Meanwhile, the pea-throwing episode and the general, live chaos at the table, viewed from a variety of angles, continues on the other screens.

Robin and I share a glance.

Eon stops making adjustments and sits back in the chair to watch the screens, letting the four looped sequences—the isolated conversants and the wild-haired girl flinging the peas, then getting yanked up and walloped—run again and again.

Without taking his eyes from the action, Eon unfolds himself from the chair, releases a long, cryptic sigh, and stretches his arms out toward the images in a curious way, spreading and letting tremble the fingers of his right hand, leaving those of his left still, as if he means to freeze the images in place even as he enjoins them to further, spontaneous motion. He has just bent over the controls to make more adjustments when Robin ventures, "Eon?"

In reaction to which he leaps and ducks at once, then turns to see we've been watching, his eyes asking *for how long.* "You scared me," he says, glancing up at the screen showing the empty room behind us. "I didn't see you come in." His face flushes; he turns and bends to switch the screens away from their former, more limited subject to a variety of general views of all the rooms below. "I was just doing a little mingling," he says with a small laugh followed by an intense, imploring look. "Now, if you'll both go back out to the Gold Room. There's something I'd like to show you."

"Yes!" says Robin, taking my hand and leading us at a brisk walk through the sliding doors, back into the empty room, where I ask in a whisper as we move to the center of the clear floor, "Eon the documentarian? Was that his family?"

She nods: "The Newcomb clan," she says, shaking her head, "in crisper color than the real thing and a heck of a lot easier to take, I'll wager."

While we wait for something to happen in the quiet, empty room, I look down at the kaleidoscopic movement of people on the floors below us, distantly remembering the face of Eon's father at the construction site of the very house in which I spun around with a sledgehammer a few nights ago. I see an image of the young Eon before he was Eon, bringing his father lunch, the angry, diminishing faces around the trailer the day little Elvis Newcomb gave me and Bradley rides in the go-cart he'd made.

The room is suddenly alive with noise and shapes. I duck and make to flatten myself out against the floor. Robin laugh-gasps, grabs my hand, and squeezes. Three-dimensional images of scantily clad, hip-shaking, hip-looking people have us surrounded—a sudden party gyrating to a frantic, pulsing beat. In three other quadrants of the room, overalled hillbillies square-dance; wigged, Age of Reason types carry out the formal intricacies of a proper waltz; tall, long-necked Masai warriors in red robes and long jangly earrings leap and shimmy.

"Wow," I say, in spite of myself, feeling a rush of surprise and delight.

"Holograms!" Robin says. "They look so real!"

In addition to the isolated movements they're making, the images begin to slowly circle, en masse, around the room, so that even as we stand where we are, we'll soon leave the hipsters' gyrations to join the hillbillies' exuberant do-si-doing.

"You've never seen these?"

"Never," she says. "I knew about them. This is the surprise I was telling you about."

Robin kicks off her shoes and dances among the images, happy as a peasant girl at a Mayfair, her real, solid body giving lie to the illusions, passing through them like movie wraiths. After a time the hologram dancers begin to move more slowly, the warriors suspended in the air for several seconds before they fall. I imagine Eon watching us as he was watching his family, on a monitor, from various angles, slowing the images with the movement of a switch, taking pleasure in our delight. Robin keeps dancing to the pulsing beat for a time. Then she, too, slows to match the asynchronous movement of the hollow forms. She throws back her head and laughs, full-throated. "Isn't this magical?" she says.

As she continues to dance, I hear—or think I hear—a quick, sharp *Look up!*

When I do, I see a three-dimensional Pinkmellon trademark, projected in a corner of the room, about fifteen feet up—a coil that looks like a bedspring drilling into a watermelon, a representation of Eon's secret, the microchip that speeds up the inner processings of Pinkmellon's computers. Then, one foot below and doubled in the ceiling mirror, in the center of the room, I see a black-and-white hologramic image of Merritt Wilson standing on a bridge spanning a canal, her head cocked slightly to one side, a playful, if slightly annoyed, expression on her face, as if she's about to mildly scold the photographer. The image rotates, so that I see that its back, Merritt's back, is incomplete—a grid of green lasers with numbers where the lines intersect. When it disappears, I stare for a few moments at the place where it was spinning, then look to see if Robin has seen it. She gives no sign, occupied as she is with trying, unsuccessfully, to outleap the Masai.

After some moments in which some isolated dancers from each group are mixed together, flickering in and out of each other's midst—Masai leaping among hillbillies; hillbillies at the waltz; waltzers among the Masai, spinning through the hoedown—the scene changes to an underwater tableau, accompanied by a tingly harp score. Whales cross and recross in the air above us, waving barnacled flukes. Schools of bright fish—jacks, angel- and clownfish, slow, tough-guy groupers, and brilliant, blinking guppies—fin and glimmer through the room. Seaweed projections and big, shimmering bubbles rise from the floor, which looks to be made of coral and sand. A few seals rise to the surface, then dive to sport in the depths. A tremendous tiger shark, with jagged, protruding teeth, hugs the floor. A sea snake, some species of Hydrophiddea, judging from the jailbird stripes, probably a sea krait (*Laticauda, colubrina*), whose venom is up to ten times more deadly than most land species', swims in circles above me, dipping down to curl in and out of a football helmet; a dolphin glides back and forth in easy sweeps over Robin.

As suddenly as they appeared, the images disappear, returning the room to stillness. A few moments later Eon—the real Eon, not a hologram, I look closely to make sure—strides out of the doorway, a look of supreme accomplishment on his face and in his walk. "Now, even you have to admit to enjoying my little hologram dance, Mr. Caldwell," he says, grinning with a sly certainty. "We have twelve more scenes we can do, but I thought these would give you the picture."

I smile and nod. "That was something," I say, wondering if I should ask now about the image of Merritt Wilson.

Robin rushes over from the other side of the dance floor, throws her arms around Eon's shoulders and kisses him on the lips. "Thank-you," she says. "That was wonderful! I wish everyone could've seen it tonight."

Eon pulls a handkerchief from the front pocket of his suit jacket and dabs at his mouth with it—an odd gesture, I think, for someone who grew up in a double-wide under catalpa trees. "It's not quite ready for the masses," he says. "We're trying to figure out the optimal number of people who can be up here to enjoy it at the same time, before we start selling tickets."

His dark, generously lashed eyes land on me. He begins to speak, pauses, the quick movement of his eyes suggesting something of the binary magic in his mind—*if this, then this; if this, not this* a million times. He asks, "What do you hear from Merritt Wilson?"

I look at him to see if I can tell how much he knows.

Robin shakes her head, crosses and uncrosses her eyes. "Ah-ha," she says, "got it." She points at Eon and says, "Venice," and thrusts the thumb of her other hand at me and says, "ancient history."

I nod twice at Robin, to reassure her, then look at Eon and say, "I haven't heard anything from her in a long time," as calm and flatly as I can, considering whether I should ask him if he's written any letters to Angola care of the Red Cross.

"That's a shame," he says and looks at me as if he means to detect a lie. "I know she thinks—or used to think—a lot of you. I'd like to show her this place, someday—when it's completely finished. So, if you'd heard from her or knew where to reach her . . ."

"I want to go all the way up, Eon. As high as it goes," Robin says, to spare us from the futility of remembering a girl long gone and best forgotten.

Eon pauses before answering, not wanting to let the former matter drop, but then lets it go with an eye-click of resignation. "Those floors aren't finished yet, as you know," he says, "I was just up there. When they're finished, they'll blow the other floors away. Including this one. We're just getting started. There's no limit to the wonders this place will contain."

"I don't care if it's not finished. I want to show Tobia the view from the top. Is it still a clear night?"

Eon shrugs. "Here's a master keycard. Don't lose it," he says. "Go where you like. I have something to arrange below. Which may be where you, especially, should direct your attention, Mr. Caldwell." He winks, turns, and walks backs to the panel in the wall, which slides open to let him step through it.

Before the doors close, I call out, "Eon, I hope we can expect you at our reclamation party in a few weeks. You'll get an invitation in the mail," in response to which he waves without turning around, the *E* on his hand wiggling, as the doors slide shut.

IN THE ELEVATOR, Robin inserts the new keycard and we move up to the next level. As Eon said, the next floor is incomplete. Strange platinum wiring juts in tangles from the concrete walls. We glance in, and then continue all the way to the top, the seventh floor. Robin flicks off the switch for a single spotlight that had been streaming from the center of the ceiling to make a circle of light on the clear floor. We walk over and stand in the darkness where the light had been.

Robin takes my hand and settles down against the clear plastic floor, then pulls me down beside her, giggling throatily, like a little girl. I wonder if she's drunk. Her head falls back with a soft crush of hair onto the floor, and she trains her burner-flame gaze on the creamy swirls of the Milky Way light-years above us through the glass ceiling. Satellites wink down at her. Red and green lights on planes wave to her across the sky. Looking up at the stars, I think of the swamp below; between them, human revelers on different levels.

We start kissing and there's no pretending necessary. Am I drunk; is it this place? Our breathing starts to promise more. After a time, I withdraw from Robin, lean on an elbow, and look down through all the floors and ceilings below us to the lighted atrium six floors down.

It's unclear, very difficult to see anything through the people and tables, on all the levels, but for a moment I think I can just make out on the atrium level a wiry form floating onto the pond in a small boat. Before the crowds flock over for a better view, blocking my own line of sight with their leanings-in to see an imminent spectacle, I think I can just see, squirming in the figure's hands, something that looks like a piglet.

"Robin," I say, and I'm going to tell her we have to leave right away before anyone can accuse us of being complicit in this, whatever it is, and that if she won't leave with me, I'll have to leave on my own. But before I say anything, Robin stands up.

I look up at her. Keeping her gaze on me, she unzips her dress and lets it fall in a pile to the floor. It's difficult, initially, to say whether I'm frightened or excited. Shortly afterward she's out of her black, lacy underthings and, with the exception of the snakehead clasp, naked and golden in the star- and moonlight streaming in through the glass ceiling.

FOURTEEN

ARLY IN THE FOOTBALL SEASON of my senior year in college, some sportswriters and -casters, who'd dug a little into what it meant to be a Caldwell of my particular stripe and observed what they took to be my equanimity on and off the field, nicknamed me "the Gentleman" and it stuck.

To calm myself between huddle and line and to help project the appropriate, leader-among-men mien to teammates, opponents, and fans, I used to whisper the names of Confederate generals.

And one crisp October day in particular, I took the snap and jogged back a few paces behind good coverage and threw a high arcing spiral. My fingers caressed the strings. The ball left my hand on an auspicious-looking trajectory, and from my obstructed vantage, looked to be tight-spiraling en route to Clint Jarvis's outstretched arms, where it would be cradled, just before the end of the end zone.

A big lineman hit me. I took the blow on chest and shoulders, felt a heavy jarring of earth to helmet. Looked up to see a shiny black, facemask-intersected visage inches from my own. Despite the shade between us, saw his gameday stubble whorled out on his cheek, the wideness of his flat nose, the whiteness of his eyes and teeth. He pushed up to stand out of view with a whispered, "How you like that, Fauntleroy?"

A plane trailed a banner advertising a bank across the scrubbed blue sky. I watched it and in my dazed state wondered if Merritt Wilson was in the stands or watching on a television in Charlottesville. I had not spoken to her or seen her since our goodbye on the porch of the old house, if you discounted three letters she'd sent, all of which I'd read several times and kept in a shoe box under my bed, but only one of which I'd answered—to tell her I thought it best we didn't see each other ever again.

The crowd erupted. I sat up, looking side to side. All around the stadium, walls of our fans had risen, cheering, to their feet. In the visitors' section everyone was seated, silenced.

The band lit exuberantly into our fight song, swinging instruments as they played. Bright sun glinted in blurry stars off the brass, and the students sang fight fight fight for good old university and the refs upthrust their arms to look exactly how a quarterback was supposed to make them look: bipedal zebras on point at God.

I stood up, brushed myself off, surveyed my crowd, and stood firm, self-possessed, slightly bemused at the ridiculousness of it all, as Jarvis ran back and threw himself, full-bodied, into me, and pounded my helmet with his glorious hands and showed the world his wide, inimitable smile and told me I was the man.

Afterward, at a dinner on the town with family and friends, Father said, "And to think. Not all that long ago he was mucking around after crawdads down in a creek in front of our house. What this sport *has done for you*, Tobia Caldwell!" He shook his head and the veins pulsed at neck and temple; his face was red from the bourbon. His eyes sparkled a little vacantly. Mother pinched my cheeks and said, "He's still our precious little boy, though. Always will be. Won't he?" Yes. Yes, of course I would. Everyone laughed. Some people in the restaurant stood to applaud as we walked out.

The coaches used me as an example in their bootstraps speeches, told the benchwarmers and grunts how I'd started out third string and stuck with it. Coach didn't call me the Gentleman like the others; he called me Senator's Son because of Grandfather Thomas. The boosters came to look upon me as their savior. It had been several years since they'd had a winning team to boast about in the locker room of the country club and to the out-of-state boys they did business with. They all had sons and nephews they wanted me to meet, almost all of whom, according to their fathers, wanted to be quarterbacks someday. There was some talk of a Heisman. It was an outside possibility—as a senior I'd come to prominence late—but my numbers were awfully good, my passing yards highest in the NCAA for the season to that point. If I continued to play as I had for the first couple games, who knew what might happen?

My fame gathered momentum. We won three, four games. Already nicknamed the Gentleman, with each new game we won, the fans tacked on a number so that I was the One . . . Two . . . Three . . . Four Game Gentleman—as if I would cease being a gentleman the moment the streak stopped. My contemporaries and teammates expressed surprise at my atavistic forbearance. I had my studies, my work-out regimen, my playbook, church on Sunday, early to bed and rise. I carefully measured what I said before speaking, kept my drawers and closet in apple-pie order, made my bed every morning, allowed myself a night of drinking with the boys on occasion. Never had too much.

Fans of both sexes, young and old, clamored for autographs or just to smile and see me smile back at them. That was all they expected of me as long as I had done my job on the field—standing, nodding, smiling, signing whatever they proffered. It was easy to deliver on such small after-game expectations, and during the games it was mostly learned instinct. I was carried along in the momentum of it.

I received so many breathy letters from young women that it put me in mind of my namesake, Tobit, who had been with John Hunt Morgan when the women of Richmond swarmed the Kentucky Raider, so sure were they that his method of guerilla warfare would do to the Federals what Marion, the Swamp Fox, had done to the Redcoats.

Some of my teammates said, *You mean to tell me—and don't lie to me, TC—you never sleep with any of these girls who try to throw themselves at you?* I did not. I dated them, kissed them goodnight afterward, turned on my heel to walk home and get a good night's sleep. The well-heeled belles I dated seemed to understand that I was not insulting them.

All of it ended on a cold, late October day when we were ahead of Penn State by six. They lined up showing blitz and did. I called a play to counter it, but three of them broke through our line and barreled for me like blue bellies after Lee in the Wilderness. I sprang away, pitched the ball to Hamilton. He ran gamely but, unable to round the end, was dropped close to the line of scrimmage. Just after the ball had left my hand I felt a jolt at my right heel. As I watched the play fizzle, I came to the awareness that something was very wrong. Though I could see my foot touching the ground, I could not feel the sensation of it having touched. Instead, an angry tingling there, more strange than painful. I looked down at my leg in rapt confusion.

"What's up, Caldwell? Y'alright?" one of the linemen asked.

"I'll walk it off," I said, thinking it a twisted ankle. But it didn't walk off, and I couldn't feel my foot touch the ground though I could see it touching. There was no spring or lift. Later, tendrilly currents of sharp pain shot all the way up my leg to pulse and writhe along its course.

A balding orthopedist told me, somberly, through a veneer of bedside-manner sincerity, that I had ruptured my Achilles tendon. No doubt in his mind. Complete tear. He had me feel the gap there, had me feel the good one: "See the difference?" I did. It would require surgery. I thanked him for his diagnosis and nodded.

After the prescribed surgery, I faded back into consciousness in the recovery room and remembered how, drifting out of consciousness, I'd listened to the anesthesiologist talk football in low tones while he looked down at my leg where they had, at that moment, been making the incision.

When I first came to, no one was around. The beds beside mine were empty. I appreciated my moment of solitude and felt oddly disconnected from myself.

A nurse came in to ask how I was feeling. I smiled at her and told her I was fine, that I thought I'd come through it all right. She said she thought the same and, blushing, asked if I would sign a football with an indelible marker, for her son. Of course I would, but I warned her my signature would soon be worthless. Later, the surgeon came in to tell me things had gone well, but had taken slightly longer than anticipated. I didn't ask him what he thought of my chances of playing again.

After a time, my family, all the coaches, and some of my teammates came by to cheer me up. Fenton Monroe said, "Well. I guess that, like Thetis, your mother must've dipped all but that pesky heel in the River Styx, eh, son? Old Penn State Paris hit his mark out there."

They filed through like pilgrims to a crumbling shrine with their jokes and well-wishings, and I smiled up at them and put on a good show for them with my nods and stiff upper lip and smiles till they left me alone again, which is what I found I'd been craving all along.

I stayed in the hospital that night, unable to sleep. I was feverish, and after a time the sheets turned wet and heavy with my sweat. As the anesthetic wore off, the pain seeped in. All that night when the pain crept in, I pushed a button to summon morphine and felt the pain overtaken by a melting heaviness. All night: the ebb and flow. Jagged pain and, with the push of a button, its smooth, liquid-leaden lack.

Still, I couldn't sleep. With flushed face and wide-open eyes, feeling oddly enlightened, as if the ceiling might open up to let me rise and gain the utmost vantage, with what turned out to be accurate foresight I saw myself hobbling up and down the sidelines for the rest of the season, pacing back and forth, dazed and distant, brokenhearted, oddly relieved. Free to think what was next for Tobia Banes Caldwell if it did not have to do with football, which it likely would not.

Just before dawn, with my new neighbor snoring raspily beyond the cloth partition and the old nurse making repeated visits to threaten us with catheterization if we were unable to urinate into small plastic jugs, I saw Ben Wilson facedown in the creek, his hair waving like eelgrass, his eyes wide before he drew his last breath. I saw the snap-action of cottonmouth strike, eyes slit, hypodermic fangs sinking into forearm flesh, and then I saw and remembered feeling the eccentric loading that had ruptured my tendon. The cottonmouth striking, the tendon snapping: cottonmouth strike, tendon snap. Again and again till dawn.

Released from the hospital and just before sleep, back in the old house, in my dream the next night, the cottonmouth that had bitten Ben Wilson, its head rejoined to its body, slithered up one of the columns and into my childhood bedroom through the open window, moonlight heavy on its scales. It coiled up on my chest, a weight like a large stone, and whisper-hissed, *Ben Wilson is coming is Wilson Ben.*

A COUPLE DAYS LATER I was sitting in the parlor of the old house reading an editorial speculating about my team's prospects without me, when Mother called from the back of the room to say I had visitors. I could tell from the excitement in her voice that these were not ordinary visitors. Since I'd been home, I'd had many visits from Haven folk: family friends and pseudo-friends who'd seen me grow up or had known me when I was little or claimed to have and wanted to deliver their condolences and see the fallen hero, the Five Game Gentleman himself, in his gentlemanly convalescence at the Old White Manse who was doomed never to increase the number of his wins. It was odd that I didn't resent these visits. I'd been enjoying their attention perhaps because I knew my days of receiving such attention were also numbered.

I stood and hobbled a distance with my crutches. When I looked up, I saw Merritt Wilson and Robin Sackett standing in the doorway together and smiling as if aware of their power. Their dual-radiance filled the doorway and splashed into the room and, since I was in the room, washed over me, a wave of sweet light, and after the backsweep of the wave, some droplets remained to shine through the thick fog in my chest and throat. I in- and exhaled, swallowed, could think of not one thing to say in the presence of such unexpected, late afternoon magnificence.

"We heard what happened," said Robin and stepped out of the doorway into the room.

"So we came by to see how you're doing," said Merritt and also stepped forward so that it almost seemed for a moment as if they had choreographed some sort of presentation. Seeing Merritt made me think of the cool water down at the creek, the golden glints on its surface, the unanswered letters she'd written to ask for an explanation for my final letter to her.

They hugged me, in turn, as best they could, given the crutches. I smiled and felt dizzy in their midst, looked from one to the other, thanked them for coming, looked down at my lower leg in its heavy cast, nodded, unsure what to say or do.

"Yes," I finally said and nodded, slowly, and looked up, forcing myself to brighten outwardly, even as I hid the brightness I felt: "How nice of y'all to come by. I'm surprised to see . . . both of you."

"We're really very very sorry. It's such a huge shame," said Robin.

In the doorway, behind the girls, my mother appeared and made her eyebrows dance for my benefit. She disappeared when the girls noticed me noticing something behind them. Shortly afterward she brought us some coffee on the Phinster china.

I looked at Merritt, and she allowed a small smile, an ironic flash in her hazelgrey eyes that seemed to say, *Yes I'm here, despite the letter.* I looked down at my cast.

They told me the story of how they had renewed their friendship and traveled in Europe together after graduating from college. Now, they were both living together, both working downtown. Robin was at a bank. Merritt had returned to work for a debt consolidation business. Robin said she liked what she was doing. Merritt admitted to being miserable. Merritt talked about her parents, how they were settling into a new life in New Orleans. Robin said her parents had both remarried and were living with their new spouses less than a mile from each other—both still in Haven.

"So, what will you do now?" Merritt asked, following a pause in the conversation.

I looked at her and felt pleasantly torn down and wondered if she could tell I had no idea what I would do next beyond graduating and that it was exhilarating to see her. Robin fidgeted.

I shrugged. "I'll probably just come back and bag groceries at the Piggly Wiggly," I said and winked—a habit I'd developed as the Five Game Gentleman.

Merrit allowed a smile.

Robin looked distressed and said, "I have a feeling there are better things than that in store for Haven's own Five Game Gentleman," and smiled, her burner-flame blues sparkling in the flat, late fall light coming in through the windows.

"Yes. Let's see. All-night stock boy? Cashier? Deli boy? Butcher?" said Merritt. Our eyes met and held a moment. I was impacted by the simple presence of her, sitting beside me so comfortably holding a coffee cup with her thumb and index finger, taking sips, tearing me down so pleasantly. I wondered if she felt it, what ground we might have covered or recovered, if Robin hadn't been there. I wondered if we could have made a start, if I would have managed an apology, an explanation for what I'd written.

Robin said she had to go, and Merritt said she had better go, too. As I crutched along beside them, out of the living room, I asked them to stay for dinner, but they both refused, arguing too much to do back at their apartment.

"We just wanted to make sure you were keeping your chin up, Tobia Caldwell. We wanted to let you know no one's forgotten you just because you're injured," said Robin and dimpled. "You're actually not as bad off as we thought you'd be."

And neither are you, I thought, but did not say.

"We expected you to be bedridden at least. Or we never would have come," said Merritt, narrowing her eyes and smiling.

"Sorry to disappoint you," I said and looked at her.

Through the blurred glass of one of the front windows, I watched them wind down the driveway between the black frozen limbs of the trees, the warm colors of their clothing glowing out of the windows.

TOWARD THE END of my time at college, when I was able to move around in a heavy walking cast, I woke up early one April day and, having little schoolwork and nothing better to do, went alone to the zoo, where I wandered among the enclosures and cages looking in at the bored-seeming animals. The sky was grey and most of the animals were sleeping and not at all interested in entertaining me, except for (or especially not) a cougar who turned from its manic pacing along a fence to bare its fangs and growl.

Toward the end of the afternoon, just before closing, I wandered into the herpetology building, where it didn't take me long to find the cottonmouth. I stared through the aquarium glass at the specimen they had on display. Its head was hidden behind a plastic bowl, it was small and the color of charcoal, and it disappointed me that it looked more dead than deadly. With a refocusing I could look at my own, thin reflection on the surface of the glass in front of the snake. There he was in thin guise over the moccasin—the Five Game Gentleman with no games left to play—Tobia the-sorry-for-self.

After a time, a thickset zoo employee approached me. He looked to be in his mid-fifties and wore a khaki jumpsuit. "Excuse me," he asked in a thick mountain twang, "but aren't you the Five Game Gentleman?"

I looked up into two small, watery blue eyes set thinly in a thick red face and nodded. I was.

"I'll be," he said. "Sorry 'bout the leg. We were going good before that happened, though, weren't we?"

"Yes we were. Thanks."

"We all thought that was a real shame."

"I guess it was."

"How's it doing now?"

"Can walk on it. But it's a step slow. Not NFL material."

He looked to see what had captured my interest.

"That's Sam," he said and looked at me. "Sleepy this afternoon. Cottonmouth," he said. "Old *Agkistrodon piscivorus.*"

"I know," I said. We looked at the snake for a time. After another space of conversation I asked on a whim, "Does the zoo need any help? Here in the herpetology department?"

He chuckled.

"I'm serious."

"Well, if we did, I'd be the one to talk to," he said. "Henley Dempster." He thrust out a meaty hand. I stood and we shook. "No relation to the Dempster Dumpster folks, though some might say we Dempsters came out of one." He smiled.

I started working with Henley part-time at the herpetology building at the zoo. Caring for the snakes. After I'd worked there for a time, the zoo managers asked me to do an advertisement. With a python slung across my shoulders, I played the part of the Five Game Gentleman one last time. Told folks, *Come on out to the zoo, y'all!* The paper wrote a

"Where are they now?" article (even though this was only six months after the football season) about my new interest. Zoo visits increased, I'm told. I autographed zoo maps.

MY PARENTS did not approve. Word got back to my father, and one night he called to ask me what manner of tomfoolery this might be. "Tell me now," he said, "and we'll laugh about it together, tuck this *phase* away—sooner better—and move on." Then, he told me he thought he could get me into a law school if he dusted off some old connections despite the fact I had no interest in going to law school and hadn't applied or even taken the LSATs. When he put her on the line, Mother asked what I was doing over the weekend, and I told her I was going up into the hills with Henley Dempster of the Happy, Kentucky, Dempsters to hunt for rattlers. I listened to the heavy silence packed into the phone lines, which scarcely seemed to be connecting us.

A month after I'd started working at the zoo, I rode in Henley Dempster's rattling '66 Ford F-250 with a cracked windshield and springs poking through the vinyl seats, to a snake-handling church near Happy, Kentucky, not far from the cabin where he'd been born and raised, to witness the brave, faithful, deadly earnest folk there feel the spirit move on them and take up timber rattlers and copperheads and drink doses of strychnine because Mark 16:18 recommended it as a way to prove their faith.

We stepped out of a cold, piercing rain into the back of the church and sat on the backmost pew to watch as the strong-believers were moved by the spirit to stand up, testify, and, later, to speak in tongues. When even this was not enough to prove their ecstasy and faith, they reached into pinewood crates inside of which writhed big, healthy timber rattlers and copperheads and from which was issuing a cacophony of rattles and hisses, the strong scent of the musk they secrete when they're scared.

When the preacher had read enough of the gospel to get the people riled up and had made mention of the special guest, *an honest-to-goodness sports he-ro worshiping with us today, praise the Lord!,* the people in the church, undaunted, speaking in tongues and looking genuinely motivated by something beyond mere bravery or foolishness so that I couldn't tell and wasn't sure I wanted to speculate if their trancelike states were inner or outer motivated, lifted snakes out of crates and did slow, stilted, narcoleptic dances with them. They held the thick, flat-headed pit vipers aloft and, in some cases, moved bunches of them from hand to hand. The snakes elevated themselves and in-and-outed their tongues to taste the air of the hot room so that it seemed as if the snakes thought this exploration would help them discover what strange human rite required their presence and how they fit into it and how they might best escape it.

Henley's aunt, a vibrant older woman who looked upon the world as if she meant to scare its mysteries into immediate confession, ropy hair down to her knees, looked across the aisle at me and, with piercing eyes, pale and blue like Henley's, told me if the spirit took me, not to hesitate to take up some snakes. No thanks, I thought but did not say. I nodded to her and attempted a smile and sat there, transfixed and frozen to my pew throughout the service, certain that if I took up a snake it would immediately sense something in me and strike.

Henley kept snakes in his basement. One day he showed me the makeshift laboratory he'd fashioned for the purpose of learning more about the venoms of poisonous snakes. He developed antivenins for rare species and sold them at great profit. In a back room adjoining the basement he had several tanks, each of which contained some of the most poisonous snakes in the world. I walked the floor of the basement reading the labels: Tiger Snake, Bushmaster, Fer-de-lance, Jaracara, Indian Cobra, Banded Krait, Black Mamba, Gaboon Viper, Taipan, Death Adder, Vibora De La Cruz, European Asp. Looking at them and thinking of the deadly potential in those cages made my heart pound, my fingertips tingle.

I stopped in front of the banded krait and watched it coil its body, moving it as if to tie its black and brilliant gold bands into a knot, all the while seeming to watch me out of its wise, impassive, vertical-slit eyes.

Henley spoke about some of the snakes in the cages. He said the Gaboon viper's fangs were two inches long. He hoped the black mamba never escaped because they were the fastest snakes on earth. The Indian cobra, up to that point, was proving to be the most valuable snake of all to the projects he was working on.

He motioned for me to follow him to a tank in the corner of the room. He lifted its top and, with some prodding, the snake inside elevated half of itself out of the aquarium. It rose up to the height of Henley's neck, and when Henley grazed its head with his palm, it inflated its head. An Indian cobra. Henley explained that it puffed itself up like that by pushing out ribs it had in its neck to tighten, to menacing fullness, the loose skin of its hood.

Henley moved his hand from side to side in front of the cobra and it hissed and followed the motion.

"You're charming it?" I whispered.

Henley nodded. He kept moving his hand back and forth and the cobra kept following it, as if transfixed. He slowed the movement of his hand and, so, the cobra's head. Then he leaned his head in close to the snake and whispered an incantation that I could barely hear: "With my eye do I slay thy eye, with poison do I slay thy poison," Henley said.

His mouth was so close to the cobra's back-and-forthing head now, to its deadly mouth, that I winced as I looked on.

"Oh, Serpent, die, do not live; back upon thee shall thy poison return," he said.

He kissed the cobra's hood. And then, as he lowered his hand outside the glass of the case, the snake relaxed its neck ribs and let its hood fall and settled down onto the aquarium floor. When the cobra was resting on the bottom of its cage and Henley had covered it, he looked at me and smiled.

I shook my head. "Where'd these snakes come from?" I asked. "How did you acquire an Indian cobra, for example?"

"Mail order," he said. "Got most of these out of a herpetology catalog. I put the cobra on MasterCard. Arrived two weeks later. Delivered to my door." He grinned. "Easy as that. I'd appreciate your secrecy," he said.

"Understandable," I said. "Count on it."

Stored in a refrigerator in the basement Henley kept several jars labeled for the different kinds of venom they contained, the effects of which Henley was monitoring with an eye to medicinal and pharmaceutical uses. In addition to the snake tanks there were a few smaller cages in the basement filled with white mice and hamsters. He also had several vials of freeze-dried antivenin labeled for the kind of venoms they counteracted. On a shelf rested a stack of back issues of the *Journal of Toxicology.*

A stack of notebooks and computer printouts chronicled his experiments with the venom. There were several tables against the wall opposite the snakes themselves filled with beakers and tongs, canvas sacks and crates, vials, and rubber material, Bunsen burners, mortars and pestles. Henley told me he was working on several things at once.

"Cobra venom," Henley said, lifting a beaker, "is a neurotoxin. It affects the nervous system. People have known for years that in the venom of the cobra there's an enzyme called lecithinase that can dissolve cell walls and membranes surrounding viruses. It's putting these findings to greater use and focusing them to that use that remains largely untapped. Down here, and out at the farm where we keep the Welsh sheep, I accelerate things, is all. I go smart, but I go fast. I'm working at finding a polyvalent antivenin that uses the blood of sheep instead of horses. One that will work for every kind of possible venom. A Nashville company is going to back my research. It's in the works."

"What about cottonmouth venom?" I asked, attempting to sound casual.

"Pit viper. Hemotoxin." We walked over to the tank with a cottonmouth in it. It was coiled up and staring stonily so that it was difficult to imagine its eyes seeing anything at all, out of the glass in front of it. "The venom is released into the victim—typically a fish, frog, rat—through tubular fangs that work in much the same way as a hypodermic needle. Hemotoxins affect the circulatory system, heart and blood vessels. The snake's victim dies when its heart stops."

"Is a cottonmouth bite deadly?" I asked him.

"To humans?"

I nodded.

"Typically, no. But it's difficult to predict what effect it'll have. It depends on the person and what they've been doing. If they've been real active, running or something or they run afterwards, the venom could spread more quickly through the bloodstream and end up being fatal. In other cases, it might just be very painful, make someone sore and sick a few days. Why?"

I shook my head. "No," I said. "No reason. There are stories of them falling into hunters' boats off cypress at Reelfoot Lake. The hunter panics and shoots at the snake, misses it, and puts a hole in the bottom of his boat. The boat sinks, and the hunter drowns."

Henley nodded, smiled. "Sometimes our conditioned fear of these suckers is out of all proportion," he said.

Henley told me he could use the help in his lab and gave me a job there in addition to my work at the zoo as long as I promised to keep quiet about it. There was good, cottage-industry money in the antivenins of some of the rarer species. It thrilled and terrified me to feel their rough scales on my own skin, to feel them squirm in my hand for an opportunity to escape or bite.

In the basement lab Henley and I milked his deadly snakes of their venom and attempted to isolate enzymes in order to break down the composition of the proteins, and injected mice, rabbits, and Welsh sheep to observe the effects of the venom on the cells and innumerable other procedures. Henley was both manic and pragmatic in his scientific exploration. He taught me the proper techniques for capturing and milking the snakes. We worked often with Welsh sheep he kept at a farm some distance into the country. We monitored the injected animals' blood to determine its makeup and how it had been altered by the presence of the venom. We brainstormed possible medicinal uses for the venom, tried to come up with newer, better ways of testing it.

On several nights I found myself poring over books of toxicology, sometimes till the sun came up. I bought my own subscription to the *Journal of Toxicology*. I lost myself in the formulas that represented the elements of the world. I began to break down everything I saw into the isolated elements from which they were composed, and I thought a lot about the ability of toxins to play havoc with that makeup, to pull apart and stymie living tissue. The bite of the bushmaster had been known to cause people to bleed from the eyes.

One morning, as the sun began to warm the air, Henley and I made our way up a dry creekbed, overturning rocks with metal tongs as we went. The night before we'd camped out under a limestone outcropping. When it rained, a waterfall formed a wall in front of us. We tipped stones carefully and stood back to wait for a timber rattler or copperhead to slither out from underneath or coil up and bare its fangs in defense. I enjoyed the fear and anticipation brought on by the tipping of the rocks. Every now and then Henley would call out, "Well, football he-ro, where're they hiding at?"

As we moved up the draw, Henley began a lecture on the difference between snakes and serpents. In his mountain twang and drawl he spoke as if he were addressing a colloquium of colleagues. During the time I'd known and worked with him, I'd gained a deep respect for Henley. It delighted me to think of him at the academic conferences he attended, in overalls and flannel with his scarred, cracked workingman's hands, politely, in his nasal, of-the-deep-hills brogue, coaching disbelieving, bottle-glassed Ivy Leaguers on the finer points of an already very nuanced avenue of toxicology. I felt very lucky to have been taken under his wing. Over time our having met at the zoo took on the glow of a destined thing.

He said, "A snake is just an animal—a slithering, cold-blooded reptile. Nothing more. But a *serpent,* now, a *serpent* is more than just a snake. The serpent has greater meaning. The serpent is the snake plus what human beings have invested in the snake for thousands of years. Snakes become serpents through the stories we tell. They become serpents when they're given a cultural depth, the symbolism and extra po-tency we weave for them—myth, legend, folktale, religion, sign, symbol."

I thought about the cottonmouth that had bitten Ben Wilson, how it visited to whisper in my dreams, and was certain it had transformed into serpent-hood.

"What happens, over a period of years and years," Henley continued, "is that this cultural buildup becomes a biological fact in our brains, comes to be inextricable from our reaction to the animal. We cannot see the snake without it suggesting something of the serpent. That make sense to you, Mr. Five Game Gentleman?"

I said that it did.

"The serpent has always been the richest of symbols," he continued as we made our way up the slough, toppling rocks, each time expecting to see a snake (serpent?) dart out at us. "It has been adopted to represent many different things to many different cultures. Let's see . . . it's represented immortality, craftiness, healing, water, wisdom, fertility, evil, power, vengeance, goodness, gentleness, deception, complexity, duplicitousness. It's as if snakes were created for the purpose of being prime candidates for symbolic use. Crawling dream-fodder, if you will. The prime material of myth. Cultures worldwide have adopted the snake into their religions, have used the snake's inherent symbolic power to serve them symbolically. It was the serpent in the garden of Eden that offered humankind its first taste of knowledge. It was the serpent in the Egyptian Book of the Dead that snuffed eternal life from Gilgamesh. There are the two serpents on the medical insignia. The Aztec god, Quetzalcoatl, the plumed serpent, was the creator of humankind. We took the snake and made it into a serpent. The question, then, is . . . ," he said, so engrossed in his own musings, the delivery of which were taking on a nearly ecclesiastical zeal, that he was oblivious of his small audience. It almost seemed as if he were speaking to a larger, imaginary one, or to the rocks and trees. "Is . . . whoa, lookee there!" He deftly grabbed and lifted up a timber rattler, which writhed, rattling, in his capable grasp.

I had to ask, "Well, what is it, Henley? Snake or serpent?"

He looked at me, the rattler writhing at the end of his thick, ropy arm. "Both," he said.

That night the fire cast our shadows on the cave wall. When we'd gotten the food cooking over the fire, Henley settled back and picked at his banjo, his playing conjuring an image of a confluence of water droplets trickling together into a clear mountain stream. He sang to accompany his playing some sad old mountain songs about abandoned homeplaces and dead or otherwise lost sweethearts, about wandering lonesome and homesick across the land. For some reason I was reminded I hadn't heard anything about Merritt Wilson since she'd come to visit me at the house. I saw her holding the coffee cup, the ironic twinkle in her eyes. Looking into the fire, I thought again about the story I wasn't going to tell Henley and wondered what Merritt Wilson might have been doing that very moment.

HENLEY HELPED make the final arrangements for a grant based on an idea I'd had to work with the venom of cottonmouths. I was going to live rent-free in exchange for leading tourists on swamp walks for the Park Service at Reelfoot Lake.

So, one early fall afternoon, I packed my meager belongings, double-checked my small, post-graduation apartment to make sure I wasn't leaving anything important, and set out.

But before I went up to Reelfoot, I went back to Haven. Mother had insisted I visit the old house before I began my research, and when I'd protested, arguing lack of time, pressing matters at the lake, important research to begin, she paused briefly before asking, "So you would rather rush off to live with snakes in that horrible old swamp that has already swallowed two of your relatives than come home to visit your wonderful charming beautiful mother who loves you very much?"

I thought about telling her how astute she was in her sarcasm but reconsidered; it wouldn't have been altogether true. In the same conversation she told me they'd sold fifty more acres to Martin Felter. The new development was to be called Golfhurst. I had seen developments sprout up on other parts of our land, had seen childhood haunts ripped apart and reconfigured into cul-de-sacs feeding cluster mansions. A turmoil of smoke, mud, sawdust, construction worker shouts, growls, back-up beeps of bulldozers, dump trucks, and backhoes—the sounds of progress.

The subdivision houses took shape one by one. Cement basements, skeleton scaffolding, the meat and cosmetics. Up they went. A new project had been undertaken on land even closer to the old house, and many of the homes in it, here and there, had been pastiche-constructed to subtly echo the Grand Old Caldwell Place. Every time I returned after having been away, I was surprised at the level of encroachment. When this section of the subdivision was completed, the old house would be surrounded in every direction except the front.

"You can't see the other homes from this side," my mother liked to say at the time. "So you can still pretend nothing's changed."

In this same conversation she also told me that a few months earlier my father had been squeezed out of his own firm by partners he'd trusted too much and had only just found new, less lucrative, work.

When I asked why she hadn't phoned to tell me sooner, she told me she'd been waiting for me to call her. Which, she added, I did entirely too rarely.

I felt compelled to return home because my mother had insisted and her insistence still had a hold on me—would until she had the stroke. Even after. Especially then. Plus, so much seemed to have changed since I'd last been home. I wanted to see how Father was doing in the wake of his setback. I didn't understand how they could have squeezed him out of the firm that had borne the Caldwell name for nearly a century.

I swept home on a wave of the brand of guilt that I knew would have intensified had I ignored her insistence and headed in another direction. As I neared the old house, I decided to make my visit run with a polite, shallow efficiency. I planned to say nothing that would pierce the facade of propriety, nothing my parents didn't want to hear, but I would not let them dissuade me from going to Reelfoot, which I knew they would try to do.

I wound up the driveway. From the front, the estate looked much the same as it always had, the driveway lined with the great trees. Approaching the house I was often overtaken by a heavy whiff of nostalgia, an awareness of lurking ghosts, half-buried events, memories awaiting their chance to pounce. It sometimes seemed as if the place might fasten me to it with old vines and hold me down to better whisper stories in my ears forever.

On that day the place was at rest in the slowness of a late July dusk, a certain violet light. A warm breeze caressed the leaves on the branches of the overarching trees and snaked through the close-mown grass that was still kept that way by a team of men and boys on riding mowers. Between the trees, my mother had embellished the curving driveway with daffodils and crocuses.

The wheels on the pavement said *youcanneverseverneverseverneversever* just before I stopped the car under the porte cochere. I stepped out, stretched. Mother was at the kitchen window, waving. I waved back and took my time walking up the porch steps to the door, glancing down at the stream running through its dark little valley.

She flung open the door.

"Tobia, welcome home! It's so nice to see you! Oh, look at your hair." Meaning, you need a haircut. And "You're so thin!" Meaning, you could stand to gain a few pounds. Often, when I returned home to visit my parents, I was reminded of having read once that parents have a deep-seated need to have their children near them and that this need is not necessarily connected with love.

"Your daddy's not home from work yet. Come in. Have some sweet tea. I had Tonorah clean up your room. There are fresh linens on your bed. I picked these flowers this morning. And, oh, guess what? I finally got one of those Nabokov Blues. It's in the new case up in my room. Let me show you. I'll fix the tea while you run up and get it for me. Okay, sweetheart?" We hugged and she kissed me.

I went upstairs and put my bags in my old room where, looking around at the things in it—the silver dollars from Aunt Marcy, a stack of recruitment letters and football trophies, my collection of arrowheads—I was ambushed by a close, murky feeling that welled up and pulsed—almost made me wince as if I'd had a shot of hundred-eighty-proof whiskey.

I got her latest butterfly collection case and met her on the front porch facing the yard and the stream.

"Do you remember how we used to wonder why butterflies are called butterflies? Remember? You told me it was because . . . what was it you used to say, Tobia?" she asked.

"I don't remember."

"Yes you do. You have such a good memory."

"Why don't you just go on and tell me," I said.

"All right. I think I remember. I think you said they were called butterflies because in the sun it looked like somebody'd smeared colored butter on their wings. Remember?"

"No."

"Well. I suppose I have to remember for you and your father. What I was going to say is that last week Professor Sullivan—an expert on birds or some old thing—came over here with Ms. Martin to the tea I had for the Garden Club. And he said, with conviction, that butterflies are called butterflies because people used to think that they were witches in disguise and that they would flutter in and make off with people's cream and butter. Isn't that wonderful!"

"I like what you used to say better."

"What did I used to say? I don't recall."

"I thought you had to remember for everyone."

"Well, I do. But, tell me, Tobia. What was it I used to say?"

"You used to say they were the most successful beetles and ants or something like that. You told me the hardest-working crawling insects eventually got wings. The harder they worked as plain insects the more beautiful a pair of wings they got. You tied it in with Karma and multiple lives or something."

"See! You remember. I knew you did. And you believed me, didn't you?"

"Never once," I said. Which wasn't exactly true. There is a time in every son's life when he believes every word his mother says.

We sat out on the porch until twilight waiting for my father to come home. We sipped the sweet tea. She told me about her friends and what was happening to them. They were aging and getting operations to combat that aging. She talked about tennis and golf at SCC and her work on the historic preservation committee, their fight against tacky growth. They were at least going to make sure it was respectable, that no charming older places would be demolished or ill-altered.

Listening and looking down into the darkening shadows of my little creek's valley at the bottom of the hill, I felt myself slipping into a sort of semi-pleasurable numbness that felt as if it had conferred invisibility.

When you have a mother who talks a lot, and who likes to order your life, and you're her quiet, thoughtful child, you learn over time to listen on the surface without any effort. I probably learned it from my father. As long as you have tuned into the correct drift of what's being said to you, it's not difficult to nod, shake your head, or register surprise at the correct times even if you don't expend energy listening. On the porch that night I heard myself making the grunts of acknowledgment that served as my father's principal communication to her, especially now that things weren't going well for him. We both loved to hear her talk, I think. Her voice rose and fell with a lilting musicality, and maybe that's exactly why we never chimed in much with our own.

He walked up onto the porch and materialized into a shade of dusk only a few shades separated from the surrounding grey. I glanced over to the gap in the railing where the steps came up, and there he was, in his suit, tie loosened, looking more thin and ragged than I remembered him being. He'd lost some hair, and his face looked gaunt and somber. He looked to have the hunger and ambitions of a younger man. I took it to be a result of his having been betrayed by his old partners and having had to start over. He looked like he wasn't sure if he could trust anyone. My injury had had an effect on him as well—he'd been so hopeful for me, so energized about my prospects. When I was away I usually imagined him tall, with longer hair, filled out and athletic-looking and with a red tinge to his cheeks so this new look hit me. He smiled. I stood up and walked over to him. He offered his hand and we shook. It had been months since I'd talked to him.

"You need a haircut," he said. "You look like General Custer."

"Yessir. Getting a little long."

"Now, I hear you're planning on going down to a swamp or something?"

"Yes, I am going. Out to Reelfoot. To work on—"

"What's there? Snakes?"

"Cottonmouths."

He glanced down at the stream.

"Where will you live?"

I thought he must have been thinking of how we sold the family house at Reelfoot after Grandmother Pearl's death and how it was no place to which I should want to return. "In a little cabin. On an island," I said.

"Who with?"

"No one. Alone."

"I see. I guess you heard about my old job."

"I did. And I'm sorry."

He nodded. "Those ungrateful bastards'll be the sorry ones, T. In addition to our now egregiously profaned legacy in that firm, I was also the best lawyer they had. You believe that?" There was a hint of the angel-demon mischief in his eyes that I liked seeing and that made me wonder if his ousting might prove a blessing over time.

"I believe it."

"What do you think of the old place?"

"Looks good."

"I think so, too. As long as you don't go around back where all that crap is going on. Good old T. Erstwhile football star come snake handler." He shook his head. "Where in the world did we fail, Lord. " He smiled like an ecstatic preacher and looked up at the blueblack sky and raised up his new thin arms. The smile didn't last long. The excess material of his suit hung down and his sharp bony wrists jutted out. He dropped his arms. Then he hugged me—shoulder to shoulder—and tussled my hair as if I were eleven or younger.

We all went inside for dinner. To keep us from silence, she told me how excited she was about all the new restaurants they'd gotten since I'd last been home and all about her upcoming trip to Aix-en-Provence. When she was going to get dessert, my father said, "I'd like to discuss a few matters with you up in the den after dinner." She brought in some strawberry shortcake, which we all ate in silence, sipping coffee. Outside, the crickets produced a tranquil, almost tangible sound. I thanked her for the dinner and asked if I might be excused.

"All right, sweetheart. You must be tired from your drive."

I said I was and stood from the table and kissed the top of her lilac-smelling hair and walked up to my room and sat on my childhood bed. A short time later I heard him come up the steps.

"Tobia," he said. "Can I see you in the den?"

When I walked in he was seated behind the desk. He had poured himself a drink. The Tennessee Turtle looked down with his stern reproachfulness.

"Well, you're in law school," he said and looked pleased with himself for showing me how smoothly things could work if you kept to the inside track. "And I can't tell you what to do with your life, but as your father I feel I should strongly recommend law as the course you chart for yourself. It's been good to me and to our family, in spite of my recent setback." While he delivered this opinion, he gazed down at the desk, and after he had loosed it on the room, he looked up at me, reminding me that his eyes are my eyes saddened by disappointment and time.

"Thank-you, sir. I appreciate whatever it is you had to do to get me into law school without having applied, but I'm charting a different course."

He nodded. "In that swamp. With snakes." He kept nodding.

"Yes," I said. "Doing antivenin research."

"You are too old for me to forbid it, but I would like you to know now that I strongly discourage it. It has the feel of an abandonment, I have to say, especially since I'll need you to help us get going again. What sort of thing is this to do with your life? I have no idea. It surprises me you will so easily abandon your family and give up the dignity of your birthright." There was something about the old den, the ancestors' weighty gaze, that pushed you into antiquated phrasings.

"I don't see it that way."

"We both know what this is about. Nevertheless, I would like to hear your explanation for why you are abandoning your family and your birthright to muck around in a swamp with poisonous snakes." His voice was calm; the ice clinked against the glass as he sipped.

"Let's just say we do both know what this is about, at least in part, and leave it at that," I said.

He nodded out the window in the direction of the creek. "If you leave now, it may be difficult for you to return to a more respectable path." He was staring into his glass as if the pattern of ice and bourbon were his script.

I nodded. A long silence passed between us set against the crickets' cacophony, which I was suddenly conscious had found us in the room through the windows. When it seemed as if he wasn't going to say anything else, I turned and left the room.

NEITHER OF THEM could believe it when I told them I had to leave the next morning. They had expected me to stay at least a little longer. It surprised *me* when I first announced it.

"Snakes can't wait, son?" my father said.

"At least stay and come to church with us tomorrow," she said.

"That's a powerful motivation for someone who doesn't believe in God," he said, which I thought odd since he knew that as the Five Game Gentleman I'd gone to church every Sunday.

"Tobia?"

"Sure," I said. "I believe in God."

"What a thing to say about your own son," she scolded.

"'And ye shall take up serpents,' huh T? When's the last time you went to church? Just out of curiosity," he asked.

"Oh, leave him alone and let him eat his breakfast," she said.

"It has been a while. During the season, when I was playing, you'll remember I went every Sunday," I said.

I wanted to get on the road and up to Reelfoot. I felt I needed to leave the old house before I was forced into an old dynamic, before I found my lips reading from a script that was not buried deeply enough inside me, left far enough behind me on the road upon which I thought I'd made progress. I stood from the table and said goodbye right after breakfast. A fear, perhaps irrational, had overtaken me that unless I left the old house immediately I would never be able to leave.

I went upstairs and packed what little I had taken out of my bags, their questions and pleas pursuing me. She was crying; he was feeling guilty because he felt like he'd driven me away when that was the last thing he wanted to do just then.

"At least wait till tomorrow, T," he said and fixed on me with his heavy eyes.

"I cannot stand it!" I heard my mother say.

He met me at the bottom of the stairs and blocked my way. He found my eyes and met them. I looked at him for a time, then looked away.

"Come on, T, for your mother's sake, son." When I managed to look up, he gave me a wink. "I can't allow you to do this to yourself. I can't stand by while you do this with your life."

I put the back of my hand on his shoulder and proceeded to the front door, opened it, walked down the steps, strode across the driveway, hopped in the station wagon, started the engine, stepped down on the accelerator and was on my way toward an uncertain future at Reelfoot with my snakes.

FIFTEEN

DOWN THROUGH THE WATER of Reelfoot Lake the stumps and halved trees of the old forest, almost two hundred years denuded of leaves and branches, loomed in the places where they'd been covered with water after the February 1812 rumblings of the New Madrid. After a time, seeing their ghostly forms below the surface fixed an image in my mind of my paternal grandparents, Thomas and Pearl, walking, easy as you please, through a path in that underwater forest—grey hair and clothing undulating, both of them smiling and waving the smiles and waves of a politician and his wife up at me.

Sometimes, when the bottom of my old Wabash brushed a stump or the top of a tree, it froze me for a few seconds, made me doubly conscious of their presence at the lake. At these times, I wondered for some time afterward what they thought of the work I'd come there to do—if it pleased or angered them or if they were indifferent that I had returned to the place where they'd disappeared. Other times I let my imagination run wild with fantasies that they'd staged their deaths to make a clean getaway, as Fenton Monroe has once suggested to me, sewn up their Tennessee lives to begin again someplace far away.

For days, especially in the beginning of my time at Reelfoot, before I started leading groups of tourists on swamp walks, or collecting and identifying butterfly and moth samples for my mother, I put off my research, did no work, lay down in the shack or under one of the cottonwood branches, absentmindedly kneading the scar on my left heel, and engaged in the otiose counting of clouds, the sifting of years and days. At night I'd lie listening to the throaty bellowing of frogs, the wing-flapping sounds of flocks of bats and birds, the splashes of bass going after moths, stinkpots falling off logs, or whatever I cared to imagine the splashes were.

After the idling time passed, I threw myself into a whirlwind of work. The swamp tours began, and I started using my growing expertise, the detailed notes Henley had given me, and my own intuition, my growing sense for things, to set up a lab on the island. Once the lab was up and running, I began working on developing a new kind of antivenin for the venom of the cottonmouth—and, in the near future, I hoped, several other species of poisonous snake—by doing a series of injections with sheep I'd had boated in for that purpose.

When I was out looking for snakes to milk for my research, all at once, the awareness that a cottonmouth was close by would come to me. This, before ever seeing one. It was a gift, an unbidden bond we'd developed. It was official. I was becoming a hardcore weirdo, a loony denizen of the swamp, Tobia-creepy-snake-catcher.

This was my home. I loved the snakes darkly. Darkly loved the way they sank underwater and blurred into nonexistence for a few seconds to reappear twenty or thirty feet away, their heads putting tiny algae into spin. Darkly loved the way they moved atop the water, the chills every time I saw one and it only retreated a short distance before stopping, as if to express a challenge. I darkly came to love the way they coiled up and aimed their white-mouthed displays at the sky, how they wiggled their fish lure tails when I caught them, sending chills down my spine and fingertips that never came when I'd see a water snake or a rat snake, or even a copperhead or rattler.

A RED CANOE with a lone paddler came into view and approached by steady, graceful strokes.

I was standing knee-deep between cypress, not far from my shack, a one-eyed moccasin I'd named The Pirate writhing like a high-pressure firehose in my right hand, twisting to try to escape and displaying the white interior of his mouth and fangs.

I watched the canoe's slow approach, expecting it to turn in another direction at any moment while I pulled out the milking cup and thrust The Pirate's fangs through its top, and applied pressure, glancing down to see an irroration of venom on the clear plastic.

When the canoe was closer, I saw that the paddler was a woman and when it was close enough for me to hear the paddle break and swirl the water, *Merritt Wilson Merritt Wilson Merritt Wilson* sliced the air, encircling me in soft whisper. I lowered The Pirate and watched him s-curve a distance before slipping soundlessly underwater between cypress knees, the green lure at the tip of his tail the last thing to wiggle out of sight.

The canoe, whose rider I was still unwilling to grant actuality, glided closer. I watched the space of The Pirate's disappearance for three beats, feeling dizzy, half-expecting the apparition I'd seen to have disappeared. When I looked up, it was not gone.

Merritt Wilson was taking in my speechlessness. A triumphant electricity played through her hazelgrey eyes—an excitement edged with some concern about the degree of surprise her visit had evidently caused. She wore jeans and a mint green REM concert T-shirt emblazoned with a monkey and a parrot riding a bicycle over the caption *We are having a heavenly time.* Her forearms were tan below which her hands gripped the quarter-dipped paddle in two places. Her hair darkened where it met her face and was swept back into a braid. Droplets of sweat beaded out on her forehead.

I was amazed at how someone I encountered so often as a thought and in imaginary conversations could suddenly appear as a real person to stand before me, suddenly filling my erstwhile solitary swampscape, as if my thoughts or fears had willed her there.

"Howdy, stranger," she said with a guarded smile.

I raised into a wave the hand that had held The Pirate.

"Are you all right?" she asked.

I nodded, thinking, *Yes, no—I am and am not all right.*

She paddled another stroke and rested the paddle across her lap and held out a hand, to comfort me, I guessed—to show me she was not an apparition. The stroke propelled the canoe too quickly toward my half-submerged legs, so she took up the paddle again and thrust it into the water to stop her progress. The canoe wheeled around. Reaching down to steady it, my hands on the gunwale, I realized it was an actual boat and thought, *Ergo, real Merritt.*

"Hello," I managed to say. "Welcome to Starlight."

She laughed. "Thanks," she said, and smiled, her expression still saying, *I'm here and it pleases me to see you're as surprised as I thought you'd be—maybe more.* She dimmed her eyes and asked, "Was that a snake in your hands, back then?"

I nodded, and seeing her knowing expression, said, "It's a long story."

"I think I may know some of it."

"You probably do."

After I'd gathered myself enough to stammer a better greeting and had helped her tie her canoe next to mine at the rickety, half-sunken dock, where they rested beside each other, red and blue, trailing in the wind at the end of their leads like restless horses—I gave her a tour of the island. After that, we had lemonade and catfish and tomato sandwiches on the front porch of the shack, in front of the four steps leading down to the dock.

As with the last time I'd seen her, in the living room of the old house, I was troubled by a hyperawareness of the in-the-flesh Merritt as opposed to the easier-to-deal-with Merritt of my dreams—the one with whom I interacted subconsciously while I daydreamed or slept.

As we stumbled into our first talk, I noticed that the lines and darkness under her quick, intelligent eyes were more pronounced than the last time I'd seen her, or than I remembered, or than the lines and darkness under the eyes of the Merritt of my dreams. What was going on behind them seemed to have deepened.

"I thought I'd give you a surprise," she said.

"Congratulations."

"I've come a long way. You weren't easy to find," she said.

"I guess I've tried to disappear a little."

She looked around, nodding at the live cypress and black walnut, the blasted, skeleton trees rising from the water like stalagmites. "I guess there are more obscure places you could've run off to."

I nodded, remembering our globe-spinning game in the study of the old house, fingertips landing on Akaba, Pompuraaw, spinning her by her ankles in the yard till the trees blurred and the blood rushed.

"Why do you want to disappear? What from?" she asked.

"I have my reasons," I said. "Plus, I have my research. I give tours for the Park Service."

"What kind of tours?"

"Reptile tours," I said. "Swamp walks."

She nodded, knowingly.

We ate for a time in silence before I asked her, "So, how did you find me? How'd you know to look here?"

"I have my ways," she said and looked at me in the sideways, playful-appraising way I remembered. The look hit its mark; my heart contracted, my head ballooned.

The trace of an idea rippled across her face. She smiled and shook her head: "I didn't want to say this so soon," she said and smiled, looking into the rippling water as if it might help summon or erase whatever it was she didn't want to say so soon but was going to anyway. "For some reason," she said, looking from the water up into my eyes, "I'm so curious about you, Tobia Caldwell. Still. It seems like I should've gotten you out of my system by now. Doesn't it?" She shook her head. "No. You're tucked in there—pretty deep in my psyche, I'm afraid."

And you in mine, I thought.

She looked around, smiled, let her palms point at low-hanging clouds: "What are you doing here? You. Tobia Caldwell, Five Game Gentleman?" It had the right hint of irony, I thought, appropriately deflating the hype of my exhausted fifteen minutes.

"I sometimes ask myself the same question," I said. "And most of the time, believe it or not, I find some answers. And now, I guess I could ask the same question of you."

"Oh," she said, smiling, impish electricity lighting up her hazelgreys, "I'm on a mission," she said. "I've had several moments of doubt and some setbacks on the way, but the woman who rented me the canoe back there was very forthcoming, and ever since I paddled away from the dock, I think things have gone quite well—at least so far."

I smiled. "So the woman at Uncle Kurt's sang like a canary about the loony snake handler out on Starlight."

She chuckled. After another silence, her expression turned suddenly serious: "I'm out to change my life, Tobia."

I didn't know what to say to that.

"Can I stay here, just for a while?"

I nodded.

"I won't take up too much time. And I don't take up much space. I can sleep on the floor," she said.

"All right," I said, "Welcome. Make yourself at home."

Later that night, as she was getting settled into our shared space, she pulled a portion of rolled-up material from her backpack, held it in front of her, above her head, and let it unroll in the Coleman light.

When it had fallen, she was standing behind a piece of material as big as a beach towel, in the center of which a pattern of stitched, interlaced strands formed a multicolored serpent on an off-white background—a serpent biting its own tail.

"I got this for you," she said, looking down at it, at me. "Well, first I got it. Then, when I found out what you were doing and set out to find you, I decided I'd gotten it for you." She handed it to me.

I held it away from myself to better take it in. The serpent's head met its tail where the fangs dug in and urged the viewer's eye to follow the body around again to the tail in an endless cycle. "It's impressive," I said.

"It's an Egyptian uroboros."

I'd heard Henley say the word. I said it myself: "Uroboros," and thanked her again and felt her watching me taking in the serpentine interlace, my eyes caught in its cycle, the multicolored strands bound together, woven into the circular form.

"Word's out on you, TC," she said.

"Word?" I asked, looking up.

"Bradley Sackett told me you're obsessed with snakes—and venom." She gave me a look that suggested she felt sorry for me because of this obsession, that she thought my métier a curse. She seemed to be waiting for me to say something in reply—to deny or accept it, perhaps admit I *was* dangerously obsessed.

"Here," I said and took up the tapestry and opened the shack door and lay the top of the tapestry over the uneven wood and shut it so the tapestry could be seen from inside. "There," I said and looked back at her. "The uroboros is up. It has been hung. Let it remind us of what needs remembering and let it keep away what needs keeping away," I said and, then, for some reason, widened my eyes and flourished my hands in a manner meant to be vaguely Egyptian.

She laughed and appraised me in the Coleman light with her hazel-grey eyes.

———

THAT NIGHT, after I was settled on the floor in a sleeping bag (after insisting several times she take the cot whose spring sounded like the cry of an animal) I asked what manner of life-change she meant to enact by coming to see me on the island.

"I don't know," she said. "I'm still reeling from breaking away from my life, though there wasn't much to break away from. I quit my job and moved out of the apartment I was sharing with Robin Sackett."

I nodded.

"She and I were growing apart, anyway, naturally . . . tending in different directions. She's on the fast track at that bank. And I was . . . I had to get out."

We fell silent for a time.

"Merritt, I'm sorry about what I said in that letter. And that I didn't answer the last couple of letters you wrote. I wanted to say it then, or when you came to see me at the house, but . . . so I'm saying it now."

She waited for a time in silence. "It's okay, now. I think. Whatever I felt back then—I was angry for a while—all of it's distilled into this potent . . . *curiosity*."

"There's nothing all that interesting about me," I said. "Certainly nothing worth traveling all this way, doing whatever it is you had to do—bribing honest canoe rental outfits, for example—to see me," I said and drew a breath for further confession in the dark shack, in the wide open gap of another silence. But before I spoke, it occurred to me that she'd traveled a long way that day, and that her voice had begun to sound sleepy, and that the time wasn't right for a proper telling. I felt I needed to rehearse the words to do it right. I told her goodnight and, feeling shielded and comforted by the prospect of imminent confession, fell asleep more quickly than I'd expected given the discomfiting energy with which she had supercharged the room.

THE NEXT DAY she told me she was curious how I occupied myself on the island. So, on my invitation she shadowed me for the day as I gave the sheep their injections (she suggested we think of names for them) and took blood samples and cared for the delicate rats and mice, and logged results. She also went along on that day's swamp tour, taking up the rear of the group as we waded through cypress. It made me almost debilitatingly self-conscious to see Merritt standing in the water in her khaki shorts behind the rest of the group I had that day—mostly a collection of middle-aged ladies from Mayfield, Kentucky. She watched with bemused irony while I answered questions about bald eagle nests, seasonal migrations of ducks and geese, the eating habits of snapping turtles, the size of catfish. I made sure to avoid her eyes while I debunked a few of the inevitable, apocryphal cottonmouth tales the women brought up.

I faltered slightly, despite Merritt's encouraging expression, as I told my guests the Indian legend of the formation of Reelfoot Lake. How the gimp-footed Chickasaw chief Reelfoot fell in love with a Choctaw maiden named Starlight, who was promised to a Choctaw warrior. How Reelfoot kidnapped her, angering the gods, who stamped the earth so furiously that water from the Mississippi, Father of Waters, rushed into the cavity to bury Reelfoot, Starlight, and the whole Chickasaw tribe.

Later that night, over a dish I called Spicy Crappie Gumbo Surprise, and rice, she said, "Let me tell you what's happened in my life since we were last together. Since the time we visited after you hurt your leg. I'll fill you in from your exit from me to my entrance to you. Okay? Then, it'll be your turn."

I smiled and slowly nodded.

"Okay," she began. "After I graduated from college, I went to Europe with Robin and Bradley Sackett," she said. "And his friend—Eon. He used to go by Elvis Orville Newcomb. But now he wants everyone to call him Eon."

I smiled to hear the name again. "Elvis Newcomb," I said. "I knew him when we were kids. He lived on the outskirts of Haven. One time he came over to the new development behind our house and gave me and Bradley rides out into the country on a little go-cart he'd made."

"I didn't know you knew him," she said. "I think he's brilliant. I'd never met him before I went to Europe with the Sacketts. He's gotten to be very close with Bradley. They got reacquainted at college. Eon showed up in one of his classes. He also ended up being part of the reason why I left to travel on my own."

She stopped talking. Her eyes retreated a level to recover something, then returned again, to see the curiosity in my face. She sighed and continued: "Eon and I got very close, very quickly over there. I admired the way he soaked up everything he saw, aggressively drank it in, with a sort of wide open innocence. I think he was seeing how he could use what he saw to make himself into somebody new. I was the same way. We seemed to want to drink more deeply of Venice than Bradley and Robin, to take it less for granted. I know it's such an awful cliché to say it and we knew we were far from the first people ever to do it—but we were hungry for the experience. We both wanted what we saw there to make us into something other than what we were. The Sacketts helped pay for his trip, and he was always asking Bradley for money, promising he would pay him back, that he would make up for it someday. Anyway, we spent a lot of time together." She trailed off again, as if remembering something in great detail.

"How was it he caused you to leave?" I asked, hoping I wasn't going too far by asking.

"He became too . . . avid, too caught up in . . . me, too quickly," she said and blushed, faintly.

An uncomfortable warmth spread through my chest. I hadn't spoken to Bradley in some time, and I hadn't seen Elvis Newcomb in years. It seemed strange to me that Bradley had reconnected with him. I tried to imagine the boy I'd known so briefly back in Haven and had trouble seeing him outside the pall of go-cart smoke, a dented helmet on his head. I couldn't get that boy to grow up and be with Merritt, in Venice.

"Anyway," she said, "we had fun—all of us did. But, strange as it sounds, the part of the trip I came to love the most were the dangerous situations we ran across—and that I later sought out, on my own. The bombing of a Metro station in Paris was the first one. Just after we'd stepped out into the sunlight and crossed the street, the earth shook. My heart beat in my ears. Whiny French sirens came closer and closer. Gendarmes and firemen sealed off the area. Bloodied people, burned black, filthy with wreckage, were brought up from the cavity, some dead, hanging limp in the rescuers' arms. The media zoomed in. I stood at the edge of the barricade and stared. Transfixed. I was high on it, Tobia. No other way to say it. The excitement of it. The rest of the group had to tug at my arm and practically yell in my ear before I'd go with them.

"Later in the trip, we stopped in a station on the Slovenian border on our way from Venice to Prague. Eon was pressing. He wanted . . . a lot from me. A lot of my time. I was feeling claustrophobic."

I had difficulty seeing him with Merritt in any capacity. A warmth spread through my chest.

"I thought I could hear guns in the distance. Everyone else was asleep. I grabbed my backpack, safety-pinned a note to Robin's collar, and hopped off the train. It was dark and rainy. I waited and jumped on the first train that came along. It was full of French UN soldiers heading to Bosnia. Some of the soldiers offered me cigarettes and tried to hit on me in broken English.

"On the outskirts of Sarajevo I met an American news crew and asked if I could tag along. They asked me if I was their intern. They were very confused, obviously. I lied and told them I was. We moved through the blasted city, ducking from wall to wall. Snipers' guns cracked from hidden perches.

"Finally, the reporter asked me what I was doing there. The intern had gotten notice to them she wasn't coming. 'We've gotta get you outta here,' he said.

"So they did. I spent the rest of the trip missing the total exhilaration I'd felt when I was under fire. When I was in Santorini in a café high up in the white cliffs overlooking the Mediterranean, halfway hoping to find the rest of the crew, I felt detached and guilty, as if I was cheating myself, failing to take a bite out of life. I felt the same way in Nice and Monte Carlo, those drowsy places, on my way back up to Paris for the flight home. I felt numb, only partially present. I floated along through the museums, next to the hypnotic water, craving new disasters, fresh adrenaline fixes that would bring me back to the . . . still-state I experienced when I was in the thick of it."

She shifted her position, and her eyes deepened. She seemed to need the telling regardless of whether or not I was listening.

She sighed before continuing: "Back in the States I moved into an apartment with Robin Sackett. She was mad for a while about how I'd abandoned them over there, but she forgave me. Eon was not upset about it, I found out, so much as intrigued. He said leaving the train at just that moment was an almost perfect act. I took a job as a mortgage broker—just something to make money, while I tried to figure out something better. I worked for a company that basically cheated poor people by making them think we were helping them by consolidating their debts. Maybe we did help them a little, took a load off their minds by simplifying things for them. But it started to feel like we were putting the screws to people who'd already been screwed or had screwed themselves by chasing after something they felt they had to have but didn't need. It lasted about six months.

"One day, I woke up and knew I was finished with that phase. You know what I mean? One day you just know it's over. I had no idea what was next, but I was relieved to have made a decision. I gave notice and went down to visit my parents to tell them the news. Which they took with a mixture of disappointment and hopefulness at a new beginning. They didn't ever see me as a mortgage broker. Thank God.

"I spent three weeks with them in New Orleans, until I got tired of them asking what was wrong, where I went on my long walks, what I planned to do. I didn't tell them I was sometimes wandering the streets in the Magnolia projects where white girls aren't ever supposed to go alone after dark, in search of the thrill I got from placing myself in danger. Striking up conversations to try to see if I could find something that felt real. I spent a lot of time in the French Quarter, drinking coffee, eating beignets and muffulettas, drinking lots of Pimm's, moping, looking for a sign.

"On Ash Wednesday, oddly enough, I got a call from Eon. He and Bradley had come to Mardi Gras to let off steam—to take a break from working on some big computer thing they're developing together. I went and met them for breakfast. Eon talked about everything that had happened in Venice. It was funny how he carried on. He wanted me to come back to Haven and work with them. He went on and on about all the schemes he and Bradley had worked up, how bright the future was with their computers. He said something about taking speech lessons to get rid of his accent so he could wheel and deal with the Silicon Valley crowd. He got an *E* tattooed on one of his hands. Somehow, in the midst of this . . . fugue Eon was creating, Bradley told me, in a by-the-way manner, that you were living here and what you were doing and it set an idea buzzing around in my head. If you'd been doing just about anything else, I don't think I would have been quite so curious. But this—this got me interested. I thought about coming here for weeks. Then, one day, I just packed a bag and set out to find you."

"Did you tell your parents where you were going?"

"I left a note saying I was going to visit a friend for a few weeks. I should call them, so they won't get worried. They still get stony-faced when they hear your name."

I nodded. "And here you are," I said and smiled.

"Here I am." She took a bite of the gumbo, chewed thoughtfully for a time, swallowed, and looked up at me. "Your turn," she said.

"There's no way I can match that," I said. "I'm not sure I want to play."

"After the way I spilled. Not a chance. It's very much your turn, Mr. Five Game Gentleman," she said.

I started talking. About college and football, my early struggles, sitting on the bench, working my way up, what it had been like riding high as the Five Game Gentleman, the Heisman talk, the attention from all those girls. I told her about the injury and how surprised I'd been when she and Robin came to visit. I told her how I'd met Henley by chance and volunteered at the zoo. And how, through a pharmaceuticals company outside Nashville, Henley had helped get me the grant I was working on at Reelfoot.

I answered all her questions very carefully. It occurred to me while I talked it had been a long time since I'd been with someone who was willing to listen like that. By the end of it, the things I'd told her were clearer in my own mind. But, as I talked, the story I hadn't told her began to coil and uncoil as if under dark leaves, in cavernous depths of my chest. Again, I drew a breath to speak, thinking it might be the moment when I would tell her a new version of the story she must have replayed so often herself. "Merritt," I began.

But as soon as I'd said her name, her eyes glazed for a moment so that it seemed as if she'd shut off a major internal receptor. I guessed something in my voice, a glimmer of anticipation on my face, had let her know what was coming. I stopped speaking.

She said, "I need you to help me decide what to do with my life, Tobia Caldwell."

I expelled the air I'd drawn for the telling: "I live in a shack, in a swamp, and work with sheep, rats, mice, snakes, and tourists for a living," I said, "and you're asking me for advice?"

She laughed. "Can I swim with your snakes one of these days?" she asked, hazelgreys asparkle.

"Absolutely not," I said.

"I think it'd be thrilling. Wouldn't it? A real rush. Oh, let me do it!"

I shook my head. "You'll have to get your thrills elsewhere on this island."

"You could save me with your antivenin, right? All you'd have to do is inject me with it, and I'd be safe."

"Let's not put it to the test," I said.

THERE WAS A CHANNEL I knew, to the south of the island. After some winding between dense hummocks, the intrepid canoeist would come to an islet even smaller than Starlight, surrounded by cypress, encased on all sides by moss and vine so dense it had taken me two afternoons to cut a narrow passage through it with a machete. Once I'd opened the passage, further travel revealed a sawgrass meadow on firm ground which, at its lowest places, fell to soggy marshland on the outer sides.

I remembered the place one morning after I'd made my rounds, so we packed a picnic and paddled out to the island. We talked a lot in the beginning as we moved over the water, refinding the rhythm we'd developed during our one, distant summer together. Later, we fell silent except for our breathing and the small splashes and murmurs of the dark water. Sometimes there was a stillness that came over you when you were far back in a channel of the lake like that, a presence-in-silence you felt it would be a sacrilege to disturb.

We pushed our way onto the island and worked through the path I'd cut, wound through the labyrinthine passage until we came to a bank on which we beached the canoe. When we found the highest point, we flattened down some of the grass with an old blanket and corkscrewed the bottom portion of a Y-shaped log into the grass beside it, let some mosquito netting depend from it, and had our picnic underneath.

After we'd eaten, we decided to leave the netting to explore the area. When the sun was higher, the mosquitoes and no-see-ums, born in the ample water all around, found us and moved in for blood. Not wanting to get our clothes muddy and not wanting to turn back to the netting, we fell upon a plan that seems very strange upon reflection but that made sense to us at the time, perhaps because we knew that its ends were from the beginning other than the ones we professed. I don't re- member whose idea it was—it must have been mutual. We undressed, self-consciously at first, until we were entirely naked in front of each other and exposed to the bloodhunger of the insects.

Then we grabbed up heaps of mud from the bog and smeared it over our bare skin. The mutual coating gradually evolved from a genuine- seeming effort to protect ourselves from the insects, to a tentative, breathy exploration that circled into something else.

We kissed, forming a charge in our lips that spread through our bod- ies and seemed to increase the earth's gravitational pull. The mud was wetly viscous between us. In some other places it was already thickly dry and coarse to the touch over skin and muscle. When we started to sweat, it became wet again and clicked with our motion. We fell to our knees; the impact made a squishing sound. Merritt laughed, and I felt the ex- pulsion of her breath on my face—lemonade and something deeper. She turned and crawled away, looking mischievously over her shoulder. Water droplets rose and were run through with sunlight from the impact of her hands and knees and feet in the ooze.

I crawled after her and caught her. We had both been cut and were bleeding from the sawgrass. I could feel her laughter bubbling inside her. My fingers fitted the spaces between her ribs and traced firm circles on her runneled back. Our sweat wet the mud and our bodies became slick and slid easily—chest to back.

"What're we doing," she whispered breathily, head turned back toward me, eyes mostly closed.

Later, my head sunk underwater. My mouth was open in undone animal wonderment. I looked up at the sky, and my hearing came and went with Merritt's rise and fall as my ears submerged in and rose from the ooze, rose and submerged, sending tiny algae into spin. Merritt's silhouette was black against the full-on blaze of noon.

In the hollow, guilty aftermath, when we were patching our sawgrass wounds with more mud under the netting, she said, "I didn't think places like this existed anymore."

"They don't," I said.

"Why do I feel like this with only you?"

I shook my head. "I know what you mean."

"Tobia?"

"Yes."

"Do you ever think about Ben?"

My skin tingled under the coating of mud and sweat. "He's grown up with me. I used to stare at people on the street who conformed to my image of what the grown-up Ben might look like. And I sometimes see him in dreams." I thought of the cottonmouth crawling in, finding me some nights to whisper of Ben's return.

"I see him in you," she said. "I feel his presence when I'm with you. You were there, no one else was. No one else knows. It's hard to lose a twin, like losing a part of yourself. You walk around unbalanced. Go in circles like a boat with one oar."

We sat for a time in silence, the un-aired story coiling, uncoiling in the ooze in my chest, under dark, rotting leaves. I only needed to find a beginning.

"Do you know the story of Orpheus?" she asked.

"Remind me," I said, my own snakebite story preparing itself in me.

"Orpheus is a musician whose music is so incredible it charms the rocks and trees. He marries a wood nymph named Eurydice. But, not long after they're married, she's bitten by a poisonous asp and goes to the underworld. Orpheus is beside himself with grief. He can't live without her. He figures out how to travel to Hades to get her back—he actually travels to the underworld to find her. The ruler of the underworld is so surprised Orpheus has come for Eurydice—he's so impressed—that he lets him take her back up. But, there's a catch, as there always is in these myths. If he looks back at all, even once, on the way out of the underworld, he'll lose her forever. Right when they're almost out of Hades, he looks back, and Eurydice vanishes.

"After that Orpheus gives up human company. In the end he's torn to shreds by Dionysian furies. That story's stuck with me because of Ben, I think. I guess the lesson is that we should get over his death, travel to the underworld and deal with the darkness once and for all, recover what we can of him, then never look back again or we'll lose him as he was alive by losing our own lives to his death. I think sometimes, it seems like all of us—my parents, me, and, it sounds like, you, too—can't help looking back."

"How can you tell when you've dealt with everything, once and for all?" I asked.

She stared into one then the other of my eyes, as if trying to see some part of Ben, a trace of my having known him.

"There's something I . . . ," I said and started to say more, but she stopped me with a kiss and said, "Let's take a swim and get rid of this muck."

We swam over the submerged trees and stumps, above the bones of my paternal grandparents, still wrapped in the memory of Ben and the presence of the coiling, uncoiling story I hadn't told, brushing mud from our bodies with odd strokes until we were mostly cleansed.

At night, over the next couple of weeks, we would lie naked on the cot, sometimes intertwined and enjoying the close communion of skin, often not, to keep cooler. I'd lie awake and listen to her enigmatic snores rise and fall and mysteriously cease and wonder what she was dreaming. Sometimes she spoke in a soft and wonderful gibberish I thought I might one day be able to translate.

One night Merritt eased closer to me in bed and I felt her warmth and the sharp prickle of the stubble on her legs and realized, with a heartsink, that I wasn't feeling the usual stirrings in the usual places. It was a hot night, and she was very close. A claustrophobia constricted my chest. A jolt of hot fear ran its course from heart to head. What was wrong? What did this mean? Was it over so soon?

I decided I needed a walk, rolled away from her, and let myself fall to the floor. She stirred, but seemed not to awaken. I stood and walked out the door and onto the dock, the constriction still at work in my chest, making me feel as if I wasn't getting enough oxygen with each breath. Moonlight was riding the surface of the water. An image of Ben Wilson running through the creek came to me as clearly as if I had been there again at stream edge in my seventh summer and watching it for the first time instead of the thousandth, his hair wafting in the eelgrass. There were debts to pay. *Debts to pay debts to pay debts to pay* susurrated over my dendrites. I shot my hands through my hair and took a series of deep breaths to try to restore myself.

You knew this would come, I told myself, this reckoning, and looked up at the moon and followed its light across the uneven floor of the shack.

Merritt was sitting up in the bed, looking out at me. "What's wrong?" she called.

I took a breath and shook my head. "Nothing."

"Come back come back, TC, TC," she sang.

I drew a deep breath, swallowed, went inside, and sat down on the cot. She reached up and ran her hand from my cheek down my neck and across my ribs. "You sure you're okay?" She kneeled on the bed, twisted around me to look into my eyes.

I nodded. "Just having trouble sleeping." I flattened out on the bed, very carefully, and she shifted to give me room. I looked up at the mismatched slats and through a hole at clouds in motion over Venus.

I slept for a time and dreamed I'd been swallowed and was surrounded by an oozy warmth that muscled me down into a greater, more viscous warmth, some ultimate intima where I would encounter a beak, and a bite—a slow and deadly venom. I sat up in bed, pouring sweat, gasped, and looked around the room in the hope that my gaze would alight on an object that could steady me.

Merritt startled me when she spoke: "What's wrong?"

"A dream."

"What about?"

"I don't know."

"Was I in it?"

"Not really."

"Then I was."

I shook my head and let it rest in my hand. "There's something always there, always in the way of this," I mumbled.

"You mean us?"

I nodded. "It won't go away unless I— But . . ."

She stayed silent.

When I found her eyes, they were glazed, as if against hearing any further confession. "Merritt, I'm afraid I wronged you," I said and looked at her and held her gaze.

She nodded, slowly, her eyes moving back and forth very slightly as if searching internally for an expected ambush.

"I wronged you before I knew you."

She sat up, brought one thin-wristed hand to her chin, and mouthed a word, without giving the word her voice, that looked like "Ben."

I stood out of bed and paced what little floor there was to pace, working up my courage and planning, yet again, how to accomplish the delicate task of telling her everything, while avoiding her disappointment and possible rage. But the more I turned it over in my mind, the more my telling her anything at all began to seem an impossibility. Any admission about the silver dollar seemed inaccessible given where Merritt and I had arrived. I convinced myself, in that pacing moment, if I told her anything, the sanctuary we'd built would explode, and the fallout would do more damage to both of us than the airing was worth. And yet even after I'd predicted the damage and decided against the telling, the cathartic prospect of confession reasserted itself to keep me pacing.

"You look crazed," she said. "You're scaring me, Tobia."

I released the air in my lungs and brought my hand up to cover my eyes and massage my temples. "Merritt," I said as evenly as I could, "back in Haven when you and—"

"No," she said and stood in front of me and took up my wrists in her fingers to stop my pacing. "Don't say anything else."

"It was hot that day, and you and Ben and your mother came over to the old house and—"

"I love you," she said and held my gaze till I looked away.

"Merritt," I said, slowly shaking my head, "wait. I think this is something—"

"No. It's okay. Please." She looked from one to the other of my eyes.

"I need to tell—"

"Please," she said.

"Especially since—"

She dropped my left hand and brought the fingers of her right hand to my lips. The nails of the middle and index fingers of her left hand pressed almost imperceptibly into the veins of my right inner wrist, as if she meant to take my pulse.

I collapsed onto the cot, the room seeming to wheel and loom. I heard her leave the shack for the dock and, after a time, heard her come back and sit beside me. She let her hands slowly trickle through my hair, saying, "Shh, shh. Sleep, TC, TC. Sleep and nothing. Just sleep."

———

THE NEXT MORNING, after I'd returned from extracting blood from the sheep, Merritt Wilson was gone, the only trace of her visit the uroboros hanging on the door, a note safety-pinned beside the ever-circling serpent:

T,

 Have to go and find my way now. On my own. Painful as it is to leave. Hope you understand. I think you will. Good luck with all you're doing. Someday . . . who knows?

Love,

M.

I stepped onto the dock, hoping to see another trace of her, even a fleeting one—the canoe on the water, a glimpse of color through cypress branches—but the lake was empty. And the island seemed suddenly so heavy with her absence, and the weight of the story I hadn't been able to tell had attained such a mass, a dying star mass—coiling, uncoiling under dark leaves in my chest—that I thought I might sink, along with all traces of the island, beneath Reelfoot.

SIXTEEN

I STAYED AT REELFOOT through Thanksgiving and Christmas and on into spring without once going back to visit the old house. I was so wrapped up in my work and in Merritt, and, after she'd left, in the contemplation of her absence, that I only sent home a few cards and notes with the most cursory of messages and no return address.

One day that spring I heard the motor of a boat approach the shack, fall silent, footsteps on the dock, knocking at the door, which I opened to reveal my father. Sweat streaked his brow and soaked his white polo shirt, which clung to his new, hungry-looking frame. His eyes shone cloudy blue in the sunlight, and his old, stained Sweet Hollow Country Club golf hat perched atop his head, a few strands of hair bunched darkly together across his freckled, sunburned forehead. He looked strangely ecstatic and vaguely troubled.

"Dad!" I said, genuinely surprised to see him. This was not something I thought he would ever do.

He nodded, unsmiling, looking faintly troubled: "Hello, T. You weren't kidding when you said you're working at Reelfoot. *In it's* more like it." He looked around us at the cypress jutting out of the lake.

Behind him, Chock, our family's and Fenton's old hunting and fishing guide from the time before the deaths of my grandparents, held a bassboat to the dock with a ropy brown forearm, his face hidden beneath the low brim of a baseball cap. I'd heard scores of stories about hunting and fishing trips with "good old Chockee." I knew that he was part Choctaw and had always wondered if that was his real name or one that had been given him by his clients. I hadn't seen him in twenty years. For a moment I thought a fishing trip was in the offing.

"I came to get you," my father said, preoccupied for a moment by the uroboros on the inside of the shack door.

"Well," I said. "Listen, Dad, I'm sorry I haven't been home in so long. I . . . Well, you made it here. Welcome." I stood out of the doorway and gestured him inside.

He stayed where he was. "Come on," he said, "I'll buy you a steak in Union City."

"Why don't we eat here? Since you've come all this way? I should have some catfish on the trot lines," I said, "and I'm teaching myself to make bread in the earth oven in the yard." I was surprised, as always, at the degree to which I wanted to prove myself to him, to show him my self-sufficiency, that I was making it. "Besides," I said, "it'd take us till late tonight to get there."

He looked troubled a moment, as if he was thinking hard to discover the passage that would help him escape a dead end in a maze. It was so surprising to see him standing on the cypress floorboards of my shack— this man, my dad.

"I would have called if you had a phone, Tobia, and I would have let you know sooner but . . . ," he said and gestured as if to say, *Look at where the hell you're living.* He took a breath and fixed me with the puzzled-looking, older, sadder version of the cool blue eyes he'd given me. "Your mother had a stroke, not long after you left," he said and watched it hit me. "Not too bad, but it's . . . scrambled things up. She can't walk. And the part of her brain in charge of speech has . . . suffered a blow, so if she did try, it would come out all jumbled up. And"—he paused—"she and I won't be living together anymore. I may as well tell you right here and now—I was guilty of an indiscretion."

The news rendered me speechless for a few moments. I looked down at Chock, holding the boat to the cypress boards, back up at my father. I shook my head. Things seemed suddenly blurry. "By 'indiscretion' you mean you had an affair?"

He sighed and looked down at my feet, then up past my eyes, just above my head, toward the roof of the shack and shut his eyes: "I love your mother, T. I'll explain when we're in a more appropriate place. I've come here to bring you back to see her," he said. "It would mean a great deal to her. And to me."

After I'd packed a bag, shut some things up, gathered the moth and butterfly samples I'd been collecting and identifying for my mother, and made a list in my head of all that needed to be done to keep the research running while I was away, I stepped into the boat in front of my father.

"You remember Chockee?" my father said as he also stepped into the boat and pushed us off. I nodded, and Chock smiled tight and briefly and nodded in my general direction and said, "Shore," then fixed his black eyes on the nearest channel through the cypress and black walnut, pulled the Evinrude started, backed us up, then motored us across the lake.

The wind pushed back my hair, and a sunset bled red and orange all over the rippled water and clotted up in the clouds and against the branches and moss in the trees. A flock of nesting double-breasted cormorants, a relatively rare sight at the lake, lifted from a hundred-foot cypress they had formerly filled, one level of branches at a time, and flew alongside us as we passed, the remnants of the bleeding sun on their flexing wings, and I thought about how much Mother would have loved seeing it, how later her voice would have risen and fallen to do it justice. I looked over at my father's distant, worried expression—the puzzled look that had taken up residence on his face, his eyes seeming to say, *Where's the way out?* He held the Sweet Hollow hat to his head with one of his wiry hands, and with the other produced a flask from a pocket of his khakis, took a gulp, and gazed off into the distance beyond the line of trees at lake edge.

My father handed Chock some cash at the take-out point at Uncle Kurt's, which was also where I'd left my car, and we caravanned back to Haven to see her. I drove the station wagon behind the immortal silver Mercedes trying to imagine the stroke as I drove.

The taillights of my father's car glowed in front of me on the highway. We were going to drive straight through, back to Haven. I thought about my father with a younger woman in the old house, his conquest, temporary slaker of desire, quick meal of skin and flesh. I wondered if she was my age or younger and tried to imagine what she looked like. I thought she must be someone impressed by the old mansion, someone who bragged to her friends about having snagged her very own big-shot, old-school lawyer. Perhaps because of his contrition and my first-hand knowledge of male desire, there was a part of me that understood him and wanted to forgive him, but not yet. It would take more time.

As we drove, I grew angry, not so much because of what he'd done as at his hypocrisy. After all his talk about honor and family, here, he'd hopped in the sack with this girl, whoever she was, as soon as my mother was incapacitated. Maybe their rift had started before the stroke and the affair after, but I wondered as I drove—was that an excuse?

I gave in to a sudden compulsion to pass him and stepped down on the gas. I wanted to blow by him and leave him far behind, to beat him back to Haven and see my mother at Aunt Marcy's and not speak to him again until I wasn't angry at him anymore. I had no idea how long that might take.

When I tried to pass him on that dark stretch of 78 near Bogota, he surprised me by swerving abruptly to block me. My headlights lit his angry, frightened face looking over his shoulder. I cursed him and swerved onto the shoulder and pressed down on the brake. On the second attempt, I surprised him—he'd thought I would stay behind, I suppose—and I did get past him. I stepped down on the accelerator. There was nothing but empty highway in front of me so that it seemed that the only people in the world were a father left behind, a son with an indeterminate future, an ailing mother at road's end. Speeding along, I thought it was possible I would never talk to him again. I kept the pedal down and watched his headlights fade.

Early that morning I wound up the driveway of our old house. I would have gone to see her right away if it hadn't been so late. I knew there would be a key under a stone at the old pump, and there was. I let myself into the house, smelled that old smell. It felt odd when she wasn't there to greet me. The house seemed too dark and quiet, whispery, not in the way it had always been, but in a quieter, more menacing way. The house was messier and dirtier than it had been when she was there. Dust had settled onto all the furniture and flat surfaces. The sink was filled with dishes, and the counters were lined with empty beer and whiskey bottles. This came to me: *Without her, the house is a body with no heart.* Just when I was about to drift into sleep, I heard my father coming into the house, and soon after I fell asleep.

The next morning, after a restless sleep with troubled dreams, and without telling Father I was going, I drove over to Aunt Marcy's. My mother was still asleep and when I went down the back hallway to see her, Marcy stood in the bedroom doorway and assured me, with a smile and a little wave, that it would be all right if I awakened her.

I walked into her bedroom, reached down, and shook my mother gently, once, by the shoulder. I was surprised at how thin she was, her shoulder nearly all bone.

It took her a second to register who I was, but once she did—I could see the recognition filter into her features—she smiled, then started to shake and cry. She looked into my eyes and with them said, *Hello, Tobia! Can you believe this? Shame on you for not coming home a whole lot sooner when I'm like this.* She clung to my arm and smiled up through tears and shook my forearm, clutched with a firm grip, her nails biting into my skin.

"He doesn't mean it," I said. "He still loves you."

I produced from my backpack some of the butterfly and moth samples I'd collected on the island and pressed into Ziploc bags, the Latin names on pieces of tape affixed to each bag.

She trembled slightly and looked up at me—her solid grey eyes tearing up—as I flipped through the lepidopteran samples. She even seemed pleased with the moths. I read off the Latin names as I showed her each one, remembering how she loved the difficult, magical names, their dusty, arcane grandeur and remembering, too—perhaps appreciating for the first time—how beautiful her recently stolen voice had been in reading them to me when I'd been much younger and had not recognized how much it was worth to me to hear her voice and feel beloved.

I felt a wave of emotion rise in me. I looked away from her and shook my head—shook it off. She didn't need to see me break down. I was aware that everything was changed between us. The stroke had reversed our roles. It had been occurring to me, lately, down in the swamp, even before I knew about the stroke, that I'd already been two years old by the time she was my age. We had come to that overlap, and looking down at her, childless myself, this seemed significant.

Before I left the house, Aunt Marcy whispered to me about her condition in the kitchen over cups of coffee, and told me, for the first time, the details of what had happened. After I'd heard, I began to see it happen, and to replay it in my mind, as if it were happening to me.

My mother returned from a trip she took with friends to Aix-en-Provence, a trip Aunt Marcy helped her afford. By all accounts this trip rejuvenated her and looked as though it might be a turning point in her life. Upon her return, she walked more often and farther, spent more time in her garden.

She went out the back door in the late morning. She'd just had a bowl of high-fiber cereal with banana slices and a tall glass of orange juice. She was going to pull weeds for a few hours before the noon-to-two heat. On her way to the garden, she stopped to take in a great gulp of the already thick morning air.

On her hands and knees she pulled weeds from the dirt that had come in to compete with her tomato plants. She stood occasionally to stretch her neck and back. The dirt was moist and fell easily from the roots after she got a good grip on the plant and lifted. She worked for some time, till there was dirt on her gloves. She mopped sweat from her brow with the backs of her hands and arms.

My father called from the house. There was a phone call for her. One of the women from the Aix-en-Provence trip had had her pictures developed and wanted my mother to come over and see them.

My mother rose to her knees, stood. There was a slight dizziness—she was reminded of a faint queasiness that washed over her briefly the day before—then something else, an intense pressure. Sunlight shot through the gaps in the leaves of the trees. An overwhelming dizziness. She must have seen a single green tomato leaf, a blur of sky and tree and then only dirt. Her cheek came to rest on firm, moist clods of earth. She tried to make a noise, tried to shout, but it was unclear whether or not anything issued forth.

Aunt Marcy said, "Your mother can learn to speak again, it's possible. She has a year-and-a-half window to recover as much as she can. The doctors and the therapists have all said that her ability to join her abstract thoughts with concrete expression has not been completely lost. She's all there inside, Tobia. Maybe more sharply now than ever. We've got to remember that. She understands everything we say to her."

For the time being, though, her vanity wouldn't suffer it. I remembered how her voice had always been so smooth, deep, strong, expressive in a lilting way that made anything she had to say a pleasure to listen to—even if she was intruding uninvited into your life. Now, she preferred the relative aesthetics of silence to spending the remainder of her life struggling to achieve what had always been so effortless. But it was taking its toll and would continue to; she seemed depressed, and Marcy described times when she would depart from herself, her gone times.

She had Broca's aphasia. A sudden lack of blood flow to a certain area of the left hemisphere of her brain had resulted in the death of neurons. The doctor had used a plastic brain to explain it to my father, Marcy, and my mother. The Broca's area was here, he'd said, pointing to the plastic brain to indicate the area where the precious cells had been destroyed. "It lies," he said, "in the third frontal convolution just anterior to the face of the motor cortex and just above the sylvan fissure. This is the motor and speech center of the brain." And Marcy and my father stood looking at the plastic brain, nodding and stunned at how delicate and strange a piece of equipment it had been revealed to be in their wife and sister.

When she woke up in the hospital room, she looked up at Aunt Marcy and my father and tried to speak, but only managed to make small grunts and chirps.

Later, she managed to say real words, which were not the words she meant to say. She would gesture with her eyes at a spoon and say, "Airplane." Aunt Marcy told me that during the beginning of this phase my father pretended my mother was making sense even though she herself knew she wasn't. Aunt Marcy said you could see the strain on his face as he leaned in over her and nodded, as if in understanding, at the nonsensical words she produced. Finally, even he admitted he didn't understand. He shook his head, while she sat in bed frustrated, bewildered, and fuming.

Her insurance covered the services of a speech therapist and a pre-scription for a relatively new drug called dextroamphetamine that was meant to excite her stricken neurons back into hyper-synaptic action, but she refused to let some stranger come into her bedroom to hear, an-alyze, and coach her rocky first attempts at speech. After a few weeks, by the time I came to visit her, she had stopped taking the medications as well.

I wasn't able to stay long. I didn't see my father the morning I left, but he left a note and some letters that had come for me. The note tried once again to convince me to stay and prepare for law school. I hadn't been able to talk with him the whole time I'd been back, though I'd wanted to before I left. I wanted to convince him that he ought to keep trying to see Mother. He was so busy using old connections to build himself a new life then, I doubt anything I might have said would have had any effect. It was a singular and indisputable sign that he did still care about her, though, that he had journeyed to find me at Reelfoot. I would always remember my surprise when I opened the door to my shack and saw my father.

I drove over to Aunt Marcy's before I left and told my mother I had to go despite her wordless, but nonetheless eloquent, case against my leaving, which she made with small shakes of her head and tiny move-ments of her eyebrows and the corner of her mouth.

SEVENTEEN

WITH OUR RECLAMATION party fast approaching, my father has given me a dual mission: I am to convince my mother to attend the party as our special guest of honor (though he has not told me what, exactly, this title means), and, to make sure she opens the gifts he's been sending her.

"If you can't convince her to open them herself," he tells me when I'm about to leave the old house to drive over to Aunt Marcy's, "I want you to open them in front of her. They need to be opened sometime this week or . . . they may die," he says.

"What may die?" I ask.

"You'll see. Just make sure they get opened today."

With mission in mind, I drive over to Aunt Marcy's, stopping at the bottom of the driveway to check the mailbox in which rests a second letter from Merritt Wilson:

T,

Today, I watched a group of lepers race down a dirt road. One of the missionaries thought it would be therapeutic for them. They resisted at first, complaining of their missing toes, ulcerated feet, but he persisted until he'd convinced many of them to give it a shot. After someone said "go," they shambled awkwardly toward the ribbon, moving as best they could, kicking a cloud of dust into the air, shouting and laughing.

On vacation from Angola and what do I do? Go to Brindizi and from there get a photographer friend to take me to Albania. There, the country's in ruin. Anybody who can is getting out on anything that floats. We'd seen the crowded boats of refugees in Brindizi. There was rioting in the streets after the collapse of the pyramid schemes. Gunshots at night. My friend had some friends over there who harbored us and told us we were crazy to have come when all other foreign nationals were being evacuated.

But, strange, I was strangely entranced by the madness of it, Tobia. It wasn't so much an adrenaline rush as a pleasurable frozenness that I let wash over me. A stillness that made me forget myself and the passage of time. To the people streaming by, I was invisible, wrapped up in a black shawl. I let them stream by, some of them rioting, looting, trying by any means necessary to get a boat out of there.

I wanted to give you a hint of what the Merritt you'll be seeing has been seeing.

M.

The traffic is light this afternoon so it's only about ten minutes of cruising under traffic lights—my mind filled with images of laughing lepers and rioting Albanians—before I'm pulling into Aunt Marcy's driveway. I step out of the car and stand firm for the inevitable onslaught of cats and dogs. Marcy has accumulated here what must be some of the friendliest animals in the state of Tennessee.

Walking to the house, I'm surprised to see that the greenhouse has been completed since my last visit. It's even full of flowers. Splashes of red, violet, pink, and green blur through the condensation on the windows. The greenhouse is unusual for its oval shape. I've never seen one quite like it. My father still hasn't told me anything about it, and I haven't asked him. All the window panels are clear except for one of stained glass set at a forty-five-degree angle above the door—a translucent red-bodied butterfly with royal blue wings dotted with mantis-green polka dots. It looks like it's about to fly away.

With a pack of dogs and cats following me, almost knocking me down in their playful exuberance, I walk to the greenhouse, open the door, and step inside. The warmth and humidity, the stillness, contrasts sharply with the blustery cool March day outside. It smells like wet mulch and spearmint. I look up at the sunlight coming through the blue, red, and green of the butterfly and think of my father wandering through an antique store, looking for the perfect thing to win back his wife.

Standing in the greenhouse, imagining my father actively engaged in winning back my mother, I remember seeing him when I returned to the old house from Reelfoot, my detailed notes and a few vials of the finished antivenin on ice in a cooler.

As I wound up the driveway, I saw that a profusion of tall, tenacious-looking weeds had overtaken the lawn, giving the impression their assault on the property had only just begun. The exterior of the old house hadn't been painted since sometime in my infancy, probably since before Thomas and Pearl had moved out and we'd moved in. Strips of paint had peeled away from the facade, revealing various grey and off-white strata. Little brown mushrooms were growing out of the kitchen wallpaper.

I called out for my father and heard no answer.

I found him seated at the dining room table, wearing an old magenta robe. I could smell the liquor on his breath at ten paces. His hair was mussed, and he was mumbling to himself, oblivious to my presence for some time, over a mess—paperwork, books, bills, notebooks, stray loose-leaf pages, dishes, silverware, glasses, and liquor bottles in various states of depletion—that completely covered the table.

"Dad?"

He turned, slowly, toward the French doorframe in which I stood. When he saw me, he laughed till his body shook.

"You aren't working?" I asked.

"Son," he said, "there are certain kinds of people who are worthy of leisure," he said with a flourish of his arms and released a violent volley of laughter. "I've actually been using my time to write my memoirs. I have been setting down for posterity the history of our esteemed family. Much as your great-grandfather Gabriel did, but I think I've discovered some new insights. See?" He held up a notebook filled with his artful script.

"What happened to Tonorah?" I asked him.

"Had to let her go. Can't afford such luxuries," he said and laughed till he was coughing. He rummaged through the pile in front of him and located a stack of bills thick as a phone book held together with a rubber band. He held up the stack and shook them over his head. "Bills," he said. "I've sold everything to the developers but the five acres immediately surrounding the Graand Oold Caaldwell Place. And still these bills. Mortgaged the son of a bitch, and still these bills, bills, bills."

"Seems to me you're proving how much you need Mother," I said, stepping forward to take the stack of bills from his hand, thumbing through, shaking my head.

"A woman is rarely as good for a man as she is brought up by this society to *think* she is," he said with another flourish and looked at me with wild eyes.

"Well, when you're sober I'd like to discuss getting a patent for the antivenin I've developed with Henley Dempster. I hope you'll help us."

He threw back his head and laughed. "Tobia, my son, erstwhile football star cum great snake charmer, home from the swamp and seeking legal advice from good old Dad."

I helped him up the stairs and into his bed and left a large glass of ice-water on the nightstand. Before I left to unpack the car, he grabbed my sleeve. "Promise you'll forget seeing me like this," he said.

I looked into his heavy, sad eyes and nodded.

"Good to see you, T. Welcome home," he said. "Tomorrow . . ."

"Sleep it off," I said.

The next morning, before he was up, I found and let the lawn drink every drop of liquor I could find and padlocked the wine in the cellar. I gathered the dishes scattered through the rooms of the house and washed them and arranged the cluttered papers into neat piles. I vacuumed, dusted, mopped, and did loads of laundry.

I leave the warmth and the remembrance that has frozen me for a time inside the greenhouse and walk back into the cool air and wind and over to Aunt Marcy's house with the animals clamoring for my attention. I stop to pet some of them and watch others get excited and jealous.

Marcy is standing in the foyer in jeans and a white blouse. She's had her auburn hair cropped short and is wearing owlish glasses with blue translucent frames. A smile comes easily to her benign face. Cats swirl around her, some of them looking up to her for a treat or as if to see how they're meant to act toward this familiar visitor. They rub themselves against her calves; a few dogs sit and stand by—lolling, wagging, panting, offering their paws for shaking.

"I believe she's reading," Marcy says.

The loud whining of a vacuum suffuses the house. When I look into the living room, I see Tonorah, humming and pushing the source of the sound over a floral rug under a clear-topped coffee table with magazines— *Southern Living, Architectural Digest, Smithsonian*—spread across the top.

"Go right on back, Tobia. She'll be excited to see you today—a special surprise," Marcy says and smiles.

"Yes, ma'am. Thanks," I say, walking toward the back hallway. I stop and turn. "What do you think of the greenhouse?" I ask.

She pauses before answering, which makes me think she's considering my closeness to my father and how I might feel if she says something derogatory. "It's actually lovely," she says. "Makes me wonder what he's up to, though, I must say."

"He wants her back. There's no secret; that's what he's up to."

"Yes. Well . . . ," she says.

I pass a few slinking cats en route down the dark hallway. My mother's room has a southern exposure and is well lit. A small portion of light has leaked onto the Persian rug outside her door. Just when I'm about to turn the knob, I hear a strange sound, a foreign voice, that freezes my hand.

"Heee. Lll. Oooh. Hhh. Elll. Oooh. Hh. Eell. Oh."

I stand outside, listening for a time before I knock, then wait to give her time to compose herself before opening the door. When I enter her room she sees me, recognizes who it is, and turns her face shyly, girlishly, away. She looks mischievous. Her face is flushed in the light streaming in from the window. Her skin is smooth, thin-looking, and pale in a healthy way, slightly translucent. She sits up straight in her wheelchair.

"Hello," I say and wait for a time, just in case. "How you feeling today?"

She smiles with her eyes, a slight narrowing to release a sparkle. I walk to her and kiss the top of her head, her soft hair that smells like lilacs.

"You know about our party?"

She manages a small, suspicious nod.

"Did you get the invitation?"

She nods again and turns her head to regard me skeptically out of the corners of her eyes. I see our open invitation on her nightstand next to a copy of *The Complete Collected Short Stories of Flannery O'Connor.*

"Are you planning to come? We'd like for you to be there. Father said to remind you—a lot of the old November Ball crowd will be there. It would mean the world to both of us if you would come. You could see some of your old friends. And . . ."

I watch her eyes cloud and glaze. She would rather this visit have been spontaneous, that its inspiration had been the prospect of spending time with her, than have anything to do with my father. She doesn't like the sullying agenda she's sniffed behind this. She looks out the window where the leaves of a maple are shaking in the breeze, a brindled tabby perched in the fork between bough and lowest limb, looking up, with wide desirous eyes, at some nervous grackles in the upper branches. A few dogs run by. I can see my mother slowly departing from herself, can see her fade till she's gone, right before my eyes.

"You'd be our guest of honor, of course. The grand and graceful charming and tasteful belle of the ball. Just like the old days. You're still the soul of that house, you know. And . . ."

She remains still, her attention fixed on the tree outside, the cat calculating his chances of having one of the grackles for lunch. Or, maybe my mother's eyes are fixed on something far beyond the tree, a faraway place where loss is better contemplated.

"Well," I say. "At least think about it."

We sit for a long time in the silence of her gone-ness while I try to think what it's like for her now, what words from me might speed her recovery, how I heard her trying to speak, how to segue to the next portion of my mission here today.

"Father," I say and pause, regretting having mentioned him again, "wanted me to ask you if you'd open some of his gifts today. He's given me the impression that some, or all, of them require attention. That they're perishable."

She doesn't say anything, keeps staring, giving no indication whether or not she's heard me.

"Would you mind if I opened them for you, then? Right here where you can see." It seems to me that she gives her head the slightest of shakes, no. No, I don't mind or no, don't do it? It's difficult to tell. I wonder for a time before deciding it was the former.

I place my hand on her shoulder and squeeze, lightly, and walk into the closet and see the gifts that have piled up in it, unopened where she's left them. It's a large walk-in closet. Some of the gifts are stacked in the corner, others occupy space on the uppermost shelf. Looking at them, in their colorful wrapping, it occurs to me how stubborn both of my parents are: my father doggedly sending these packages when he's long known about their non-reception here; my mother continuing to refuse to open them because they've come and keep coming from *him,* but, nevertheless leaving them here instead of throwing them away, tossing them in the fire.

My father's gift-giving campaign has been going on for about twenty-five weeks, and there are at least as many of the perfectly wrapped packages stacked in the closet. I move them out of the closet to the bedroom and set them down in front of my mother, who shows no signs of noticing what I'm doing. None of the gifts are very heavy; it almost seems possible the paper and ribbons are disguising nothing but empty boxes. It occurs to me, again, how interesting it is that my mother hasn't thrown these gifts away. It's almost as if she's waiting for something, biding her time. It takes four trips to stack them in front of her. I wonder, also, how much my willingness to open these gifts is a function of my own curiosity about them.

"I'm going to open these now," I say. "Do you want to help me?"

She remains departed.

"All right. I'm going to start now. Okay? Here I go. All right." I look up at her.

She remains still and fixed in a rapt and expressionless contemplation of some beyond-the-tree place, grappling with loss there.

I unwrap the first package, marveling, as I do so, once again, at my father's meticulous wrapping job. Maybe he should have been a surgeon, a sculptor, someone who makes a living with his hands. With the ribbons and wrapping off, I come to a cardboard box. I lift its top.

Facing me on the top of the box is a pamphlet that says: WE WELCOME NEW BUTTERFLY MOTHER OR FATHER TO WONDERFUL HAPPY BUTTERFLY WORLD!!! HERE ARE EASY FOLLOWING FUN HAPPY BUTTERFLY INSTRUCTION. Underneath this there is a black-and-white depiction of a large butterfly lit on a tiger lily. In the package itself under the piece of paper are several plastic containers with holes punched in their tops, each one containing wiggly white larvae. Good, I think, at least these are still alive. I lift out one of the containers and hold it up for my mother to see. She looks down and scowls at the contents. *What the hell is that— mealy worms, he got me mealy worms!?* her withering look seems to say. *I should have known that fool would send me something like this.* Perhaps she expected jewelry. There is evidence of indignation despite her former pretended disinterest.

When I say, "Butterflies. They'll . . . become butterflies," her look softens immediately. It says, *Oh, well, that's different.* Then, with a furrowed brow and a sigh, her expression changes to pensive consternation, her eyes take on new depths. At least she's returned to the room, I think.

Fenton and I were right on the money about what was in these packages. Once they're all opened and spread out on the floor in front of us, the packages are revealed to contain, in larva form, twenty-five different species of butterfly and moth from around the world. There are painted ladies, monarchs, spring azures, swallowtails, Gulf fritillaries, clouded sulfurs, black and tiger swallowtails from North America, emerald moths from Peru, sunset moths from Madagascar, blue morphos from Brazil, purple jays from New Guinea, lacewings from the Philippines, giant

Atlas moths and "Neros" (apparently named for the Roman emperor because of their fiery color) from Malaysia, the nocturnal Eversmannia Exornata from Siberia, malachites from Costa Rica, green commas from Nova Scotia among others. Each has come with its own instructions for how the larvae are to be fed, how the material for the cocoons (twigs and leaves) is to be introduced into their environment, the details of their life cycles, what they will look like before they fly away. My mother has several of these species etherized and dead, pinned to the felt backing of her collection cases, but she's never dealt with live ones.

The instructions for the care of these butterflies are not necessarily difficult taken by themselves, but with so many species it occurs to me that it will take some doing and quite a lot of time to see them through to when they'll crawl out of the chrysalis and wait for their wings to dry before fluttering themselves, shakily at first, into the air. According to the instructions some larvae prefer potatoes, others nettles, still others guava nectar, Japanese hops, fennel, heather. I shake my head at how, in his dream for how perfect and beautiful this gift would be, my father seems to have overlooked the work necessary to see it completed properly. Some of the more exotic tropical species will require the atmosphere of the greenhouse, and some rare species of flower, to survive their brief lives.

Or, maybe my father knew what he was doing. Maybe he did some thinking about how raising these butterflies would be good for the stubborn convalescent he knew his wife to be.

The gifts do seem to have surprised her. She's fully returned to the room, now. In her stilted way she indicates the instructions and descriptions on top of each opened package and asks by pointing if she can see this one, now, that one. After looking at each one she shakes her head slightly. Some tears begin to roll down her cheeks. And then after she's seen most of the descriptions of the butterflies, she retreats again into her contemplation of the yard. I suddenly feel I've been with her in the room for hours.

"We need to figure out how we're going to raise these things, I suppose," I say, shaking my head. "Now that you have them, we can't just let them die, can we? I'll take them down and show Aunt Marcy." I make four trips to the kitchen with the packages and set them on the kitchen counter and table before I go back to my mother's room to say goodbye.

"I love you," I tell her. There have only been a handful of times I've said this to her, almost always after she's said it first, so this is different.

She doesn't stir. This surprises me, scares me. She stays still and staring far away. I leave her there in the rippling shadows and sunlight of her silent room, remembering how I heard her relearning to speak. Leaving the room I smile at how she has her own secrets—probably more than me or my father.

Before I get in the car to drive back to the old house, I show Marcy the butterfly larvae. We're in the kitchen. I say hello to Tonorah, who's doing the dishes and, seeing her, have an idea for the raising of the butterflies.

"So, *that's* what those packages were all about. Hmm. I've been wondering for some time now. Your mother didn't even like for me to talk to her about them. It's good to finally know." She shakes her head, chuckles. "He's trying. You've got to give him that," she says, looking through the boxes and the instruction/descriptions. "Oh, I like this one," she says.

"They'll take some raising, it sounds like," I say and look at her to see if I can tell what she thinks of the idea of her raising them here, as if she doesn't have enough creatures to care for with all the dogs and cats.

"Yes, they will," she says in a way that is not encouraging.

"Tonorah?" I say.

She turns from the running sink, looking surprised to have been brought into the conversation. "Is Jacob still looking for work?"

She nods.

"How does he feel about butterflies?" I ask her.

"I don't think he feels one way or the other," she says and chuckles.

Before I leave, Tonorah agrees to approach Jacob about raising the larvae over the next few weeks for which he will be paid fair wages. Marcy agrees to supervise. This, if my mother does not rouse to raise them herself, which, considering the state she was in when I left her in her room, seems unlikely.

EIGHTEEN

I N COUNTERPOINT, my father and I rock in wicker chairs on the
front porch and watch our guests arrive. The upper porch shadow
and the newly fallen darkness have hidden us from the guests' view. The
headlights either zoom down Caldwell Trace or slow down, turn into
the drive, float over the creek, and wind up toward, then past us to the
backfields to be parked by Jacob and his friends.

Earlier today some workmen set up the white canvas tent where our
party will take place and which I imagine must now be softly awash
in light given by the Japanese lanterns and candles on the tables. This
morning I set up other lanterns demarcating the former foundations of
those Golfhurst houses we have erased. And this afternoon I strung
white lights across the ruin of the half-demolished Golfhurst house. I'm
looking forward to seeing how my work looks in the dark when my
father and I leave off with our rocking to take up hosting. This will
happen soon.

A bluegrass band composed mostly of local physicians with whom my father is acquainted (two of whom grew up in the Clinch Mountains of West Virginia) are playing something they call Classy Grass—a sort of tongue-in-cheek bluegrass for sophisticates. There is an equally good chance of the band playing "Foggy Mountain Breakdown" as tearing into a Bach concerto. They also play good old rock 'n' roll. The sound of the banjo, mandolin, Dobro, fiddle, bass, and drums rises from the backfield to blend with the chirring of the crickets. The crickets are honorary percussion tonight. My father and I decided Around the Bend was perfect for our purposes. Culturally astute without having forgotten their laid-back roots. Not afraid to get dirty; not afraid to recite a sonnet.

It was Robin's idea that my father and I wait till all the guests have assembled before we make our entrance. She thought it would underscore the official business of the evening. That was the first of many suggestions she's made about this party, which has impressed my father and solidified his thinking that Robin's the one. It's amazing how she's taken charge of this party: buzzing around, arranging things all day, greeting our guests, introducing herself to everyone as my girlfriend.

We're going to be fashionably late for our own party. For now, we're just waiting, watching the headlights' slow glide up the drive. I rock, slowly, steadily, sipping a Maker's and water, enjoying the clink of ice on glass, the burnt syrup of the bourbon. I feel calm, numbed. Whence this numbness? We watch the car lights wind up the drive. My father's knee bounces like an expectant promster's. The toe of his right shoe flexes against the porch boards, catching light from someplace and glinting. This project has become more his than mine. Our heritage is shared; it is as much mine to shoulder as his. But my part feels watered down, of less value despite the trees and my as yet dim gentleman-farmer aspirations. What absolves me? What is my role? I ask for the hundredth time: Whence this numbness? The drink? I am Tobia-the-relaxed, the laissez-faire, the abstracted-from-self, Tobia the wait-and-see, tonight, in spite of myself.

About now, I'd love to see Fenton wheel up in his old Caddy to alight with an elegant, still-graceful octogenarian on his arm, her earrings pouring from her ears like portions of waterfall, facets and eyes glimmering, some woman who will recall us all to the sealed-off, neverland glory and dignified grace of a bygone time. Yes, I'd like to see that. I'd also like to see the Goodhopes show up to witness our bid to oust them from their house, to send them on their way, albeit with a fistful of bills. And of course I'm curious about Brandon Campbell, the NAACP and John Redbear, the American Indian Movement representative. How will they mix here at WASP central? Angrily? Peacefully? Not at all?

I'm expecting to see Henley Dempster, who called to say, "Wouldn't miss it, football he-ro. If I can swing it."

My father watches the approaching cars, his knee bouncing, his eyes by turns alert and dismissive. I'm sure he'd most like to see Aunt Marcy's old cream LeBaron creep up the drive bearing my mother. When I returned from my mission the other day, he grilled me slowly, in his own smooth, casual, surreptitious way, about the visit. *What did she think of them?* I gave him a full report and told him about my arrangement with Jacob, which—once I reminded him who Jacob was—made his blood pressure rise. I told him not to worry because Aunt Marcy wouldn't let any living thing die on her watch.

"You reminded your mother about this evening, didn't you?"

"I did. But it didn't look very promising. I don't think she's ready for her debut." I haven't told him I heard her relearning to speak. That's her secret.

I'd like to see my mother tonight as much as my father, for his sake and for hers, but I don't think it'll happen even though she was invited and did not regret.

There are enough revelers assembled in the tent to have raised a steady, pleasant hum of human voices in the backfield. It occurs to me that if crickets were more intelligent, they might sit out on their leaves and muse on the ebb and flow of human tones as we sometimes use their chirps as background for our own musings. Our voices are no less mating calls than their sawings. I must be half-drunk to be thinking such things. At any rate, the human sounds bode well for this evening. Clips of laughter intertwine with the crickets' bowing, the fiddle, bass, mandolin, Dobro, banjo, drums. Women's voices rise an octave when they greet one another—"Why, hello, Kelly-Jean Driscoll! How are *you!*" A particular man's laughter—it sounds like Wardell Pierce, a corpulent red-faced insurance tycoon—booms out in baritone under and louder than the rest.

I would like to see Eon show up tonight. His appearance would bode well for our fund-raising. I'm counting on Bradley Sackett out of the Pinkmellon crowd, but Eon is a question mark. It's not difficult to imagine him sneaking around in the woods, on the periphery, hiding out in the half-demolished Golfhurst house. Maybe he's already mounted cameras in the elms, positioned mikes among the azaleas to ensure his enjoying the party secondhand, in his chosen medium—film, television, hologram, videogame?—piped into his mansion, the sound crisp as bacon sizzling, the images dancing in laser-sharp color. Realer than real. He may be eavesdropping on us from multiple angles right now, from the plush acoustic perfection of his entertainment chamber. With a press of a button availing himself of a new shot, a more provocative angle, another take on what we must experience with what God gave us. Or . . . will Eon dare take the air tonight and party like folks.

A small army of valet parkers are waiting in the backfield to make sure these floating headlights that have been drifting by from time to time are parked in an orderly fashion on the lawn, and to ensure that our guests are escorted to the tent. The parkers are Jacob and some of his friends. Earlier I walked back to give them their instructions. I intro-

duced myself to all of them, wide-eyed kids between sixteen and eighteen, trying to look serious in front of me.

"How are things going with those butterflies?" I asked Jacob.

He looked down at his Hush Puppies and smiled, chuckled like his
mother but did not answer. I could understand that. At sixteen, raising
butterflies is not the coolest of jobs. I assumed he felt uncomfortable answering it in front of his friends, so I let it go and got on with advising
them how to best park the cars on the lawn and how to organize the
keys, as if I knew.

After I'd briefed Jacob and company, I experienced reservations
about this crew doing the job. I had no doubt they could do it as well as
anyone, but I was concerned about what Brandon Campbell and his
NAACP friends would think. I saw the party through their eyes—
mostly white guests, mostly black people serving them. To worsen the
situation, the caterer, a white woman named Nancy Pitchfork, employs
an all-black serving staff. I imagined them seeing Nancy's crew of ten to
fifteen black men and women in their twenties and thirties racing
around under her direction, Jacob and his friends waiting in their positions on the back lawn to park the cars. I clutched my head briefly with
the realization, but it was too late to do anything about it.

Robin and her friend Pam are welcoming the guests as they reach
the tent.

When the time comes, very soon now, my father and I—one of the
unlikeliest pair of hosts in the history of genteel parties—will rise and
stroll through the lawn and back to the tent, where we will greet our
guests and, later, at the appropriate time, subtly and firmly make our
plea for money for Rollback Inc. The time has almost come.

Three cars are creeping up the drive, the back two a safe distance behind a black Range Rover. Behind the cars comes Henley Dempster in
his shiny 1966 F-250, refurbished with money from our patent, bringing to mind the first and only time Henley came to the old house be-

fore now—coughing and sputtering up the driveway in the same truck.
On that day, I let him into the old house and offered him refreshment.
He stood in the front parlor in his overalls, looking at the pineapple-
patterned latticework in the windows, running his hands over the white
oak paneling on the French doors, and looking out at the trees and the
houses going up where the fields had been.

I told Henley to wait there and went to find my father, who was still
feeling the effects of having recently climbed on the wagon. Then I
stood and watched as Henley and my father moved toward each other
to shake hands, my father smiling with icy politeness, Henley, in cau-
tious, thin-eyed appraisal.

"I've enjoyed working with your boy here—he's a fine boy," said
Henley.

"Thank-you," my father said. "He speaks highly of you."

We moved into the living room, sat around a coffee table, and discussed how we would go about getting a patent for the antivenin. I was
impressed by how professional my father sounded in presenting his
ideas, how he'd glued himself together for the meeting. As he talked,
Henley seemed to relax, nodding and taking everything in with his
cold, blue eyes.

"What do you think?" I ask my father. He half-turns, revealing the
white of his tuxedo shirt, the mother-of-pearl buttons running down
the middle, an outward curve just above the cummerbund. The black tie
is neat and tight under the well-defined veins of his neck.

"Yes," he says, nods. "Just 'bout time."

"What're you thinking about?"

He shrugs, looks back down the driveway.

"You think Mom'll show up?" I ask.

He makes the neck gesture of looking back at me, then looks back
down the driveway. The white of his shirt disappears. Some new headlights—not the lights of Aunt Marcy's LeBaron bearing my mother, but
the lights of the Goodhopes' silver Lexus—wind up the driveway. I look

to see if the Goodhopes' appearance has registered with him, but he seems not to have noticed.

"Let's do it," I say. "You ready?"

"What?" he says. "Yes, okay, yes," he says and lets his feet fall on the porch boards. He sighs, looks at me, manages a brief, tired smile, winks.

Inside the tent, the guests have assembled beautifully thanks to Robin and Pam. They stand when we enter the glowing tent. Tables have been set up and adorned with white cloth, candles, and glass jars filled with arrangements of apple and chinablossoms, dogwood branches, magnolia flowers, tulips. Our two hostesses greet us with smiles equally as broad, if a little more ironic, than the ones they must have worn for the guests. Pam, who is a few years older than Robin and was also a Tri-Delt at Vandy, has seated herself toward the back of the room with a table of young lawyers, politicians, and businessmen, many of them male and single. There's an audible hush upon our entry. This is what Robin, our spin doctor, our own private marketing guru, must have had in mind.

We walk to our seats through the buzz of human voices. If crickets were intelligent . . . Robin sits down next to me. Bradley and Clarice are also at our table as is Fenton and some other old friends of the family who we managed to relocate and stir. There are four empty places where my mother and Aunt Marcy and Eon and his date would have been. I try to catch my father looking at the empty places, but he has made a remarkable transformation into host mode. He wears his graceful, gentlemanly persona like a transparent suit of armor, the fake, all-purpose smile precedes him like a cattleguard. He stands up straight, shoulders back, chin high, a real pretender. I look around the room at all of our guests.

Nancy Pitchfork's white-gloved crew delivers the meals like the professionals they are. I cringe when I see that not one of them is white and scan the tent in the hope of gauging the intensity of a future confrontation with an NAACP representative. The salad is excellent—fresh and green. The balsamic vinaigrette has just the right tang. Everyone's eating, talking, laughing. The cocktail servers are moving to and from the bar and back to the tables. A soft breeze has found its way into the tent. What a night for a party!

Shortly after the meal, I am captured by Betty Ison. Betty was in garden club, investment club, and on the preservation committee with my mother. Betty's husband, Randy, plays bass for Around the Bend, otherwise she would not be here. Betty shows no signs of ever being finished with me though I'm giving her nothing to go on but nods and smiles. I look at her, really look at her, for perhaps the first time. She is one of those heavily made-up surface-happy women with short, dyed, and mercilessly teased hair who approach conversation, even with the newly-met, as if there is already an inside joke between conversants. Betty won't tell you a thing of any interest about her own life, but she is certain of her right to wheedle in and squeeze a polite young man by something vital until he gushes useful information about his family's private affairs. I think I know Betty without knowing much about her. She is an interior decorator; she worked on several of the erased houses. Judging from the taste she demonstrates in her own dress, the overabundance of hairspray and makeup, I wouldn't let her decorate a barn. Betty thinks she knows me because she used to hear my mother talk about me ten years ago. She heard me read "The Serpent" that day. But, really, our conversation contains not one morsel of substantive exchange.

Betty is just beginning to angle in like a practiced interviewer, alert for new information about my parents when I'm amazed to see, or to think I see . . . *Merritt Wilson* . . . stepping through the center aisle between tables. I gasp. Is she back, now? Is she here? *Merritt Wilson.*

Betty knows I didn't gasp because of anything she's said. Merritt is barefoot. Her legs look smooth and tan against her loose-flowing white dress, the lower folds of which are rippling in the breeze. She's smiling, not at me, but somewhere behind me, over toward the bandstand. She's too far away for me to tell. Is it really her or someone else, some other girl who has unexpectedly stirred my heart? When Betty notices my distraction, what must look like nothing less than shock, she shoots her eyes to the source, then looks back at me. I understand, her look says, you naughty devil. I excuse myself to gain a better vantage of . . . Merritt?!? pretending not to hear Betty's last effort—which is her most brazen—to get her scoop.

"What about your mom and dad?" she says and her conspiratorial expression says: *He wants her back doesn't he and how could she refuse, considering?* My father must still be of interest to Betty's crowd. His contrition and his being on the wagon has redeemed him, and he never lost his gossip value because of our name and his handsomeness and fallenness.

I've heard Betty, but I pretend I haven't. I keep walking, following Merritt?!? out of the tent and onto the lawn, where other jaunters are strolling between the orange lantern–defined paths to have a look at the former foundations and the white-light-strewn ruin farther back.

Robin appears in front of me and, noticing the distractedness of my gaze, follows it, then finds my eyes. A second later I look at her.

"What's shakin', bacon?" Robin asks. "Having fun? You okay?"

I nod and look at Robin.

"The lights are a nice touch, I think. Don't you think so? I think they turned out really great."

"Yes." I've lost Merritt behind a group of revelers talking and drinking in a bend of the lanterned path.

"What's the matter?"

"I'm nervous about my speech, I think."

"You'll ace it. Come on. You'll knock 'em dead," she says and sees someone she wants to talk to. I see it come into her eyes, and she moves off to say hello to the person, trailing her hand behind her as if to say, *Wait there* or *I want to introduce you to someone.* She says her hello with typical enthusiasm and grace. When she turns to find me, I'm not there.

Merritt—or, who looks like Merritt—walks toward the half-demolished house. I hold back. She steps, gracefully, like someone remembering something, like someone who has been away and returned and is thoughtful about what she has seen in the faraway place she's been. The breeze lifts the folds of her dress, her hair. I have yet to get a good look at her face. I expect her to turn around, now, and head back to the party. When she does, I'll see her face and know and either speak or act as if I'm also out for a look at the ruin. She doesn't turn around. Instead, she walks through the quivering white lights at the doorway.

My immediate thought is for her barefootedness. The inside of the wreckage is strewn with nails and shards of glass. I move toward the house, immediately. The white lights streak in my sight as my head shakes from jogging.

"Hello," I shout into the doorway, my breath in my ears. "I noticed you're barefoot," I say. "There are a lot of nails on the floor. And glass. A lot of glass. It's not safe." My words fall emptily in the ruin. There is no answer. I can hear the tiny glass bulbs of the lights tinkling in the wind. I enter the house. Back at the tent, Around the Bend is playing "Like a Hurricane."

I check all the rooms on the ground floor. No one. The soles of my tuxedo shoes rasp against glass shards and nails. I step over the sledge-hammer and walk up the raw steps.

"Hello? Are you up there? . . . Merritt?" I check all the rooms on the upper floor. All the windows are broken. The little white lights clink in the wind. All the rooms are empty. I look down at my almost empty Maker's and water like a cartoon drunk—as if the drink might have caused this illusion. I check the rooms again, before descending the stairs and returning to the party thinking, *The house was empty, yes, it certainly was empty. But how?*

BACK IN THE TENT, the band is taking a refreshment break. My father looks over as if to say where have you been? He nods. It's time.

We approach the stage. I walk behind him. The numbness, deeper than a Maker's and water numbness, remains, even as we gain the stage, stand behind the mike, and look out over the assembled. There they are, our wonderful guests. I look to see if the mystery girl is among them and she's not. I shake my head.

My father welcomes our guests, tells a brief anecdote—the one about how a squirrel could once climb from tree to tree—from somewhere to somewhere else in the United States, some unbelievably great distance—and then a more personal anecdote about how he grew up on this property and was able to ramble like Thoreau, with a trusted dog, for miles through wilderness in every direction. I catch only snippets of his speech, engaged as I am with trying to see if I can detect something in the audience that might explain the apparition I followed into the blasted house. I hear: ". . . make this land into a park . . . a noble return to its native greenery . . . so please enjoy yourselves to the hilt . . . dance if you're inclined to the music of Around the Bend . . . please consider making a donation to our cause, if you feel so moved. . . ." A smattering of mild applause awakens me to the fact that my father is gesturing at me and our guests are awaiting a second speech.

I step to the mike, all numbness receding, as if on cue, and talk about the value of green spaces, oxygen-producing trees, and what a tragedy it would be to lose them altogether in our mad, greedy push to cover the globe in strip complexes and individually owned demi-urban bungalows, to bury the earth in asphalt and steel. Just as I'm picking up momentum, I hear a disturbance from somewhere in the back of the tent and realize someone's been shouting something at me I didn't hear in my soapboxing. Guests' heads swivel, murmuring, to see who it is.

"Why don't you and your father go all the way, then?" John Redbear is shouting from the back of the tent. "If you really and truly are interested in this land being returned to its pristine state, then why not tear down the plantation house over there and give all the land back to my people?" He's smiling, though, even from here, I can see the challenge in his eyes and posture.

I don't know how to answer him with our guests looking on. My father is squinting toward the back of the tent. "Because you'd turn it into a goddamned casino," he says, under his breath.

Some joker in the crowd says, "Who invited the injuns?"

"For those of you who might not know him, this is John Redbear. He's . . . here tonight representing the American Indian Movement. John, would you like to say something?" I say, dodging his question to save myself.

"Well," he says. "I already said a lot of what I wanted to say. I'd just like to know your answer."

"Yes, and after you've answered Mr. Redbear's question I have something to say as well," says Brandon Campbell in a hearty baritone and stands up next to John Redbear at the back of the tent. "I'd like to inform the crowd about the history of slavery on the Jackson and Caldwell plantations in Tennessee and Mississippi. Some of my people lived here on this land and worked it without pay, as slaves for this evening's gracious hosts. There are some who say they might owe us reparations," he says, with an ironic bow in our direction.

The murmur turns to a buzz and ripples through the crowd. They seem to be pleasantly scandalized.

My numbness has returned to freeze me in place. I feel caught in the middle and torn. My immediate impulse is to reach out to John and Brandon, to help them feel better about our project. At the same time, here is my father, standing beside me who would rather John and Brandon were a thousand miles away and blaming me for their presence. I'm torn, afraid to say anything at all. Afraid if I open my mouth I'll say something drastic like, "Yes, take the land. It's yours. You're right. Tear down our house. You, John, were here first. If we believe the current thinking, your people lived as peaceful stewards of the land. And you, Brandon, your people were taken from your African homeland and brought here to work the land without pay for the great profit of my ancestors while they stood by sipping whiskey. You deserve it. Yes. Have it." On the other hand, I'm equally as concerned I'll hear myself say something out of character like, "Off our land! Get trucking! Both of you! Out of my line of sight before my daddy and I whup the living shit out of you like our ancestors did before us and you know good and well we still can! This ain't no university! Now get before we put shot in your tails!"

My father steps up to the mike. "Good evening, gentlemen," he says. "We *will* be keeping the house and the acreage that has been in our family for the better part of two hundred years." He chuckles. "The rest will be, as I said, a park for everyone to use, regardless of race, color, or creed." He laughs and scans our guests. I wonder if they can hear the undercurrents of rage in his calm voice. "The land we have in mind for the park will be protected in the public interest for everyone to use. And let me also add that we are proud of our Anglo-Saxon heritage, and we will not apologize for it, thank-you, sirs," my father says in a voice of strained calm. It's strange to hear him resorting to these antiquated "sirs" as if we've stepped into an antebellum film and a duel is brewing. I look out at Brandon and John, wondering if this is a planned ambush or a spontaneous outburst.

I step to the mike. "Please," I say. "Why don't you both come up here and say what you like into the microphone?" My father grumbles as John and Brandon walk to the stage through the assembled white guests. In the interest of being fair I have betrayed him. I step back and brace myself, feeling I've made a mistake.

A flash goes off, another. The society columnist and her photographer are sniffing a bigger story.

John Redbear steps to the microphone. He's wearing a silver bolo tie with his tux. "I didn't expect to be given an opportunity to speak tonight. I'll try to keep this brief. Aside from the question which our hosts seem not to want to answer," he says and smiles, "I suppose I would like to inform all of you that there has been some recent research pointing to our hosts' relative Joshua Jackson and his involvement in organizing a brutal massacre on land near here whose professed goal was to rid this area of its 'Indian problem.' These were peaceful hunting parties that had been looking for game in this part of Tennessee for centuries before Joshua Jackson was even born. I thought you should know," he says and nods. "When I heard about this Rollback project, I thought it sounded good, but then I thought, well, we Native Americans would like a rollback of our own to a time before whites ever set foot on this land. I thought I would raise these issues here. That's all," he says, smiles, and looks over at Brandon Campbell.

My father takes the mike, his teeth looking sharp for the anger in his smile. "Okay, all right, thank-you, that was fascinating. As far as I know, there is evidence of no such massacre," my father says. "And if there was, well, the West was won the way it was. I'm sorry, but I won't stand by and let you turn this into a guilt-administering session, gentlemen. God knows there's enough of that going on out there. I've heard quite enough of this," he says with a glance to the audience that says, *Don't you agree, please agree with me, that we've heard enough of this kind of talk so we can get back to our party and writing our checks?* "Thank-you very much, gentlemen. Thank-you for your opinions, but really that's more than enough." He smiles at both of them and nods.

John Redbear is about to say something more without the benefit of the mike, perhaps about to introduce Brandon Campbell, who is looking impatient and ready to take the podium himself, when a gun explodes in the back of the tent.

At least five women and two men scream. When I come up from my crouch on the stage, I look to the back and left of the tent. It's Fenton. He stands in back of our table, a smoking .38 revolver in his right hand. Is this the way they got people's attention in his day? *My Lord, this is turning into one hell of a party,* I think. One of the wits at a nearby table says, "Now, that's one thing that would *not* have happened if the old bastard'd ever got himself married."

John Redbear and Brandon Campbell have both flattened on the stage. They look out at the partygoers and, with wide, frightened eyes, at the crazy old white man with a gun. There's a healthy hole in the roof of the tent, a Florida-shaped flap has come loose and is fluttering down.

"Give 'em hell, Fenton!" someone shouts. Fenton grins, scans for the yeller, approaches the stage reholstering the .38 in his jacket. John Redbear and Brandon Campbell stand, watching Fenton carefully, as he positions himself behind the mike. My father shakes his head.

"Gentlemen," Fenton says. "I hope you will forgive this intrusion, but I have some news of the future that may offset the present wrangling over the past and which concerns all of us alike, regardless of color or creed. As many of you know, I have, for some time, been monitoring seismic activity in this area in the hope of ascertaining the next manifestation of the New Madrid Earthquake," he begins. The room is oddly silent. You can hear the crickets percussing outside the tent. Amazing what a gun can do. "If you have not yet been informed of my search, well, then, I'm telling you now."

Someone in Fenton's audience bursts out laughing. "What's the news, Fenton? Break it to us gently." Fenton seems to like this boisterous atmosphere for his revelation. I was afraid he might expect, or, worse, demand, with racing heart and shaking gun, a reverent silence.

"I am pleased, and, I must admit, somewhat chastened to be able to announce to you this evening that the next major occurrence of the New Madrid Earthquake, a manifestation not to be taken lightly by any stretch of the imagination, and which I believe will measure something above a seven on the Richter scale, will occur on April twenty-third. At about two-thirty P.M."

A few seconds of silence. The crickets chirrup. Fenton scans his rapt crowd. Then: cheers and laughter, especially from some of the drunker members of the crowd, some of them openly mocking his prediction. I cringe, hoping Fenton's just myopic enough not to notice or good-natured enough not to care.

"Now . . . ," Fenton says. "Now . . . ," a consoling hand up, his expression serious now. Has he mistaken their hilarity for panic? The crowd quiets, I'm afraid, more in the tone of an expectant stand-up comedy crowd, than that of an earthquake symposium.

"Now, don't worry. In ancient Rome, when the leaders were informed of certain auguries, they weighed them carefully and then decided on a course of action. They racked their brains to come up with something to appease the gods. I don't think there's anything that will stop our God from sending this quake. It's too late. We've put ourselves in a position to need to be taught a lesson about our insignificance. However, I would like, now, to dedicate the rest of this party, with the permission of our hosts"—he looks at me, and I nod, hands out—sure, whatever you say, Fenton—"to God. A celebration of fellowship and"—he looks at John Redbear and Brandon Campbell—"brotherhood. For, let us not forget that we are but small, insignificant specks on this great and mysterious earth and we are—every one of us—*in this thing together.*" Fenton steps back from the mike and goes over to John Redbear and Brandon Campbell and gives them unreciprocated hugs. Then, he comes over and hugs me and my father, who looks more surprised to have been hugged this way than any of us.

Fenton steps back to the podium and reaches into his jacket pocket for the gun. I see my father's horrified expression. He lunges forward, trying to stop Fenton from shooting again. Several guests put hands to their ears. John and Brandon once again hunker down. My father is too late. The shot rings out, and the party is reborn with the sulfur smell of gunsmoke, regardless of whether or not our guests feel like giving our project a cent or not. At least they've seen a good show, I think. My father manages to wrest the gun from Fenton the moment after it has gone off.

There are enough of Fenton's golfing buddies and their progeny in the tent to know he's harmless, and this is the crowd that raises a cheer. We hastily give the stage back to Around the Bend, who light into a lively rendition of "It's the End of the World As We Know It." When I hop from the stage, Robin shakes her head and goes cross-eyed. I watch my father move through the stageward-rushing crowd like a soldier at the end of a lost battle. Fenton is beaming, swaying slowly, out of time with the jumpy rhythm, in the front row amid a throng of other guests. Robin finds the center and dances with Fenton, holds his hand and helps him execute spins.

There are others who haven't taken so kindly to Fenton's display. Some are leaving, many of them in a huff, John Redbear and Brandon Campbell and their friends among them. I walk quickly after them, shouting apologies.

"I hope you know this was not planned. You were not in any danger. It's Fenton, he's harmless. He . . . ," I call after them as they walk in a tight cluster toward their cars. I stand watching them go, feeling surprised and frustrated that they won't even turn around to talk. As they arrive at the place where Jacob and his friends are waiting to retrieve people's cars, I stand in the field, shake my head, and shrug.

"How 'bout all that?" I ask my stunned father when I catch up with him. I'm smiling like an idiot, hoping he's adopted a similarly light view of the incident. When he doesn't answer, I grab his shoulders to make him see me. "It's not necessarily a disaster. We'll have to wait and see what happens."

He doesn't speak, gives me a forlorn look, and shakes loose from my grasp. He grabs a bottle of bourbon from the bar table and, with the bottle in one hand, Fenton's confiscated gun in the other, walks like a zombie out of the tent, scarcely acknowledging his guests, who are mostly ignoring him.

When I see all the people milling around, looking as if they'd like to have a word with me—Martin Felter, Nancy Pitchfork, Tom Good-

hope, Tracey Roister, a local society columnist and her photographer—
I turn quickly and follow my father.

Nancy: "Mr. Caldwell . . ."

Tom: "Tobia, could I have a word . . ."

Martin: "Interesting little speech about development there, Cald-well, but . . ."

Tracey: "Mr. Caldwell, Mr. Caldwell . . ."

"Excuse me, I'll be back in a moment," I tell them all and smile.

My father moves down the orange-lantern-lit path at the same dogged somnambulistic pace at which he walked through the tent, the same stunned steps. Before he reaches the ruin, he takes a sharp right, steps over the lanterns, and heads for the Goodhopes'.

When I come to the Caldwell graves in the Goodhopes' backyard, I see him sitting on a bench in front of Grandfather Thomas's small mau-soleum. A child is sitting on the other end of the bench, Kippy Good-hope. The whiskey bottle sits, still unopened, between them. Back at the party I can hear the band playing "Man of Constant Sorrow."

I stand behind them and focus my hearing toward them; they aren't speaking.

I walk around the side of the bench. When Kippy Goodhope sees me, his eyes widen. I am the lunatic with the sledgehammer in the half-demolished house. He gasps, stands, and, with a shout, runs back toward his house. Go on and run, you little bastard, I think. What did I ever do to you? Father turns his head from the graves to watch Kippy's greyish form colorize in the Goodhopes' back porch light. Kippy opens the door, looks back at us where we're lost to darkness between the porch-light and the party lights—strange grown men in a graveyard with whiskey and a gun.

"Fan of yours?" my father asks with a thrust of his chin in Kippy's direction.

The gun is resting, black on grey, in the blueish light beside the bot-tle, the barrel pointing toward him. Both the bourbon and the gun insinuate their potentials. I sit down on the other side of the bench, the gun and the booze between us.

"This is a pretty lethal duo you've brought down here with you," I say.

He chuckles again. "That duo's what gave we Caldwells our place in the world if you listen to your buddies up there. May be some truth to it. Who knows?"

I look at the grass at grave edge. There they are. Joshua and the Tennessee Turtle and my namesake buried beside his loyal slave Granger and the three Jackson sisters Charlotte, Lucille, and Grace. All the way up to Grandfather Thomas and Grandmother Pearl. They're all there except for the ones who escaped and went off to exotic places and were never heard from again.

"When I walked down here I didn't know what I was going to do," he says. "That boy was hiding among the graves and spying on me. He asked me if I was a ghost. And I told him, 'Yes—a living ghost.'" He looks at me, the full weight of the sadness behind his eyes like a bottom-bound anchor in him. I wonder if and when my eyes will look like his. He looks at the ground and sighs. Then stands with the bourbon and twists the cap and walks to the decomposing graves in the oldest section. He pours a dollop on the graves there, lets Joshua Jackson have some and Mary Bean (Joshua's favorite slave), and moves on to the others from oldest to youngest, ending with Grandfather Thomas and Grandmother Pearl Caldwell. By the time he's given them their due, there are only a few swallows left in the bottle. He tilts it and winces as he downs a swallow. He turns to me, holds out the bottle, and his sad, weighty eyes—my eyes but heavier—ask, *will you take it?*

This ritual is not a real ritual for its spontaneity—or does that make it more authentic? We've never done this before. It seems to me, in a part of myself, maudlin and sad and almost laughable. But I stand and take the bottle, tilt it back, and join my ancestors by drinking the last.

He takes up the gun and the empty bottle and starts to walk back, not in the direction of the party, but toward the old house by a side path, beneath the great, dark trees. "I trust," he says, "you'll manage the end of this fiasco?"

I nod that I will. And return to the fiasco, which I don't consider to be a fiasco at all except for the hasty retreat of the Brandon Campbell and John Redbear parties, and which is continuing unabated without its hosts, although its numbers have thinned considerably to reveal a hard core. I search the tent for someone or something that might require my attention and see nothing. Things seem to have sorted themselves out while we were down in the graveyard.

A little after midnight, the electricity goes out. The band members are undaunted, even exultant, especially the drummer, Dr. Jenkins, who's been keeping a steady stream of planter's punch on a small nightstand next to his drums all night. "Jinx" throws his prominent, ruddy forehead up at the roof and keeps up the beat. A beautiful heiress/lawyer twirls on the floor with her fiancé, who, she said earlier, doesn't like to dance. Maybe Fenton's warning has had its effect on him? Better dance while there's a solid earth on which to do it. Around the Bend starts playing "Let the Circle Be Unbroken" when there is a snap and a white flash from the sound system. The music suddenly stops, the electric lights go out, but Jinx keeps the beat.

And, wonder of wonders, our guests, *our guests* (I'm proud of them) keep singing, clapping in unison, dancing despite the loss of power. Bradley and Clarice laugh and stomp the floor. After a time someone fixes the problem, and Around the Bend finishes the song with amplification behind them.

"Do you know what this is?" Fenton says, his blue eyes wide, a lithe girl, no more than twenty-five years old, with warm brown eyes and soft, smooth, tan skin clutching with both of her chubby little hands at Fenton's, tug, tug, tugging him back to the dance floor, not at all happy with me for delaying him.

"This," Fenton says. "This. All of this. Is a last gasp," he says. And then he stops resisting. She pulls him onto the dance floor. He looks back at me, shrugs.

Henley comes up to say thanks and goodbye. "Y'uns throw quite a set-to in these parts," he says, offering a hand. "It was good to see you again."

"Thanks, Henley. What did you make of the unplanned speeches?"

"Well. I suppose by some accounts I could've been the next one in line to leap on up and express a grievance or two. I like the old man's point." We both look out at Fenton, who's trying to keep up with his plump, young belle.

"Are you sure you don't want to stay here tonight. It's a long drive."

"No, thank-you-much, football he-ro. Think I'll be on my way." We say some more thank-yous and let's stay in touches, before he nods, turns, and I watch him walk off for a time before turning back to the dancing.

Robin and Pam are turning around the floor with two young lawyers. I watch them twirl across the floor and for a moment wonder if I should vanish from the picture, let Robin and this lawyer start something. I'm still young enough to be surprised when people my age and younger—now, some of them people about whom I remember thinking, He or she will never make much of him- or herself—go around calling themselves lawyers. I sit at a table near the back and tell one of Nancy Pitchfork's workers to keep bringing me Maker's and waters. I do that for a time before I decide to join the dancing. I go to the floor and begin to dance by myself in the vicinity of Robin. I'm pleased when she leaves her lawyer, who almost winces to see her go, to dance with me. *Me.*

Fenton and his young partner are still dancing at such a pace that I'm concerned for his health. The lawyer, who is drunk, stares at Robin and me, stunned and stubbornly gauging his chances. A little later I see him staggering, head down, across the field toward the cars.

After the band has played its last song, a small, sweaty group of us remain on the dance floor. Fenton's friend leaves with some of her friends, and he comes over and says, "If you think I won't be feeling the effects of this tomorrow, you should have your head examined. Goodnight, all. Thank-you, TC." I walk Fenton across the lawn toward the valets. The last of the stragglers, most of them sweaty from their effort on the dance floor, come up and thank me.

Pam and her lawyer have arrived at a state of drunken touchy-feelyness, her right hand in the pocket of his sport coat, his left hand on her left hip. "Let's go out," he says, Pam's lawyer. "Let's go to that new place . . . that Dipsy-Do Club."

Robin looks at me, widens her eyes. "Yes. Let's go there," she says.

I shake my head. "I'm going to stay here and make sure everything gets settled properly."

"Come on, the party's over here, my man," says Pam's lawyer. "We need to keep it rolling somewhere else."

"Come on, Tobia," says Pam.

Robin comes in close and puts a finger between my ribs and tries to tickle me.

Laughing, I say, "What're you doing?"

"There's nothing to settle here. What happened there, before, could always happen again," she whispers into my ear and licks it.

My knees weaken. I take a deep breath. "No," I say. "Ya'll go on ahead."

Robin backs away a step and pouts. Then, they move across the field and away from me. Pam, in the middle, initiates their skipping. Arms draped across one another's shoulders, they skip away, in their finery, toward the cars in the backfield. God knows who's going to try and drive. Both Pam and Robin have removed their shoes and are letting them dangle from a few fingers of their free hands at the end of their extended arms. Robin turns to look back at me, her eyes smiling. She purses her lips and gives me a long-distance kiss-pout.

"Thanks for everything, ya'll," I call after them. "Have fun."

I watch the last few of the cars start up, the white head- and red tail-lights coming on. I watch them pull across the field to the driveway and disappear. I give Jacob and his buddies each a fifty-dollar bill, and they thank me quietly.

Jacob holds back when the others have gone to the two cars they've arrived in.

"How'd it go tonight?" I ask.

"Smooth," he says. "Pretty smooth."

"Tips?"

"Hundred dollars about. You asked me about the butterflies back then."

"That's right. How are they doing?"

"They're doing all right. They're a bitch though. Just 'cause there's so many kinds of 'em," he says and nods. "And 'specially since your mamma's on the case, it's not easy."

"Is that right," I say. "What do you mean, 'on the case'?"

"I mean she's down there watching me when I'm feeding them. In that wheelchair, looking like she'll do I don't know what if I screw up, and never saying anything. And I got to feed this one nectar, and that one nettle and this one over here other stuff. It's nerve-racking, I'm telling you. Ya'll might not be paying me enough money," he says and smiles and shakes his head.

The car with his friends pulls up alongside us, and Jacob opens one of the back doors and hops inside. A rap song thumps from the speakers and the boys inside are nodding their heads to its rhythm and the rapper is pouring forth a stream of punch-like words about the trials of life deep in the 'hood and the importance of authenticity and remembering your roots.

"Thanks, guys," I say.

Jacob and his crew nod from inside the darkness of the car and then they pull away and disappear down the driveway.

I walk back out to the tent and sit in a chair at one of the tables. The band has finished disassembling their equipment. It is silent except for the crickets, who are still at work.

IT'S THREE O'CLOCK in the morning. I have awakened from a brief nap. I'm still sitting at the table. I thought everyone had left but here is Devon Highfield. He must have passed out under one of the tables. He smacks at his neck. He is now the last guest splayed out at one of the tables in the wreck of the tent. A recently divorced high-profile attorney with a well-known drinking habit, Devon is true to form. I wonder where his date is. Could it be she was the young tender with whom Fenton was dancing earlier?

"Gallinippers!" Devon yells.

"What's that?" I say.

"You need to do something about these bloodthirsty gallinippers, Caldwell, for the love of sweet God," he says and, once again, smacks his neck, hard, perhaps killing the offending insect, which is probably reeling from his alcohol-thinned blood anyway.

NINETEEN

M Y FATHER SITS at the kitchen table sorting through the returns from last night's party, shuffling the envelopes, opening them to reveal the contents, and tabulating the results on a calculator.

I walk into the dining room, watch him, and try to decide from his expression how well we did last night. He doesn't look dejected, or particularly elated.

"What's the take?" I ask.

I seem to have startled him. He does a little in-seat jump before he looks up at me. "Considering what happened last night, it's not too bad. Your friends the Sacketts are our heroes. I think I'll kiss him—scratch that—I'll definitely kiss *her,* the next time I see them. Inviting the Goodhopes turned out to be a good idea." He lifts a note and says, "'Make an offer and it will be entertained, regardless. Signed, Tom Goodhope.' I assume that means they'll entertain something lower than three million."

I nod. "I think that's exactly what that means. What's the total?"

"Five hundred thousand. Give or take. Which—Robin was right—is more than we would have gotten had we charged a thousand dollars a plate."

"How much of that is from Bradley and Robin?"

"Two."

I nod and feel a rush of gratitude for Bradley and Robin.

"You know who we haven't heard from?"

"Who?"

"The other part of the Pinkmellon triumvirate. That genius nutball who doesn't know how to RSVP."

I nod. "Eon. Right."

"I think you ought to go by and see him. See if old moneybags over there is willing to help us finish this thing up the right way."

"Look at this," he says and slides the morning paper across the table. It's folded back to an article. FUND-RAISER TAINTED BY GUNFIRE, RACIAL TENSION.

I shake my head.

"That quick," he says. "Can you believe it? And, of course they got the whole thing bassackwards. These guys imply in here that shots were taken *at them*.

"And look at this," he says and slides another section of the paper over to me. LOCAL MAN PREDICTS DATE AND TIME OF NEXT QUAKE.

AFTERNOON'S GIVING WAY to dusk when I drive over to Eon's house to talk to him about a possible donation. I stop at the bottom of the drive to check the mail. In the box, among many forgettable items, is an airmail envelope from Merritt Wilson containing another letter. "Can't Buy Me Love" is on the radio. I switch it off and turn off the ignition:

T,

Now that my time here is almost over, I've been recalling things, sifting them. I woke up one night on the metal berth of a boat, going up the Congo, and I found I was covered, head to toe, with large, winged insects. My breath came for a while in small gasps then settled down as I relaxed into a stillpoint acceptance of it.

It was not the most disturbing thing I've seen, not by a long shot, but it was a galvanizing one. I saw a woman making soup out of barely edible, boot-trampled plants. The look on her face of determination to live, to feed her children.

A twenty-seven-year-old man told me that his grandfather had known of a time before war and had tried to tell him what it was like. The younger man didn't believe him.

Very Soon I Hope,

M.

Very soon . . .

I start the car and drive—in light traffic, between the chain of chains, past collections of townhouses, not really seeing any of it for thoughts of large, winged insects; a barefoot Merritt in a breeze-blown gown stepping toward Haven—to Eon's house.

Which is a sprawling conglomeration of multileveled rectangles—all smooth stretches of dark wood and long wide sheets of glass that reflect the surrounding trees during the day and, as now, at dusk, glow through the branches invitingly, allowing glimpses into the interior, as a visitor winds up the wooded ridge. The house is perched on a hill in a wealthy wooded community spiraled through with access roads. I glimpse pieces of imperious houses, some of them seeming to eye me suspiciously through the bough, leaf, and branch gaps. What are *you* doing here? they seem to say. Who *are* you?

It's easy to imagine that the architect's objective was to have the house blend with the wooded hillside. And, at this, he was remarkably successful. It's not the house I would have expected Eon to live in, though, especially given the bells and whistles of the Dipsy-Do Club.

I park and step from the car, walk to and knock on the door—the house spilling, in several levels, down the hill.

Eon opens the door and stands looking at me for a moment. I called before I came over, but he looks surprised to see me.

We exchange a greeting, I follow him into his minimalist living room, and we both sit on black leather chairs. I'm surprised at the sparseness of his house. It still looks only partially moved-into. I find myself wondering if it's some sort of new-century minimalism. Only flat screens on the walls with mesmerizing patterns swimming across them reveal this to be the home of the CFO of Pinkmellon Computers. The one in the foyer shows a dance of blue triangles, green circles, lavender squares, and what look to be wiggly black-and-white sperm.

"Good to see you, Tobia. I thought about coming to your party last night, but at the last minute I decided there were things I needed to do. You know how it is."

"I know how it is."

"Good. Of course you do, you must. Can I . . . Something to drink? Anything you'd like to drink, I have it."

"No thanks, Eon."

"Are you sure? I have it somewhere here. In the kitchen or the bar. I have a fully-stalked bar—and I mean, sta*l*ked, with an *l*—with celery for Bloody Marys. Have a seat."

"I'm already sitting down."

"How was the party? Did people have fun? Will it enable you to turn back time? Will you soon be in the market for slaves again?" he asks and starts to laugh. He whistles a few bars of Dixie.

"I thought it was a success."

"I saw the paper this morning. The press," he says and throws up his hands. Eon has had his own problems with the press. After the Dipsy-Do party, an animal rights interest complained about Eon's making the feeding of the pig to the python into such a spectacle. Eon issued an apology to anyone who was disturbed and promised never to do it again. "And what a shame about the . . . And the New Madrid's coming according to the old man. April something, isn't it? Twenty-third at two-thirty. This place won't be any good in an earthquake. I think I got the insurance, but I don't recall, really. Have to check into that."

"Yes," I say. "Who knows when it might happen?"

"We're not so different as you might think, Tobia," he says. "'The way up and the way down are one and the same.' Heraclitus. You and I will meet where back becomes forward and forward back." He smiles at this application of the ancient paradox.

I nod, and we continue on like this for some time before I excuse myself on the pretense of needing to use one of his restrooms, meaning to see more of his house without him seeing me seeing it.

"Sure, sure," he says. "Down the hall, a left, and then it's on the right," he says. "A left then it's on the right."

I walk down the hall, take a left, then a right, and find myself in Eon's bedroom, where on the wall facing the bed hangs a giant flat screen featuring the same image of Merritt Wilson I'd seen at the Dipsy-Do Club blown up to four or five times life-size and covered in a panoply of bloom and dispersing shades of green—shifting, dripping, overlapping atop the image. The greens fade and dis- and reappear in differently shaped patches elsewhere on her face and on her body. Behind her, Venetian buildings, a portion of bridge, a slice of canal, also roil in verdancy. She's smiling a slightly perturbed smile under the percolating spectrum and has cocked her head in a manner that suggests she's humoring the photographer. The green dance roils over the steady lines of her face and across the small, blurry shops, and washes over the cobblestone street in the background. I stand and watch the shapes reconfigure themselves for some time.

"Find it all right?" Eon asks with a hint of anticipation, when I return to the living room.

"Yes. Thanks," I say. "Eon, I actually came over here to discuss something with you. You didn't come to our party, but I thought you might consider making a donation. I wanted to ask. Please don't feel any pressure."

"Ahh," he says and looks at once deflated and triumphant, which makes me guess that, in part, he wanted my visit to be a social call, that he would like to think we're just hanging out. At the same time, now that I've revealed the true nature of my visit, another part of him is declaring victory and is satisfied at my having confirmed the notion he holds dear that everybody wants something,

He immediately walks over to a drawer, pulls it open, and withdraws a checkbook. He takes a pen from a pocket of his black chinos and holds it over a check.

"How much?" he asks.

"Two million dollars," I shoot back at him without a pause and smile.

He lets the hand holding the pen fall to his side and stands looking at me. "Ahh," he says. "That's a big number."

"It is."

"This seems a good time for me to admit something, in light of this big number," he says.

"You have something you'd like to admit to me? All right."

"I wrote a letter to Merritt Wilson. Well . . . I wrote her several letters and never heard back from her. So, then, as an experiment, I decided to, and did, write her a single letter . . . from you. As you. Before you left Pinkmellon, I went into your office and found a notebook in which you'd written some . . . notes. I xeroxed a few pages and duplicated your lettering and wrote her a letter from you, in an approximation of your handwriting. Don't worry. There were no confessions. I kept it very safe and bland. Except, I did tell her—speaking as you—that I—you—wanted to see her. I put my own return address on the letter. Now, I've waited for some time with no response. It seems you carry no more weight with her than me after all. I wanted to clear that up before—"

"She wrote back," I say.

"What?"

"She wrote back."

"What?"

"She corresponded."

"Oh. Oh?"

"She said she misplaced the return address."

"What else?"

"There's a good chance she'll be coming back to Haven."

"When?"

"She hasn't said yet, for sure."

"Ah, ah, ah. There's something. There's an idea I have for what. Yes. What do you think of . . . This will be easy . . . I think. Let me know how this . . . How about this? Yes, what about, how about, think about this. I'll give you this check, a big, big—this huge check. It's only money. We understand that between us, you and I. What is money in the face of things like this? I'll give you this big check. And you will . . . give Merritt to me when she returns. You'll influence her in my favor. Deliver her."

I begin shaking my head in the middle of his speech and keep shaking it after he's finished. "I can't influence her, Eon, even if I wanted to. And I sure as hell can't *deliver* her."

"Yes," he says. "But you can promise to eliminate yourself from the equation. That's all we could ask," he says and lifts the pen and lets it hover over the check, regarding me.

"This is ridiculous," I say.

"Think, though. Think. You really aren't in the equation anyway. If

I hadn't written the letter, she wouldn't be returning, in any case, would she? Most likely, not. And, from what I understand, in the past you've tried to keep your distance from her. Unlike me. Perhaps, you even have a reason to keep her from stirring up some dirty things from your past. Right? What is the issue, then? Where is the sticking point? The way I see it, you're getting a good deal. You're cleansed of someone tied to a messy episode from your past. Everything back to green over there, Caldwell graves under Caldwell control."

I look at him. "Why her, Eon? I've seen some of these women who throw themselves at you."

"Gold diggers. Whores and harlots all," he says. "There is no one else. If you had seen Merritt in the café off the Piazza San Marco that night you'd understand."

"And why is that?"

He begins to pace the sparse room, crossing back and forth in front of the screen on which orange and white clownfish fin over and through white coral. "When she talked and even when she laughed, there was a deep sadness in her voice and in the way she carried herself. It was clear she looked at things dead-on, courageously, without any delusion, without any static, a clean, clear line—nothing in the way." He stops and turns to look out the floor-to-ceiling window in front of him, the trees almost lost to darkness spilling down the hill.

His phone rings; the fishtank turns blue and a name, phone number, and image (Ferdinand De La Garza's face) appear on the screen: Ferdinand 555-7777. Eon glances at it and continues, "That night we talked about who close to us had died. She told us how she'd lost her twin brother when he was only eight years old. He was bitten by a . . ." He stops and looks at me, as if he expects me to continue the story.

I remain silent.

He nods, continues: "There was no self-pity in her story. Hers was a sadness that had been filtered into better things—enthusiasm, truth, wisdom. It was like she'd distilled her sorrow into a strain of joy. I dreamed of her all that night. And when I woke up the next morning, my mind was filled with her. I felt blessed as I never had before, to be with her in Venice. We had long, intense conversations. She told me her dreams. One night I kissed her on a sidewalk paralleling the grand canal."

He looks at me for a time in silence. Then: "There was something else Merritt said on that first night in the café. When we asked her about it, she told us she suspected you knew something more than you'd told her, or her parents. She said she wanted to get close to you again to find out what you knew. She implied that after she'd found out what you knew, your hold on her would be broken." He looks at me, to see how I'm handling it, the dark circles under his eyes making him look sadder than I've ever seen him before. "Bradley told me about the silver dollar," he says.

It feels as if something heavy is moving in my gut and chest. In my mind I see Bradley Sackett, beaming. I have to swallow in order to keep the movement from spilling out into the open in some guise. We sit for a time in silence before I manage to say, "You realize, Eon, that I can guarantee you nothing. I'm in no way the keeper of Merritt Wilson. I have no control whatsoever over her. I haven't even seen her in over six years. She may stay a few days and take off again—if she comes back at all. She might go right back to Africa or some other place to continue her work. I can't keep her from doing that. My influence will be dicey at best. Negligible."

He shakes his head as if to say not to worry. "If she returns, she'll have me," he says. "I'll make sure of it. I'll show her the Dipsy-Do. She's all I lack." He gestures around him as if to convince me that this spartan, if spacious, house with all its screens and gadgets, speakers, and oddly shaped furniture along with his growing empire, is everything.

"You're right, I'm convinced," I say as calmly as I can, hearing myself say it as if with a disembodied voice. "Would you like me to sign something? Should we draw up a contract?"

He looks at me for a time, sensing, or trying to sense, what he knows

I must be burying. "A handshake should suffice," he says. "You're an honorable man."

I try not to let him see any recognition on my face of the irony of this remark or the deep heartsink I'm experiencing as I stand and shake his hand.

Which he releases from my own to slowly lift the pen and casually write a check, *E* flexing, for two million dollars (two million dollars!). He signs it and begins to hand it to me, pulling it away as I try to grasp it.

"You'll show me the letters?"

I nod.

"You're certain she's coming back?"

"It's in the letters, but . . ."

"And when she gets back you promise to do everything in your power to sway her in my favor, if she requires it."

I nod.

He hands me the check, and I look down at it in disbelief. In the comments section at the bottom left-hand side he's written:

M.W. ♥ *E.O.N.*

TWENTY

O LD HAVOC GRUMBLES to a start, shakes into motion, and crawls over the lawn toward the Goodhopes' house. It's just started to rain, so we considered postponing this, but, in the end, decided it was time.

My father is at the helm. Even from a distance, through the rain-pelted window, I can see his expression of cold determination. He is not undertaking the destruction of this house blindly. Sometimes, even the most important acts pass without our grasping them. This isn't happening to my father in this case. He knows what this means. He has willed the house gone, the graves recovered, and now, as Old Havoc comes within striking distance, he's got it clasped tightly in heart and mind clutching the moment, seeing it through. The old machine lurches forward.

The house seems to have made itself more vivid, somehow, against the green lawn, under the grey sky, against the rain. It seems aquiver with an energy; this house slotted for demolition has marshaled all of its birr to the fore in a last-ditch effort to save itself on the day of its de-struction. You can feel the vitality the house has soaked up in its seven years, vibrating through the facade with an extra pleading intensity, for a forgiveness my father will not grant it.

There are no witnesses to watch the long swing of the great demol-ishing ball through the slategrey sky. The house takes its blows with no fanfare, though it seems to say, in its last efforts to save itself, *There's been a mistake there's been a terrible mistake.* The ball swings through sheets of rain and finds its mark again and again. The house finally buckles and shatters and caves in on itself, saying, *There's been a mistake there's been a terrible mistake I'm a new house a new house.* Says this until it's rubble and the rubble beaten by the rain insists the same thing. *I'm a new house a new house.*

Later, we have BLTs—the *T*s of which are from our own garden—and lemonade in the kitchen. The wind pushes the rain against the windowpane.

Neither of us is talking. I break the silence with a question. "I was over at Fenton's a while ago. And he told me something that I was just going to keep to myself. But I've been wondering what you'd make of it."

He looks up at me as if he forgot I was in the room, nods.

"You know the story about the cave. You know how it always ended with Grandfather Thomas and Fenton leaving the cave to go back home after getting directions from the enemy. Well, Fenton said Grandfather Thomas tossed a grenade back in the cave and blew those Germans to kingdom come."

He shakes his head. "That man's losing his mind. I've heard that story hundreds of times from both of them. They had a nice wine party in that cave with the enemy and the Germans told them how to get back safely to their lines. They followed the instructions and left and went back behind their lines. Period. Fenton's cracking up, I'm afraid. Not

long before someone—one of us, I suppose—will have to put him in
a home."

"Why would he say *that,* though? You don't think there might be
something to it."

"I won't get into the psychology of that man. He's been slowly unraveling for years, ever since your grandfather died. He never got over
it. It's an obsession with him. Hell, it's even linked to all this earthquake
nonsense."

"You think that's nonsense, too? The earthquake's going to happen
sometime. And, as for the cave, if Fenton was such a friend to Grandfather Thomas, why would he tell this version of the story now? Don't
you think the story would go in the opposite direction as he got older?
Make Grandfather Thomas look better?"

He chuckles. "You want to know what I think? I think everyone's
humoring that man and has been for years. I wouldn't let that story dis-
parage a great man. And I also wouldn't let it make you think any less of
Fenton. Bury that version of the story's what I think. Let it lie. Your
grandfather was a great man. He was a great man. I think Fenton
might've tried to tell me that story once. I ignored it; I'd advise you to
do the same." He stands up and takes his dishes to the sink and rinses
them in a stream of water. The rain is still rattling on the windowpane.
He glances up from the dishes briefly to look through the blurred window out at the dark, impressionistic green of the trees.

"Great work today, T. In fact, great work throughout. I'm proud of
you, son," he says. "We've done it, haven't we?" he says and raises a fist
and mock-scowls. "Your father's going to sleep well for the first time in
a long time." He spends a real smile, the lines at the sides of his eyes furrowed with it. There is at the same time a hint of the old angel-demon
mischief and a magnanimous hint of the father he wished he could have
been in the smile. His sharp blue eyes, which often make him look ruthless and unforgiving and lately have seemed heavy and sad, appear, at the

moment, to be merely and honestly kind. He holds the smile for a second or two and stands there in the doorway. Looking at him, it occurs to me for some reason that even unto death and no matter how much they appear to have been lost, we carry buried in us the unrealized hopes and dreams of our youth. Standing in the doorway, he looks to be eighteen or younger, smiling with some mischief and hope at having recovered a portion of lost time.

"All right, Dad," I say. "Thanks. Goodnight."

TWENTY-ONE

ROBIN AND I ride in the cockpit of Old Havoc over the shiny backfield grass. Weeks ago, I joked about taking her for a spin in Old Havoc and to my surprise when she came over this afternoon, she remembered and insisted I make good on my promise.

We roll slowly toward the outskirts of the expanded Grand Old Caldwell Place. Roll past the rubble of the Goodhope house that Bank and his crew will begin to cart away tomorrow. Roll to the crest of a hill. Down the rise Old Cherokee runs its course, the life-vein of the chain of chains, the links of which feed on its steady traffic, as it runs unbroken for twenty or so miles toward the city to our right. Cars with newly switched-on lights glimmer by in both directions, going somewhere (home?) in haste. At its end the road is being widened to match the rest. Stoplights are going up. At the fringe, to our left, are the mud and debris of construction sites with scattered materials, sleeping equipment.

I turn off Old Havoc's ignition. Robin and I climb out and stand in the relative silence at the crest of the hill and look out over the well-traveled artery. The car sounds are surf-like from this distance—far off, innocuous, faintly mesmeric. One of the gates of the Golfhurst subdivision stands on either side of the entryway that joins Old Cherokee. Soon, we'll take off the lettering that says Golfhurst and put up the sign for our park. The road still winds through the field and the new trees and driveways branch from it, leading to spaces of shiny grass blowing in the wind.

"Tobia?" Robin asks after a time.

"Yes."

"We've been together for how long now?"

"Let's see . . ."

"Six months."

I nod.

"It's not all that long, but we've known each other for a long time. I feel like I've gotten to know you pretty well in that time."

I nod and look at her.

"I just want to know where I stand. Where you stand in this. Where we stand. I think we should talk about where we're going with this. I want to know what you're thinking."

"Well. I think things are all right," I say. "Who else do you know who can give you rides in a demolition machine? I was actually just thinking of where I could get some good pigs. And maybe some chickens and a cow for milking. Some seeds for planting. And I need to call that horticulturist to talk about starting a tree farm out here."

"Pigs," she says. "And a cow for milking." She pouts and looks at the ground. A long silence passes between us. I think she wants me, now, to reel her in, and I'm not sure whether or not I want to do it.

The silence lengthens. I watch the steady stream of cars coming at us out of the semidarkness with their lights on and blurred and wonder when Merritt will get back to Haven and what will happen when she does. I think I can feel her on the way. The silence grows heavier between Robin and me.

"If I wasn't here at all," she says, "you could have all the time you wanted to plot becoming a farmer."

I look at her to judge the timbre of the remark and decide it's safe and put my arm around her shoulder. We start to walk across the lawn. "I'm sorry," I say.

She sighs and shakes her head. "Aren't we driving back?" she asks.

"No. Let's let them see Old Havoc up here. Let them see it and be afraid. Let them think about what they've done. Maybe someday, we'll push it all back. Erase our mistakes and start over, keeping the good things, going at a slower, more careful pace the second time around."

She laughs. "That's a nice idea. A pretty pipe dream," she says. "Do you know how many farms fail every year? Do you know what happens when people don't have jobs?"

I surprise myself by smiling. "You're right," I say, "it is crazy, a foolish dream." I squeeze her shoulder, even though I feel a distance spreading between us. "And it seems ridiculous right now. But tearing down this part of Golfhurst seemed ridiculous, too, and—look at this field."

We leave Old Havoc sitting within view of Old Cherokee and walk across the field in silence between the young trees, some of them still surrounded by wire rims. We stroll back toward the old house. Again, I'm surprised when the question comes into my head. *Will you marry me will you marry me will you marry me.* I suppose the question is usually preceded by a speech and accompanied by a ring. Close to the graveyard, whispers are calling for me to ask it, ask it. It's all I can do to keep myself from tripping and dropping to a knee.

TWENTY-TWO

MAY FIFTH, Kentucky Derby Day.

Fenton's date and time for the quake has come and gone. There was an article in the paper about Fenton and his prediction, his animals, and his small following, most of whom were planning to leave the area the day before.

Fenton spent the day of the twenty-third over here where he was certain he would be safe. I spent a few hours in the cellar with him, Tango, Treffen, and Turtle Eddie, who I helped carry, hissing, down the steps along with some dog biscuits and a mason jar full of minnows.

From two o'clock to three-thirty, when it seemed unlikely the quake was going to happen, we sat waiting. I wasn't sure if I was just doing it to make him feel good or if at any moment I expected to feel a shaking.

We sat in a pair of old Adirondack chairs and waited in the musty basement next to the padlocked wine cellar, intent on every sound. After a time Fenton convinced me to go get the key and unlock the cellar so we could have some of the port he remembered Grandfather

Thomas's having bought a few years before his death. So, we sat there, awaiting cataclysm, sipping a rich, wonderful vintage. At a little after two-thirty my father, who thought we were ridiculous and had refused to join us, beat on the ceiling directly above us with a Louisville slugger, which I thought for a time was going to be the end of old Fenton—he got so excited.

So, no, it's May fifth and there was no quake. This afternoon we're having another picnic to celebrate the destruction and greening of the Goodhopes' house, the recovery of the Caldwell graves.

Our guests begin to arrive. Around the tables, on either side of gold-blossomed forsythia branches in fishbowls of water, are gathered Bank Shankhorn and his crew, benefactors, sympathizers, friends of Rollback Inc., old friends of the family. I reach into my glass of icewater to fish out one of the tiny gold forsythia blossoms and raise it up, a gold thimble cupping my fingertip, to have a better look.

Tom and Trish Goodhope, Kippy, and their daughter, Beth-Ann, have come from their new house in Eon's neighborhood. Tonorah has also joined us this afternoon, though we're missing Brandon Campbell and John Redbear, who I invited as a goodwill gesture. Not far from the tables, the Caldwell graves, newly festooned with dahlias and chrysanthemums, rest in the shadows of their great ash trees. We have begun (my father especially) going by old photographs and records, to bring about the complete replacement of the Confederate graves precisely as they had been.

Eon is seated to my right, Robin to my left. Bradley and Clarice Sackett are directly across from me.

"So, who do you like in the derby this afternoon?" Bradley asks the table.

Eon nudges me, and when I give him a look meant to convey my annoyance, he shrugs. He's eager to see Merritt's letters, which I told him might happen later this afternoon when everyone else, especially Robin, has left. I look at Robin and see that she noticed something pass between us. She tries not to let me see her noticing, and I try not to let her see me noticing her having noticed.

A short time later, Fenton walks toward us over the lawn, late as usual, Turtle Eddie with him on one leash and Treffen on another. Seeing the three of them coming toward us, I know something's up, at least in Fenton's mind. In addition to the obvious signs, I feel a vague presentiment, some faint stirring of the air. I stand from the table and stare at them as they come toward us, slowly, for Eddie's reluctant steps at the end of the old red leash. Fenton stops and turns to look behind him. I look past him to see what has captured his interest.

And see Aunt Marcy wheeling my mother over the grass toward Fenton. Jacob is with them and carrying an old hatbox with a green ribbon. All three of them look grave, as if they are envoys sent forth on behalf of a neighboring country to declare war or negotiate a precisely worded peace.

I turn to look at my father. He's seen them; he stands and watches them come. Then, like a man under the effects of a still-remembered dream, he moves toward my mother. Everyone gathered around the tables knows the backstory of this meeting so many of our guests, too, stand and follow my father at a distance to see how it will end, or, how it will begin again.

He approaches her across the staggeringly green lawn and stops about ten yards short of where she is waiting for him. He makes the sort of vague hand and face gesture that says, *I am overwhelmed and there are no words to say what I would like to convey to you so here is . . . this—forgive its lack.*

"Helen," he says.

She fixes him with a bursting glance and places her feet on the ground and stands from the chair, a little shakily. Marcy comes over and hands her a cane, which she uses to steady herself. She clears her throat and says very clearly, loud enough for all to hear, the words sounding as if they have been pulled up at great effort from a deep and treacherous mine shaft within her.

"Th—o—m—as," she says, only his name, in a tone both reproach-ful and forgiving; she beckons him forward.

There is a hushed gasp, an expellation of air, from the audience both at her having spoken and at the degree of command she has been able to infuse into her pseudo-voice. Heads turn, tennis match style, to see how he will react.

He comes to her and falls to his knees in the lush grass in front of her and clasps her calves. He begins to mutter apologies. I've never seen him this undone and never thought I would.

"Eeee-rrre," she says in the new voice she's been working on in private, once again pulling up the words in a feat of concentration. "Hhh—eere," she says and holds out her right hand. Jacob walks up alongside her with the hatbox and hands it to her and retreats to where he'd been standing, all very formally, his face giving nothing away.

Looking at my father, who is still on his knees, on his knees before her or anyone else for the first time since he asked her to marry him, I have to imagine. She unties the ribbon, lets it fall to the grass, and lifts the oval lid. There is a moment during which nothing happens. Then, a first butterfly, one with wings of incandescent blue, crawls up onto the edge of the box, pauses on the lip for a moment, and flutters, dipping and climbing as if drunk, into the May day.

This first one is followed by several others. Here are the painted ladies, monarchs, spring azures, swallowtails, Gulf fritillaries, clouded sulfurs, black and tiger swallowtails—all the North American species. I wonder at the fate of the more exotic species. Most of the ones that have been released remain concentrated over the box for a time before gradually spreading out over our lawn.

"S—tt-aa-nd," my mother says with great force, and he does. She puts her arms around him. She's crying now and so is he. I've never seen him cry. I look at Fenton.

"I'll be damned," Fenton says very quietly. A painted lady flits over and lights on his shoulder. Eddie snaps at one of the butterflies when it dips too low; Treffen, who looks nervous and jumpy, follows them with bored eyes. "Never in all my days," says Fenton in the same quiet voice.

After the initial excitement over the butterflies and moths, which are still fluttering, demonstrating their small splendor in every direction over the yard, a look of deep concern passes over Fenton's features. He begins, and people don't seem to hear him at first, but by the end of his speech he has everyone's attention:

"Now," he says. "It occurs to me that my breaking in right now, just after this . . . moment might very well sound rude and crass. I certainly do not want to put a damper on this reconciliation and this wonderful natural spectacle," he says, indicating the butterflies and moths aflutter all around us. "Or, for that matter, I hate to interrupt this fete-in-progress," he says with a flourish in the direction of the set table. "However . . . I feel it is my duty to inform all of you that this particular section of earth is about to shift. Shift . . . hell—that's not adequate—it's about to start doing the tango. I realize I sound like the boy who cried quake, but this time, as they say, I mean it. We are, I need to let all of you know, standing atop a powder keg here, my friends, and we'd best adjourn, and quickly, to the Old Caldwell Place yonder and weather it in the limestone cellar. Do you see how Treffen's shaking?" The dog is, indeed, quivering and casting quick glances left and right. "This is a dog that could take a nap in a dynamite factory. This is not a nervous hound." He looks around at all of us, with his white eyebrows raised.

"Well," my father says, his eyes still brimming, tear tracks in evidence, smiling. He comes over and puts his hands on Fenton's shoulders. He is red-faced but quickly recovering himself, reeling in his pride. "Why don't we, at least, eat first, Mr. Monroe? Then, later in the afternoon, we'll see about taking cover. We've got some food over there that needs to be eaten. We'll sit out the quake with full stomachs. How does that sound?"

"Well, I suppose we could but . . . ," Fenton says, the rest of what he says is lost to mumbling and head shaking.

I step toward my mother and hug her. She grips hard as if to say, *You still love me despite this awful new voice, don't you, Tobia? Don't you? You still love your wonderful, beautiful, charming, graceful mother.*

"We'll need a few new chairs for our guests," my father says. "Tobia. You mind? Let's see, four more?"

"Sure," I say. "Just a moment."

Robin says, "I'll help you get them."

"That's all right. I've got it."

She shrugs. "You sure?"

"Yes."

I move across the grass. At first I'm walking and then, before I know what I'm doing, as if any time lost in procuring the chairs might result in the dissolution of my parents' apparent reconciliation, I'm running as I haven't run in a long time, wondering if it's possible her return is already restoring some lost youth to me, unburdening me in some unforeseen way. I don't know when I last ran over grass, under trees, for no reason, toward the old house.

I go through the side yard under the trees and around to the front of the house. I'm just about to turn and take the first step onto the moss-covered, cracked front steps when some movement catches my eye. A blur of color down by the stream turns my head. It is a woman walking beside the creek with sunlight playing in her hair and forming shadows in the folds of her clothing. I know immediately, before my mind has confirmed my knowing, that it is Merritt Wilson.

She's walking beside the creek under the dead limbs of grandmother oak. She shows no signs of having seen me. She steps slowly, her movement suggesting a deep preoccupation. Like my father in Old Havoc moving to erase the Goodhopes' house, she owns this moment and she's clutching it close, letting this place say whatever it might still have to say to her. She looks down at the rippling creekwater as if she thinks she might see Ben there, will him to a second life. Call him forth from the water.

A blue swallowtail lands on my shoulder and sits there slowly flexing its wings.

It occurs to me that keys to the car are resting in the kitchen, above the desk, next to the phone. It would be so easy to go in and pick them up and run down the hill to her and have her come and hop into the car with me. There's enough money left in my account to make a clean break and a new start far away from the old house and its ghosts, if that's what I decide within the next couple seconds. I could do it, *we* could do it. From mind to body, I fill with the energy of this possibility until I am tingling with it and feel as if I'm levitating.

Our lives together flash in front of me. We're in some desert hellzone. There are towering oil fires on the horizon. They're slashing and burning the rain forest. The refugees look to us so we must be strong. We're huddled together and oddly exhilarated by it all—the lack of sleep, the selfless giving (does our exhilaration make it, somehow, selfish?), the way our own bodies are gaunt and tan, our cheekbones sharp, intellects engaged—made still by the whizzing of bullets, butting heads with some intractable purveyors of injustice, made strong by the way the people need us. Merritt will show me how to live this life.

Or, no, we're here on the Old Caldwell Place going backward, learning to be agrarian, to be yeoman farmers, despite the slick allure of conformity, with a parcel of roly-poly kids who get muddy down at the creek and trace crinoid stems with their fat little fingers and fill bottles with fireflies and bring them in to show us on summer nights. We raise what we eat here, live close to the land, circle through its seasons. And there are times when we can't stand each other and struggle to get through an ordinary Tuesday afternoon, other times when we remember how it should be and apply ourselves, wholeheartedly, to making it good again. But . . . is that Merritt or Robin with me in this second scenario at the old house? Merritt or Robin? Neither? Why would either one have me?

At the most it would take fifteen seconds to get the keys. A minute later we could be doing eighty toward anywhere. We could go away until the interested parties have forgotten their interest. We could go away and never come back like couples in nineteenth-century Romantic poems. Into the storm together, arm-in-arm, oppressive foes in hot pursuit, not knowing where we'll spend the night, faithful in serendipity, full of road energy, all that. Or maybe, it's just me on the road, speeding away from everyone, everything here. Clean slate. The final incarnation—Tobia-the-Cleansed-of-Past? Now would be the time.

I watch her walking. One of her brown boots hits the grass, and she lifts it and, in that moment, looks up the hill and sees me looking down at her and lets the boot rest on the grass and takes a deep breath. I can see myself registering with her and guess that she's wondering how it will be between us now. Nearly seven years. I can't read her expression from this distance. I don't know her anymore; she doesn't know me. Has she ever? Have I ever? Will she ever? Will I ever? Will we have the chance? Do we want to have the chance? Standing at the bottom of the hill she makes a gesture that says, *Come down here. I want to show you something.*

I let gravity pull me into a jog down the hill and stop, leaving some distance between us. "There's something I have to tell you," I say.

"I know," she says.

"You know?"

"That's why you wrote the letters."

"I didn't write any letters."

She looks down into the gurgling water of the creek, shakes her head, looks up again. "It doesn't matter. I'm here."

"I'm glad you're here."

We each take a step toward the other. A shudder runs through the earth.